Also by Brenda Novak

For a full list of Brenda's books,
visit www.brendanovak.com.

Look for Brenda Novak's next novel
THE TALK OF COYOTE CANYON
available soon from MIRA.

Brenda Novak

Talulah's Back in Town

mira

mira™

Recycling programs
for this product may
not exist in your area.

ISBN-13: 978-0-7783-8617-9

Talulah's Back in Town

Mira
22 Adelaide St. West, 41st Floor
Toronto, Ontario M5H 4E3, Canada
www.Harlequin.com

Printed in U.S.A.

To Maureen Fink...

It was so wonderful to meet you at my signing in Boston. Thank you for your love of my books, for introducing your friends to my work and for writing to me with such enthusiasm after reading each new release. I've enjoyed the family pictures you've shown me and interacting with you since then via email and in my book group on Facebook. It's always such a pleasure when a faithful reader becomes a wonderful friend.

One

"Well, if it isn't the runaway bride."

Talulah Barclay glanced up to find the reason a shadow had just fallen across her plate. She'd been hoping to ease back into the small community of Coyote Canyon, Montana, without drawing any attention. But Brant Elway, of all people, had happened to come into the café where she was having breakfast and stopped at her booth.

"Of course you'd be the first to bring up my past sins," she grumbled. They hadn't seen each other for nearly fourteen years, and he'd certainly changed—filled out what had once been a spare frame, grown a couple of inches, even though he'd been tall to begin with, and taken on a rugged, slightly weathered look from spending so much time outdoors. But she would've recognized him anywhere.

The crooked smile that curved his lips suggested he was hardly repentant. "I'm not likely to forget that day. I was the best man, remember?"

She wasn't likely to forget that day, either. Only bumping into her ex, Charlie Gerhart, would be more cringeworthy.

She felt terrible about what she'd done to Charlie. She also felt terrible that she'd repeated the same mistake with two other men since. Admittedly, jilting her fiancés at the altar hadn't been among her finest moments, but she'd had every intention of following through—until the panic grew so powerful it simply took over and there was no other way to cope.

It said something that, while she regretted the pain she'd caused others, especially her prospective grooms, she didn't regret walking out on those weddings. That clearly indicated she'd made the right choice—a little late, perhaps, but better not to make such a huge mistake than try to unravel it later.

She doubted Brant would ever view the situation from that perspective, however. He'd naturally feel defensive of Charlie. He and Charlie had been friends for as long as she could remember. She'd hung out with Charlie's younger sister, Averil, since kindergarten and could remember seeing Brant over at the Gerhart house way back when she and Averil were in fifth grade, and he and Charlie were in seventh.

Dressed in a soft cotton Elway Ranch T-shirt that stretched slightly at the sleeves to accommodate his biceps, a pair of faded Wranglers and boots that were worn and dirty enough to prove they weren't just for show, he rested his hands on his narrow hips as he studied her with the cornflower-blue eyes that'd been the subject of so much slumber-party talk when she was growing up. Those eyes were even more startling now that his face was so tanned. Had he lived in Seattle, like her, she'd assume he spent time cultivating that golden glow. But she knew he hadn't put any effort into his appearance. According to Jane Tanner, another friend who'd hung out with her and Averil—the three of them had been inseparable—Brant's parents had retired, and he and his three younger brothers had taken over the running of their two-thousand-acre cattle ranch.

"What brings you back to town?" he asked. "You've laid low for so long, I thought we'd seen the last of you."

Pretending that running into him was no more remarkable to her than running into anyone else, she lifted her orange juice to take a sip before returning the glass to the heavily varnished table. "My aunt Phoebe died."

"That's the old lady who lived in the farmhouse on Mill Creek Road, right? The one with the blue hair?"

Her great-aunt had been a diminutive woman, only five feet tall and less than a hundred pounds. But she'd had her hair done once a week like clockwork—still used the blue rinse she'd grown fond of in her early twenties when platinum blond had been all the rage—and dressed in her Sunday best, including nylons, whenever she came to town. So she'd stood out. "That's her."

"What happened?"

Talulah got the impression he was assessing the changes in her, just as she was assessing the changes in him, and wished she'd put more effort into her appearance today. She didn't want to come off the worse for wear after what she'd done. But when she'd rolled out of bed, pulled on her yoga pants and a sleeveless knit top and piled her long blond hair on top of her head before coming to the diner for breakfast, she'd assumed she'd be early enough to miss the younger crowd, which included the people she'd rather avoid.

That had proven mostly to be true; except for Brant, almost everyone else in the diner was over sixty. But he worked on a ranch, so he was probably up even before the birds that'd been chirping loudly outside her window, making it impossible for her to sleep another second. "She died of old age. Aunt Phoebe was almost a hundred."

"I'm sorry to hear you lost her." He sounded sincere, at least. "Were you close?"

"No, actually, we weren't," Talulah admitted. "She never liked me." Phoebe hadn't liked children in general—they were too loud, too unruly and too messy. And once Talulah had become a teenager, and her mother had allowed her to quit taking piano lessons from her great-aunt, they'd never really connected, other than seeing each other at various family functions during which Talulah and her sister, Debbie, had gone out of their way to avoid their mother's crotchety aunt.

His teeth flashed in a wider smile. "Maybe she was a friend of the Gerharts."

Talulah gave him a dirty look. "So were you. But unfortunately, you're standing here talking to me."

He chuckled instead of being offended, which soothed some of her ire. He was willing to take what he was dishing out; she had to respect that.

"I'm more generous than most," he teased, pressing a hand to his muscular chest. "But if it makes you feel any better, you're not the only one who struggled to get along with your aunt."

"You knew her personally?" she asked in surprise.

"Not well, but I'll never forget the day someone had the audacity to honk at her because she was driving at the speed of a horse and buggy down the middle of the highway, holding up traffic for miles."

"What happened?"

"Once I got around her, I found she was capable of driving a lot faster. She tailgated me to the bank, where she climbed out and swung her purse at me while giving me a piece of her mind for scaring her while she was behind the wheel."

Talulah had to laugh at the mental picture that created. "You're the one who honked at her?"

"The bank was about to close." He gave a low whistle

as he rubbed the beard growth on his squarish chin. "But after that, I decided if I was ever in the same situation again, I'd skip the bank."

Most people in Coyote Canyon probably had a similar story about Aunt Phoebe, maybe more than one. She might've been small, but she was mighty and wouldn't "take any guff," as she put it, from anyone. "Yeah, well, imagine being a little girl on the receiving end of that sharp tongue. I'd dread my weekly piano lesson and cry whenever my mother left me with her."

"I'll have to let Ellen know that," he said.

Talulah didn't remember anyone by that name in Coyote Canyon. "Who's Ellen?"

"I assume you're staying at your aunt's place?"

She nodded. "My folks moved to Reno a couple of years after I embarrassed them at the wedding," she said glumly.

He laughed at her response. "Ellen lives on the property next to you. She and I used to go out now and then, when she first moved to town, and she told me the old lady would knock on her door to complain about everything—the weeds near the fence, trees that were dropping leaves on her side of the property line, the barking of the dogs."

"But they both live on several acres. How could those small things bother Aunt Phoebe?"

"Exactly Ellen's point. Heaven forbid she ever decided to have a dinner party and someone parked too close to your aunt's driveway."

Talulah found herself more distracted by the mention of his relationship with this Ellen woman than she should've been, given that it wasn't the point of the anecdote. Brant had always been so hard to attract. Most girls she knew had tried to gain his interest, including her own sister, and failed. So she couldn't help being curious about how he'd come to date her new neighbor—and why and how their relationship had ended. "Sounds like Phoebe."

A waitress called out to tell Brant hello, and he waved at her before returning his attention to Talulah. "How long will you be in town?"

She arched an eyebrow at him. "Are you running recognizance for my enemies?"

"Just curious." He winked. "Word will spread fast enough without me."

"You can assure everyone who cares that it'll only be for a month or so," she said. "Until I can clean out my great aunt's house and put it on the market."

"If you weren't close to her, how come you were unlucky enough to get that job?" he asked.

"My parents are in Africa on a mission."

"For the Church of the Good Shepherd?"

"Yeah."

"I didn't realize they sent people out on organized missions."

"Sometimes they do, but this one is self-funded, something my dad has wanted to do ever since hearing a particularly rousing sermon." Talulah wasn't religious at all—much to the chagrin of her parents. But a good portion of the town belonged to her folks' evangelical church or one of the other churches in the area.

"What about your sister?" Brant asked. "She can't help?"

"Debbie's married and living in Billings. She's about to have her fourth child any day now."

He feigned shock. "*Married?* Fear of commitment doesn't run in the family, I guess."

She scowled. "It's a good thing I didn't go through with it, Brant. I was only eighteen—way too young."

"I never said I thought it was a good idea," he responded.

"If you'll remember, I made the same argument way back when."

"How could I ever forget?" They'd always been adversaries. He'd hated the amount of time his best friend had devoted to her, and she'd resented that he was often trying to talk Charlie into playing pool or going hunting or something with him instead. "But let's be fair. I doubt I'm the only one with commitment issues." She glanced at his hand. "I don't see a ring on *your* finger."

"I've never left anyone standing at the altar."

She could tell he was joking, but he'd hit a nerve. "Because you bail out before it even gets that far."

He seemed to enjoy provoking her. "That's what you're supposed to do. I can teach you how, if you want me to."

"Oh, leave me alone," she muttered with a shooing motion.

He chuckled but didn't go. "How much are you hoping to get for your aunt's house?"

"I have no idea what it's worth," she replied. "I live in Washington these days, where prices are a lot different, and haven't met with a real estate agent yet."

"You know Charlie's an agent, right?"

Slumping back against the booth, she sighed. "Here we go again…"

He widened those gorgeous blue eyes of his. "That wasn't a jab! I just thought you should be aware of it."

"I'm aware of it, okay? Jane Tanner told me."

"You still in touch with Jane?"

"We've been friends since kindergarten," she said as if he should've taken that for granted. But she'd been equally close to Charlie's sister, and they hadn't spoken since Talulah had tried to apologize for what she'd done at the wedding and Averil had told her she never wanted to see her again.

"Maybe it'd help patch things up if you listed your aunt's house with him," Brant suggested.

"You're kidding. I can't imagine he'd want to see me— not even to make a buck."

His eyes flicked to the compass tattoo she'd gotten on the inside of her forearm shortly after she'd left Coyote Canyon. "Does he know you're in town?"

She shrugged. "Jane might've told him I was coming. Why?"

He studied her for a long moment. "I have a feeling things are about to get interesting around here. Thanks for breaking the monotony," he said, and that maddening grin reappeared as he nodded in parting and walked over to the bar, where he took a stool and ordered his breakfast.

Disgruntled, Talulah eyed his back. He'd removed his baseball cap—that was a bit old-fashioned, perhaps, but her parents would certainly approve of his manners—so his hair was matted in places, but he didn't seem to care. He came off more comfortable in his own skin than any man she'd ever known, which sort of bugged her. She couldn't say why. He'd always seemed to avoid the foibles that everyone else got caught up in. For a change, she wanted to see *him* unable to stop himself from falling in love, do something stupid because he couldn't help it or make a mistake he later regretted.

"Would you like a refill?"

The waitress had approached with a pot of coffee.

Talulah shoved her cup away. "No, thanks. I'm finished."

"Okay, hon. Let me put this down, and I'll be right back with your check."

Leaving twenty-five bucks on the table, more than enough to cover the bill, Talulah got up and walked out.

The last thing she wanted was to run into someone else she knew.

Most of the town had been at that wedding.

Aunt Phoebe's house was going to take some work. Two stories tall, it was a Victorian farmhouse with a wide front porch, a drawing room/living room off the entry, a music room tucked to the left, a formal dining area in the middle and a tiny kitchen—tiny by today's standards— at the back, with a mudroom where the "menfolk" could clean up before coming in from the fields at dinner. Probably 2,400 square feet in total, it was divided into thirteen small rooms that were packed with furniture, rugs, decorations, books, lamps and magazines. The attic held objects that'd been handed down for generations, as well as steamer trunks of old clothes, quilts and needlepoint— even a dressmaker's dummy that'd given Talulah a fright when she first went up to take a look because she'd thought someone was in the attic with her.

The basement held shelf upon shelf of canned goods, a deep freezer full of meat that'd most likely been butchered at a local ranch, which meant there would be certain cuts— like tongue and liver—Talulah would have no idea what to do with, and stacks of old newspapers and various other flotsam Phoebe had collected throughout her long life.

Even if she started right away, it'd take a week or more to sort through everything, and the house wasn't the most comfortable place to work. The windows, while beautiful with their old-fashioned casings and heavy panes, weren't energy-efficient. There was hardly any insulation in the attic and no air-conditioning to combat the heat. Typically, summers in Coyote Canyon were quite mild, with temperatures ranging between fifty and ninety degrees, but they were in a heat wave. It was mid-August, the hottest part of the year to begin with, and they were setting records.

A bead of sweat rolled between Talulah's breasts as she surveyed the basement. Even the coolest part of the house felt stifling. And it was only noon. She couldn't imagine how Aunt Phoebe had managed in this heat. But her aunt could handle just about anything. She'd had a will of iron and more grit than anyone Talulah had ever met.

"How am I going to get through all this junk—and what am I going to do with it?" Talulah muttered, disheartened by the sheer volume of things her great-aunt had collected over the years.

Her phone vibrated in the pocket of her yoga pants. Pulling it out, she saw that her sister was calling. "Hey," she answered.

"How's Coyote Canyon?" Debbie asked.

"I just got in last night, but from what I've seen so far, it hasn't changed much." The town's population had stayed at about three thousand since the end of the nineteenth century, when the railroad came to town and Coyote Canyon had its big boom.

She chuckled. "It never does. Bozeman is growing like crazy, though. I read somewhere that it's the fastest growing town in America. You should see how much it's changed."

"No kidding? Who's moving there?"

"Mostly families, I guess, but enough millennials and nature-lovers to change the whole vibe from Western to trendy."

Only forty minutes away, Bozeman had been where their parents would take them to buy school clothes and other supplies. But she'd had no reason to go there since she'd left Coyote Canyon. Thanks to the stigma caused by the wedding, she'd tried to forget the whole area. "Did you guys come for Rodeo Days this year?" The week before the Fourth of July, Coyote Canyon held seven days of celebration that included rodeos, a 10K/5K run, a Mountain Man Rendezvous, parades, tractor pulls and bake-offs. Everything culminated in the fireworks of Independence Day.

"No. I wanted to," Debbie said, "but Scott was under too much pressure at work to take the time, and I didn't want to try to manage the kids on my own."

"I'm sorry that Paul and I couldn't make it."

"Has something changed I'm not aware of? Are you two together now?"

He'd been trying to get with her since she met him, especially after they started the diner. But it was only recently that she'd gone on the pill and slept with him for the first time. "Not really. We've started dating. Sort of."

"Sort of?" her sister echoed.

"You know how hard it is for me to know when I really like a guy. Anyway, how've you been feeling? Any news on the baby?" She asked because she was interested, but she was also eager to change the subject.

"I'm fine," Debbie said. "Just tired."

"It shouldn't be much longer, right?"

"I'm due in a week, and the doctor won't let me go more than a few days over."

"Call me as soon as labor starts. I'll come for the birth." Billings was only a hundred miles to the east. Part of the reason Talulah had agreed to handle her aunt's funeral and belongings was because it put her in closer proximity to Debbie. She wanted to be there for the arrival of the new addition, especially since their parents couldn't be.

"I will. I can't wait until this pregnancy is over." She groaned. "I'm getting so uncomfortable."

"You've done this three times before. I'm sure the birth will be routine."

Maybe not *strictly* routine. Debbie had developed gestational diabetes, so there was a good chance this child would have to be delivered by Caesarean section. But they were pretending there'd be no complications. Neither of them cared to consider all the things that could go wrong.

"I feel bad that you're having to take so much time away from the dessert diner," she said. "Maybe I should drive over for the funeral, at least, and help while I can."

"Don't you dare!" Talulah said. "I don't want you going into labor while you're here. Your husband, your doctor, everyone and everything you need are there."

"But I'm just sitting around with my swollen ankles while you deal with everything in that musty house."

Musty, *sweltering* house. But Talulah didn't want to make Debbie feel any guiltier. Besides, her sister wasn't just sitting around. She was watching her other kids. Talulah could hear them, and the TV, in the background and knew that Debbie would have to bring her young nieces and nephew if she came here. Having them underfoot would only make it harder to get anything done. "The church is stepping in to organize the funeral. You set that up yourself. So you *have* been involved. Besides, much to our parents' dismay, you're the only one giving them grandkids. This is the least I can do for Mom and Dad."

Debbie laughed. "Have you heard from them?"

"They called last night to make sure I got in okay."

"How long did the drive take you?"

"Ten hours."

"Ugh!"

"It wasn't a big deal. I couldn't fly—I knew I'd need a car while I was here." She'd made the trip to Reno several times since her family moved from Coyote Canyon, so she was used to driving even farther. They'd only visited Seattle once, but Talulah had been so busy with college, then culinary school, then working in various restaurants before launching Talulah's Dessert Diner with Paul, whom she'd met along the way, that she didn't mind.

"I'm surprised they aren't coming home for the funeral," Debbie mused.

Not to mention the birth of their latest grandchild. Talulah thought she could hear the disappointment in her sister's voice, but Debbie would never complain, especially to a defector like Talulah. Debbie remained as committed to their parents' faith as they did. "I'm not surprised," Talulah said. "Africa is so far away, and they'd only have to turn around and go right back. They want to remain focused on their mission, at least until they're officially released."

"Aunt Phoebe was so prickly, she and Mom were never very close, anyway," Debbie added.

That wasn't strictly true. Phoebe used to have them over for dinner every Sunday, and Carolyn brought Talulah and Debbie over for piano lessons. It was only later that they had a bit of a falling-out and quit talking. Despite that, Talulah guessed their mother felt conflicted about missing her aunt's funeral. She also understood that Carolyn wasn't going to change her mind. Choosing her mission over her family was almost a matter of pride; it showcased the level of her belief. "When we visited Aunt Phoebe, and we weren't there for piano lessons, we had to sit on chairs in the cramped dining room or living room, and she'd snap at us to quit wiggling, remember?"

"That was if she'd let us in the house at all," Debbie said drily. "She used to tell us to go out front and play."

"With no toys."

"She was the sternest person I've ever met."

"She also never threw anything away."

"She was a *hoarder*?"

"Kind of. She somehow managed to be fastidious and

clean at the same time, so it's not the type of hoarding you imagine when you hear the word, but it's so cluttered in here I can barely move from room to room."

"If it's that bad, I should come over, after all."

Talulah blew a wisp of hair that'd fallen from the clip on top of her head away from her mouth. "No, I've got it. Really." There was no way Debbie would survive the heat, not in her condition.

"But you must be feeling some pressure to get back to Seattle," Debbie said. "You told me you have a line of people every night trying to get into the diner."

"We do, but Paul's there." She couldn't have taken off for a whole month in any prior year. In the beginning, their business had required too much time, energy and focus— from both of them. She'd come up with the concept and had the name, the website, the logo, the location and the recipes figured out when Paul decided to come on board to help with the capital, credit and muscle required to get the rest of the way. It'd been touch and go for a while, but the place was running smoothly now, following a familiar routine. They had employees they could trust, and with her partner managing the day-to-day details, she wasn't too worried.

"He doesn't resent you being gone so long?" Debbie asked.

"He has a family reunion in Iowa at the end of September. Then he'll be hiking in Europe for three weeks with a couple of friends. So I'll be returning the favor soon enough."

"He gets to go to Europe while you have to spend your vacation in Coyote Canyon, attending a funeral and cleaning out a house that was built in the 1800s?"

Talulah didn't mind the work. It was facing the past

and all the people she hadn't seen or heard from in years that would be difficult. "It's not a big deal," she insisted.

"Okay." There was a slight pause. Then her sister said, "I hate to bring up a sensitive subject, but…what are you going to do when you see Charlie?"

"I don't know." She certainly wasn't looking forward to it.

"It'd be a lot easier if he was married."

Talulah agreed. If he had a wife, he'd be able to believe she'd saved him for the woman he was really supposed to marry. His family and friends would then be more likely to forgive her, too. But according to Jane, he wasn't even seeing anyone, so she had no idea how he'd feel toward her. "I ran into Brant," she volunteered, simply because she knew her sister would be interested.

"How'd he look?"

Too good for the emotional well-being of the women around him. But such an admission would never pass Talulah's lips. She preferred not to acknowledge his incredible good looks. "Haven't you seen him fairly recently?" She knew her sister came back to Coyote Canyon occasionally.

"Four or five years ago."

"He probably hasn't changed much since then."

"He married?"

"No."

"Somehow that doesn't surprise me. I doubt he'll ever settle down. What'd he say when he saw you?"

"Just gave me a hard time about Charlie."

"When I was in high school, I was *so* disappointed I couldn't get his attention. Now I'm glad he had no interest in me. He would only have broken my heart."

"Probably," Talulah agreed. But, truth be told, she felt sort of bad talking about Brant that way. It was a case of "the pot calling the kettle black," as her aunt would've said. She'd broken her share of hearts, too, and possibly in worse ways, as he'd intimated. But she couldn't seem to settle down. No matter how hard she tried to force the issue and be more like her sister—to do what her parents expected of her—she wound up having such terrible anxiety attacks she literally had to flee. Maybe Brant had the same problem when it came to making a lifelong commitment. Maybe he was just better at accepting his limitations.

The doorbell rang as her sister finished telling her about little Casey, her three-year-old niece, who'd gotten hold of a pair of scissors and cut her bangs off at the scalp. "That's probably the woman from the church now," Talulah said. "I need to go over the funeral with her. I'll call you later, okay?"

Her sister said goodbye, and Talulah disconnected as she hurried up the narrow, creaking stairs. There was a woman standing on the stoop, all right. But before she pushed open the screen door—the regular door was already standing open because she'd been trying to catch even the slightest breeze—Talulah could see enough to know it wasn't anyone from the church.

This woman had a cigarette in one hand and a bottle of wine in the other.

Two

Ellen had purple hair cut in a short, jagged style, a heart-shaped face, bottle-green eyes, a ring through her nose and a tattoo sleeve on one arm featuring mermaids and dragons. She was also wearing army boots with a pair of short shorts and a spaghetti-strap top. She reminded Talulah a little of Miley Cyrus. She was certainly beautiful, but Talulah couldn't imagine anyone standing out more in this small, traditional community.

"It's nice of you to walk over and introduce yourself," Talulah said. "I was wondering if I'd get to meet you."

One thin eyebrow slid up. "You've already heard of me?"

Talulah couldn't resist laughing, especially since she could tell Ellen wasn't all that surprised to think people were talking about her. "I ran into Brant this morning. He mentioned you weren't exactly on the best of terms with my great aunt."

Ellen took a drag of her cigarette while considering Talulah's response. "Yeah, well, I won't lie to you. I didn't care much for her. She was the reason I took up smoking. I needed something to calm my nerves. But—" she formed her china-doll face into a more sympathetic expression "—if you loved her, I'm sorry for your loss." She handed over the wine while being careful to blow her cigarette smoke in the opposite direction.

Talulah read the label: Orin Swift Papillon. "Thank you."

"Call it a bribe," she said. "I'm hoping you'll like me better than your great aunt did, and I can finally have some peace."

Although Talulah laughed again, she could tell Ellen was only partly joking. "You don't have to worry about me. I figure you've been through enough. Would you like to come in?"

She wrinkled her button nose. "Are you kidding? It's too fucking hot in there."

Wiping the sweat running down the side of her face, Talulah gestured at the wicker chairs on the porch. "What if we sit out here?"

"It's hot here, too. But I might as well stay until I finish my cigarette."

"When I was growing up, there was an older couple who lived on the adjacent property," Talulah said. "My great aunt actually liked them. She used to take them various things she'd canned—peaches and dill pickles and beets. And the man would come over and fix a leaky faucet now and then or shovel her walks in the winter, that sort of thing."

"That had to be my grandpa. He'd do anything for anybody. It's too bad you didn't get to know him. How often did you visit your aunt?"

"Often enough. I grew up in Coyote Canyon."

"I didn't realize that. When I saw you pull into the garage, I thought you were family from out of town, coming to take care of things."

"That's basically what's happening. But I'm familiar with the town because I lived here until I graduated from high school. Then I went to San Diego State University,"

Talulah explained. "I wanted to spend a few years close to the beach."

"What kind of degree did you get?"

"None. Regular college wasn't for me. After two and a half years, I dropped out and enrolled in culinary school in Denver."

Ellen got up to flick her ashes over the porch railing. "Did you like that better?"

"Much better. I now own a dessert diner, together with a partner, in Seattle. We specialize in fancy cakes, pies and other pastries."

"Sounds like you found your calling."

"Feels that way." Talulah watched Ellen closely, trying to figure out what about her had attracted Brant. Was it because she looked like a hard chick in the sea of softer good girls who made a play for him?

If so, her sweet-faced sister, who'd never dream of getting a tattoo, let alone wearing a nose ring, never had a chance. "What's your story?" she asked. "How'd you come to live in such a sleepy town—and on the property next to my mother's peevish aunt?"

"When my grandparents moved to Phoenix two years ago, they offered me their house."

"That was nice of them."

"I like it. And I immediately added air-conditioning. So if you get too uncomfortable over here, feel free to come on over."

"I would take you up on that, except it'd be pretty hard to sort through things from there. Where'd you live before Coyote Canyon?"

"Anaconda. Have you heard of it? It's a small town, too, only about an hour from here."

"I've heard of it, but I would've guessed somewhere more like LA…"

"Because I don't look like I fit into any small town, especially one in Montana, but that's okay. I don't care what people think."

"Why didn't you choose somewhere like Bozeman? Judging by what my sister just told me, folks there might be a bit more open-minded."

"I go over there occasionally. But I've decided to settle here. This is where I'm building my business."

"What kind of business?"

"I drill wells for a living."

"No kidding?" That was the last occupation Talulah had expected Ellen to have. She didn't know of one other female well-driller.

Ellen shrugged. "It's a living."

"How'd you get into that?"

"Runs in the family. My father's a driller. So was his father."

"He taught you everything he knows?"

She grimaced. "No. He saved that for one of his stepsons. But I don't need him. I figured it out myself."

"Brant told me you and he used to date."

"It's been over a year, but…yeah."

"Have you…gotten with someone else since?" She was prodding, but she was so curious she couldn't resist.

"No. When you've been with Brant Elway, it's not easy to find someone who measures up," she joked.

Her response prompted Talulah to dig a little deeper. "Would you mind a personal question from a total stranger?"

Fresh interest glittered in Ellen's eyes. "You and I aren't strangers anymore. You already like me better than your great aunt did, right? You said so yourself."

There was a transparency to Ellen that made Talulah feel comfortable asking almost anything. "Then I'll go ahead. What happened between you and Brant?"

"I wish I could tell you." Dropping her cigarette, she crushed it beneath her boot. "We're still friends. He treats me great whenever he sees me and stops by to visit now and then. The only thing I can figure is that he didn't want to lead me on when he was just trying to make a statement."

"A *statement*?" Talulah echoed.

"I'm guessing the reason he asked me out in the first place was because he wanted me to feel accepted and welcome. By being seen with me, he was putting everyone here on notice that different isn't always bad, essentially trying to make it a little easier for me to fit in and become part of the community."

Talulah wasn't convinced Brant was that perceptive, that kind or that deep. And even if he was, she didn't want to think so flatteringly of her old archenemy. She'd never *hated* him, exactly. But they'd battled over Charlie for two years, and she'd prided herself on being one of the few women in town he couldn't count among his many admirers. "Are you sure he wasn't just after a piece of ass?" she joked.

Ellen picked up the stub of her cigarette. "I'm sure, since I would've gladly given him one had he ever made a move," she said. "Let me know when you're ready to open that bottle. I'll come over again."

Brant hadn't tried to sleep with her? Talulah hadn't anticipated that. "I will," she said and lifted the wine in farewell.

Brant had been expecting a call from Charlie, so he wasn't surprised when his phone went off while he was fixing the roof on the barn closest to the house. He rocked back on his haunches, removed his gloves and used the bottom of his T-shirt to mop the sweat from his face before he answered. "What's up?"

"Talulah's back in town, man. I just ran into Marie Christensen at the grocery store. She said she waited on her at the diner this morning."

Brant probably should've been the one to tell Charlie about Talulah. But he'd put off relaying that bit of news. There'd been something in her eyes that reminded him of a cornered animal, and that had made him want to cut her a break in spite of what she'd done at the wedding.

It shouldn't have stopped him, though. She had no excuse for hurting Charlie so deeply. Even if she had to break up with him, why couldn't she have done it *before* the wedding? Putting it off until the very last second had heaped so much embarrassment on top of the rejection. "Is that all Marie said?" he asked tentatively.

"What do you mean?"

Apparently, the waitress hadn't mentioned that Brant had been in the restaurant at the same time. He wondered if he needed to divulge that information, but ultimately chose not to say anything. He'd get grilled if he did: *Why didn't you tell me? Did you talk to her? What'd she say? What does she look like? Did she mention me? What's she doing these days? Is she seeing anyone?*

The fact that Charlie still compared every woman he dated to Talulah, and the new prospect always came up short, indicated that he hadn't gotten over her, even after all this time. That became more apparent than ever when he was drunk. Then he'd ramble on, crying in his beer about the various things he'd seen her post on Instagram, especially the pics that included some guy named Paul. "You gotta forget her, man—move on," Brant said. "I've told you that before."

Conveniently ignoring his advice, Charlie asked, "Why do you think she's here?"

Since Brant knew the answer to that question, he had

to be careful how he responded. "I heard her great-aunt died, so there must be a funeral, right?"

"I heard about that, too. But I didn't expect Talulah to come back for her funeral. They were never close. Her aunt was a miserable person to be around."

"They were still family."

"True." He hesitated for a moment before revealing what was really going through his mind. "I wonder how she'd react if we were to bump into each other. Do you think she regrets what she did to me?"

If she regretted not going through with the wedding, Charlie probably would've heard about it long before now. But wishful thinking could blind a person to the most obvious truth. "I have no idea. Does it matter? You'll only get hurt again if you go back to her."

"I've decided to attend the funeral."

"What?"

"I knew her great aunt," he said, somewhat defensively. "She was my Sunday School teacher way back in the day."

She'd also been Brant's Sunday School teacher. Brant and his family weren't religious, but he'd often attended church functions with Charlie. "Considering the circumstances, it'd be perfectly understandable if you skipped out on the funeral."

"But it would also be understandable if I went. That's the point."

Brant could tell he was getting sunburned. He hadn't planned to be on the roof for so long. "You're kidding, right?"

"I'm curious about what Talulah's like these days. That's all."

"You follow her on Instagram. You see what she posts."

"You know about social media. Everything's designed

to be flattering to whoever's putting it up. You can only believe about half of what you see."

Which was part of the reason Brant hardly ever went on Instagram. He checked it out occasionally, when he was bored, but he rarely posted anything. "Seriously? It's been fourteen years since you two were a thing."

"You never really get over your first love."

Maybe there was something wrong with him, but Brant had never been unable to get over a woman. Did Charlie think Talulah was secretly pining for him?

"I wonder where she's staying," he mused. "Her parents sold their house to the Willoughbys years ago when they moved to Reno, so she can't be there. She must be at one of the motels. Or maybe she's at Phoebe's."

"I'm up on the barn," Brant said, trying to put a stop to the conversation before it went any further in the wrong direction. "I have to finish patching this roof."

"I'll let you go, then. But let's play some pool tonight."

"Okay, I'll call you later." Brant disconnected but before he could put his phone back in his pocket he received a text.

It was from Ellen, which was a surprise. She didn't contact him very often these days.

Hey, remember that portable AC unit you brought over when I first came to town? If no one's using it right now, my new neighbor doesn't have any AC. I was wondering if you'd let her borrow it while she sorts through her aunt's belongings.

Brant squinted up at the broiling sun. It didn't usually get this hot in Coyote Canyon, but the heat wave wasn't supposed to break until Wednesday.

I can do that. No problem.

Thank you. And can you deliver it, too? I'm going out of town for a wedding and won't be back for a week or more.

No problem. I know Talulah. I'll throw it in the back of my truck and swing by in an hour or two.

I'm sure she'll be grateful. She seems like a nice person.

After what Talulah had done to Charlie, at least half the community would argue with Ellen about Talulah being "a nice person," but he didn't feel it was his place to tell her what'd happened. How'd you meet her? Did she come over?

I took her a bottle of wine an hour ago. That's how I know it's sweltering over there.

It was sweltering on the damn roof, too. Awful neighborly of you to bring the wine.

I would've been happy to share it with you instead, but you never come around anymore. ;)

We'll have a drink together someday soon.

When she didn't press him for a date and time, he breathed a sigh of relief. Ellen was attractive, unique, open-minded and perceptive. She was tough as nails, too. He'd enjoyed getting to know her. But as soon as he could tell she was beginning to have feelings for him, he'd backed away. The last thing he wanted was to hurt her.

"Damn, it's hot," he muttered and mopped his face

again. Then he finished patching the roof, took a shower so he wouldn't smell like the cattle he worked with and found the portable cooler in the storage closet off the bunkhouse.

He had no doubt Charlie would want to be included on this errand—or at least know about it—but after the way he'd behaved on the phone, Brant wasn't going to call him.

When Brant arrived at the farmhouse on Mill Creek Road, he found a dusty Lexus SUV with Washington license plates in the garage. That told him Talulah was home, but it would've been obvious, regardless. Music was blasting through the house so loudly he knew it wouldn't do any good to knock. There was no way Talulah would hear him.

He could text her—if only he had her number.

He glanced at the property next door, but trees blocked his view of the house. He could ask Ellen for Talulah's number, although he doubted she'd have it, either. The two women had just met. Besides, he didn't want to be here for too long. This was supposed to be a quick errand. If he could get Talulah's attention, it still could be.

The screen door hung crookedly on its hinges, leaving a gap that made it obvious the hook could no longer latch even if someone tried to lock it, so he stepped into the living room and called her name.

There was no response, but he wasn't surprised. The music was even louder inside.

"Talulah?" He went from room to room, looking for her, but he didn't see anyone. She wasn't upstairs, either, which meant she had to be in the attic or the basement—and in this heat he was willing to bet on the basement.

Planning to make sure she'd accept the portable air conditioner before he hauled it inside, he'd left it in his truck, so he was unencumbered when he jogged down the narrow stairs. "Talulah?" he called again and had to bow his head as he reached the basement because of the low ceiling.

Since the music was coming from upstairs, it wasn't quite as loud down here. He heard Talulah when she gasped and dropped the box she'd been lifting. Something that sounded like dishes broke, but neither of them paid any attention to that. Her eyes flew wide and so did his. She wasn't wearing anything except a pair of panties and some slippers.

He immediately spun around to charge back up the stairs. But he forgot about the low ceiling. Whacking his head so hard he saw stars, he felt his legs crumple beneath him—and the next thing he knew, he was laid out on the floor.

Three

Torn between darting around Brant so she could run upstairs and get her clothes, which she'd taken off because of the heat, and making sure he was okay, Talulah froze. The second she realized he was bleeding, however, his well-being became more important than her modesty. "Are you okay?" she said, trying to cover her breasts with one hand while she dropped down beside him.

He squinted at her. "Are you really naked? Because if you're not, I hit my head harder than I thought."

She was tempted to laugh but couldn't. She was too concerned. He'd hit his forehead near the temple and nearly knocked himself out. "I'm sorry. I wasn't expecting company. Should I call an ambulance?"

He closed his eyes. "No. Just…give me a minute."

"Okay. I'm going to get dressed. Don't move. I'll be right back."

She ran upstairs to where she'd shed her clothing one piece at a time. Then she turned off the music and found her yoga pants where she'd tossed them while throwing out the dated food in the pantry, but she was so panicked and sweaty it wasn't easy to get them back on. She cursed as she struggled to pull them all the way up, but she didn't want to take the time to go upstairs and rummage through her luggage to find something else.

Once she'd finally succeeded, she spotted her shirt thrown across the back of a kitchen chair, but didn't bother looking for her bra. At least she was covered.

After filling one of her aunt's flour-sack dish towels with all the ice that was left in the freezer, she hurried back to the basement to find Brant trying to get up.

"No, don't," she told him. "I have ice."

He allowed her to press him back down and groaned when she set the makeshift cold pack gently on the knot forming on his head. "What are you doing here?" she asked, but he was so disoriented he couldn't give her a coherent answer.

She bit her lip as she studied his face. How serious was this? Should she call for help?

"What's wrong?" he said. "Am I dying?"

Her heart leaped into her throat. "Why would you ask that? How bad do you feel?"

She knew he'd been joking when he tried to chuckle. "The look on your face..."

"I'm a little stunned. That's all. Let's get you upstairs."

"I'm not sure I can stand. I feel pretty woozy," he admitted. "I was out in the sun all morning. I think that's making matters worse."

"I'll help you." She draped his arm around her shoulders so she could support him, but he was too big and heavy. Fortunately, he was able to grab hold of the railing and use it to pull himself to his feet.

They made slow progress, but with her support, he managed to climb the stairs. She would've put him on the couch in the living room, but her aunt's Victorian settee was way too small for him and would've been almost as uncomfortable as the dirt floor in the basement. "Can you make it up one more flight?" she asked.

"What?" he said as if he didn't comprehend the question, but he allowed her to guide him up to her aunt's room, where she eased him onto the bed and removed his boots.

"I'm going to call a doctor," she said.

"Don't." He waved her off. "I'll be fine—" he winced as he touched the cut on his head "—in a minute."

Was that true? She'd heard that head wounds typically bled a lot, but the sight of so much blood dripping onto the pillow scared her.

She went into the bathroom, ran some cool water onto a washcloth and returned to clean him up.

"Where am I?" he asked, looking around the unfamiliar room, with its collection of hatpins and hatboxes, as though he'd fallen down the rabbit hole in *Alice in Wonderland.*

"You're in Aunt Phoebe's bed. I bet you never thought you'd find yourself here."

He looked confused. "I have an aunt Phoebe?"

"No. She's *my* aunt. Do you know who *I* am?"

"Of course."

"What's my name?"

He held her gaze. "Talulah."

"Good answer."

"I've always liked that name," he volunteered and repeated it a few more times, as though he enjoyed the way it rolled off his tongue: "Talulah... Talulah... Talulah..."

That he remembered her was reassuring; she tried to ignore the rest because it was odd. Obviously, he didn't know what he was saying. But when she heard her name with a question mark at the end, she pulled the washcloth away. "What?"

"You are so *beautiful.*"

She had a feeling he wasn't talking exclusively about her

face—could tell it was a reaction to what he'd seen right before he hit his head—and felt her cheeks start to burn. But it was so hot in the room she doubted he'd realize he'd embarrassed her. "When you come back to yourself, you're going to be mortified you said that to me," she told him.

He blinked at her, obviously perplexed. "Why? I'm just being honest."

"Because you don't like me, remember?"

"I never said that."

"You didn't have to."

"You're wrong. I like you a lot."

She found this earnest, boyish version of Brant rather endearing, despite everything that'd happened, and tried to galvanize herself against the effect he was having on her as she worked to wash him up. Then she wrapped his head in a bath towel along with the ice.

When she was finished and had changed the pillowcase, too, he looked up at her and said, "*Where* am I again?"

He couldn't remember from five minutes ago. "That's it," she said. "I'm calling for help."

"No, I'm okay," he argued, but she went to find her phone anyway and used it to ask Google what to do in the case of a head injury.

"It says to seek medical attention if there's been a loss of consciousness, even a brief one," she told him. "Do you think you lost consciousness?"

"When?" he asked.

She shook her head. "Never mind. How are you feeling?"

"My head is killing me."

"According to what I'm reading, I can give you some painkillers—if I can find some in this house."

She ran downstairs and rifled through the cupboards and drawers, eventually coming up with a small bottle of ibuprofen. It'd expired last year, but she figured even if it wasn't as effective as usual, something was better than nothing. She got a glass of water and carried that up with two tablets.

His eyes were closed when she got back. "You're not going to sleep, are you?" she asked in alarm. If he had a concussion, she couldn't let him drift off. Everything she'd ever heard about blows to the head made that clear.

When he didn't answer, she jiggled his arm. "Brant?"

His eyelashes fluttered, as if it was a major effort to lift his eyelids. But he eventually managed to look up at her. "Talulah?"

He still knew who she was, although he sounded surprised she was there. "What?" she asked.

"I like your name."

"You've already told me that," she said, hoping he wouldn't say she was beautiful again.

He tried to finger the gash on his forehead, but she pushed his hands away. "Did you hit me with something?" he asked.

"No, of course not!" He definitely needed to be checked, she decided. Was a knock on the head like this one serious enough to bring him to the emergency room?

She was about to get him up so she could help him to her car when she remembered that there'd been a doctor in her family's church, and she'd seen a telephone list of the members—the entire congregation—in a kitchen drawer when she was searching for painkiller.

What was the guy's name? She knew him from when she used to attend services. Gregory... Or Gregor... Dr. Gregor!

Hopefully, he still lived in town.

After returning to the kitchen, she located the list. Sure enough, Dr. Joseph Gregor was on it.

She used her aunt's ancient rotary phone to make the call. She thought he'd be more likely to pick up if he saw a number he recognized.

Thankfully, someone—a man—answered on the second ring. "Phoebe?" he said uncertainly.

She could tell that whoever had answered the phone found it strange to be getting a call from a woman who was supposed to be dead. "No, it's her great niece, Talulah."

"Sorry about that," he said. "Your mother's aunt played the piano for me whenever I sang in church. I couldn't imagine anyone else calling me from this number. But I remember you from when you were just a little girl."

"Is this Dr. Gregor?"

"It is."

"Then I remember you, too. And I hate to bother you on a weekend, but there's been a little accident over here."

"What happened?"

"Someone has a head injury. Can you come over right away?"

"Of course. I'll be there in about fifteen minutes."

As soon as she hung up, Talulah hurried back to the bedroom. "Don't fall asleep," she reminded Brant, grabbing his hand.

She was taken aback when he held on to her. "I'm not," he mumbled, but he was clearly on the brink of it.

"I have a doctor coming," she informed him.

"Who needs a doctor?"

"*You* do. You have a concussion, remember?"

"Oh." He seemed to mull that over for several seconds. Then he said, "Is that why my head hurts?"

"Your head hurts because you hit it on the ceiling in the basement."

"Right. And I hit my head because…" Lines formed on

his forehead as he struggled to remember. Then his expression cleared. "You were naked!"

Talulah winced. "Not *completely* naked."

"Almost naked," he insisted. "God, you're beautiful."

"Do we have to talk about this *again*?"

His teeth flashed in a roguish grin. "It certainly helps keep me awake…"

She rolled her eyes. "If that's what it's going to take, okay. But you'd better not be bringing that up again and again on purpose."

"Are you really worried about me?" he asked in surprise.

"No," she said, but with the way she was clinging to his hand, she was pretty sure he knew it was a lie.

Talulah paced at the foot of the bed while Dr. Gregor took Brant's blood pressure, listened to his heart and checked the dilation of his pupils with a penlight. Since Brant had asked her the same questions over and over, despite the number of times she'd answered him, she knew something was wrong with his brain and hoped he was going to be okay. She also hoped he had the presence of mind not to mention *why* he hit his head. He liked talking about it, but that was more information than she wanted circulating in Coyote Canyon.

So far, Brant had let her handle the conversation with the doctor, except when Dr. Gregor posed a direct question to him.

"Brant, can you tell me what month it is?" the doctor asked.

Brant took a moment to reflect on it. Then he said, "June?"

The doctor glanced at Talulah; it was August 11.

"What do you think?" she murmured as he put his instruments away.

"He's got a concussion, all right," he replied. "But from what I can tell it's a mild one. His pupils are reacting as they should, and the cut on his forehead isn't deep. I'm guessing he'll be fine tomorrow, but you'll have to watch him during the night."

"How do I do that?" she asked. "Do I need to keep him awake?"

"No. They've proven there's no benefit to that. He can sleep, but if he gets nauseous, acts uncoordinated or throws up, take him to the hospital right away."

The prospect of a middle-of-the-night trek to the emergency room because his brain was bleeding or swelling was more than a little daunting. She hoped it wouldn't be necessary. "Before you got here, he was saying he'd been on the roof of a barn in the hot sun," she said. "Could he also have heatstroke?"

"It's possible. But his temperature, pulse and breathing are normal, so I think it's a plain old concussion. Just keep a cool cloth on his forehead and make sure he gets plenty of liquids. He should be okay."

A gentle breeze was coming through the windows. That, together with the shade provided by the box elder trees now that the sun had migrated into the west, was bringing down the temperature. But it was still too hot for comfort in the small, cramped room. "Should I take him home, where it's got to be cooler?"

The doctor frowned as he looked over at Brant, who'd already drifted off to sleep. Then he checked his watch. "There's no guarantee he has air-conditioning. A lot of people in this area don't. And I doubt it'd be worth waking him, not when it's already starting to cool off here. Once the sun goes down, it'll be temperate enough."

Getting both Brant and his truck home would mean she'd have to involve someone else, and she preferred not to do that, anyway. Jane was the person she'd call if she needed help, but her childhood friend was with her cousins at Glacier National Park until Tuesday night. "Okay," she said. "Thank you. How much do I owe you for coming out?"

"There's no charge," he said. "It wasn't a far drive, and my exam only took a few minutes."

"Are you sure? I feel I owe you something—"

He lifted his hand to stop her when she reached for her purse, which was sitting on the dresser. "No, please. I want to do this in memory of your great aunt—for all the times she accompanied me when I sang. And she used to bring us pickled beets whenever she canned them. The least I can do to repay her kindness is be of some service to you."

"I appreciate that."

"She was a fixture in this town," he said. "Such a strong, determined woman."

Talulah smiled, somewhat surprised to find he genuinely seemed to admire Phoebe. "There are beets in the cellar. Let me get you some."

She ran downstairs, grabbed as many jars as she could carry and brought them to Dr. Gregor as he stood waiting on the porch, dabbing his sweat-dampened forehead with a handkerchief.

"Well, will you look at this," he said, sliding his thick-rimmed glasses higher on his nose. "I'll really enjoy them. And I'll think of Phoebe every time I open a jar."

"Thank you for coming."

Talulah watched him get into his Suburban before she went back inside, retrieved the fan she'd been using in the basement and carried it to the bedroom.

Brant seemed to be sleeping deeply as she plugged it in

and turned it on. He moved when she refreshed the rag on his forehead, but he didn't wake up, so she sat at her aunt's desk in the corner and read a suspense novel, some news and surfed the internet on her phone for a couple of hours. She had so much to do, but if she went very far from the room, she wouldn't be able to hear if Brant needed her, especially with the fan on.

It was only eight when she grew bored. While refreshing the rag on his forehead yet again, she felt his cheeks with the back of her hand to judge his temperature. He seemed to be cooling off. She wondered if she should remove his shirt and possibly his jeans. She had no doubt he'd be more comfortable. But she wasn't convinced that getting his clothes off would be worth waking him.

She was just trying to think of something else she could do to entertain herself when she saw that his eyes were open and tracking her.

"How do you feel?" she asked.

"Like someone's taking a sledgehammer to my head," he muttered.

"I'll get you some more painkillers." She was no longer worried about the bottle of ibuprofen being past its expiration date. While she was on her phone, she'd learned that most tablet medications remain effective years after opening them.

She hurried to the kitchen and returned with two more tablets and a glass of cold lemonade. "Are you hungry?" she asked as she helped him sit up so he could take the pills.

"No," he said. "But I do need to go to the bathroom."

He managed to swing his legs over the side and sit up straight, but she stopped him there. "You'll be cooler if we can get some of these clothes off you," she said, and he held up his arms as she tugged off his T-shirt.

She tried not to admire his chest and shoulders, but they were a work of art—even with such a marked farmer's tan. "Now for the bathroom," she said as she pulled him to his feet.

"You okay?" she asked, quickly steadying him when he swayed.

"I think so."

She guided him to the bathroom, which was out in the hall.

"I'm guessing you can manage now," she said, once he grabbed onto the sink.

"Yeah. I got it."

She waited in the hall until she heard the toilet flush and the taps go on as he washed his hands.

When he came out, she saw that he hadn't bothered to zip or button the fly of his jeans. "We might as well get rid of these, too," she said. "You'll be a lot more comfortable."

He didn't argue. He just leaned against the wall as she removed his socks and peeled off his jeans, which she tossed aside.

"All set?" she asked when he was wearing nothing but his boxers.

"That feels *a lot* better," he admitted. "It's fucking hot in here."

"No kidding," she agreed as they moved back to the bed. "But it's cooling down."

"Where are you going?" he mumbled when she turned to leave the room.

"I'll be downstairs for a bit."

He grimaced as he fingered the dried blood in his hair. "I'm sorry that you're having to take care of me."

"I don't mind." She certainly couldn't complain about the view, especially now that he was almost naked.

"What time is it?" he asked. "Aren't you tired? Why don't you come sleep with me?"

There were two other bedrooms in the house, so she had options, but she planned on staying much closer to him than that. "Maybe I will later, if you don't take up the whole bed," she joked.

"Just push me over."

"We'll see. Are you sure you're not hungry?"

"I don't feel like eating."

Renewed concern made her hesitate at the door. "That isn't because you're nauseous, is it?"

"I don't think so. All I want to do is sleep," he said and a few minutes later, he'd drifted off again.

Talulah went to the kitchen and tossed herself a salad. Then she decided to bake homemade croissants stuffed with ham and Gruyère cheese, using the dough she'd made and chilled last night. They didn't sell croissants at the dessert diner, so it'd been ages since she'd attempted them and was in the mood for a challenge. They could be tricky. The secret was adding a little brown sugar to the recipe, which tasted wonderful with all those buttery layers.

As she worked, she checked on Brant periodically. Fortunately, he seemed fine.

The croissants filled the house with the yeasty smell of fresh bread as they baked. Once they were done, Talulah put one on a plate and took it upstairs to see if she could tempt Brant to eat.

He stirred as she pressed a hand to his forehead.

"What's that incredible smell?" he muttered.

"I made ham and cheese croissants."

"You *made* them? No one makes croissants. I don't know where they come from. Heaven, maybe."

She had to admit he was cute when he was at a disadvantage. "Are you hungry? Because you might feel better if you eat a few bites."

"In the morning."

"You don't want anything tonight?"

His eyes latched onto her. "Does what I want matter?"

She could tell he was setting her up. "Maybe... Why?"

"I want you to come to bed with me."

When she hesitated, he said, "I'm harmless. What could I do? Look at me."

She *had* been looking at him. That was part of the problem. He looked pretty damn good to her, and she didn't want to fall into the same trap so many other women had fallen into, wanting Brant when he was unobtainable.

But she had such a hard time falling in love she couldn't believe that would be a serious concern—not for her—so she shrugged off her reservations. Sleeping in the same bed would be better than waking up every hour or two to cross the hall and check on him.

"Okay. I'll be up soon."

She went down to the kitchen to eat and take care of the mess, and when she returned, he was asleep again.

Grabbing the tank top she normally wore to bed, and a pair of pajama shorts she usually didn't bother with, she changed in the bathroom before creeping back into the room and lying next to him.

She'd been careful not to jiggle the mattress when she crawled in, and she was being mindful about staying on her side. So she was surprised when he reached over and pulled her into the curve of his body. "There you are," he mumbled into her hair.

Thankfully, it'd cooled off enough that she didn't mind being so close. She held her breath, waiting to see what he'd do next. But he didn't do anything. Within seconds, she could hear his breathing deepen and feel the steady rise and fall of his chest. And before she knew it, she found herself relaxing into the comfort of his body.

Four

Brant wasn't in bed with her anymore. That was the first thing Talulah noticed as she slowly came awake. She thought maybe it was morning. That he'd simply gotten up and left and she no longer needed to take care of him.

But when she forced her heavy eyelids to open, she saw that it was still pitch-black outside.

Had he gotten sick? Was he throwing up?

The doctor had warned her that would mean a trip to the hospital.

Jumping out of bed, she called his name but got no response.

It was then that she heard the sound of running water coming from the bathroom.

He was in the shower.

Shoving a hand through her hair, she padded quickly out of the bedroom into the hall and knocked to check on him.

No answer.

She cracked open the door, improving the odds of him hearing her. "Brant?" she called. "Are you okay?"

"Talulah?" he responded. "Are you up?"

Now that he knew she was there, she felt safe poking her head into the room, and he poked his head through the crack in the shower curtain that enclosed the old-time, claw-foot tub.

"You weren't in bed and… I was worried about you," she explained.

"I'm fine."

She covered a yawn. "How's your head?"

"Still hurts, but I'm doing better."

Relieved that there was no emergency, she sagged against the door frame—until she noticed her toothbrush on the side of the sink. *"You used my toothbrush?"* she cried.

"Sorry," he said with a sheepish expression. "I *had* to brush my teeth. I would've used your great aunt's if that was all I could find."

She laughed in spite of her outrage.

"I'll buy you a new one tomorrow," he added.

She didn't really mind that he'd used it; she was just surprised he'd be bold enough to help himself to such a personal possession. "There's no need. I'm sure I'll survive your germs."

Their eyes connected and something passed between them that sent a wave of pleasure through Talulah. When his gaze moved down over her, speculatively but with obvious interest, she knew he'd felt it, too.

"Well, if you're going to let me use your toothbrush, maybe you won't mind a few more of my germs," he said.

She told herself she'd better get out of there—*fast*. They were alone in the middle of the night, he was naked and she was barely dressed. But her feet wouldn't carry her. "What do you mean?" she asked.

"Would you like to join me?"

She felt her jaw drop. "Are you propositioning me?"

When she stated it that baldly, she figured he'd laugh it off and say he was just messing around. Brant Elway had never shown any interest in her. Even if he was attracted to her—although she'd never gotten that feeling—his loyalty to Charlie would've kept him from making any sort of move. But they were just kids when she was with Charlie. The wedding was so long ago it probably seemed like a moot point now.

He maintained eye contact. "Yeah. I guess I am."

She felt her breath rush out of her lungs. Why her? And why not Ellen? "You must've hit your head even harder than I thought."

"You don't want to?"

"*You* don't want to!" she clarified.

He blinked at her. "I invited you, didn't I?"

"Yes, but…you've never liked me."

"That's not true," he said. "You just…got in the way sometimes." He grinned. "And now you're not in the way anymore. Are you seeing anyone?"

Talulah thought of Paul. She knew he'd like a commitment, and she hoped she could give him one eventually. But after breaking as many hearts as she had, she was going to take it slow. Maybe even *very* slow. She didn't want to end up in another relationship that progressed toward a wedding she couldn't follow through with. "I've recently started seeing my business partner," she said.

"Are you…exclusive?"

"No, it's a brand-new development."

His gaze lowered to her white tank, and she realized he could see the outline of her nipples through the thin fabric. "So you wouldn't be hurting anybody…"

Paul wouldn't be happy about it, of course. But she didn't see why he'd even have to know. He could be out with another woman right now; they had no claim on each other.

"You're thinking about it…" Brant said.

She nibbled on her bottom lip. "I'm looking for pitfalls."

"You're only here for, what…a few weeks? You won't be around long enough for this to go wrong."

That sounded like a reasonable argument…

"And I'm pretty sure we'd have one hell of a good time," he added, his smile widening.

His blue eyes, with those thick black eyelashes, were so beautiful she told herself not to look at them. She didn't need to complicate her life by sleeping with her old arch-enemy.

Then again… If *she* didn't expect anything to come of it, and *he* didn't expect anything to come of it, would it be so terrible to have a last hurrah before going back to Seattle and trying to devote herself to a more serious relationship with Paul, who'd make a wonderful life partner?

"If you get in this shower and you're not enjoying yourself, you can always change your mind," he offered.

Her heart was pounding so hard she was afraid he could hear it. She wondered why she'd never felt this excited about Paul. Maybe it was because she and Brant hadn't seen each other in years and had once been adversaries. Or maybe it was the temporary nature of a fling—the taboo of it. It could even be simpler than that. Raw lust wasn't a minor consideration with a man as virile as Brant. "You won't tell anyone…"

"It'll be like it never happened," he said. "So…what do you say?"

She didn't say anything. She shimmied out of her pajama shorts and panties. Then she paused, suddenly feeling a little panicked, even though the length of her shirt meant he couldn't see anything quite yet. Did she really want to do this and then possibly run into him in town over the next few weeks?

She didn't have an answer for that, but before she could

change her mind, he pulled the curtain back the rest of the way, taking the risk of baring it all first.

After gathering her nerve, she lifted her shirt over her head and dropped it on the floor.

Although Talulah had always been attractive, with a smattering of freckles across her small, upturned nose, thick honey-blond hair and wide, hazel eyes, Brant had never let himself think too much about her. She'd been with his best friend. That had put her out of bounds.

But it'd been fourteen years since her relationship with Charlie. And when he'd spotted her at the diner with no makeup and her hair piled loosely on top of her head, a few long strands falling around her face, he'd realized she'd gotten even prettier.

Not only was he attracted to her in a physical sense, he was beginning to like her. She'd been kind, gentle and diligent in taking care of him. Of course, that didn't absolve her of standing his best friend up at the altar. But he wasn't looking for anything long-term, so it wasn't necessary to heed that warning sign.

As he helped her into the tub, he couldn't take his eyes off her face—even though there were a lot of other beautiful things to look at now that she wasn't wearing any clothes. She seemed hesitant and uncertain, which concerned him.

"What's wrong?" he asked. "If you don't want to do this—"

She shook her head. "That's not it."

"Then what's going on?"

"I'm nervous," she admitted. "I've been so involved with my business for the past few years, I've had no social life. Other than sleeping with Paul once, a week ago, I haven't been with anyone since my last fiancé as a kind of...self-imposed punishment."

There was a lot to unpack in that statement. A long period of celibacy she attributed to a self-imposed punishment was one thing. The guy she'd mentioned she was starting a relationship with was her partner in the dessert diner, which seemed like an unnecessary risk to her business. But Brant was most interested in her use of the words *last fiancé.*

"How many have fiancés have you had?" he asked.

She frowned. "Three."

He felt his eyebrows slide up. "And you've broken each engagement?"

"At the altar," she admitted with a wince.

He gaped at her. *"Like what you did to Charlie?"*

"Something's wrong with me," she told him. "I get close and then I just...can't go through with it. Why does everyone want to get married, anyway? It's so permanent and...and terrifying. It ruins a good thing. Whenever I imagine saying 'I do' to that kind of lifelong commitment, I have such a terrible anxiety attack that I have no choice but to bolt."

"No kidding?" he said. "So it wasn't just Charlie."

"No."

He could tell she felt absolutely miserable about what she'd done. But the numbers were still shocking. "And you're telling me this because..."

"You need to know. Before we...before we go any further. I realize you're not interested in anything long-term, but I feel it's only right to warn you." She blinked quickly, evidence that she was tearing up. "I can't stand the thought of hurting anyone else."

"Then...why do you say yes to the men who propose to you?" he asked.

"I don't know!" she replied. "Because I'm a pleaser, I guess. I have trouble saying no to the people I care about. With Charlie and Tim and Jason—they just kept at me until I finally gave in."

"You didn't learn your lesson with Charlie?"

"I was so young. And Tim and Jason came right after, when I was still too young, and promised it would be different with them. That I'd finally be happy to go through with it."

"And they were wrong. *Both* of them."

"Yes."

The reservations he'd had about her—the residual anger and outrage from fourteen years ago—melted into compassion. She seemed completely sincere, even traumatized by her own behavior. If she *didn't* have a guilty conscience, she wouldn't have felt the need to make such a confession. She hadn't left Charlie or anyone else at the altar because she was indifferent or callous. She'd *tried* to give the men who'd asked her to marry them what they wanted.

"Well… You can relax." He grinned. "I'm not even going to mention marriage."

Instead of laughing at his response, she seemed genuinely relieved. "Okay. That sounds good. You have a concussion, anyway, so you'll probably forget all about this in the morning."

He brought her naked body up against his, groaning as her soft breasts came into contact with his bare chest. "That would be tragic. I hope I won't forget a second of it," he said and bent his head to kiss her.

Talulah's heart began to pound even harder as Brant's lips met hers. She'd made fun of her sister and every other woman she knew who'd ever dreamed of kissing him— and here she was kissing him herself. But he was so good at physical intimacy that she couldn't regret taking advantage of the opportunity. His lips were firm yet pliable, his hand came up to brace the back of her head, and he didn't immediately overpower her and invade her mouth with a greedy tongue. His kiss was restrained, respectful and delicious all at the same time.

To her surprise, and probably his, too, she caught his face in her hands and was the first to take the kiss deeper.

When he obliged and added more intensity, she thought, This *is what a kiss should be like*, and hated that she immediately compared Brant to Paul and found Paul wanting.

Paul is a good man, she reminded herself and tried to shove him out of her mind. She wasn't going to ruin this by thinking about anyone or anything except Brant. By warning him of her past, she'd set herself free. It wasn't that she believed she had to worry he'd fall in love with her. She suspected he was probably as incapable of commitment as she was. She'd been honest for her own peace of mind, and she was glad she'd said what she had. Now she could cast off her fears and inhibitions, let loose for one night and simply enjoy Brant.

"Wow," he said on a long breath and looked slightly dazed as he stared down at her.

"What is it?" she asked.

"I just..." He gave his head a slight shake. "This is going to be even better than I thought," he said and the next kiss proved to be as carefully crafted and perfectly executed as the first.

"It's the little things," she said.

He rested his forehead against hers. "What?"

She hadn't meant to say that out loud. It was simply what she'd been thinking. But she didn't mind paying him the compliment; he deserved it. "It's the little things that take something like a kiss from good to great."

He seemed unsure of how she meant that statement. "And the way I kiss is…okay?"

She chuckled. "It's better than okay. It's fucking *great*," she said and the next kiss—and the kiss after that—grew even more intense until she was so eager to feel him inside her she was trembling.

But it was almost impossible to make love in a claw-foot tub, so he stopped himself and grabbed a towel for each of them.

They didn't take the time to dry off very well. They weren't willing to be apart for even a few seconds. They dropped their towels along the way and bumped into the walls and furniture while they continued to touch and kiss until they reached the bedroom.

"Thank God," he said when they fell into bed. "If this room had been any farther away, we would've had to do it up against the wall."

She would've laughed, but she was feeling too many other things. He'd quit being so deliberate, had lost the ability to control himself to the same degree as he could in the beginning. But that only made everything more exciting. She was a little out of control herself, so she wanted him to be out of control with her. His ragged breathing and eager movements confirmed that she wasn't alone in her need for release.

"What about birth control?" he asked as he rolled her beneath him.

She barely had the breath to speak. "I'm on the pill, and I'm clean."

"Me, too."

She managed another gulp of air. "Good, because I don't think I could stop now if I wanted to," she said and gasped as he immediately pressed inside her.

Once he was settled between her legs, he paused to look

down at her for a few seconds before starting to thrust. He smoothed the hair out of her face, which seemed more intimate, in a way, than what they were doing below the waist. She smiled at him, and the smile he gave her in return left her breathless. They weren't just having sex, she realized. They were sharing a level of intimacy that required trust, and he seemed to recognize and appreciate that.

He continued to watch her as he began to move, and she wrapped her legs around his hips, allowing the tension to build higher and higher. This had to be the best sex of her life. She thought it was odd that it would be with Brant and not with any of the men she'd tried to marry. The irony didn't escape her, but she wasn't willing to think about it right now. Giving herself completely over to Brant, she cried out when she hit climax, and saw him close his eyes in relief.

"I made it," he muttered and let himself go.

When Brant woke up, pale shafts of sunlight were just beginning to come through the windows, the bed was a complete mess and Talulah was all tangled up with him.

Holding still so he wouldn't wake her, he took a few minutes to enjoy the satisfying pressure of her head resting on his shoulder, having her leg wrapped around his and her arm flung casually across his chest. He'd never dreamed he'd have sex with "Talulah the Runaway Bride," but she'd been surprisingly responsive and exciting—and yet real and vulnerable, too. When he looked at her now, gone was the girl who'd frustrated him so many nights in high school by stealing Charlie away when it would've been more fun to have his best friend along as a wingman. Making love with *this* person had been absolutely intoxicating.

Unable to resist, he lifted a hand to cup her bare breast,

and that caused her to stir. "Hey," she mumbled, opening her eyes.

He rolled her beneath him again, resting his weight on his elbows while running his lips up her throat. "I'm sorry for waking you, but I can't help it."

She let her fingers delve into his hair while being careful to avoid the cut high on his forehead. "What time is it?"

"Early," he said and kissed her.

"How're you feeling?"

"Better."

"Can you tell me what month it is yet?"

"August."

"Hallelujah!" She covered a yawn. "Do you remember telling the doctor it was June?"

"I remember not being able to figure it out."

"So you're not shocked to find yourself in my bed."

He grinned at her. "Nope. I can recall every detail— from the birthmark on your perfect round ass to the sounds you make when you come."

Her face flushed. "Spare me the details. I'm not sure how we ended up like this. We don't even know each other that well."

"We've known each other since we were kids. You're just embarrassed. But you shouldn't be, because thinking about last night makes me want you again." He slid off her so he could move his hand down the plane of her stomach.

Her expression grew more serious. "Aren't you too tired for this?"

"No. I've been sleeping since I hit my head. You're the one who probably needs more rest. But I'm hoping you'll be able to stay in bed once I go to work."

She scowled. "You're not going to work today."

"There's some things I have to get done."

"It's Sunday."

"Cows don't know that."

"Can't your brothers fill in for you? You just had a concussion. You should take some time off."

He found the spot he was looking for and felt himself grow hard when she gasped at the contact. "I'll be careful."

She closed her eyes as if she could no longer think straight, but managed to add, "What brought you here in the first place?"

"Ellen asked me to let you use my portable air conditioner."

"That was nice of her."

"I'm about to show you how nice *I* can be," he joked and took her nipple in his mouth as he pressed a finger inside her.

Her breathing went shallow and her hands gripped his forearm as he leaned back to watch the emotions play across her face. "You're beautiful, Talulah Barclay," he said. "I hope you know that."

Her eyes grew clear and focused as she looked at him. He got the impression that she'd never dreamed he'd consider her that attractive. He must've done a better job of selling his dislike of her in high school than he'd thought. But she didn't explain what she was thinking or feeling. Pushing him onto his back, she got on top and straddled his hips as she took him inside her. Then she stared down at him, watching him as intently as he'd been watching her while slowly riding him—so slowly he almost begged her to pick up the speed.

In the end, however, he was glad he held off and let her do it her way. The climax she gave him was more than worth the wait.

Five

When Brant opened his eyes again it was nearly nine thirty according to the clock radio by the bed. He blinked at the ceiling, trying to remember where he was, but then his hand encountered the soft body of a woman next to him and the memories came tumbling back. After waking Talulah earlier, he hadn't planned on sleeping longer, since he normally got up by six. But last night had been anything except normal, and Talulah was partially right when she said his brothers could fill in for him—they *could* do that, at least for a while.

Careful not to wake her, he slid out of bed, went to the bathroom and pulled on his jeans, which he found in the hall. His shirt and boots were still in the bedroom, but he didn't go back for them. It was already growing warm. He wanted to grab the AC unit from his truck and get it working so Talulah would be as comfortable as possible when the temperature rose today.

But he was so hungry as he started down the stairs that the scent of the ham and cheese croissants she'd made last night drew him to the kitchen.

As soon as he found them in the fridge, he put one in

the microwave and, while he waited for it to heat up, felt his pockets for his phone.

It wasn't there. He must've left it in his truck. His brothers were probably freaking out, wondering where he was, but he supposed a few more minutes without checking in wouldn't change anything.

The croissant oozed a white cheese he'd never tasted before, but he loved it—so much that he put another one in the microwave while he walked outside to get the air conditioner. He was yawning and scratching his chest as he stepped off the porch when he caught sight of a familiar vehicle parked behind his truck. Charlie's.

Brant froze. He'd completely forgotten that he'd told Charlie they'd play pool last night. "Damn it," he muttered as his best friend climbed out of the Explorer he'd been driving for years.

"*Really*, Brant?" he said. "You can have almost any woman you want, and you have to sneak around with Talulah?"

Brant wished he hadn't been so lackadaisical about putting on the rest of his clothes. He knew this didn't look good. But he'd never dreamed he'd have to worry about being seen. Aunt Phoebe's house was out in the country. Ellen was the only neighbor within half a mile, and she was out of town.

"Charlie, before you get too upset, let me take this inside," he said. "Then you and I can go somewhere else and talk."

"And say what?" he demanded.

Not since the canceled wedding had Brant seen Charlie so upset. The way he held his body—like a tightly coiled snake—and the venom in his voice was something Brant had never experienced. Charlie had always been fairly easygoing. "This isn't what you think."

"You *didn't* fuck her? Because that's all I care about."

Brant wished he could answer that question the way Charlie wanted him to answer it. Given the concussion, he probably would've been in a similar state of undress even if he hadn't had sex with Talulah. But he couldn't deny it. That would be a blatant lie. "Can you lower your voice?" he asked. "She's sleeping, and she doesn't need to wake up to this."

"You think I care if she's sleeping?" he cried. "After what she did to me? After what you've *both* done to me?"

"Charlie, you and Talulah haven't been together for fourteen years!"

"So that means *you* can move in on her? She was my *fiancée*, Brant. She's the only woman I've ever loved!"

"It's been fourteen years! You have to get over her."

"Why?" he retorted. "So *you* can have her?"

"We're not together. You're jumping to the wrong conclusions."

"I'm going by the obvious! And I can't believe it. She just got back in town and you're already sleeping with her."

"I'm telling you, I didn't come over here for that," Brant said. "It just sort of…happened. I came over to let her borrow an air conditioner." He gestured at his truck. "See that?"

"Yeah, I see it. If you came over to deliver it, why the hell is it still in your truck?"

"Because I hit my head! I had no plans to… I mean, I didn't come over here with the intention of—"

"Getting her into bed?" he finished.

"Exactly!"

"Then why did you do it?"

This was going from bad to worse. Brant had to get Charlie away from Aunt Phoebe's house before Talulah realized he was there. "Just…stay where you are for a second, okay? I'll be right back. Then we can go somewhere else and talk, like I said before."

Brant's mind was buzzing as he grabbed the air conditioner and hauled it into the house. He wanted to carry it upstairs for Talulah. He figured she'd need it most in the bedroom, and the darn thing was heavy, probably too heavy for her to lift. But at least she'd have it in the house while he dealt with Charlie. He didn't know how long it would take him to convince Charlie to calm down, but he could try to come back later—sneak over in the middle of the night if he had to.

Setting it in the living room, he whipped around to stride back out, only to find that Charlie had followed him in.

"Seriously? You feel that comfortable with her now?" Charlie asked. "You can just…come into her house whenever you want? As if you live here?"

Brant's clothes were upstairs and his second croissant was in the microwave, but he was willing to leave both— even his boots. Charlie was too worked up. Brant didn't want this to play out here, didn't want to make Talulah feel the kind of panic and guilt he was feeling right now.

"Come on, Charlie, let's go," he said, but Charlie's attention suddenly shifted to the stairs as they heard Talulah say, "What's going on?"

"I can't believe you'd come back to town and fuck my best friend," he snapped. "How could you do that after what you did to me?"

Talulah had pulled on Brant's T-shirt. It was backward— she must've grabbed it off the floor since her own clothes were in the bathroom—but the fact that it hit her mid-thigh made it obvious it wasn't hers.

The second she realized they had company, she stretched

the soft cotton down even lower. "I didn't come back here for Brant. I came for my great aunt Phoebe's funeral."

"So that *isn't* Brant's shirt?"

She looked down. "I… I—" she started but couldn't seem to come up with the rest of that sentence.

"Don't bring Talulah into this, Charlie," Brant said. "It's me you're mad at."

"No, I'm mad at her, too. The last time I saw her, she was wearing my ring," Charlie said. "I thought I'd be spending the rest of my life with her."

"I sent the ring back to you," Talulah said, "along with a check for the tuxedo rental and any other expenses my parents didn't cover for the wedding."

"You think this is about money?"

"I know it's not. I'm just saying that I tried to make it right."

"How can a few hundred dollars and returning the ring make what you did right?"

"Not right exactly," she hedged, "but…the best I could do. I sent you an apology, too."

"Yeah, I got your letter. For not intending to hurt me, you certainly did a damn fine job of it," he scoffed as his eyes ran over her tousled hair, Brant's T-shirt and her bare legs and feet. "So what are you these days? Some kind of whore?"

"Charlie, that's enough!" Brant said, but those words acted like a match to a stick of dynamite—minus the long wick. The next thing he knew, his best friend took a swing at him, and it was so unexpected that Brant wasn't able to dodge it entirely. "What the hell's wrong with you?" he asked after Charlie's fist glanced off his cheekbone.

"What's wrong with *me*?" Charlie echoed. "What's wrong with *you*? I trusted you. You *know* how I've always felt about her."

"I also know it's been over for fourteen years!" Brant said, but that didn't seem to make any difference. Charlie tried to hit him again, forcing Brant to defend himself.

Talulah cried out as they crashed into the wall and a picture fell while Brant was taking Charlie to the floor. From there, they wrestled with each other until Brant finally managed to pin him down.

Charlie was breathing so hard he could barely speak as he glared up into Brant's face. "Get off me!"

"I'll be happy to do that," Brant said. "But…is this over?"

"It's over," Charlie muttered. "She's not worth it. And neither are you. We're done. Don't ever call me again."

"Charlie, will you calm down?"

Charlie's stony expression didn't change. "I said to get off me."

Brant stood up slowly, in case Charlie started swinging again.

Fortunately, that didn't happen. Charlie wiped his nose, discovered that it was bleeding and gave Brant a dirty look. "Fuck you," he said. "Fuck you both."

"Wait," Brant said, but Charlie grabbed a lamp off the entry table and threw it down, causing it to shatter into a million pieces, before stomping out.

Talulah's jaw had dropped, and her hand was covering her mouth.

"I'm sorry," Brant said. That was all he could get out before a loud bang drew him to the front window. He was barefoot, so he couldn't reach the door because of the broken glass.

Charlie had rammed Brant's brand-new Ford F-250 before peeling off.

"Did he just hit your truck?" Talulah asked.

Brant stretched his neck, watching a plume of dust fan

out behind Charlie as he rocketed down the driveway. "Yeah."

"How'd he know you were here?" She sounded confused, and he could understand why. She would have no way of knowing that Charlie had never gotten over her—that she'd moved on, but he hadn't.

"I was supposed to play pool with him last night. When he didn't hear from me, he probably started to look around."

Her eyes widened. "But why would he look *here*?"

Because he knew she was back and staying at her great aunt's place. Brant could easily imagine Charlie driving past the house—several times—even if he *hadn't* been actively looking for anyone. But Brant didn't volunteer that. He was too loyal to Charlie to make him sound like a stalker and too mad at himself for hurting his best friend. Somehow, Talulah hadn't seemed off-limits eight hours ago. For one thing, he knew she'd never go back to Charlie, regardless of anything he did. And he'd seen their time together as a night no one would ever have to know about. He certainly hadn't planned on *this*. "He probably looked everywhere."

"Did he do much damage?" she asked, coming up to peer out the window with him.

"Hard to tell from here." Brant didn't want to go out and examine the damage, wasn't quite ready to face it. He was still grappling with what had occurred.

"Are you okay?" she asked, but from the way she was hugging herself, he got the impression she was the one who was rattled.

"Yeah. I'm fine." His cheek was tender. But it could've been a lot worse.

"He was bleeding," she said, staring through the window at the now-empty drive. "Do you think he'll be okay, too?"

"Physically? I'm sure he will. I tried not to hit him, especially in the face. I have no idea how he got a bloody nose."

She turned away from the window. "I couldn't tell you, either. It—it happened so fast."

"It's over now," he said, hoping to reassure her.

She nodded as she stared at the broken lamp. The frame of the picture that'd fallen was cracked, but there'd been no glass in it. So that was good, at least. "Maybe I owe you an apology," she muttered. "You probably weren't thinking straight when you were in the shower last night. I should've said no."

He pinched the bridge of his nose. "I'm the one who should be apologizing. It was my fault."

"You'd hit your head. You had a concussion."

He touched her arm so she'd look up at him. "I knew what I was doing."

"Still, that's how we'll have to play it," she said, sounding more and more assured as she spoke. "It's the only way we *can* play it. Or he'll never forgive you."

Brant remembered promising her he wouldn't tell a soul. Now she was volunteering to be the fall guy? "What are you talking about? I'm not going to blame you. That wouldn't be fair."

She went to the kitchen and came back with a broom, which he took from her.

"You need to go put on some shoes first," he said.

She didn't argue. But neither did she go after her shoes. Stepping away from the glass, she found a chair. "I'm already a lost cause where Charlie and the rest of Coyote Canyon are concerned. But if you act as though you didn't know what was going on, this shouldn't affect you."

"How do I act as if I didn't know what was going on?" he asked.

"You just make a big deal of the concussion, say you were out of it."

He grimaced. "No way. I'm not going to make it sound like you took advantage of me. That's ridiculous!"

Her chest lifted as she drew a deep breath. "Then just… refuse to address it."

"How will that solve anything?"

"I'll have Jane spread the word that you had a concussion when you stayed over, and town gossip and conjecture will take care of the rest."

"People will ask me about it."

"And you'll tell them you don't remember what happened. You're one of Coyote Canyon's own. In their eyes, I'm already a pariah. Why *not* have it go this way?"

"Because it's wrong."

Raising her chin in a show of stubbornness, she held his gaze. "Do you want to lose your best friend?"

Squeezing his eyes closed, he rubbed his temples. "Of course not. But the truth is the truth. I was the one who asked you."

"I hurt Charlie when I stood him up at the altar," she said softly. "I don't want to take his best friend away from him, too."

Brant could see the logic in what she was saying. If she was never going back to Charlie, it didn't matter if Charlie blamed her for this. Plus, she was only in town for a month, so the pain, for her, would be short-lived. But then he'd come out of this with no real consequences while she was made to look opportunistic and sexually aggressive—embarrassingly so.

He sighed as he touched the cut on his head from when he'd hit the low ceiling. "I hear what you're saying. It just feels so creepy."

"You can do it for Charlie, can't you?"

"For Charlie, yes. But I'd benefit, too."

"That's okay. At this point, it's about damage control. The punishment doesn't have to be evenly distributed. So…are you in?"

Punishment. Last night shouldn't have cost her anything. She didn't owe Charlie her fidelity fourteen years after breaking off their relationship. But maybe this was her attempt to make up, at least a little, for what she'd done before. She was pushing him down the path that would hurt Charlie the least. But it was also the path that would hurt her the most.

He couldn't help admiring her for trying to take the fall, but he also couldn't accept her offer. "That won't work, Talulah. Charlie, me, you…we'll just have to deal with the truth."

Six

Talulah was still shaken by Charlie's visit when she left Brant in the living room, sweeping up the broken glass, and went upstairs to change. She'd known Coyote Canyon was small enough that she'd probably have to face her ex-fiancé eventually, but she'd never dreamed he'd come to her house, especially at such an inopportune time.

After gathering up her clothes from the bathroom, she carried them into the bedroom and was digging through her suitcase, looking for something to wear, when she heard Brant come up the stairs. She'd closed the door, but he knocked and said, "Talulah? Can I come in?"

She hesitated. He'd already seen all there was to see of her. But that was last night. Today was different—wasn't it?

"Talulah?" he said when she didn't answer right away.

"You can come in." Turning her back to him, she pulled off his shirt and tossed it on the bed where he could grab it, but before she could take hold of her own clothes, he came up behind her, rested his hands gently on her waist and slowly turned her to face him.

"I'm sorry," he said, and since he was looking into her eyes and not at anything else, she believed him.

"It is what it is." She was trying to play it off, but he must've known she felt crappy inside because he pulled her into his arms and rested his chin on the top of her head.

"Having Charlie show up is definitely not the way I wanted last night to end," he said.

"It'll only be a few weeks before I'm gone," she reminded him, but despite her desire to get dressed after what had just happened, being chest to chest was somehow more comforting without clothes. "Hopefully, he didn't do too much damage to your truck."

"I'm almost afraid to go look," he admitted.

"If you can't drive it, I'll give you a ride home."

"Okay." He surprised her by pressing a kiss to her forehead before releasing her. "Do you want me to bring that portable air conditioner up here, or are you going to be working elsewhere today?"

"You could put it in the basement for me. I'm going to try to make some progress down there. I'll wait until this damn heat wave is over before tackling the bedrooms or even the main floor."

"I was thinking it might make you more comfortable when you sleep tonight."

She selected a red summer dress from her suitcase and shimmied into it. "I'd rather it helped me through the hottest part of the day."

"You got it."

While he put on his shirt, her phone went off and she took it from the charger.

When she immediately set it back down, he glanced over. "You're not going to answer?"

"Not right now."

"Why not?"

When she pretended to be too preoccupied digging around in her suitcase to reply, he said, "Was it Paul?"

She was shocked he could remember Paul's name. She'd only mentioned it once. "Yeah. I'll call him later."

He pulled on his socks and picked up his boots while she slipped on a pair of panties under her dress. "Will you tell him about last night?" he asked.

She felt less self-conscious now that she was dressed and somehow emotionally safer, too. Brant didn't act as if nudity was any big deal. But in the light of day, sleeping with him didn't seem like the best decision she'd ever made. Given their background, she almost couldn't believe it'd happened. She certainly hadn't seen it coming. "I don't know. Probably not."

"Because it'll make him angry?"

"Because it'll make him jealous." And it would be an awkward conversation, one that would most likely start a fight. She didn't need that right now, not when they still had several weeks apart and she was relying on Paul to take care of the diner.

He yanked on his boots. "Is he…possessive?" Brant asked.

"Not really. Or…maybe a little." Remembering her last conversation with Paul, after she'd finally slept with him, she amended her answer yet again. "Actually, yeah, I guess he is. He's been pushing harder and harder for us to be exclusive."

"Do you plan to move in that direction?"

"Eventually. If I can. We have a lot in common. And he claims he loves me."

Fully dressed, he sat back as he looked at her. "How do *you* feel?"

"He's a good guy," she said to avoid answering that question more directly. "A girl could do a lot worse."

Brant gave her a funny look. "That's your answer? *A*

girl could do a lot worse? I'd be destroyed if the woman I loved was that dispassionate about me."

She threw up her hands. "I don't know how I feel, Brant. That's the problem with me. That's how I've made so many mistakes in the past."

He stood and faced her, but, fortunately, changed the subject. "When's your great aunt's funeral?"

"I won't know for sure until I talk to the lady from the church. But since my parents are in Africa and my sister can't come, it's just me, so I can be flexible. I'll do it whenever the building's available, although I'd rather it not conflict with the birth of my new niece. I plan on driving to Billings to be there when Debbie goes into labor."

If he remembered Debbie, he didn't say. Like so many other girls, Debbie had noticed every move he'd made, but it seemed that, for him, she'd always been part of the background. "Doesn't your aunt have any other family?"

"None. She never married, never had any kids."

He walked over to where she'd left her phone and flashed it at her face to get past the identity lock.

"What're you doing?" she asked.

"Making sure you have my number, in case you need anything while you're here."

She watched as he called himself so he'd have her number, too. "There won't be any reason for me to bother you—unless I can't get the AC unit you brought into my car when it's time to return it."

"You don't have to worry about that. I'll pick it up. Just let me know when you're done with it."

"Okay. Thanks for…for bringing it over. I'm sorry about your head and…all the rest of it."

He propped his hands on his hips as he studied her. She wished she could tell what he was thinking, but his expression didn't give anything away. After a few seconds, he sighed and said, "I guess I'd better go take a look at my truck."

She found a pair of sandals and slipped them on before heading down herself.

Although he'd swept up the glass, he pointed at the floor. "Be careful. You need a vacuum here. I'm not a hundred percent sure I got everything."

"I'll take care of it," she said. Then he carried the air conditioner to the basement, plugged it in and showed her how to run it before they went outside.

She followed as he strode immediately to the front of his truck. "What do you think?" she asked.

He crouched to examine the damage. "It's not nearly as bad as I expected from the sound of the crash."

Charlie had made a sizable dent in the bumper, but it didn't look as though the engine had been affected. "Is this truck brand-new?"

"Yeah. I only bought it a few months ago."

"That makes this even worse."

"It's a work truck. I would've beat it up eventually," he said, but she didn't find that entirely convincing. If she had her guess, he was more upset than he was showing.

He left the door open as he got in and started the engine. "Sounds fine," he said when it fired right up.

"Good." She stepped back so he could close the door, but he didn't. He squinted against the sun as he looked at her the same way he'd looked at her when they were inside a few minutes earlier—speculatively, as though a lot more was going through his mind than she could read on his face.

"What is it?" she asked.

"It's hard to regret last night," he replied. "I enjoyed every second of it—well, the part that came after I hit my head."

"Fear of commitment doesn't necessarily make me bad in bed," she joked.

His gaze lowered over her as though he was savoring the memory. "You're a long way from bad in bed."

She couldn't help smiling. "I could say the same about you."

He grinned at her. Then he nodded goodbye and closed his door, and she stood in the driveway, watching as he drove off.

"Holy shit," she muttered as she started toward the house. He'd said he was having a hard time regretting what they'd done, and truth be told, so was she.

But how would last night affect the rest of her stay in Coyote Canyon?

Brant didn't know whether he should try to call Charlie or not. He felt bad about what'd happened, had certainly never intended to hurt his best friend. It'd been so long since the wedding, he hadn't thought of Charlie as having any claim on Talulah. Maybe how Charlie would react should've been more obvious to him. He would've expected it if she was planning to move back to town or there was even a remote chance of a reconciliation between them. But she didn't regret leaving Charlie behind. Spending one night with her, when neither of them was committed to someone else, simply hadn't seemed like *that* big a deal.

Until Charlie found out, of course. Now it seemed like a really big deal—so big Brant couldn't believe he'd gotten himself into such a mess. He'd always been careful when it came to women, especially the women in Coyote Canyon. The ranch was his livelihood, his future; he couldn't imagine he'd ever leave the small town he called home. That made it imperative he protect the relationships he had here, so it was pretty ironic that his first major scandal would involve Charlie.

After he pulled into his own drive, he found his phone, which was right where he'd left it yesterday, charging in his truck, and scrolled through his missed calls and messages. There were a few from his brothers, wondering where he was. But the majority had come from Charlie.

We still on for tonight?

Where are you, bro?

Are we playing pool or not?

That was how Charlie's first few texts had gone. Then there'd been a lull for several hours—during which Brant imagined him growing bored and more and more curious and obsessed with Talulah. Once it was late enough that he felt he could safely drive past her aunt's place without being noticed, the tone of his messages had drastically changed.

Are you freaking kidding me?

That had come in at 2:00 a.m.

No way are you with Talulah! You'd better not be fucking her.

4:30 a.m.

You bastard! I'm never going to forgive you for this.

6:00 a.m.

He must've sat in front of her house all night, waiting to ambush Brant as soon as he came out.

In addition to those texts, Charlie had left several profanity-filled voice mails, telling Brant what a lousy friend he was.

With a sigh, he got out and slid his phone in his pocket. He wasn't going to call Charlie. Charlie wouldn't listen to him right now, anyway.

"There you are!" His youngest brother, Kurt, who was twenty-five, had spotted him from the closest paddock and nudged Fancy, one of their best horses, into a gallop to reach him. "Where the hell have you been?" he asked, bringing the horse to a stop a few feet away. "I thought you were going to move the cattle this morning."

Brant didn't want to talk about what'd happened. But he *had* committed to moving the cattle, which his brother had obviously just done for him. And with all the drama involving Charlie, he knew his brothers would hear about Talulah sooner or later. Everyone would. It would be better—for Charlie—if he did what Talulah had asked him to. Otherwise, what she said later wouldn't ring true. But it was going to be difficult to navigate the next few days without resorting to outright lies. "Talulah Barclay's great aunt's house."

Kurt took off his baseball cap and beat the dust off it while his horse threw its head, trying to force enough slack in the reins to nibble at a dandelion coming up through the gravel. "I heard she was back in town. Everyone's talking about it. But…what were you doing with her?"

"Ellen texted to ask if Talulah could borrow the portable air conditioner we've been storing in the bunkhouse, so I drove it over."

"And that took all night?"

Brant indicated the gouge on his forehead. "I hit my

head hard enough to get a concussion while I was there," he replied. "I couldn't exactly drive."

"Why didn't you call one of us? We would've come to get you."

"Talulah had a doctor check me out. He felt it was better if I just rested there until morning."

"Oh." His brother gave him the once-over. "So...are you okay?"

"I am now." Physically, anyway. Inside, he felt like shit—had no idea how he'd repair his relationship with Charlie.

Lines of consternation appeared on Kurt's forehead as he put his hat back on. "What was it you ran into? Because it looks like you hit your face, too."

"I smacked into the ceiling of the basement. The damn thing was too low. Charlie did the rest."

Kurt forced his horse's head back up, which made Fancy prance around. "Did you say *Charlie*? Was it an accident?"

"It was intentional. But I don't want to make a big deal of it." Eager to get into the house, if only to avoid more questions, Brant tried to go around the horse and his brother, but Kurt urged Fancy forward, cutting him off.

"Dude, how is it not a big deal that your best friend punched you in the face?"

"I dodged the brunt of it," he replied. "Didn't even hurt."

"What made him mad in the first place?"

"Finding my truck at Talulah's."

"You didn't tell him about the concussion?"

"Didn't have the chance."

"He wouldn't even let you explain? What an asshole!"

Brant hated playing the innocent. Kurt was only making the guilt he felt worse. He didn't want his brothers rising to his defense when he really *had* done what Charlie was upset about. But he kept going back to that conversation with Talulah and telling himself that handling the situation as she'd requested would hurt Charlie less, even though it made him feel like the biggest jerk on earth. "He's not an asshole. I can see why he'd be mad."

"Why? You didn't sleep with her, did you?"

"I don't want to talk about it anymore, Kurt. Will you get out of my way?"

His little brother's eyes narrowed in suspicion. "You *did* sleep with her."

"That's none of your business."

"But that's why Charlie's mad, isn't it? Has he even spoken to her since she left?" He leaned on the horn of his saddle, rubbing his beard growth with one gloved hand. "Jeez, I was, what…ten or eleven when that whole thing went down. He still cares that much after so long?"

"Obviously." He gestured at the damage to his truck. "He backed into the front of my truck on purpose, too."

Kurt's jaw dropped. "Oh, man, I'd kick his ass."

"He's my best friend."

"I don't care who he is. That right there would be the line."

"I'm not going to kick his ass. Will you move?" he asked again.

"One more sec," his brother said. "Are you and Talulah together now?"

"Of course not," he replied. "She's only in town for her great aunt's funeral."

"So…you and Charlie will be able to get beyond this?"

"I hope so," he said as Kurt finally allowed him to circumvent Fancy. But there was no way to be sure. He'd never seen his friend quite that upset, not since the wedding.

He'd been a shortsighted idiot. But that didn't change the fact that he'd enjoyed every second of it.

* * *

Talulah sat on the floor of the basement, hugging her knees to her chest in front of the portable air conditioner. She was trying to block out the thoughts bombarding her brain by simply listening to the whir of the fan. What had she been thinking? Why had she allowed herself to get involved with Brant? While she and Paul weren't officially together, she knew he wouldn't be happy about her sleeping with another man.

And there was Charlie, of course.

Except…she'd never dreamed she could still hurt Charlie.

Lifting the skirt of her dress to capture more of the cool air, she told herself last night was over and there wasn't anything she could do about it now. The past was the past.

Yet she couldn't stop dwelling on the ramifications. Charlie had always been close to his mother, and his mother and hers were dear friends. For years they'd served together in various community programs. That was part of the reason her mother had been so mortified when she'd run away instead of taking her wedding vows. Talulah didn't want Carolyn to know what'd happened with Brant. But she had no doubt Charlie would tell Dinah, who would email if not call her mother.

Here she was in Coyote Canyon, a place she'd sworn she'd never return to, because she was trying to help her family. She'd thought that maybe, finally, she'd get to be the hero for a change.

Instead, she'd embarrassed her parents again—and on almost her very first night. To make everything worse, Charlie would tell his sister, too, and Averil would be glad she'd cut off all contact with Talulah.

"I do *not* know what I was thinking," she mumbled.

Her phone buzzed more loudly than usual because she'd

left it on a cardboard box. Paul was calling back. He'd tried three times so far. She had to pick up eventually, and the longer she waited, the odder it would seem that she hadn't checked in with him.

Drawing a deep breath, she tried to put some energy into her voice as she answered. "Hello?"

"There you are! Where've you been? I've been trying to reach you."

"Sorry about that. I don't always keep my phone with me while I work."

"No problem. I was just…missing you."

"I miss you, too," she said, feeling guiltier than ever. "How's the diner?"

"Everything's going great. We were absolutely slammed last night. We should consider opening another location."

He'd mentioned that before, many times. He could be so insistent. "I'm not ready for that," she said.

"It won't be as hard to get up and running as this place was."

"I think we need to pay off our debts and get in a stronger financial position before we take on more risk."

"By then we could lose first-mover advantage."

She couldn't think about those kinds of business decisions right now. "We can look into it when I'm back, if you want. Provided we find the perfect location, and it's in a spot we can afford…maybe," she said, putting him off for the time being just to avoid an argument.

"Okay. At least you're open to it. Have you run into Charlie yet?"

"Charlie?" she repeated as if she didn't recognize the name.

"Yeah. The guy you almost married. He's the reason you didn't want to go back to Coyote Canyon, isn't he?"

She'd been completely transparent about her history

and her difficulty with commitment, so at least he'd been warned. She'd also rebuffed every advance he'd made—refused to even let him take her out—until the past year. "Oh, yeah. I just…" She squeezed her eyes closed as the memory of Charlie calling her a whore only a few hours ago echoed through her mind. "I don't think I'll see him."

"But it's such a small town. You said you were almost guaranteed to run into him."

"I'm hoping that's not the case."

"You don't think he'll come to the funeral?"

"He was part of my great aunt's church, so…it's a possibility. It'll depend on how well he knew her. A lot of church members will be there." Including his mother and possibly other members of his large family. Talulah had no doubt of that.

"I wish I could be standing by your side."

That didn't ring entirely true. She'd sort of wanted him to come, had mentioned it once or twice, and he'd said it would be better if he stayed to manage the diner. Anyway, if Paul came, he'd probably be the *only* person by her side, especially now. The fact that Charlie had found Brant at Phoebe's house—her house at the moment—had pulled the past into the present. "It's much more important that you look after the diner, like you said before. Thanks for holding up that end of things."

"Of course. When will the funeral be?"

"Someone from Phoebe's church is coming over today and we'll decide."

"It's nice the church helps out."

"It really is. There're a lot of good people here."

"No one's better than you."

She winced. "Thank you."

"You know how I feel about you. We're meant to be together, Talulah Ray," he said, using her middle name, "and I hope you'll realize that soon."

She tensed. When he started pressing her, she often felt overwhelmed and claustrophobic. It wasn't so much the things he said; it was knowing what he wanted and being unable to give it to him. Why wasn't *he* more skittish? After all, he was the one who'd already been through a divorce. "Don't…don't put any pressure on me, okay?" she said. "I'm sorry, but…dealing with all of this makes me especially sensitive. I—I can't offer you a commitment right now."

"I understand. You do what you have to do and know that I'm eager to see you when you get home."

Slightly surprised and relieved that he'd backed off so easily—that wasn't always the case—she felt some of her anxiety fade away. "Thanks."

She asked if he'd finalized the travel plans for his trip and listened as he went over his itinerary. Then they talked about his mother, who'd had a knee replacement two weeks ago.

"The pain is easing," he assured her just as someone banged on the door upstairs.

She checked the time on her phone. It was her understanding that church didn't let out until two. So…who was this?

Afraid it might be Charlie, or even Averil or Dinah, coming to vent their long-simmering resentment, she told Paul that she had to go. But by the time she'd hurried upstairs, moved the vacuum she'd used to finish cleaning up the shards of glass in the entry and answered the door, there was no one there—just a beautiful bouquet of pink, white and orange peonies with small bits of greenery.

Although it didn't look like the typical funeral arrangement, she assumed that someone had sent it after hearing the news of her great aunt's passing—until she saw a new toothbrush sticking out among the flowers.

Then she knew it had to be from Brant.

Taking the card from its small envelope, she read, "I forgot to tell you I loved your croissants and you might find one in the microwave I never got to eat. Thanks for letting me use your toothbrush."

She put the flowers on the coffee table and sank into a nearby chair, staring at the arrangement for several minutes before navigating to the number he'd typed into her phone this morning and texting him a response.

Thank you.

Life was so unpredictable. Brant Elway was the last man she'd ever thought she'd sleep with. He was also the last man she'd ever thought she'd like.

Yet…she'd wanted to sleep with him. She'd enjoyed sleeping with him. And she definitely liked him.

Seven

A tall, willowy-looking woman in her midfifties, wearing a dress and heels, her soft brown hair curled under, arrived not long after the flowers. Identifying herself as Sarah Carrier from Aunt Phoebe's church, she mentioned how beautiful Brant's arrangement was as she took the seat across from Talulah in the cramped sitting room. She also said that funeral arrangements had come a long way, but Talulah didn't correct the assumption that what Brant had sent was an example of that. The last thing she needed to do was mention his name.

"I'm so sorry for your loss," Mrs. Carrier said as she tucked her purse at her feet.

Talulah nodded. "Thank you. Aunt Phoebe was almost a century old, so it wasn't unexpected, at least."

"She lived a long and good life. I'm sure you'll miss her, but I hope it'll be a comfort to know she's in a better place."

Since this woman belonged to Charlie's church, Talulah guessed she'd heard some of their history. Debbie might even have told her about the wedding. "It's nice of you to help with the funeral."

"Phoebe was part of our church family. Of course we'll help. I bet having you come all the way from Washington to be here at this time means a lot to your mother and sister. It must be difficult for Carolyn to miss the funeral, and Debbie wishes she could do more to help. She told me so on the phone."

"She told me that, too, but she has enough to worry about with the new baby coming," Talulah said. "I can manage here."

"Of course you can, especially because we're happy to fill in wherever you need us."

The "we" in that statement referred to the church generally, Talulah supposed. "I appreciate that."

"Of course." Mrs. Carrier bent to withdraw a piece of paper from her purse, which she held in her lap as she continued. "The building is available on Thursday, as we discussed. I was thinking we'd start at two. That should allow time for the graveside service afterward before we return to the church for dinner."

"That sounds good."

She smiled as she handed Talulah the paper she'd taken out of her purse. "This is the sign-up sheet I circulated during services today, asking for volunteers to contribute to the meal."

Talulah gazed at the names of the various people who'd answered that call. A few of them she recognized as friends of her parents' or people she'd known from childhood. Five of eight slots had been taken for "Potatoes," six of eight for "Green Salad," five of five for "Dinner Rolls," only three of eight for "Gelatin Fruit Salad" and eight out of eight for "Brownies."

"I'm going to make a double batch of potatoes myself," Mrs. Carrier said. "That should give us enough. And the church will provide the ham."

"What a great menu," Talulah said. "It's nice of everyone to contribute."

"Many hands make light work," she chirped.

Talulah glanced down the list again. Aunt Phoebe would have the standard church funeral, which she probably would've liked. That so many people were willing to share the work and expense was deeply touching. But it also made Talulah feel a greater responsibility to her own flesh and blood. She could do more for her great aunt herself. There wasn't any reason to lean on these people where she didn't have to.

"I'll email everyone the recipe for each item so that the meal's consistent," Mrs. Carrier informed her.

Talulah folded the paper and handed it back to her. "This is *very* gracious. But could you email to tell them they won't have to bring anything this time?"

"Excuse me?"

"I could use your help with getting the speakers and arranging any musical numbers for the service, plus setting up the tables and chairs for dinner. But while it was so kind of you to gather volunteers, I'll handle the meal myself."

She blinked several times. "The whole meal?"

"I've been to culinary school and can do it if I start tomorrow. Will I be able to use the kitchen at the church Thursday morning?"

"Of course. I can let you in as early as you'd like."

"That's fantastic."

"You're signing up for a lot of work…"

She was obviously giving Talulah the chance to change her mind. But Talulah was set on making the best meal Coyote Canyon had ever tasted. She wanted to do it for her late mother's aunt, to prove to Phoebe that she was no slouch, even though Phoebe had always preferred her church family. And, she supposed, she was also hoping to show Charlie and those who hated her for what she'd done fourteen years ago that she'd made good. So many had believed that breaking off the engagement and leaving Coyote Canyon meant her judgment was lacking and she'd never amount to anything.

"Would you like to speak at the funeral?" Mrs. Carrier asked.

Talulah opened her mouth to say no. She didn't want to speak, especially in front of people who would be eager to criticize her. The meal was enough of a statement, she told herself. At least she knew she could do that well.

But then she glanced down at the compass tattooed on her arm and remembered what it stood for. She would follow her own conscience regardless of the pressure of "group think," and she wouldn't allow anyone to intimidate her or make her feel "less than." She'd come too far from the self-doubt she'd experienced when she first left her hometown.

"I'll speak," she said. "Since I'm the only representative of the family, I feel it's my duty to say a few words."

Mrs. Carrier beamed at her. "Your aunt would be so proud."

Talulah wasn't convinced of that. Aunt Phoebe had always believed her way was the only way and Talulah's life philosophy was wrong just because it was different from hers.

But Talulah hoped she'd be able to contribute something meaningful.

After Charlie's sister Averil went through a divorce four years ago, she'd brought her son, Mitch, back to Coyote Canyon, and this summer Brant had been giving the boy horseback riding lessons. Averil was working paycheck to paycheck at the bank and living with her parents again, and Mitch didn't have a lot of interaction with his father, who'd moved to California. So, along with Charlie, Brant was trying to help her out and be a good role model for her son.

Charlie was usually the one who brought Mitch to the ranch on Sunday evenings. But after what'd happened this morning, Brant hadn't expected to see either of them today. He was surprised when Averil's old Nissan Altima came trundling down the long gravel drive to his house.

He dropped the sledgehammer he'd been using in an attempt to straighten out his bumper as she noticed him by the detached garage and pulled up next to him.

"Hey," she said as she got out, but there was no smile in the greeting. He could tell by her subdued voice that Charlie had told her about Talulah.

"Hey." He bent slightly, trying to peer into the back seat. "You bring Mitch?"

She tucked her thick dark hair behind her ears. "Not tonight. I thought you might not be in the mood to deal with riding lessons."

Brant wasn't in the mood, but he would've done it. "He's usually pretty excited to come. How'd skipping a week go over with him?"

She tightened the knot on the button-up blouse that was tied above her high-waisted cutoffs. "He'll live through the disappointment. It's important for him to learn that we don't always get what we want."

"You're a good mother," he said. After the loss of her marriage, it would've been easy for her to make Mitch her whole world and spoil him rotten, especially in a small town like Coyote Canyon, where there wasn't much of a social scene. But she had a way of loving him without going too far, and Brant respected her for it.

"I heard about this morning," she said, leaning up against her car.

Brant adjusted his baseball cap to better shade his eyes from the late-afternoon sun. "Figured."

"What happened?"

"I don't want to talk about it."

She toed the small rocks beneath her red flip-flops. "Your brother called about an hour ago."

"Which one?" he asked as he went back to trying to straighten out his bumper with the crowbar.

"Kurt."

"He shouldn't have," he said and meant it.

She sidled closer, trying to get into his line of vision, and jammed her hands in the pockets of her shorts. "He told us you had a concussion and didn't know what you were doing. That true?"

He straightened while deliberating on his response. If he couldn't tell the truth, he didn't want to say anything. "Last night isn't something I'm willing to discuss."

Ignoring his gruff response, Averil indicated the bruise on his cheek. "Charlie went too far. He should've given you the chance to explain."

"There's nothing to explain. What happened happened. There's no changing it now. But I can guarantee you that no one was out to hurt Charlie."

Her lips compressed into a thin, straight line. "God, I hate her."

"Why?" he asked, taken aback by the vitriol in that statement.

"First, she broke Charlie's heart—and as if that wasn't bad enough, now she's after yours."

"She's not after my heart," he scoffed. All Talulah had tried to do was take care of him. *He* was the one who'd turned his stay at her place into more.

"She only wants a man until she gets him, Brant. You

understand that, right? Jane told me she's done the same thing she did to Charlie to two other men. *Two!*"

Standing up so many grooms was excessive, and yet Brant felt slightly defensive of Talulah. After what she'd told him, he sort of understood why she'd done what she'd done and believed she wasn't being malicious. "She obviously has commitment issues. She'd probably be the first to tell you that."

"She doesn't need to tell me. I was a witness to just how big those issues are. She leads the guy on until he goes all in and then—" she snapped her fingers "—it's over."

"It's been fourteen years since the wedding, Averil. When are you going to let that shit go?"

"Emotions aren't that simple, Brant. She's a man-eater. And if you're not careful, you might find that out the hard way."

"Trust me, I can take care of myself."

"That's what you think."

He rolled his eyes at her. "Aren't you being a little overly dramatic?"

Ignoring that comment, she said, "Why'd you go there, anyway?" The sulky sound of her voice suddenly made him uncomfortable. Was she *jealous*? Every once in a while, he got the impression she was hoping for more than the friendship he'd offered her. But then, assuming he'd misread the cues, he'd always been able to talk himself out of it. She'd been like a sister to him since they were both kids, and his feelings in that regard hadn't changed. He couldn't truly imagine hers had, either.

"I was just trying to deliver an air conditioner."

"And she got you into bed that easily?"

He dropped the crowbar next to the sledgehammer. "It's a long story, okay? Can't we let it go? She didn't do anything wrong, and I don't want to make her stay here any more uncomfortable than it already is."

Shock registered on Averil's face, and she stepped back. "Oh my God. You *like* her."

He couldn't deny it, so he kept his mouth shut.

"Are you kidding me?" she continued. "You've always hated her!"

"*Hate*'s *far* too strong a word."

"Are you saying you were friends when we were in high school? Because that's not the way I remember it. Neither of you had anything nice to say about the other."

He shrugged. "That was then."

"What does that mean?"

"It means there's no reason to hold a grudge."

"What about Charlie? What she did at the wedding is a reason."

"That's between the two of them. Charlie's a big boy. He doesn't need us taking up for him against an ex-girlfriend. Besides, what she and Charlie had has been over for a long time."

She barked out a humorless laugh. "I can't believe this. She's *that* good in bed?"

He had no complaints, but he knew better than to say so. "You're making too big a deal of it. That's all."

"Does that mean you're not going to see her again?"

He couldn't help glancing away. "We don't have any plans, if that's what you're asking."

"You've never had your heart broken, have you," she said.

It was a statement, not a question. "Not really. I guess I've been lucky."

"Yeah, well, let's hope your luck isn't about to run out," she said and got back in the car, her tires spewing gravel as she whipped around and shot down the drive.

Brant took off his work gloves as he watched her go. He wasn't getting anywhere with the dent in the bumper of his truck; he was only making it worse. And he had a feeling the conversation he'd just had with Charlie's sister hadn't gone his way, either.

On Sundays, almost everything was closed in Coyote Canyon, so Talulah had to wait until Monday morning to visit Terrell's Market. She hated that she'd lost so much time; it was going to take every moment of the next few days to make enough food for the funeral. Almost the whole town had known Phoebe.

"Maybe I should've thought more carefully about this," Talulah mumbled as she stared at the piles and piles of groceries she'd unloaded onto her aunt's dining table, counters and every other horizontal surface. Unlike the commercial space she was privileged to work in at the dessert diner, with its giant ovens and refrigerators, she'd be limited to her aunt's tiny kitchen. She'd have to store some of the food in the fridge at the church, in Sarah Carrier's fridge and possibly Jane's.

Besides that, she'd have to make everything during this terrible heat wave. She was already beginning to sweat. The air conditioner, which she'd requested Brant to put in the basement was too heavy for her to lift. She was afraid she'd drop it while coming up the stairs, so she didn't dare try.

Too bad she hadn't thought of making the meal *before* he'd put it in the basement…

For a brief moment, she felt overwhelmed enough to regret her decision to tackle such a big endeavor. But then she remembered what had inspired her to do it in the first place. She wanted to be there for Phoebe as a member of the family, to prove she could deliver, even though everyone considered her their weakest link.

She wouldn't renege on the commitment she'd made. She'd follow through and do her best.

After turning on some music, she scrubbed her hands and spent the next few hours making the rather unusual but delicious gelatin fruit salad her aunt had brought to almost every family function—one that, among other things, contained finely grated cheddar cheese, lots of heavy whipping cream and chopped walnuts. Talulah had decided she'd make all of Phoebe's favorites—the dishes her aunt was known for, including lasagna, which she'd make with the tomato sauce Phoebe had canned. She'd also share the dill pickles, pickled beets, peaches and pears from her aunt's cellar.

As she worked, her heart felt lighter and lighter. It made her happy to think Phoebe would be pleased with what she was doing, that her great aunt would like helping to provide one last meal to the loved ones she'd left behind.

Talulah had finished four double batches of the gelatin fruit salad, which filled eight large baking dishes. She was just trying to squeeze the last of those into the refrigerator when her phone went off.

Her heart jumped into her throat the second she saw that it was her sister. Was Debbie in labor?

"No. No, no, no," she said. Debbie couldn't have the baby while she had so much to do for the funeral!

After quickly rinsing and drying her hands, she hit the green phone button before the call could transfer to voice mail. "Is it time?" she asked without preamble.

"Sadly, no," Debbie responded.

"You're not feeling *anything*? Not even false labor?"

"I'm feeling uncomfortable. Does that count?"

"No, you were uncomfortable the last time we talked."

Debbie chuckled and Talulah wondered what it would feel like to be pregnant, especially this pregnant. Would she ever have that experience? Maybe she'd end up like her spinster aunt, with a niece one day cooking the meal for *her* funeral. "So what's up?" she asked.

Her sister sobered. "Mom called me a few minutes ago."

"Is something wrong?" she asked. "It's the middle of the night in Africa, isn't it?"

"Not quite but close."

"She must be excited about the baby."

"I think she is, but that isn't why she called."

Talulah sank into a kitchen chair. She'd been on her feet all day, and something about Debbie's response made her uneasy. "What did she want?"

"Dinah contacted her an hour ago."

"Charlie's mom?" Of course. Now Talulah knew what this was about. Word was traveling even faster than she'd expected. "To tell her about Brant?"

"So…it's true?"

Talulah dropped her head into her free hand. "I'm thirty-two, Debbie," she replied. "My sex life should not be any of my mother's concern."

"I agree with you…to a point. But you have to realize that you're not in Seattle anymore. What you do in Coyote Canyon reflects on Mom and Dad. They have so many lifelong friends who still live there."

"I understand that. It wasn't supposed to become public knowledge."

"You really slept with Brant?"

Talulah couldn't deny it. "I might have," she said softly.

Her response was met with a long moment of silence. Then Debbie said, "I thought you didn't like him."

Talulah was beginning to sweat even more than when she'd been cooking in the hot kitchen. Desperate for some fresh air, she hurried through the sitting room and burst onto the porch, slamming the crooked screen door against the house as she went. "I don't know what to say. It was… It was… I guess I made a snap decision, and it wasn't the right one."

"You *think*? How'd it happen?" her sister asked.

"I have no idea. Not really." It wasn't any cooler outside. Rivulets of sweat ran down Talulah's back and dampened her hair. Remembering the air conditioner, she went back inside, down to the basement, and sat directly in front of the unit, which was already cranked up as high as it could go.

"Did you two go out?" Debbie prodded. "Or did you invite him over for a drink or something when you saw him at the café?"

"No. It was nothing like that. He brought me a portable cooling unit because we're in the middle of a heat wave. That's all."

"Apparently, that *isn't* all," she said. "What about Paul?"

"I've told you before that Paul and I are *not* an item. I didn't cheat on him."

"Does he know what happened with Brant?"

"Of course not."

"Are you going to tell him?"

"At this point, I think he might be the only one who *doesn't* know. And he doesn't need to hear about it, certainly not right now."

"Okay, but…how'd things progress from Brant bringing over a portable cooling unit to Charlie finding you both naked yesterday morning?"

Talulah angled the vents to blow more directly on her. "We weren't *naked*."

"From what he's telling everyone, you weren't fully dressed."

She cringed as she remembered the unpleasant surprise of coming downstairs to find Charlie in the house. "I'd rather not go over the details. What happened is nobody's business but my own."

"That's easy to say, but a lot of people are talking, and they'll all be staring daggers at you during the funeral. It's not as if Charlie or any of his family feel the need to protect you or your privacy."

"They wouldn't have been friendly to me anyway."

"True, but they'll use this to make you look as bad as possible. It'll be their revenge."

"I don't care," she said, even though that wasn't remotely true. She'd always liked Dinah and the rest of Charlie's family, especially his younger sister. "I'll put in my time here, take care of Aunt Phoebe's funeral and possessions for Mom and Dad's sake, and then I'll be gone."

"That's probably easier said than done," Debbie said. "What about Averil?"

Talulah had long wished she could repair her relationship with Charlie's sister. When she agreed to come back to Coyote Canyon, she'd still been holding out hope that once Averil realized she was in town they'd be able to get past the wedding. But Charlie had probably ruined any chance of that. "What about her?"

"I know how much you miss her."

Talulah tried to ignore the pang her sister's words created in her heart and focused instead on the sweat drying on her skin and in her hair. She craved another shower, but it wouldn't do her any good to wash up until she was finished cooking. "Averil will never forgive me now."

"Should I call a few friends and ask them to look out for you while you're there? I don't want anyone to mistreat you."

Debbie had always been a good sister, which was part of

the reason Talulah felt so bad about fleeing her own wedding. She'd understood how mortified her family would be. The shame and embarrassment she knew it would cause them was part of the reason she'd felt trapped by the engagement and unable to back out sooner. "I'll survive."

"Are you sure? I could ask Joanie and Rebecca to go to the funeral with you. That way you won't feel so alone."

Joanie and Rebecca were two of Debbie's closest childhood friends and they each had their own young families to take care of. "No, thanks. Why would they want to go to a funeral for someone they barely knew? I say we forget about what happened with Brant."

"Does that mean you won't be seeing him again?"

"We might bump into each other around town. But knowing Brant, it was just another night for him. He's probably already forgotten about it."

"Okay."

But it wasn't fifteen minutes later, right after she'd gotten off the phone with Debbie and returned to the kitchen, that Talulah got a text from him.

Eight

How's the air conditioner working?

Talulah puffed her cheeks full of air she blew out as she read Brant's message. The air conditioner was working fine. It just wasn't doing her much good in the basement.

I decided to do all the cooking for my aunt's funeral, so I'm in the kitchen for the next three days. I wish I hadn't asked you to put it in the basement. Other than that, it's great.

I can come move it.

She walked into the sitting room and gazed out the window at the road. She didn't see anyone, but she suspected Charlie was keeping a close eye on her house. If Brant came over, it would only add to town gossip.

Ellen can probably help me when she gets back.

She won't be coming back until next weekend.

After the funeral. *After* all the cooking. "Damn." Still,

she needed to keep her distance from Brant. No big deal.
I can live without it.

I'm done with work for the day. I'll come by as soon as I
get cleaned up.

I don't think you should. Not if you're hoping to patch up
your relationship with Charlie.

He won't even know.

He must be checking my place, and after Saturday night,
I can only imagine he's watching it closely.

I'm aware of that. Don't worry.

   "Don't worry?" she mumbled. Why take the risk?
   He didn't answer right away. She thought he might not
answer at all. But after a few minutes, her phone dinged
again.

Because I can't quit thinking about you.

   Talulah felt her jaw drop. She'd never expected Brant
to say anything like that. She had no idea how to respond.
   Can I come? he asked. I never got to eat my other
croissant. ;-)
   She kneaded her forehead as she tried to decide. They
could be friends, couldn't they? Charlie and his family
shouldn't be able to dictate who she saw in Coyote Canyon.

Sure. I'm just about to make lasagna for the funeral. We
can have some for dinner, if you're hungry. The croissants are two days old and won't be very good anymore.

I'm definitely not going to say no to dinner. I'll bring a bottle of wine.

She had a feeling that this was a pivotal decision, another potential mistake. But despite all the fallout from Saturday night, and her family and the funeral, she couldn't quit thinking about Brant, either.

Brant was careful to watch for cars he might recognize as he drove to the other side of town, but he felt fairly confident that Charlie wouldn't be monitoring Talulah's house this evening. He spent Monday nights with his folks. His mother cooked for the whole family, and, since his father had been diagnosed with prostate cancer, he rarely missed it. Everyone was optimistic George would beat it, but he'd only just started treatment and no one knew for sure whether the chemo would be effective.

Still, to avoid causing further hurt and anger, Brant parked in the big barn behind Ellen's house where no one could see his vehicle, and walked over to Talulah's. As he climbed the stairs to the front porch, he had a final look around and didn't see anyone.

Talulah was playing her music again. It wasn't as loud as it had been the first time he'd come to the house, but he had to knock twice before she let him in.

"Where's your truck?" she asked, peering out as he slipped past her.

"In a safe place."

"Good."

She was wearing a form-fitting black dress that hit her at midthigh, with no shoes, and she had her hair pinned up, probably to help combat the heat. A light sheen of sweat covered her face and arms, and he could see a few damp tendrils of hair curling at her nape.

It was difficult not to touch her after having had full access to her body. The impulse hit him immediately and was much stronger than he'd anticipated. He'd offered to come over to move the air conditioner, and had hoped to reassure himself that she was okay after what had happened. But she'd offered dinner and she'd dressed up enough that this felt more like a date. She was wearing makeup and perfume—a scent he liked.

Those could be signals. And yet…with her bare feet and the way she'd done her hair, she came across as casual at the same time. Maybe they were getting together as friends tonight, and she wouldn't be happy if he tried to touch her. She didn't step toward him, didn't give him a hug.

"Dinner smells great," he said.

She wiped her upper lip. "I just showered, but cooking makes it even hotter in here."

"I'll take care of that right now." He put the bottle of wine he'd brought on the dining table, which was already set for dinner, and went down to get the air conditioner.

"Thank God," she said, once he'd hauled it up and she could feel the cool air it was pumping out. She indicated an appetizer she'd made that was sitting on the counter. "Try that dip and see what you think."

He scooped some up with a cracker and nearly moaned when he tasted it. "Wow."

She was cutting lasagna in a pan on the stove, but looked over her shoulder. "You like it?"

"It's incredible. What's in it?"

"You might enjoy it more if I don't tell you," she joked. "It's not very healthy."

He could tell it contained artichokes and green chilies; he knew she couldn't be talking about those. Which left sour cream or whatever the rest of it was made of. "It's worth it."

She opened the oven and pulled out a loaf of toasty garlic bread sprinkled with grated Parmesan cheese. "Would you mind cutting the bread?"

"Not at all." He was yanking out drawers, searching for a knife, when she handed him one.

"Have you heard from Charlie since he stormed out of here?" she asked.

"Nope."

She carried their lasagna to the dining table. "Have you tried calling him?"

"Not yet. I want to let him cool off first."

"How long do you think that'll take?"

He shrugged. "Don't know. We've never had anything like this happen."

She sighed. "Well, take it from me. He can hold a grudge for a *long* time. His whole family can."

He found her wounded expression sort of endearing. "You'd like to be friends with him?"

"Of course. It's not as if I never cared about him."

He dipped another cracker and took a bite. "I don't think Charlie's capable of accepting anything less than what he really wants, Talulah. In case you haven't already figured it out, he still has a thing for you."

"I can't imagine how," she said, sounding exasperated as she took a green salad out of the fridge and stuck a pair of tongs in it. "He hasn't even seen me for fourteen years."

"Maybe not in person, but he follows you on social media."

"Really?" she asked in surprise. "He's never commented on any of my posts…"

"Because he's lurking."

She handed him a corkscrew for the wine. "There's not much to see on my personal Instagram. I don't post very often. I'm too busy trying to come up with compelling content to promote the dessert diner, so I'm usually post-ing on that account instead."

He popped the cork on the J brand pinot noir he'd brought. "You've put up a few pictures of you and Paul."

She blinked at him. "*Charlie's* mentioned that?"

"I've seen them, too," he admitted.

"When?"

"Last night." He'd scrolled through her pictures again today, several times actually, since he couldn't get her off his mind, but he didn't volunteer that. "I was curious about this business partner of yours. Aren't you afraid of mess-ing up your ability to work together? What would happen to the dessert diner then?"

"It's a risk," she said. "That's partly why I resisted let-ting our relationship drift in a romantic direction. I'd hate to ruin it. But he's so adamant than we're perfect for each other. And I do like a lot of things about him."

"Name some of them," he said.

She turned off the oven and hung up the hand towel. "Well…he's sweet and attentive and conscientious and an incredible pastry chef. Because we're both committed to making the diner succeed, we have a common goal, which is nice. And we share a love of good food."

The dude he'd seen had been super fit. There'd been several pictures of them hiking. "He likes the outdoors?"

"He does. He's going on a backpacking trip to Europe with a buddy for three weeks when I get back."

"You're not going with him?"

"Someone has to stay and take care of the diner."

"I see." Brant decided he didn't much care for Paul, even though he had no good reason to feel that way. "Do you think you'll marry him?"

She stopped piling the chunks of bread he'd cut into a

serving basket and took a moment to consider the question. "I might try."

"That means he could be the next poor sucker standing at the altar while you flee your own wedding," he joked.

She gave him a dirty look. "He's fully aware of the risk he's taking."

"Meaning you warned him like you warned me?"

"Basically." Finished with the bread, she started stacking the dishes she'd used to make the meal in the sink. "It would be stupid to fall in love with me. I warn everyone I get involved with."

Folding his arms, he leaned against the counter as he watched her work. "Maybe that's your problem."

She dried her hands. "What do you mean?"

"Giving a guy a challenge is never a wise thing to do, unless you want him to try."

"I'm not giving anyone a challenge," she said. "I'm making sure the men in my life proceed with caution."

Chuckling, he shook his head at her response. It was cocky, and yet it wasn't. He could tell she was only trying to avoid hurting anyone else. And he found her honesty appealing. "I don't think I've ever met anyone like you," he said.

"I'll try to believe you mean that in a good way," she muttered.

He merely grinned. "Averil stopped by Sunday night," he said as he handed her a glass of wine.

Her eyebrows slid up. "What'd she want?"

"To tell me to stay away from you."

She'd been lifting her glass to her mouth, but at this her hand froze. "I hope she doesn't think I'd ever go back to Charlie."

"She said you'd only break my heart."

"Did you tell her that's impossible?" she said with a

laugh. "That I've found the one person who's totally safe with me?"

Had she? Was his heart that untouchable—as untouchable as hers? "I told her I can take care of myself."

"I'm happy to hear it."

He burst out laughing. "I believe you really are."

She clinked her glass against his. Then, after taking a sip, she asked tentatively, "Do you think Averil still hates me?"

"Of course not." Charlie's sister had said as much, but he didn't want to let Averil make Talulah feel any worse. "She's just protective of her brother."

"Would she rather I'd married him?" Talulah asked. "Been miserable and made him miserable, too? Maybe the Gerharts should be thanking me, because our marriage would've ended in divorce. I wasn't in love with him enough to marry him."

He took another sip of wine. "Is that true for the other guys you were with, as well?"

"I guess." She dunked a cracker in the dip. "What else did Averil say?"

It was easy to tell that she cared more about Averil than Charlie, so they were entering territory where the truth could ruin the night. Brant definitely didn't want to let things go in that direction. "Enough about the Gerharts. Let's not waste our time talking about them."

"Because Averil *does* hates me," she said sadly, seeing right through his attempt to divert her.

"She doesn't understand what you're up against."

She nodded and, again, he felt the compulsion to touch her, to draw her close. Instead, he said, "Why don't we eat? You've done a lot of work here and dinner looks incredible."

"Okay." She gestured at the bread. "Can you grab that?"

* * *

Brant ate so much that Talulah couldn't help teasing him about it. "Jeez. If you ever come over again, I'll have to make you your own pan of lasagna," she said as he finished off a second giant helping.

He flashed her a heart-stopping smile. "I might not get another invitation, so I'm making the most of this one."

"You think I should invite you back?" she asked in surprise. She hadn't been able to eat much herself. She was too busy fighting her attraction to him.

"Why not?"

"Because I'm trying to keep us out of trouble!"

"It's too late for that." Putting down his fork, he pushed the empty plate away. "Hopefully, the Gerharts will judge me on my lifelong relationship with them and not on a few weeks' involvement with you."

A few weeks? Not just one night? Charlie wasn't the only consideration. What about her family? She was determined not to get another call from Debbie tomorrow concerning her behavior. "I'm trying to do something admirable for my parents and sister."

"What does that have to do with me?" he asked.

"More than you probably realize," she grumbled, finishing her wine.

"Do you want to explain that?"

She didn't. It was too convoluted. "No." They were both unattached, both adults and should be able to decide for themselves. And yet… Coyote Canyon didn't really work that way.

He seemed disappointed she was no longer open to a physical relationship, but he didn't say anything. She could tell from the way he looked at her and flirted with her and touched her whenever possible that he was interested in a repeat of their night together. She craved the taste and feel of him, too, which was why she was reluctant to hold his gaze for more than a second, and she stepped away whenever he got close. She was afraid she'd give in.

"What are your parents up to these days?" she asked, launching into a new subject. She didn't know the Elways well, but she'd seen them around the high school and other places when she lived here and could still remember how much Brant resembled his father.

"They're living in town while they're taking care of my grandmother, who's eighty-nine. My brothers and I are buying the ranch from them."

"How often do you see your folks?"

"Fairly often. My dad drives out to look things over now and then. And my mom cooks for us three or four nights a week."

"Are you kidding?" she said with a laugh.

He didn't seem even slightly embarrassed that his mother continued to take care of him and his brothers. "It gives her something to do," he said with an unconcerned shrug. "And she knows we'd just go out to eat if she didn't. By the time we're done working, no one's eager to spend an hour or more in the kitchen—although we might grill a steak now and then."

"I bet she's a good cook."

"She is," he said without hesitation. "And so are you."

"I'm a professional. I *should* be good."

He relaxed into his seat as he finished his wine. "Tell me about your dessert diner."

"I dreamed about opening my own place—a restaurant or something—for years. So I'm excited that it's working out for me."

"Was this Paul's dream, too?"

"Once we met and became friends, and I started talking about it, he got on board. I doubt he would've done it without me."

"Why not?"

"It's much easier to tackle such a big endeavor with a partner. You can pool your money and share the work as well as the risk."

"That's the upside," he said. "The downside is that you have to compromise if you ever disagree." He poured her more wine.

"True. We don't argue very often, but we do have our differences occasionally."

He added a splash more wine to his own glass. "What types of things do you disagree on?"

"I'm a cautious person—"

"Some would say *overly* cautious," he broke in, and she knew he was teasing her about her fear of commitment.

"I'd rather not get into anything I can't get out of," she admitted. "I don't like feeling trapped."

A half smile curved his lips. "Why do you think you're so afraid of that? Has something terrible happened that's made you leery of close relationships or—"

"No. Nothing like that. I just hate disappointing others."

His eyebrows went up. "You see the irony, right?"

"Of course. But like I told you before, it's the fact that I have trouble saying no that gets me into the engagement in the first place. Then I try to convince myself it's the right thing to do and that I'll be glad I did it in the end..."

"And then the wedding comes up and you panic."

"Exactly."

He rocked back onto two legs of his chair. "How is Paul going to be any different?"

"I'm older, for one. I've learned a few things about myself since I lived here."

"You've also warned him," he said, his lips twitching as though he was tempted to laugh.

"I have," she said, scowling at him for being amused by her predicament. "I think that's only fair."

He shook his head. "He's going to have his hands full with you."

"Fortunately, he's a patient man."

"Which, no doubt, makes you feel obligated to stick with him. So how is it, exactly, that this relationship is taking a different path?"

"I want to find someone *eventually*. Get married and have a family. Don't you? And maybe he's the best guy for the job. Maybe I just don't have a good feel for when I've met the right person."

"I have a different take on that," he said, sobering.

She eyed him speculatively. "What's *your* take?"

"I think you should only commit to someone you're *dying* to be with. You shouldn't have to talk yourself into anything."

"What if I never have that experience? What if I'm not built that way?"

"Everyone's built that way. That's how you know when you've found 'the one.'" He raised his fingers to indicate quotation marks.

"Spoken like a true authority on the subject," she said, cracking up. "Have *you* ever found someone you feel that passionate about?"

"Not yet," he admitted, somewhat grudgingly. "But I'm willing to wait."

"You could be wasting your time," she pointed out.

"Then I'll remain single. That's better than trying to force something that wasn't meant to be."

"I'm not forcing anything," she said. "I admit I'm not head over heels, but I care about Paul."

"Enough to *marry* him?"

"Desire could develop over time."

"How long have you known this guy?"

She'd already told him she met Paul years ago, clear back in culinary school, so she knew he wasn't actually seeking an answer. "You're saying I should've figured that out by now."

"Bingo."

"Not every relationship takes the same course."

"I'm not suggesting that. But shouldn't you feel more than you do?"

"You asked me how Paul and I approach our business and what we might disagree on," she said, hoping to guide them to safer territory.

"And you said you were cautious. I take it he's not."

"He doesn't even consider the possibility of failure. He's pressing me to open another dessert diner, but I'm afraid that will spread us too thin. And if it doesn't work…"

"You'll be in over your head."

"We could lose it all," she agreed.

He put his empty glass back on the table. "I'd like to come see the diner sometime."

She hadn't expected that response, or his interest in general. Part of her was eager to show Brant what she'd created. It'd taken a lot of work, and she was proud of it. The other part, however, was reluctant to have him meet Paul. It was one thing to indulge in a quick fling before she committed herself to her business partner; it was another to welcome the man she'd slept with to *their* restaurant. "If you're ever in Seattle, you'll have to stop by."

He chuckled. "That was a lukewarm invitation if ever I've heard one."

"Paul will be there," she pointed out as if it should be obvious.

"If you and I are just friends, what does that matter?"

She opened her mouth to respond, but couldn't come up with a good answer. So she checked the cuckoo clock her aunt had hung on the wall after a trip to Germany—one of the few times she'd left Coyote Canyon—and said, "It's almost eight. I'd better get the dishes done so I can make some more food for the funeral."

He helped carry their plates into the kitchen and put the leftovers in plastic containers they crammed into the fridge with all the gelatin fruit salads.

She was standing at the sink, filling it with hot, soapy water when he came up behind her, penned her in with a hand on either side and looked at her through their reflection in the window. "Thanks for dinner," he murmured.

Although he wasn't actually touching her, she could feel the heat of his body and was shocked by how difficult it was not to lean back. She couldn't remember ever wanting a man so much, which added to her shock. This was Brant! But now she knew what sex with him was like—and she couldn't forget it. "Of course."

"You'd like the air conditioner to remain here in the kitchen for the next few days, right?"

Just a few inches. If she leaned back that far, she knew his arms would go around her. He'd probably turn her around and kiss her. And then…

A shiver of desire rolled down her spine, but she summoned her resolve and continued to avoid contact. "Yeah. I won't be able to go back to sorting and packing until after the funeral."

"When's that?"

She glanced down at his hands, remembering what it was like to feel them on her body. They were nice hands—large and masculine yet gentle when they should be. "Thursday."

Because she didn't respond in any way that invited him to touch her, as he'd probably hoped, he stepped back. "What time?"

After using a dish towel to dry her hands, she turned to face him. "At two. Why?"

"I was planning on attending the service."

Her gaze fell to his lips. They had to be the best lips she'd ever seen—perfectly formed. She had to force herself to look up at his eyes. "Why? You barely knew Aunt Phoebe."

"I don't want you to have to face Charlie and his family alone."

She was having trouble thinking clearly, because there was this other part of her brain that kept weighing the decision she was making right now and hoping for a different outcome. "I know at least part of his family will be there, but…surely Charlie won't come."

"I'd count on it."

"Why?"

"Because it'll be a good excuse for him to see you. I think he's hoping you'll suddenly realize what you walked out on and change your mind."

"That's ridiculous."

"Not to him."

She sighed as she imagined her ex-fiancé glaring at her across her great aunt's coffin. She was definitely making the right choice by not sleeping with Brant again, not only for her and Paul, but for Charlie, who'd been hurt badly enough. "Either way, it'll be fine," she said. "Jane's hoping to make it home by then."

"Jane can't pick sides, Talulah. That'll ruin her relationship with Averil."

What he said was true. Jane had tried to remain neutral for the past fourteen years, but since she and Averil still lived in the same small town, Talulah knew they were a lot closer than she and Jane were these days. And she knew that if Jane went to the funeral, she'd have to be very careful how she handled it. It would actually be smarter for her to stay away and avoid the whole issue.

Talulah would be by herself at the funeral. But it was only for a few hours. She'd just have to get through it, because she didn't want to endanger Jane's or Brant's relationships here in Coyote Canyon by expecting their support. "I can manage on my own, so it's nothing you need to worry about."

"It's not? Because I feel responsible for what you're going through."

"Don't. Everything started long before Sunday, remember?"

"You *really* don't want me to go to the funeral?"

"No. Don't feel duty-bound to protect me. What you need to protect is your relationship with Charlie—the same way Jane has to protect her relationship with Averil."

"Except that freezes you out—in both instances."

"If you ask any of the Gerharts, they'll tell you I deserve it," she said with a wink.

He frowned but acknowledged her wishes with a reluctant nod. "Fine. You'll call me if you need anything, though?"

"Of course." She had no intention of bothering him again, but she didn't say that.

"Okay. Good night." He dropped a kiss on top of her head before walking to the back door.

She followed him so she could lock up behind him. "Thanks for coming over." *And showing some concern*, she mentally added. She had to admit that had felt nice.

"Dinner was delicious."

She smiled, and he walked out, heading across the property toward Ellen's.

With a sigh of relief, she congratulated herself for handling the evening so well. She hadn't touched him once, let alone kissed him.

But as the seconds stretched and she imagined him getting closer and closer to his truck and driving away, her heart started to pound.

She didn't want him to leave! This could be her only chance to be with him again.

In a sudden panic, she ripped open the door. "Brant?" she called out.

She could hear the surprise in his voice when he answered. "What?"

"I've changed my mind," she blurted and held her breath as she waited for his response. Would he ask what she meant or would he know instinctively?

He didn't say anything, but he was coming back. She could hear his footsteps even before he reached the rectangle of light spilling onto the ground. And she could tell he knew exactly what she meant when he gave her a sexy smile, stepped into the house and used his foot to close the door because his hands were already pulling her to him.

Nine

Brant couldn't remember ever being so excited to touch a woman. He'd thought Talulah had sent him home and that was that. So when she'd stopped him from leaving, and he could tell she was feeling the same desire he was, a wave of relief heightened the excitement.

"I'm glad you changed your mind," he murmured against her lips. "I've been dying to get my hands on you all night."

"I hope it won't cost you your friendship with Charlie," she said, obviously worried.

Brant didn't want to think about Charlie. He wasn't out to hurt his best friend. That wasn't what this was about. If Charlie had *any* chance with Talulah, Brant wouldn't be here. But Charlie didn't. Talulah had made that clear. "I hope so, too. But I can't seem to resist you."

Her hands delved into his hair, and she parted her lips as he kissed her. "What about your truck? You don't think Charlie will find it, do you?"

Her skin was so soft. And the smell of her... He ran his lips over her collarbone, breathing in the scent he remembered and liked so well. "No. It's in Ellen's barn. There's no way he'd ever think to look there."

After helping her out of her dress, he immediately unsnapped the black sheer bra she was wearing and filled his hands with her breasts. She melted into him. But then she stiffened and twisted her head to look out the window. "He wouldn't come up to the house…"

Would Charlie go that far? After the way he'd spoken about Talulah, Brant wouldn't put it past him. To be safe, he guided her up the stairs where peering in the windows wasn't such an easy possibility.

He peeled off her panties and tossed them aside before pressing her up against the wall and kissing her again as he slid his hand between her legs. When he found the wet warmth he'd been seeking, and she gasped, he used the opportunity to deepen their kisses.

"*Your* clothes," she said breathlessly as she tried to undo his belt.

Scooping her up in his arms, he lowered her onto the bed. "We'll get to that soon enough."

He was as eager to remove his clothes as she was—to feel her naked body against his—but he knew the next few minutes would go entirely too fast if he got naked, too.

He preferred to make this last.

Climbing onto the bed, he straddled her as he took his time kissing her mouth and neck before meandering down to her breasts and sucking on one nipple and then the other.

He caressed her stomach and legs as he moved lower, settling his mouth between her legs—and felt a measure of satisfaction when she began to arch her back and grab handfuls of his hair.

"I want you inside me," she said as her muscles grew taut, but he could feel her thighs quiver and guessed she was close to climax. He planned to make that happen first.

When she groaned and her body began to spasm, he knew she'd reached that release. "That must've been good. Goose bumps broke out on your whole body."

"Don't get conceited about it," she joked.

"Will you do me a favor?" he asked.

She sobered, and when their eyes met, he thought hers were among the prettiest he'd ever seen. "What?" she asked.

"Put on my T-shirt again. It turns me on to remember you coming down the stairs in it."

"That was pretty ill-timed."

"Don't ruin this by mentioning the rest," he said.

She pulled it on as soon as he handed it to her, and by the time he'd tossed the rest of his clothes on the floor, he was staring down at the Elway Ranch logo on her chest. The only thing better than seeing her in his shirt was knowing she had nothing on underneath—and that he had complete access.

Taking a moment to admire the sight of her, he reached under the soft cotton fabric, seeking the curves and warm skin he knew he'd find, and his pulse began to race in anticipation.

It was late—Talulah had no idea what time exactly— when she felt Brant move in the bed beside her and realized he was awake. She assumed he was getting up to leave, until she felt his hands delve once again beneath the T-shirt she was wearing.

"Do you want your shirt back?" she asked, half-asleep. She knew he had to go, but was reluctant to lose the comfort and warmth of his body, especially since the weather had finally cooled off and a chill wind was blowing through the open windows.

"I can leave without it," he said. "I doubt anyone will see me this late."

"You never know. I'll give it back to you, just in case."

"Not yet," he told her when she attempted to remove it.

"Don't you have to get up early for work tomorrow?" she asked.

"I do, but I'd rather have this than sleep," he said, his voice a low rumble in her ear as he spooned her.

Nudging her hair to one side with his chin, he kissed the nape of her neck, and she felt him grow hard. "I want to take you from behind," he said as his hands moved around to cup her breasts. "Would you let me?"

She actually liked that he was eager to explore and experience her body in different ways. "Yes."

His hand slid down her stomach and he used his fingers to arouse her before pushing inside. Having a man behind her wasn't usually her favorite way of making love, but she found it erotic and exciting with Brant. And she was surprised when, after he reached climax, he stayed inside her as long as possible and continued to curl his body around hers.

"Don't you have to leave?" she whispered when his breathing evened out and he seemed to be drifting back to sleep.

"In a minute," he replied, but they must've faded off together, because the next thing she knew, early-morning sunlight poured through the bedroom window and someone was calling his name from outside.

"Who's that?"

Brant felt Talulah come awake beside him as someone shouted his name. "My brother," he mumbled, recognizing the voice as he struggled to drag himself out of a deep sleep.

"Is something wrong?" she asked, but before he could answer, Kurt yelled from outside again.

"Brant? If you're in there, bro, you'd better get your ass

out quick. Charlie called me looking for you about twenty minutes ago. I bet he'll be coming here next."

Talulah sat up instantly. "What would Charlie want with you this early in the morning?"

"I have no idea," Brant said. "But he knows I'm generally an early riser." He climbed out of bed and grabbed his jeans off the floor so he could get his phone from the front pocket. It was after seven. Damn. He was normally on the ranch by now, especially when it was hot. The earlier he got up and finished his work, the sooner he could call it a day and escape the summer heat.

"Has Charlie been trying to call you?" Talulah asked, pulling the sheet up to cover herself.

"Yeah. Several times." Charlie's calls had started last night around ten. Brant just hadn't noticed; his phone was the last thing he'd been thinking about.

"What does he want?" she asked.

"I don't know. Probably to talk about you. I can't say for sure. He didn't leave a voice mail, and there're no texts from him, either."

"Brant?" his brother called up again. "Are you there?… Hello?… Talulah? Do you know where Brant is?"

Brant crossed to the room to see Kurt, head tilted back, gazing up at the open window. "I'm coming," he called down. "You'd better leave before Charlie sees you. You have no excuse to be here, either."

"I could say the air conditioner you brought over quit working, so you sent me to take a look at it. This place— well, *Talulah*," he corrected, "is a Charlie magnet. He's obsessed with her." He glanced around as if he expected Charlie to drive up at any moment. "Where's your truck? I haven't found it anywhere."

"Then how'd you know I was here?" he asked, jamming his legs into boxers and then his jeans.

"It wasn't too hard to guess, and Charlie will guess, too, if he hasn't already."

Talulah threw his shirt to him and Brant pulled it on over his head in one quick movement, smelling enough of her and her perfume on the cotton to know he needed to change before someone else picked up on the scent. "Okay. I'll go out the back, and Talulah will let you in the front."

"Go!" his brother said simply.

Brant yanked on his boots without bothering with his socks. Talulah tried to hand them to him, but he couldn't take the time to mess with them. "Later," he said, shoving his phone back in his pocket with one hand while pulling out his truck keys with the other.

She didn't argue. She was in too much of a hurry to get dressed herself.

"I'll call you," he told her as he hurried out and took the stairs two at a time, careful to avoid the furniture, piles of books, sheet music, newspapers and lamp-topped tables as he weaved his way through the main floor.

Once he made it to the kitchen, he barged out the back door, running for the barn.

It wasn't a long-distance sprint, but his boots weren't meant for running. He was breathing heavily by the time he reached Ellen's barn and slowed to a walk. He fully believed Charlie would never find his truck. It'd been too long since Brant had dated Ellen for Charlie to guess he'd use her property. And Charlie would have no way of knowing she was out of town. Brant wouldn't have known himself if she hadn't requested the air conditioner.

Still, he held his breath as he cracked open one of the heavy, wooden doors and peered inside.

His truck was there, and it didn't appear as if anyone had come near it. He could see only his own footprints in the dirt.

Breathing a sigh of relief, he shoved the door the rest of the way, climbed behind the wheel and fired up the engine. It was a risk to leave the cover of the barn; he could easily be spotted if Charlie happened to be driving by as he pulled out. But he had to make a break for it sometime, and he figured sooner was better than later. The only thing that would stop Charlie from searching for him was finding him, and Brant couldn't let that happen until he was home.

Once he'd backed out, Brant didn't bother to close the barn. There was no time for that. He did the fastest three-point turn he'd ever done and tore down the drive.

His truck bounced and swayed over the ruts and rocks until he reached the pavement, but then he punched the gas.

He looped around town, going the opposite way he expected Charlie to be traveling and avoiding all the businesses in Coyote Canyon in the process. He was keeping an eye out for his friend's Explorer while trying to decide what he'd tell Charlie if they *did* encounter each other. If he tried to justify his actions by saying that what had happened between him and Talulah didn't mean anything, that it was only a fling, why couldn't he have had that fling with someone else? Someone Charlie *didn't* have any feelings for?

Brant wrestled with the answer to that question. She just…had this…magnetism, was more desirable than anyone he'd ever encountered, and he couldn't seem to get enough of her.

Was that what had gotten the best of Charlie? Could Averil be right? Brant had gone back to Talulah's even after being warned that he was playing with fire.

Was he falling into the same trap his best friend had never escaped?

The thought made Brant uneasy. Of course he wasn't.

He knew how to take care of himself, how to keep his emotions out of it. He'd always remained in control.

And yet…he couldn't have stopped himself from touching Talulah last night, even for Charlie, and he knew it.

Talulah held her breath so she could hear more clearly and pressed her ear to the front door. After throwing on a pair of shorts and a tank top, she'd slid her feet into her flip-flops. Then she'd brushed her teeth, combed her hair and hurried downstairs to let Kurt in. But the second her hand touched the knob, she'd heard voices and stopped. At first she'd thought Kurt was talking to Brant, that Brant hadn't gone out the back way, after all. He'd only left five minutes ago, except she could make out enough of what was being said to rule that out almost immediately.

"What are you doing here? Don't tell me you're sleeping with her, too."

That was Charlie. She recognized his voice and the bitterness that oozed through it. From what she could tell, he was standing about ten feet away from the door—maybe coming up the walkway?

"The portable air conditioner we're letting Talulah borrow isn't working," Kurt said. By the sound of his voice, he was closer to the door. Talulah assumed he'd been waiting for her to let him in when Charlie turned down the drive. "I came by to see if I could fix it before it gets too hot today."

"So where's Brant? Why didn't he do it?"

"I guess he's busy."

Talulah had to hand it to Kurt. He affected the perfect careless tone, as if there was nothing going on.

"On the ranch?" Charlie pressed.

"Far as I know."

"I looked for his truck in the drive earlier. It wasn't there."

Talulah heard the skepticism in Charlie's voice and hoped Kurt would be able to convince him.

"Maybe he drove to the lower paddock," Kurt responded. "Or he went out to get more feed. Why? What's the emergency?"

There was a moment of silence. Then Charlie said, "No emergency. I've just been thinking about what you told me—that Brant had a concussion Saturday night. I feel bad about how I acted."

"You feel bad? That's why you're here?"

"Not exactly," Charlie replied. "I thought… Well, when I couldn't find him, I thought… Never mind. I don't know what's wrong with me."

"Neither do I," Kurt said as if he was exasperated. "You need to get over Talulah, man. Why let her mess up your life fourteen years after the fact?"

She heard Charlie say, "I know you're right. But that's easier said than done."

"What's so special about her?" Kurt asked.

Stung by the question, Talulah felt her mouth drop open.

"I wish I could tell you," Charlie replied, and then they each said something else that Talulah couldn't hear, and Charlie must've gone back to his car and driven away because the conversation ended there.

Still, she was afraid to open the door, in case Charlie wasn't quite gone. The less she saw of him while she was in town the better.

A loud knock made her jump. "Talulah? Are you coming?" Kurt yelled loud enough to make himself heard all the way upstairs. "The coast is clear. Can you let me in?"

He looked startled when she swung the door open less than a second later. "Oh," he said, stepping back so they wouldn't be too close. "You're right there."

She gave him a dirty look. "Yeah, I'm right here."

His eyebrows went up. "What's wrong with you?"

"What's so special about her?" she mocked.

He had the good grace to give her a sheepish smile. "Sorry. You're pretty and all that." His gaze ran down over her. "Okay, you're *really* pretty. I can see why Brant would be attracted to you. But I've never known my brother to risk his friendship with Charlie or anyone else over a woman, especially a woman who'll be leaving in a few weeks." He scratched his head under his baseball cap. "And Charlie is *still* stuck on you. After all these years! So I wasn't just being a jerk—that was an honest question."

"Believe me, it's nothing I'm doing on purpose," she said. "I've apologized to Charlie. And I had no plans to hook up with Brant. That's not why I'm here."

He studied her for a moment. Then a crooked grin appeared on his face—a grin that made him look just like his brother. "I guess shit happens," he said and thrust out his hand. "In case you don't remember me, I'm Kurt."

She did remember him, barely. She'd only seen him in passing. "You're the youngest in the family, right?" she said as she shook his hand.

"I was barely eleven when you left. But I can still remember it."

Folding her arms, she tilted her head to the side. She knew what he was alluding to. "Because that was the only thing people were talking about?"

"For weeks," he confirmed.

She rolled her eyes. "Lovely."

"Well, for what it's worth, you seem like an okay chick to me."

Surprised by his quick bottom-line assessment, she laughed. "I guess I should be grateful for that, since you're one of only a few in this town to have a positive opinion."

"All you need is a few," he said with a wink and looked

beyond her into the house. "Since I'm supposed to be fixing an air conditioner, and I can't leave right away without risking bumping into Charlie again, is there anything else you'd like me to do?"

She waved him inside. "You might as well come in. I'll make you breakfast."

Ten

Brant was torn between calling Charlie and simply ignoring what had happened this morning. A text from Kurt said that Charlie had shown up at Talulah's after he left, so he knew the reason his best friend had been looking for him was to apologize. If he hadn't spent the night with Talulah, they would've been able to put the rift behind them and move on, provided he kept his distance from her in the future, too. That was the catch. And since he hadn't managed to stay away, he didn't care to answer any questions where she was concerned.

Or…should he simply call Charlie and tell him the truth? Lay it all out and admit that he might continue to see Talulah while she was in town? He'd never had any reason to lie to his best friend before—never had any reason to keep secrets from him, either—and it didn't feel good to start now.

But relieving his conscience might make Charlie miserable, and what purpose would that really serve? As Talulah kept pointing out, she'd be leaving soon. If he made a big deal about having the right to spend time with her, he'd damage his relationship with his best friend permanently.

"What he doesn't know won't hurt him," he mumbled.

"What'd you say?"

Brant stood up and spun around. He'd gone out to the farthest paddock to repair the watering system, so he was surprised to find Miles, the brother closest to him in age at thirty, coming up behind him. "I didn't say anything," he replied.

"Now you've started talking to yourself?"

He shot his brother a mock scowl. "At least I'm not singing all the time, like you."

"You *wish* you could sing like me," he said with a grin.

Miles *was* pretty good. He played the guitar, too, and had recently started booking gigs at various bars in Bozeman on the weekends. "What are you doing way the hell out here?" Brant asked.

"We've been having trouble with the herd in that front paddock."

"What kind of trouble?"

"Bloat."

"Every herd faces bloat now and then—"

"I'm saying we have more cows with it than normal," he broke in. "Ranson and I are thinking we might need to adjust their diet."

Ranson was the fourth brother, who was three years younger than Miles. He'd skipped college, figured he didn't need a degree to continue working on the ranch the same way he had his whole life. But Brant felt the degree he'd gotten in natural resources and rangeland ecology at the University of Montana in Missoula had helped them modernize. Although his father had resisted the changes—Clive was as old-school as a guy could get—ever since Brant and his brothers had taken over and switched to rotational grazing, they'd increased the amount of forage harvested per acre by nearly two tons. "They might be getting too much potassium," he said.

"Or not enough salt."

"Have we lost any?"

"Not yet. Thank goodness. I nearly had to call the vet a few minutes ago, though. One poor steer was in so much pain I thought he was a goner. But I finally got that damn tube down his throat and relieved the gas."

Had he not been able to do that, the steer might've suffocated. "He's okay now?"

"Seems like it."

Bloat was caused by rumen fermentation gases and wasn't uncommon in cattle who were fed alfalfa or other legume grasses. Without help, a cow with bloat could die in an hour or two, so it was a condition all ranchers took seriously. When a tube didn't work, they had to stab the animal on the left-hand side to let the gas escape. "I'll change up the feed," he promised.

"Okay. I'm going to the feed store to buy a few more salt licks in case that'll help."

"Sounds good."

Miles started to leave, but turned back at the last moment. "By the way, what was with Charlie this morning? Is he mad again?"

After getting sunburned while fixing the roof the other day, Brant had put on a long-sleeved shirt. He used his forearm to mop the sweat from his face. "It's nothing."

Miles sized him up. "Kurt told me it's about that runaway bride with the weird name."

Brant might've referred to Talulah in the same way once, but now he felt immediately defensive and was tempted to tell his brother never to refer to her like that again. Resisting the impulse, because it would only make his brother *more* interested in what was going on in his life, he said simply, "Talulah Barclay."

"Yeah, that's her. So...what's the deal? Are you really seeing her—the woman who stood Charlie up at the altar?"

"She won't be in town long," he replied. Although that didn't really answer the question, he wasn't sure how to describe their relationship. And since his loyalties were suddenly split and he didn't know what to do about it, he'd rather not have this conversation.

"But you're seeing her while she's here? Is that what you're saying?"

Brant's phone went off. Relieved to have an out, he removed one leather glove and pulled his cell from his pocket.

The second he saw who was calling, however, he wasn't nearly as pleased. "This is Charlie now," he said. "You and I will have to talk later."

Miles gave him a funny look. He'd been dismissed, something he wasn't accustomed to. Normally, Brant didn't have any secrets. Even if he did, he didn't keep anything from his brothers.

"Hello?" he said, answering his phone before it could transfer to voice mail.

"There you are," Charlie said.

"Give me one sec." Brant gestured for Miles to allow him some privacy.

"What's going on with you?" Miles grumbled but finally left.

"I'm here," Brant told Charlie when his brother was out of earshot.

"Where've you been? I've been trying to reach you all morning."

"Sorry. It's been a busy day. The watering system in the far paddock broke, so I've been knee-deep in mud, and my brothers have been fighting to save several steers with bloat. We almost lost one."

"That sucks. You were able to save it, though?"

"Looks that way," he said. "Don't *you* have to work today?"

Charlie seemed taken aback by the question, probably because Brant hadn't entirely concealed his irritation. "I have a couple of house showings, but they aren't until later."

As far as Brant was concerned, Charlie didn't have enough to keep him busy. Maybe he'd worry less about Talulah if he did. "So what's up?"

"I'd like to apologize for acting like a jealous ass the other day."

Brant didn't want an apology. That was part of the reason he hadn't called Charlie after he got back from Talulah's, as he'd planned. He'd heard from Kurt, knew his brother had covered for him, so Charlie's contrition only made him feel guiltier for sneaking around. "It was nothing. Let it go."

"Really? I mean, dude! I hit you when you already had a concussion. I can't believe I did that. But you didn't tell me you'd hit your head. How was I to know?"

He hadn't given Brant time to say much of anything. He shouldn't have hit him regardless. It wasn't as if Brant had slept with Charlie's girlfriend or wife. But Brant knew that reminding him he had no claim on Talulah would only make matters worse. "My skull's as hard as granite. I'm fine."

"How'd it happen?"

He sucked in a lungful of air he silently blew out. "I went down in the basement to see where she wanted the portable cooler and whacked my head on the ceiling as I came back up the stairs." That was close enough to the truth.

"Why'd you have to go to the basement?"

"That's where Talulah was working." Almost naked. It was a sight he'd never forget. But the less said, the better.

"So...did she come on to you or what?"

He dropped his head back to stare up at the wide blue sky. "Charlie, I don't want to talk about it."

"Why not?"

"Because there's no reason to!"

"She has a boyfriend in Seattle. You know that, right? How's he going to feel about her hooking up with you?"

Brant could easily have answered that question. He and Talulah had talked about Paul. But he wasn't going anywhere close to that land mine. "I have no idea, and it's none of my business."

"I bet he won't be happy about it."

"I don't get the impression they're exclusive."

"Did she say that?"

"Charlie, please!" Brant said.

"I'm just saying...she never posts pictures of any other guys."

"Sheila Humphrey has had a thing for you since I can remember. Why don't you give her a shot?"

"Sheila's nice. But I'm not attracted to her."

Charlie needed something or someone to help him move on. "There are other women in town," Brant said.

"Easy for you to say. You don't understand what I'm going through because you've never been in love."

Brant pinched the bridge of his nose. "I'm sorry it didn't work out for you with Talulah. I know it's been rough. But I have to get back to fixing this waterline. It's hot as hell out here."

"Okay. Should we play some pool tonight?"

Brant wished he could say no. He hadn't gotten a lot of sleep, today had been physically demanding, and he wasn't done yet. But he knew that Charlie was offering him an olive branch and would be offended if he refused.

"Sure," he heard himself say and was convinced he was

doing the right thing, because no matter how exhausted he was, he was afraid he'd sneak over to Talulah's again if he could.

And if he kept doing that, Charlie would catch him eventually.

Talulah had spent the day trying to forget about Brant, Charlie and the rest of Coyote Canyon while making eight pans of lasagna. She'd just driven them over to the church because they wouldn't fit in her refrigerator, and was contemplating the type of green salad she'd serve at the funeral when her screen door flew open and Jane Tanner rushed in like a sudden gust of wind.

"I can't believe you're back in town for the first time in fourteen freaking years, and I wasn't here when you arrived," she exclaimed.

Startled, Talulah nearly dropped her aunt's cookbook. An old, tattered tome with handwritten slips of paper and cards stuck between the pages, parts of it would've gone all over if Jane hadn't crushed it to Talulah's chest by sweeping her into an enthusiastic hug.

"I thought you wouldn't get back until later!" Talulah said. "Why didn't you text me that you'd be in town before dinner? I would've made us something to eat."

"I wanted to surprise you," she said. "Besides, we can make something together." She gestured at all the bowls and pans in the sink that were stacked almost to the ceiling. "What're you doing?"

"Getting ready for my aunt's funeral."

"It looks like you're cooking for an army."

"I am. I decided to do the dinner myself."

"I thought you said Phoebe's church would be handling it."

Talulah gave her a sheepish look. "I wanted to do it myself."

"Why?"

That was difficult to explain. To feel better about herself. To show the town she'd made good in spite of her reputation and to honor her aunt. But maybe it didn't really mean anything in the end and had been a stupid idea. "I don't know."

"Is it too late to change your mind?"

"I'm not going to back out now," Talulah said. "I've already got a lot of it done."

"I'm happy to hear that, because the funeral's on Thursday, isn't it? You only have tomorrow left."

"I'll make it."

"What can I do to help?"

It felt wonderful just to hear that question, was so good to have her friend back. Although Jane came to Seattle almost every year, those few days together weren't quite the same as spending time with the person she'd been closest to—besides Charlie's sister—where they'd grown up. "I'm happy you're here."

A worried expression jerked Jane's eyebrows together. "Has it been that rough?"

"Well, no one's run me out of town quite yet, but…"

"There's been drama. I know. What the heck were you thinking, sleeping with Brant Elway?"

"It didn't mean anything. It shouldn't have been a big deal," Talulah said, although it seemed like a much bigger deal now that she'd spent *two* nights with him. Each time they made love felt less casual than the time before.

"So…how'd it happen?"

"We're starting on this subject already?" she said.

"The whole town's talking about it."

Talulah rolled her eyes. "Great. That should make the funeral fun."

"Don't worry. I'll be there."

"No, you won't," Talulah said.

"Why not?"

"You know why not."

Jane frowned as she plopped into a chair. "Averil's got to understand that I'm friends with you, too."

"Except she won't. If you go, you'll have to choose between us, and she'll never forgive you if you choose me. I don't want to imagine you lonely and miserable after I leave."

"Well, when you put it that way," she joked.

"I'm serious. I can get through one afternoon by myself."

"But Averil will expect me to be there, too."

"Why? You barely even knew my great aunt."

"She gave me piano lessons."

"So? Come up with an excuse. Get sick or have something happen to a family member that takes you out of town for the day."

"I'll feel terrible doing that."

"It'll pass. Trust me, you need to stay away."

"Brant won't be going, will he?"

"No."

"He didn't know your aunt, either?"

"Not really. And he's in the same situation you are. It'll be best for both of you to skip it."

"But you didn't do anything wrong. It's not as if Brant's off-limits."

"Apparently to me he is. How protective of her brother can Averil be?"

"I don't think this is entirely about Charlie," Jane confided.

"What do you mean?" Talulah asked.

"The way she's been talking about Brant lately. It's sort of making me wonder if she'd like to sleep with him herself."

Talulah felt her eyes widen. "No!"

"Yes! He seems to be coming up in our conversations quite a bit. He's giving her son horseback riding lessons. He came to rescue her when she got a flat tire on the way to Bozeman and she couldn't get hold of Charlie. She thanked him by baking a giant chocolate chip cookie and taking it over to him. She talks about seeing him whenever he comes into the bank, and yet I don't hear about any other patrons. And on and on."

Talulah sank into the chair beside her. "Have you asked her if she's interested in him?"

"I have. She denies it. And he's been a close friend of the family for years, so maybe I'm reading too much into it. But when she called to give me the latest gossip yesterday, I don't know…it made me wonder all over again."

"Wow." Talulah felt a little sick inside, but she couldn't really explain why. Her whole life was in Seattle with her dessert diner and Paul. Why would she care if Averil had a thing for Brant? For all she knew, they were perfect for each other. And maybe if they got together, he could convince Averil to forgive her for what she did at the wedding.

"Talulah?"

Talulah had been staring off into space. Blinking, she shifted her gaze back to Jane. "What?"

"Let's order a pizza and open a bottle of wine."

Talulah remembered the bottle Ellen had brought over. Ellen had mentioned sharing it with her, but Talulah would simply buy another bottle. "Okay. I just happen to have some pinot noir," she said—and was somehow more eager than usual to drink it.

Charlie was particularly good at pool. But so was Brant. They enjoyed playing because they were evenly matched. "Damn, I just set you up," Charlie complained, using his cue stick to indicate the ball he'd accidentally knocked to the brink of the corner pocket.

"And I'm going to take full advantage." Brant was so immersed in the game and trying to engineer a win, even though he was currently behind, that he was glad they'd decided to come to Hank's Bar and Grill. Hanging out with Charlie reminded him of all the fun they'd had together over the years and made it possible to forget the recent strain.

He sank the nine and was sizing up a much trickier bank shot when Charlie cursed, making him flinch and send the cue ball into the side pocket. "What the hell?" Brant growled. But then he followed Charlie's gaze, saw what'd caused his reaction and lowered his stick.

Talulah and Jane had just walked in. The two women were dressed casually in jeans and flip-flops. Talulah had on a red top with short sleeves while Jane wore a pink-and-white one with straps. They were laughing and talking while waiting for the bartender to take their order, and they hadn't spotted him and Charlie. But Hank's was too small a place for them not to notice eventually.

"Let's get out of here," Brant said.

Charlie frowned. "No way. You don't have to worry. I'm not going to say anything to her. Besides, our food hasn't even come. And we're in the middle of a game."

Brant eyed his beer. If he stayed, he was going to need a lot more alcohol—except that drinking away the awkwardness he felt being around Charlie and Talulah at the same time was probably the worst thing he could do. This situation was a recipe for disaster even without the alcohol. But wild horses couldn't drag Charlie away; he was too obsessed with Talulah. "Fine. Let's finish our game," Brant said and gestured for him to proceed.

"You want your shot over again?" Charlie asked.

Brant deserved a second chance, but he shrugged. "No, it's fine."

Charlie didn't argue. He was too interested in keeping an eye on Talulah to focus on much else. The penalty Brant would receive would only help Charlie win, anyway. And that was what Charlie wanted. To win—not just the game, but the girl who'd broken his heart.

Brant stood by, watching as Charlie moved around the table, searching for his best shot. He eventually found one he seemed to like, but before bending to take it, he glanced at the bar once again, and Brant couldn't help doing the same. Talulah and Jane were speaking to the bartender.

Charlie missed, so Brant stepped up and managed to sink the fourteen in the side pocket. He didn't have a good angle on anything after that. Although he still had the ten and the thirteen on the table, the way they were positioned meant he'd be more likely to sink the eight ball and lose the game if he took a shot at them. So he simply did what he could to block Charlie, hoping he'd have a better opportunity next turn.

Brant stood waiting, on edge as Charlie tested various angles and eyed different pockets. He was taking forever, which irritated Brant, but he supposed it didn't really matter. As Charlie had said, their food hadn't even arrived yet. There was no way Brant would be able to convince him to leave, or come up with a good excuse to leave himself, until after that.

Jane caught sight of them first. She nudged Talulah as they were carrying their drinks to a table, and Brant saw Talulah stop walking the second she realized. He smiled and nodded, hoping to put her at ease, but Charlie had been keeping such a close watch on them that he immediately noticed, and she looked away and started walking again without acknowledging either of them.

What were the chances they'd show up here at the same time? Brant thought. But in a town this size, the chances were actually pretty good. There wasn't a lot of nightlife in Coyote Canyon, and because this place played music that appealed to a younger crowd, Hank's was the obvious choice for anyone under forty.

Their food couldn't take too much longer. He'd eat. Then he'd say he was exhausted and go. If Charlie wanted to stay, that was up to him, but Brant was going to remove himself from the situation, hoping that would somehow make things easier on Talulah.

"She won't even look at me," Charlie said.

Clenching his teeth, Brant had to talk himself out of telling Charlie to grow up. "She's just having a drink with an old friend, Charlie," he said, once he'd regained control. "Give her a break."

Charlie straightened, scowling at Brant's words. "Why are you always defending her?"

"I'm not defending her. I'm trying to give you a little perspective. She's moved on. You need to, as well."

"I'm sick of everyone saying that, as if I can decide and make it happen like that." He snapped his fingers. "I wish!"

"Just take your turn," Brant said, gesturing at the pool table.

Charlie threw him a dagger of a glance before sinking his last ball and following up with the eight ball to win the game. "There you go," he said tauntingly. "I took my turn."

"Good for you." Brant was about to walk out even before the food arrived. As far as he was concerned, Charlie had been feeling sorry for himself long enough, and Brant was tired of putting up with it. But after he returned his pool cue to the rack, he spotted Becky, the waitress who'd taken their order, weaving through the tables, and he could see she had their wings, fries and bacon burgers on her tray.

"Hey," Charlie said, greeting her when she reached them. "I'd like to send that woman with the long blond hair over there a note. If I give you twenty bucks, will you get me a piece of paper and a pen and take it over to her?"

"Sure," she said, enthusiastic about the big tip.

"Charlie, don't," Brant murmured after Becky scurried off to do his bidding. "Leave Talulah alone."

"Why? This might be my only chance to let her know how I feel."

"She's well aware of how you feel."

"Maybe so. But I've never really had my say, and I'd like to take this opportunity. I think I deserve it."

Brant felt his muscles tense. "What more is there to say, Charlie?"

"That, my friend, is none of your business," he said with a cocky grin.

Even if he'd finished eating, Brant couldn't leave now. No way was he going to let Charlie mistreat Talulah.

Becky returned with pen and paper and Charlie pushed his food back, even though he'd barely touched it, to make room.

Brant watched him write what seemed like a tome, but he couldn't read it, thanks to the dimly lit room and Charlie shielding the paper. Becky waited beside them. He folded it over and handed it to her as soon as he was done, but Brant snatched it out of her hand.

"What're you doing?" Charlie demanded.

"Just making sure you're not being a dick," Brant replied.

Becky covered her mouth. "I think maybe you two have had too much to drink."

Brant had only had two beers. This had nothing to do

with alcohol. "You'd better get out of here," he told her, and she hurried away.

"You don't have any say in what I do," Charlie said and his stool squealed against the concrete floor as he shoved it back and sprang to his feet.

Brant stood, too, and took a step back, bracing himself just in case. "What're you going to do? Start another fight?"

Charlie didn't answer, but his fists were clenched.

"If you do, this time I won't hold back," Brant warned him.

"You're going to let Talulah, of all people, come between us?" Charlie said.

Brant didn't bother to respond. Instead, he read the note.

Hey Lu,

Remember me? I hope so, because I won't ever forget the day you walked out on our wedding. I don't know another chick who could do something like that, but you're not going to get away with it or what you've done since you came back. I'm going to message your boyfriend on Insta and tell him you've been fucking my best friend. We'll see what happens to your dessert diner after that.

Paybacks are a bitch, aren't they? ;-)

He signed it: *The first man you stood up (now what will the others do?)*

Brant glared at Charlie as he leaned forward, held the paper over the flame of the candle that was in the middle of their table and burned it. "This is bullshit, Charlie," he said. "And you'd better *not* contact Paul."

"I've already done it," Charlie said.

Brant's heart leaped into his throat. Everything Talulah had built could be ruined—because of him. "What the hell is wrong with you?"

"With *me*! I can't believe you're on her side. That must've been one hell of a fuck."

"You know what?" Brant said. "It was."

Charlie took a swing at him, but his fist never landed. Brant caught his arm, twisted it around his back and shoved him into the table, causing everyone in the vicinity to gasp and step back. "I'm glad she didn't marry you," he gritted out. "You don't deserve her."

"Get off me," Charlie yelled.

"You got it. But this time we're really done." Giving him a final shove, Brant let go and walked out.

Eleven

"You don't think that was about me, do you?" Talulah said to Jane. After having pizza and wine at her place they'd decided to get out of the house and have a drink, but she now regretted that decision.

Jane looked as stunned as Talulah was to see Brant shove Charlie before stalking out of the bar. "Of course it was about you."

She frowned. "I was afraid you'd say that."

"Brant's a pretty chill guy." Jane spoke in a low voice. "I wonder what Charlie said to set him off." She rubbed her bare arms. The air-conditioning was making the bar too cold, but Talulah got the impression she was reacting to Charlie more than the temperature. "Look how he's glaring at us."

Talulah met Charlie's eyes. The hate that filled them almost brought her to tears. She'd honestly never meant to hurt him. She'd been a stupid, innocent girl who hadn't been assertive enough to cut off the engagement when she should have. She'd made great strides in being more up-front about her feelings, but only after living a bit longer and finally coming to believe she didn't have to please everyone.

"Uh-oh," Jane murmured. "He's going to come over here."

Talulah caught her breath. She didn't want her ex to cause a scene, wasn't prepared for any ugliness.

Fortunately, he seemed to reconsider whatever he'd had in mind. Instead, he threw a stool to the ground in a fit of temper and started to leave, but Bill Whitehead, the bartender, stopped him before he could reach the door.

Talulah sat on pins and needles while Charlie gave Bill his credit card to cover his bar tab. She wished Bill would hurry at the register so Charlie could leave. She was afraid he'd change his mind and approach her. "Come on," she muttered when Bill got waylaid by another patron.

"Maybe I should go talk to Charlie," Jane said, looking pained.

Talulah grabbed her arm before she could stand up. "No, don't. Please. Let's not provoke him."

"But he's acting like an idiot," Jane argued. "And I think he and I have known each other long enough that I might be able to get through to him."

"It's better if you don't jump into this," Talulah insisted. "If you try to defend me, or he interprets it that way, he'll go home and complain about you to Averil."

"*Someone* should say something." Jane slid her chair away from the table. But then Bill returned with the charge slip for Charlie to sign, handed him his credit card and Charlie turned on his heel and walked out.

Jane relaxed in her seat and slid forward again. "Are you okay?" she asked after he was gone.

Talulah nodded, but felt shaky inside.

"Do you want to go?" Jane asked once they'd waited long enough for Charlie to have left the parking lot.

Talulah *did* want to leave. But at the same time, she wasn't ready to go home alone. What if Charlie showed up at the house? So far, she'd been contrite where he was concerned. She'd still feel that way if he wasn't acting like such a big baby. After what she'd seen of him this trip, she had nothing more to say to him and refused to keep apologizing. "No, I'd rather stay and forget everything—the food for the funeral, the funeral itself, Averil and Charlie."

"Are you saying we should have a few more drinks?"

Talulah hesitated. It was tempting, but… "How would we get home?"

"My sister will pick us up."

"Great." Relieved to have a driver, she lifted her hand to catch Becky's attention, and when the waitress came over, Jane ordered a couple of shots for each of them.

Brant stripped off his clothes as soon as he got home and fell into bed. He preferred not to think about what had happened at Hank's. He didn't want to wonder if he'd done the right thing, and he didn't want to think about Talulah.

But, of course, everything he didn't want to think about was all he *could* think about. Had Charlie *really* sent Paul a message on Instagram? Had Paul read it? If so, when would Talulah find out that he knew about them? She had her aunt's funeral on Thursday and the arrival of her sister's baby soon after. It wasn't even as if she could rush back to Seattle to placate him.

Using the remote, he turned on the TV and propped himself up in bed. He hoped to distract himself with a baseball game—he grew up playing baseball—but only a replay of the last Cubs versus White Sox was on, and he wasn't interested in either of those teams. He let the game play in the background as he reached into his nightstand and retrieved his laptop. He wanted to take another look at Paul Pacheco.

After logging on and finding Talulah's profile on Instagram, he scrolled through her pictures, even though he'd seen them before, stopping whenever he encountered one of her business partner.

The dude wasn't only fit, he was handsome, with long brown hair he wore in a ponytail and thick eyebrows that were just a shade darker. His nose was slightly too big for his face, but he had a strong chin, too, so the nose didn't hurt him. He did seem to be older, though, closer to forty than thirty.

Pictures of his hiking and traveling adventures featured heavily in his personal feed, along with a lot of posts about cakes and pastries and cooking, of course. The dishes he'd featured looked pretty damn good.

Brant still didn't like him. As a matter of fact, he liked him even less now than he had a few days ago.

With a sigh, he navigated to the feed for the dessert diner, which reminded him of carhops on skates and the drive-ins of the fifties he'd seen in pictures growing up. With a black-and-white-checkered floor, pink walls and a jukebox opposite the register, it was clean, upbeat and appealing. And the pies and cakes were extra-fancy, the portions large.

He navigated to the diner's website and clicked on "specialty cakes," which called up pictures of cakes for almost every occasion, from weddings to anniversaries to graduations to baby showers.

It appeared that this was a very successful business, and that she and Paul were good at what they did. They seemed happy together, too—at least as far as he could tell from the photos.

Would Charlie's message to Paul spell the end of all that?

A chime signaled an incoming text, and Brant realized he'd left his phone in his jeans. Setting his computer aside, he leaned over to peer at them on the floor. But he was reluctant to get up and retrieve them. It would only upset him if Charlie was sending a bunch of incendiary bullshit.

Ignoring it, he forced himself to quit scrolling through pictures he'd already seen and did some channel surfing instead. But when another text came in, he dragged his ass out of bed and dug his phone from a front pocket. He had to put it on the charger anyway.

Charlie had sent the first text, but Talulah had sent the second. Ignoring Charlie's message, he touched hers.

Are you okay?

He climbed back into bed. I'm fine, he wrote back. You?

Trying to drown my sorrows. lol

How's that going?

Pretty well, actually. After three shots, I feel almost bullet proof.

Is Charlie still there?

No. Thank goodness.

He didn't approach you, did he?

For a minute it looked like he might—but he changed his mind.

A good choice on Charlie's part. Now that Brant had blown up their relationship, he wasn't about to let Charlie do anything more to hurt Talulah. If he bothers you, let me know, okay?

He watched a few minutes of a random *Dateline* while waiting for her response: I'm not going to do that.

Why not?

I don't want you standing up for me. I already feel terrible that you and Charlie aren't getting along.

You did what you could to save the relationship. This is on him.

It took a bit longer to receive a response. What happened? she asked. It looked like you two were having fun until I showed up. I wish I'd never come. But I had no idea you were here. I was talking to Jane when we arrived and never even thought to look for your truck.

Going to the same bar shouldn't have been a problem.

What'd Charlie say when I came in?

Should he tell her about Paul?

He decided to wait. He was still hoping Charlie had been bluffing and hadn't actually contacted Talulah's partner. Not much. Don't let him ruin your night. Just try to have some fun.

Okay.

He set his phone aside. But he could only ignore Charlie's message for so long. After watching a couple of MMA fights on YouTube, he got up to go to the bathroom and, when he came back, picked up his phone and pressed Charlie's name.

How dare you push me around!

Brant was tempted to remind him that he'd started it. But what good would that do? If Charlie had been thinking straight, nothing would've happened.

Brant started to set his phone back down, but then he got a text from Averil.

Did you really shove Charlie into a table at Hank's?

Brant rolled his eyes. Why was Averil contacting him so often? He was trying to help her out with her kid, but she seemed to call or text him for all kinds of reasons— and some were beginning to feel like excuses.

He told himself to ignore her message, too. But then she texted him a second time.

Brant?

He threw the first punch—*again*, he responded.

He must've had a good reason. You're changing.

That's not true, he wrote back. But there was something different going on with him. He cared enough about Talulah and her well-being that he wasn't about to let anyone hurt her, and that included Charlie.

It was late when Jane's younger sister, Kate, pulled up to Talulah's aunt's house. Fortunately by then, Talulah had had enough to drink that the incident she'd witnessed between Charlie and Brant seemed like nothing—or at least like an incident that'd happened so long ago it didn't matter much anymore.

She got out as a drunken Jane sang the last song they'd heard at the bar at the top of her lungs, causing Kate to grimace.

"Thank you," Talulah said, bending down to see inside the car. "Good night!"

She shut the door and they drove off as she waved. "Thank God for Jane," she muttered as she turned to the house. "And Kate."

She was unsteady enough on her feet that she had to use the handrail to climb the steps to the front porch. She also fumbled the key, dropping it twice before finally managing to open the door. Then she practically fell into the house because she'd been leaning against the panel while unlocking it.

Once she'd secured the dead bolt, she tossed her purse onto the closest chair and was crossing to the stairs to go up to her bedroom when her aunt's grand piano caught her eye, and she decided to see how much she remembered from the lessons her mother had insisted she take as a child.

The music room wasn't large, so the piano, two side chairs and a small accent table were all that could fit. After snapping on the light, Talulah navigated the furniture and other clutter, searched through the sheet music stored in the piano bench and found a book of music she recognized. It contained "Für Elise," which represented the furthest she'd ever advanced in her piano studies.

When she started playing Beethoven's popular classic, her fingers stumbled over the beginning, which was the easiest part. But she hadn't even sat at a piano for four years, maybe longer. It'd been important to her mother that she learn, probably because of the influence of Phoebe, who felt a woman wasn't properly educated until she could play an instrument. Talulah had never been particularly interested in music herself. Debbie had always been the better pianist—yet another area in which Talulah had fallen short.

After a few minutes, the piece she'd memorized so many years ago began to come back to her. She was actually playing it quite well when two beams of light caught her attention and she looked out the window to see headlights in the drive.

Was Brant coming over? she wondered, going to the window. She'd been missing him. The more she drank, the more she'd wanted to call him. But she couldn't tell who it was. All she could see were the headlights shooting into the house like lasers.

It was so late it had to be Brant. If it was Charlie, he'd turn off his headlights and creep down the drive to see if Brant was here. He wouldn't announce his presence like this.

She retrieved her phone from her purse and returned to the window, where she texted Brant. Is that you in the drive?

She was waiting for him to get out of the vehicle and come in when the window exploded.

She dropped to the floor as glass pelted her. But only after she lifted her head and saw taillights instead of headlights did she realize what'd happened. The window hadn't exploded; someone had thrown a rock through it, which had hit the piano with a solid *thunk*.

Fortunately, she'd instinctively sheltered her head, so glass hadn't gotten into her eyes or cut her face. But her arms stung from several small cuts, and there was a large shard sticking out of her left forearm.

The sight of it made her queasy. The fact that she'd drunk too much alcohol didn't help the nausea rising in her stomach. Should she pull out the glass? Or had it severed an important artery?

Regardless, she was going to need stitches. She'd have to call Dr. Gregor. He'd come to her rescue once already.

She hurried into the kitchen and found his number, but he didn't pick up. Probably because it was so late...

She stared at her arm in shock, trying to think clearly enough to solve the problem. She'd have to call an ambulance and pay an astronomical fee on top of whatever the hospital charged, she decided. But then her phone dinged with a text.

In your drive? No. Is someone there?

Brant. He was awake. Thank God!

She was beginning to shake, which made it difficult to hit the right buttons. After several tries, she managed to call him.

"Talulah?" she could hear him say. "Are you there? Hello?"

Taking a deep breath, she tried to speak over the pounding of her heart, but even she could hear the reedy quality of her voice when she said, "Brant?"

"What is it?" he asked. "What's wrong?"

Cradling her injured arm with her other hand, she watched the blood that was seeping up around the glass roll down to her wrist and drip onto the linoleum. "Can you help me?"

What had Charlie done?

Brant yanked on his clothes, grabbed his keys and jogged down the hall of the three-thousand-square-foot rambler his parents had built when they first bought the ranch. It would take ten minutes to get to Talulah's, but there was nothing he could do about that. After she told him what'd happened, she'd insisted she'd be fine waiting for him.

He hoped she was right. If not, he was going to make Charlie *very* sorry. He wanted to do that anyway.

The night air felt cool enough to suggest that the heat wave they'd been suffering was finally over. He raked his fingers through his hair, which he hadn't even bothered to comb, as he hopped into his truck and fired up the engine.

A car drove past. He wondered if it could be Charlie coming by as a sort of "fuck you" after what he'd done. But the vehicle didn't slow as it approached the house, so maybe he was imagining things. Whatever had happened to Talulah, if it was Charlie's fault or not, he was going to get to the bottom of it—after he made sure she was okay.

Fortunately, there wasn't any traffic this time of night. He barreled through town, running any stop signs where there were no other cars, and reached Talulah's great aunt's house in only seven minutes.

As soon as he pulled in, he saw her sitting on the porch steps waiting for him and left his engine running as he jumped out to help her. All she'd told him on the phone was that someone had thrown a rock through the front window and she'd been cut, but he hadn't expected to see a three-by-four-inch piece of glass sticking out of her arm. She was bleeding so badly her hand looked painted red.

She'd gotten up the moment she saw him turn onto the property, but seemed a little wobbly as she started toward him, so he simply swept her into his arms and carried her to the cab of his truck. "Goddamn it," he said. "If Charlie did this, I'm going to beat the shit out of him."

She didn't tell him not to talk like that—something he felt certain she'd do if she was feeling okay—which worried him even more. She didn't say *anything*. Her face was pale, her breathing shallow, but she had a towel to catch the blood, and she didn't complain about the pain.

"I'll get you to the hospital as fast as I can," he promised as he set her gently in the passenger seat and buckled her in before running around to climb back behind the wheel.

He would've backed out of the drive like a bat out of hell. He wanted that glass out of her arm as soon as possible. But he was afraid driving like that would cause her more pain, so he tried to take it easy. He wished he could question her—he was dying to learn more about how this had happened—but he doubted she could focus on anything except getting to a doctor.

"There's a regional hospital forty minutes from here."

She knew that, of course, but he was trying to reassure her.

She nodded to let him know she'd heard, but he could tell she wasn't really listening.

He turned on some heat, thinking she might need the added warmth, and gave the truck more gas once he hit the straightaway that led out of town. "You're going to be okay," he said. "I'll make sure of it."

She offered him a grateful smile, which only made him angrier with Charlie.

As they traveled, Brant was afraid she might pass out. He kept looking over at her, but she seemed alert. She sat still as a statue and didn't say anything until they were almost there. Then she said, "Brant?"

He glanced at her yet again. "What?"

"Thanks for coming to get me. I know it's late, and this is probably going to make it hard for you to work tomorrow, but…I appreciate it."

"I'm happy to help," he said and again felt the urge to punch Charlie in the face for doing this to her.

* * *

Talulah couldn't remember ever being so tired. She tried to keep her eyes open while Brant drove home from the hospital. It was close to four in the morning; he had to be tired, too. She hated to leave him battling fatigue without someone to help him stay alert. But the alcohol she'd drunk at the bar, combined with the trauma of getting seventeen stitches, kept dragging her down. She'd start to nod off, Brant would look over and tell her to give in and go to sleep—and then she'd sit up straighter and try harder to stay awake so she could talk to him.

Finally, exhaustion got the best of her. She didn't even realize she'd lost the battle and fallen asleep until she woke up. The truck had stopped and Brant had opened her door and released her seat belt.

"I'm sorry I faded out on you," she mumbled as he scooped her up. "I just…couldn't stay awake. Are you okay?"

"Relax. I'm fine," he assured her. "And you're going to be fine, too."

Unable to recognize their surroundings, she raised her head in confusion. "Where are we?"

"At the ranch."

"*Your* ranch? You're not taking me home?"

"And leave you there alone after what Charlie did? No way."

"I doubt he'd come back. Last night was probably…" she searched her sluggish mind for a convincing explanation "…a reaction to seeing me at the bar. He's struggling with having me back in town."

"That may be true, but no one has the right to do what he's done. I never dreamed he'd be capable of it, but now that he's proven otherwise, I'm not taking any chances."

She was too tired to argue. All she wanted to do was

go back to sleep, and she knew she'd feel safe with Brant, so there wasn't anything to complain about.

"Okay." She rested her cheek against his chest as he carried her in. She could've insisted on walking; she was capable of it. But it felt good to let someone else take care of her for a change, especially someone as strong and competent as Brant.

The beating of his heart thudded in her ear, as steady as the metronome she remembered from her music lessons— a reassuring sound—as they moved down a long hall and entered what had to be his bedroom. He didn't turn on the light. A full moon shining through the windows made it possible to see as he put her on the bed.

"It smells like you in here," she murmured.

He sniffed. "Is that a good thing or a bad thing?"

"It's a good thing. You always smell great."

"Not when I'm out on the ranch," he said with a chuckle.

His room was rather Spartan compared to her great aunt's house. There was nothing on the dresser except a large flat-screen TV, and the nightstand held only a lamp, the remote for the TV and a phone charger—until he added his wallet.

"This is a huge bed," she said while he took off his shirt.

"When you're as tall as I am, you need a big bed." He sat down beside her to remove his boots, which he tossed carelessly into the corner. "Do you have to use the bathroom?"

She shook her head. "I went before we left the hospital."

He eyed her speculatively. "Do you…plan to sleep in your clothes?"

She understood why he was asking. They'd made love several times, but they hadn't established any ground rules outside the two nights they'd spent together. They didn't owe each other anything and didn't expect anything, either.

So he had no way of knowing where the boundaries were. "Are *you* planning to sleep in your clothes?" she asked.

"Not unless you want me to."

"I don't want you to," she admitted.

He took that as his cue to help her undress. Being careful of her stitches and the bandage that covered them, he lifted her shirt over her head and held the waistband of her jeans as she stood up and wiggled out of them. When he'd stripped her down to her panties and bra, she curled onto her side and he covered her with his blankets.

He went to the bathroom off the bedroom before shucking his jeans and climbing in with her, wearing just his boxers. "Do you need any pain pills or anything?" he asked.

"No, thank you."

Seemingly satisfied, he curved his large body around her smaller one. "Okay. See you in the morning."

With the warmth and security Brant provided easing the shock, pain and upset she'd endured earlier, Talulah dragged his arm a little higher. She liked its solid weight holding her against him so much it seemed perfectly natural to kiss his knuckles before slipping gratefully into oblivion.

As tired as he was, Brant couldn't fall asleep. He was too surprised by the affection Talulah had shown him when she kissed his hand and tucked it under her chin as if they slept together every night.

Their relationship was beginning to feel like more than a sexual one, which scared the hell out of him. He'd spent the past few years hoping he could find the right woman eventually. He planned to have a family one day. But he knew better than to care too much about this particular woman. Even if she didn't have commitment issues, she lived in a different state.

Averil's words ran through his mind: *She only wants a man until she gets him, Brant.*

Was that true? Was he falling for someone who'd just break his heart?

Maybe the cockiness he'd exhibited when Averil tried to warn him would come back to bite him in the ass...

She leads a guy on until he goes all in and then it's over.

That wasn't happening here, he told himself. He felt what he felt for Talulah because they weren't only sex partners, they were friends. But the defensiveness that welled up whenever he thought of Charlie mistreating her was stronger than it should be—strong enough to suggest otherwise. And Brant didn't quite know how to explain that. Charlie had always been important to him. So why was he risking their friendship over Talulah?

She's a man-eater. And if you're not careful, you might find that out the hard way.

Was he in trouble?

No. There was no need to panic. She'd been back in town less than a week. No one fell in love that fast. That kind of thing only happened in the movies.

He waited to see what Talulah would do next, but she didn't do anything. She'd already drifted off to sleep. That kiss on the hand was probably her way of expressing gratitude for his help—except he couldn't see her doing that to just any man.

As he listened to her breathing even out, he let his lips move lightly over her bare shoulder and up under her hair. He loved the smell of her almost as much as he loved the feel of her.

She stirred, so he stopped. After what she'd been through, he didn't want to wake her. But having her bare body against his made him hard. He wanted to make love to her again, couldn't seem to get enough. She did something to him no other woman ever had, which made him worry about how he was going to feel when she returned to Seattle. Chances were good she'd never even look back, not after her most recent experience in Coyote Canyon.

He'd put some distance between them once he knew for sure she was safe, he decided. He'd pull back, stop seeing her.

But no sooner had he made that decision than she turned in his arms and sleepily found his mouth with hers—and that kiss quickly escalated into a desperate desire to get the rest of their clothes off.

Twelve

Talulah woke up alone. She'd spent an incredible night in Brant's bed, enjoying his body—both when they were making love and when they weren't—and had all but forgotten about her injury. It was the pull of her stitches as she started to stretch that reminded her. "Ouch," she grumbled, quickly drawing her arm back in.

She checked the bandage and was relieved when she didn't see any blood seeping through. That was fortunate. So was the fact that as long as she could stave off any infection, she wouldn't have to return to the doctor to have the stitches removed. She'd been told they'd disintegrate as the wound healed.

Leaning up on her elbow, she reached for the alarm clock. It was nearly nine. She hadn't planned on sleeping so late. She still had a lot to do to get ready for the funeral tomorrow.

Instead of jumping out of bed, however, she took a second to listen for Brant.

She couldn't hear anything. He didn't seem to be in the house and neither did anyone else. She assumed he and his brothers had gotten up and gone to work.

After she used the bathroom, she started to search for

her purse. She'd taken it to the hospital last night so she'd have her insurance card with her, but it didn't seem to have made it into Brant's house. Assuming she'd left it in the seat when he lifted her out of the truck, she got dressed so she could go out and grab it. She needed her phone. Her sister might've gone into labor. Or maybe her parents had been trying to call to see how things were going with the funeral arrangements.

Planning to shower as soon as she got home, she didn't bother combing her hair. It would've felt slightly intrusive to go through Brant's bathroom drawers looking for a comb. Why she'd be hesitant, when he'd helped himself to her toothbrush a few nights ago, she didn't know.

Since he was probably out on the ranch somewhere, she decided to ask Jane to come get her. But as soon as she stepped out of the house to see if she could get her phone, she found him standing in the drive arguing with someone. He was saying that what Charlie had done wasn't cool, but she couldn't see who he was talking to until the sound of the door prompted him to look over—and Averil peered around the vehicle that'd been hiding her.

This was the first time Talulah had seen her childhood friend since she'd moved away from Coyote Canyon. Her heart jumped into her throat and she tried a tentative smile, hoping that after so long Averil would be at least slightly happy to see her. But the hostility on Charlie's sister's face let Talulah know nothing had changed.

Tempted to avoid the confrontation altogether, she nearly went back inside. She wished she'd at least combed her hair. But that wouldn't have made any difference. It was obvious she'd spent the night.

Refusing to be a coward, she forced a smile to replace the one that'd wilted beneath her former friend's scorn and walked over. "Hello, Averil."

"Don't you dare approach me," Averil snapped. "Every time you come around someone gets hurt."

"Averil!" Brant's voice was filled with irritation. "*She* was the one who got hurt last night. She needed seventeen stitches to close up her arm, yet you're acting like it was nothing."

"I'm sure when Charlie threw that rock he wasn't thinking she'd be standing in front of the window!"

Talulah felt her fingernails curve into her palms at such an easy dismissal of what Charlie had done. "He could see me," she clarified. "His headlights were pointed right at me."

"And he could've hurt her much worse than he did," Brant added. "The shard that cut her arm could as easily have landed in an eye."

Averil threw up a hand to indicate she wasn't remotely concerned. "She shouldn't have come back. She knows she's not welcome here."

"All because she wouldn't marry your brother?" he asked, but Talulah spoke at the same time.

"Averil, I know you think the worst of me. I apologize *again* for walking out on the wedding. But you and Charlie and your parents should be glad I didn't go through with it. Our marriage would never have lasted. I wasn't mature enough to marry, and I wasn't in love, at least not enough to make it work."

"Because it's all about the chase for you, isn't it?" Averil said. "As soon as you own a man's heart you don't want it anymore."

"That's not true. I have a problem with commitment," Talulah said. "I admit that, but—"

"You have a problem with a lot more than that," she interrupted. "And now you think you can wrap Brant around your little finger and play him like a puppet? Come between him and his best friend?"

"No, that's not true," Talulah cried.

"Then why are you spreading your legs for him every chance you get?"

Images from last night flashed before Talulah's mind's eye and she felt herself flush. "I'm not… I mean… It hasn't been anything like you're painting it."

"Don't you dare go after her on my account," Brant growled, which made Averil turn on him.

"I never knew you were that desperate for a piece of ass!"

"Averil, you're overreacting," Talulah said. "I get it. Brant's your brother's friend. He's your friend, too, and I don't have a place in his life. I needed someone to take me to the hospital last night—"

"Oh, so now you're saying you haven't been sleeping with him?" she broke in with a shrill laugh.

"I'm not saying that—"

"You'd say it if you thought I'd believe it. You're such a manipulative bitch. But I'm telling you right now to stay away from him."

Once again, Brant started to object, but Talulah put up a hand to stop him. "Wait a second," she said to Averil. "Is this about Charlie? Or *you*?"

The blood drained from her childhood friend's face. "I don't know what you're talking about—and neither do you," she said and whipped around to climb into her beige sedan.

Brant jerked Talulah out of the way as Averil executed a quick three-point turn and nearly sprayed them with rocks and dirt as she rocketed away.

"What the hell's gotten into her?" he said. "She's never acted like that before."

Struggling to cope with all the emotions charging through her, Talulah rubbed her forehead. "You know what's going on, don't you?"

Brant looked uncertain about where she was going with that. "What?"

Talulah suspected he knew the truth, but he was dismissing the obvious because he preferred not to be in the awkward situation it would put him in. "She's in love with you."

Paul had called her at least thirty times, starting early this morning. He'd never been *that* persistent before, so Talulah assumed there had to be an emergency. Had the diner been robbed? Had it sustained fire or water damage?

She nearly called Paul right away, even in the truck with Brant driving her home. But the fact that her business partner hadn't left any voice mail messages, as he would've done if there'd been a catastrophe of some kind affecting the diner, made her uneasy. What was so important that he'd blow up her phone but not leave a message—or at least send a text?

Worried, she nibbled at her bottom lip.

"What is it?" Brant asked, noticing her preoccupation.

After what had just happened with Averil at the ranch, Talulah hadn't said much. He'd asked her to stay for breakfast, said he wanted to make sure she was okay before taking her home. But she'd said she needed to get back and start cooking, and he'd agreed to drive her right away. Other than that, she'd been kicking herself for being foolish enough to mess around with Brant. As much as she enjoyed being with him, the relationship couldn't go anywhere. Her business was in Seattle and his ranch was in Montana. She couldn't even say why this type of relationship had sprung up so suddenly between them.

When she didn't reply immediately, a pained expression appeared on his handsome face. "Is it Paul?" he asked. "Has he been trying to reach you?"

She looked over in surprise. "How'd you know?"

He sent her a sheepish glance. "I thought he might."

"Why?"

"Charlie said something to me last night," he replied. "That's what caused the fight between us."

"What'd he say?"

"He told me he sent Paul a message on Instagram, telling him about us," he said with a wince.

Her stomach felt instantly queasy. "He *what*?"

"I know. I'm sorry."

"Why didn't you warn me?"

Although they were still a mile away from Phoebe's, Brant pulled to the side of the road, presumably so he could give her his undivided attention. "Because I couldn't believe he'd really be that big an asshole. I've known him my whole life. I guess I was hoping he was only bluffing to get back at me for being with you."

Scarcely able to breathe, she pressed a hand to her chest and returned her gaze to Paul's missed calls.

Paul Pacheco 6:33 a.m.

Paul Pacheco 6:35 a.m.

Paul Pacheco 6:41 a.m.

And the list went on…

Clearing his throat, Brant shifted so he could face her more directly. "Hey," he said. When she didn't respond, he added, "Talulah?"

"What?" she asked mechanically.

"Are you okay?" He reached for her hand, but she pulled it away.

"No, I'm not okay." Talulah felt completely numb. "I have seventeen stitches in my arm. My relationship with my partner is in jeopardy. My business could be in jeopardy. My sister and parents are embarrassed and disappointed in me, even though I came here for them. And any hope I had that Averil would one day forgive me is gone. As if that isn't enough, I also have to face the entire Gerhart family at the funeral tomorrow." Squeezing her eyes closed, she let her head fall back on the seat. "What have I done?" she said with a groan.

"I didn't mean for any of this to happen," Brant said.

Visions of Paul pleading with her to get serious with him, telling her how much she meant to him and how happy he'd make her played in her mind. What was she going to say to him now? How would he react to this? He couldn't claim she'd been cheating on him; she'd made it clear they weren't even unofficially together. But until she left Seattle, their relationship had been moving in the direction he wanted. Sleeping with Paul had made him confident they'd finally turned a corner.

She'd only been gone a week, and she'd already slept with someone else when it'd taken him *years* to get her into bed.

That wasn't going to be easy to explain.

"I feel terrible," Brant said. "Will you please say something?"

She opened her eyes. "I'm not blaming you," she said dully. "It's not as if you forced me into the shower that night."

"But I did make the first move."

"We thought it would be an isolated incident, nothing anyone would ever have to know about." She frowned as she stared off into the distance, across the acres of farmland heading toward the mountains. "Neither one of us thought it would turn out like this."

He leaned forward, trying to get her to look at him, but

it was partly his striking blue eyes that'd gotten her into trouble in the first place. "What are you going to tell him?"

"The truth, I guess. I wasn't going to volunteer our involvement. I was going to leave it here in Coyote Canyon, along with everything else I've left behind. But now that he knows, I can't lie to him."

She could feel Brant's gaze on her face even though she wouldn't meet it. "Have you ever seen him angry?" he asked.

"A few times. But only at his brother, whom he's fought with since childhood, or vendors who didn't bring what they promised, or an employee who left us high and dry. Never at me. At least…not really." She'd never done anything to make him mad, and he'd been hoping to win her over, which meant she'd probably never seen his worst side.

"How does he behave when he gets angry?"

"He'll yell and then he'll withdraw. As far as I know. Like I said, his anger has always been directed at someone else."

"Maybe you should call him while I'm with you."

"That's a *terrible* idea."

"I want to be here, in case he treats you badly."

"You wouldn't be able to do anything about it anyway," she pointed out. "It'd only make him angrier if you tried."

"I get that, but… Damn. I don't know. Isn't there *anything* I can do to make things easier?"

"Nothing. It would help if I could give him a good explanation as to why this happened. But…I can't even say it was just a one-night stand. Is there such a thing as a three-night stand?"

He scratched his neck. "I think I'd steer clear of the numbers."

"I agree. Maybe I could say that I was intimidated by all my enemies here and…and I felt like I needed a friend."

"Is that true?" he asked, sounding slightly crestfallen. "Is that all it was?"

"Not really. At least I don't think so." She put down her phone and finally looked at him. "But what else can I say? That I wanted you so badly I couldn't help myself?"

"*I* like the sound of that."

She made a disgruntled face. "That'll only hurt him more. I knew him for years before I agreed to sleep with him."

His eyebrows slid up. "That's a long time to chase a woman. Why didn't he give up?"

"Because not every man has your take 'em or leave 'em attitude."

"Why weren't you interested in him sooner?"

"I don't know. I wasn't ready, I guess. But…you see the problem."

"Yeah, I see it." With a sigh, he put the truck back into gear and started driving, more slowly this time. They said nothing during the last mile, and the moment Brant pulled down the driveway, Talulah opened the door.

He caught her by the arm, well above where she'd been hurt, before she could get out. "I suppose this means you don't plan on seeing me anymore."

He sounded disappointed. She was more disappointed than she felt she should be herself. They'd spent some incredible nights together. But the fact that Charlie told Paul what was going on had been a huge wake-up call. If she didn't clean up her act, she could lose everything. "I think we've done enough damage to each other's lives, don't you?"

"Maybe that's true, but…" He released her arm and took her hand instead. "I'd rather put the pieces back together after you're gone. It'll be a lot easier."

She was tempted to agree. But she couldn't head any

farther down that road, and she knew it. "I can't wait that long, Brant. By then it might be too late to save what I've built."

Letting go, he straightened. "Okay. I don't want to push you into anything that might make things worse for you."

"Thank you." She slid to the ground and turned to take one last look at him. "Being with you was…good," she admitted. "Actually, it approached fantastic."

"I feel like it was fantastic all the way," he said.

She offered him a smile in lieu of goodbye, closed the door and started toward the house. She was under so much pressure to try to fix everything that was wrong she felt the need to hurry—and yet, at the same time, she dreaded each step, because she knew she'd have to phone Paul as soon as she got inside.

Paul didn't answer when she dialed his cell. Talulah tried three times before calling the store instead.

"Talulah's Dessert Diner."

Talulah recognized the voice as the woman they'd hired to work behind the counter during the week. "Beth? It's me."

"Oh, hey," she said.

Talulah dug nervously at her cuticles. "Have you seen Paul today?"

"No. He had all the baking done when I arrived, so he must've been in earlier, but I haven't seen him since I got here. Have you tried his cell?"

Of course she'd tried his cell. But she didn't want to make it obvious that he wasn't answering for her. The last thing she needed was for their employees to pick up on a potential problem between them. "He's probably out on a hike," she said. "How's everything at the diner?"

"It's been quiet this morning, but it's always slow before dinnertime. Then we get *crushed* until closing."

"We need the slow times to prepare for the busy ones."

"That's what I'm doing—getting ready for later," she said and covered the phone to tell someone she'd be right with them.

"Sounds like you have a customer," Talulah said. "I'll let you go."

"Okay, but…do you have any idea when you'll be back?"

"Not yet. The funeral isn't until tomorrow. Then I'll need to finish dealing with my great aunt's house and its contents." Sadly, thanks to all the distractions, as well as the cooking she'd taken on for the funeral, she hadn't gotten as much done as she'd planned.

"I hope that goes well."

"Thank you," she said and disconnected. She was just gathering the nerve to try to reach Paul again when she received a call from her sister.

Grateful for the reprieve, however short-lived, she answered immediately. "Debbie!"

"Wow," her sister said with a laugh. "You sound incredibly relieved to hear from me."

Talulah *was* relieved. As embattled as she felt, her sister's voice came across like a warm hug. "I've been waiting for you to call," she said. "You're not in labor, are you?"

Debbie's sigh made it sound as though she was just as beleaguered as Talulah was. "Not yet. At this rate, I don't think I'll *ever* have this baby."

"I don't want you to go into labor too soon. If you started now, I'd miss the birth. Wait until after the funeral, okay?"

"I'll see what I can do," she said with a chuckle. "How's life in Coyote Canyon? Are you prepared for the funeral?"

Talulah grimaced while peering around the messy

kitchen. Last night she and Jane hadn't cleaned up the salad mess they'd made to go with the pizza they'd ordered. They'd been too set on going out for more drinks after that and having a good time. And now she had to contend with the mess as well as the rest of the cooking. "Almost."

"You've got the food done?"

"Not quite, but I still have today."

"I hate that you've had to carry the entire load. How's everything else?"

Attempting to put fresh energy into her voice, Talulah drew a deep breath before she said, "Great. Fine. Perfect."

She knew her answer had rung false when Debbie said, "Oh, no," in a much lower voice. "What's wrong?"

Blinking quickly in an effort to stave off tears, Talulah meandered into the dining room. "Nothing. What do you mean?"

"Lu, come on. You can't hide anything from me. What is it?"

A single tear escaped Talulah's eyelashes and began to roll down her cheek. "It's Charlie."

"What's going on with him now?"

She sniffed. "He hates me."

"He's hated you for fourteen years. Why would that bother you enough to make you cry?"

Sinking into one of the hand-embroidered chairs that went with her aunt's Duncan Phyfe dining table, she rested her chin on the fist of her good arm. "He wrote Paul on Instagram and told him about Brant."

"No!"

"Yes," she said glumly.

"What'd Paul say?"

"He hasn't said anything yet. He won't pick up."

"I'm sorry, honey."

She straightened the large doily she and Jane had folded

back when they were eating and once again centered the vase full of dusty silk flowers that had been on her aunt's dining table since she could remember. "It's my own fault. But… I don't know why I hooked up with Brant to begin with. I'm having a tough time coping since I got here and seem to be making all the wrong decisions."

"It was one night. Surely, Paul can forgive you for *one night* when you haven't promised him your fidelity in the first place."

Except it hadn't been just one night. It'd been *three* hormone-fueled nights filled with some of the best sex she'd ever known—not that she was going to volunteer that information. "Charlie also threw a rock through the front window last night, and I have seventeen stitches to show for it."

Debbie gasped. "He *what?*"

"He hurled a rock through the window."

"And you got cut? I hope you called the cops!"

Talulah peeled back her bandage to take a look at her injury. Her skin puckered where the thread held the gash closed. "I was too busy trying to get to a hospital."

"But you're okay?"

"I'm fine. I'll heal. But it was pretty over-the-top of him."

"That's beyond over the top! That's illegal. You need to call the cops right now."

Talulah had considered it. Charlie deserved some type of consequence. But she didn't see any real hope in pursuing a criminal case. "Why? It won't do any good. All I saw was a pair of headlights and the next thing I knew I had a big piece of glass sticking out of my arm. From their perspective it could've been anybody."

"So how do you know it was him?"

"Who else would it be? But he could easily say it *wasn't* him, and I have nothing to prove otherwise."

"Do you think he was *trying* to hurt you?"

"Probably not as badly as he did. Still, he's a bastard for throwing that rock."

"I'm going to call him up and tell him he'd better back the heck off and leave you alone!"

"Back the *heck* off, Deb?" In spite of everything, Talulah started laughing. "That's the best you've got?"

"He'll get the point," she insisted.

Talulah sobered. "Look, I appreciate the support, but if he won't listen to Brant, he won't listen to you."

"Brant's been sticking up for you?"

Suddenly realizing that she'd always hated Phoebe's silk flowers, she got up and threw them away. "Not sticking up for me exactly—just trying to talk some sense into Charlie."

"That's nice. But…you're not seeing Brant anymore, are you?"

Talulah had told Brant only this morning that she wouldn't be. But she held back on the timeline. "Of course not. Like I told him, we've done enough damage to our lives."

"So he still wants to see you…"

"I'm sure he doesn't care either way, Deb."

"How do you know?"

"I just do. Brant is…Brant. He doesn't take *any* romantic relationship too seriously. Have you ever known him to have a steady girlfriend?"

"I haven't, but that was way back when. I have no idea what he's like these days."

"He's the same." Except that he was now friendly to her. More than friendly…

"So what are you going to do about Paul?"

"Tell him the truth, I guess—if I can ever get him to talk to me."

"What will you do with the diner if you can't work this out?"

"That's just it—I don't have a good answer to that question."

"The business has your name on it, Lu. He's the one who'd have to move on."

Talulah doubted Paul would think so. He was too excited about their success, too set on expanding. Losing her would be one thing; he'd never really had her to begin with. But he felt firmly in control of the diner and wouldn't easily walk away from it. "Hopefully, neither one of us will have to move on," she said.

"After you talk to him, call me and let me know how it went. I have to get going. I have a doctor's appointment, and I'll be late if I don't jump in the shower right away."

"Okay. Good luck at the doctor's." Tossing Phoebe's ugly vase into the trash along with the fake flowers made Talulah feel slightly empowered. But that feeling quickly faded as, once again, she hit the redial button to reach Paul.

Thirteen

Jane guided Mitch, Averil's son, to the edge of the pool as Averil came out of her parents' house with two glasses of iced tea.

"You thirsty?" she called over.

Jane wasn't thirsty; she was anxious. After Averil had told her Talulah had been injured, she wanted to call and check on her. But she knew if she did, or left Averil's too soon, Averil would feel she was choosing Talulah over her and would be offended. This was a test of her loyalty, one she hadn't faced before because Talulah had never come back to Coyote Canyon. Although Averil knew they got together once a year in Seattle, and Jane could tell she didn't like it, it wasn't quite the same as flaunting their continuing friendship under her nose. "Not right now."

"It'll be on the table when you're ready." Keeping her own glass, Averil sat in one of the wicker chairs in the shade of the patio, propped her bare feet up on the glass-topped coffee table and took a sip.

"You're not getting in the water?" Jane asked. Swimming had been Averil's idea.

"In a minute." Sliding her sunglasses higher on her nose, Averil checked her phone.

"You've been tethered to your phone ever since I got here," Jane said. "What's going on?" She was afraid Averil was sending scathing texts to Talulah, so she was somewhat relieved when Averil put her phone aside, leaned back and said, "Fighting with Cash—as always."

Cash was her ex-husband. Averil had met him at Montana State University and they'd settled in Bozeman where, after they graduated, he'd worked as a physician's assistant. "What's going on now?"

"He hasn't sent his child support this month."

"Why not?" Jane asked. "He knows perfectly well that he owes it."

"Claims he doesn't have the money."

"I thought he had a good job."

"Not anymore. He couldn't get along with the doctor he worked for, so he quit."

"How long ago was that?"

"Maybe…two months?"

"Why didn't you tell me?"

"I didn't realize I hadn't. I didn't keep it from you on purpose." She adjusted the straps on her blue-and-white-striped bikini. "It's just one more thing in the ongoing saga between us. To be honest, I try not to think about him anymore. But now that he's not paying his child support, I have no choice."

"He hasn't found another job? How's he been living since he quit?"

"My guess is that he's found another woman and she's supporting him. Or he's working construction with his brother and getting paid under the table."

"I can't believe he's not more of a stand-up dad." She jerked her head toward Mitch, who was holding his breath and putting his face in the water. Averil's son was still wearing floaties, but he was super proud of the way he was "swimming." "This is one special kid."

"Watch me, Aunt Jane!" Mitch said as soon as he came up for air.

She'd been watching him since she got there, but she smiled anyway. "I'm watching, buddy. Great job."

"Cash doesn't care about anyone other than himself," Averil complained once her son's head was under water again. "That's why I had to leave him."

"Is he still going to have Mitch come to Bozeman for a week before school starts?" She'd heard Averil mention that several times. They'd even discussed taking a weekend girls' trip to Vegas while Mitch was away, since it would be Averil's first opportunity in ages.

"Not if he doesn't pay me."

Mitch came up sputtering and splashing, and Jane smoothed the wet hair out of his face to keep it from dripping into his big brown eyes. "This kid deserves more."

"Cash never was big on responsibility. I should've seen the warning signs before I married him."

"How were you to know everything would turn out the way it did? He made it through college. That shows some dedication and hard work. What went wrong after that?"

"Being a full-fledged adult—and marriage. He hates being responsible for anyone else."

The sliding door opened and Charlie stepped out of the house wearing chinos, topsiders and a golf shirt. "Where's Mom and Dad?" he asked his sister.

"At a doctor's appointment," Averil said. "They haven't been home all afternoon. Why?"

He shaded his hazel eyes against the sun and dipped his head when he noticed Jane. His medium-blond hair was starting to recede in front at the temples, but he was still generally handsome, with a decent build and a ready smile—the quintessential real estate agent. "Mom wanted me to get something out of storage for her so Dad wouldn't have to."

"Hi, Charlie!" Mitch yelled, excited to see his uncle even though Charlie's appearance at his parents' house certainly wasn't a novelty. It seemed to Jane that she saw Charlie every time she visited.

Charlie mustered a smile for his nephew. "Hey, bud. You having fun?"

"I'm swimming! Watch me!" Mitch said and stuck his face back into the water.

"Looks like you swim at least as well as Jane does," Charlie teased when he came up for air.

Jane scowled at him. She wasn't in the mood to joke around. She was too mad at him for what he'd done last night. "I swim better than you do," she grumbled.

"Mommy, I have to go pee!" Mitch cried, and Averil jumped up, grabbed a towel and scooped him from the water.

As she hurried into the house with her son, Charlie helped himself to the Doritos Averil had carried out earlier, as well as Jane's iced tea. "How was Glacier?"

"Incredible. If you've never been, it's definitely a bucket list item."

"When'd you get back?"

"Yesterday."

"And rushed right over to see Talulah?" She and Charlie hadn't interacted at Hank's Bar and Grill last night, but he'd obviously seen her with his ex-fiancée.

"Why wouldn't I?" she said, challenging his statement.

"Because she's not a nice person," he said simply.

"According to *you*."

He popped another chip in his mouth. "I have reason to feel the way I do."

"Is that why you threw a rock through her window after I dropped her off last night?"

He lowered the bag. "What are you talking about?"

She rolled her eyes. "You know what I'm talking about. I can't believe you'd do such a thing. That could've hurt her much more than it did."

Tossing the bag of chips back on the table, spilling several in the process, he walked closer to her. "Talulah got hurt last night?"

Jane blinked in surprise. Was he playing her? "Yes! When you threw that rock through the window, she was hit by a piece of glass. She had to get seventeen stitches."

His eyebrows shot up. *"What?"*

Jane peered at him more closely, trying to read his eyes, his expression. If he was lying, he was damn good at it. "You're telling me you don't know anything about it?"

"I don't!" He spread out his hands as though that might somehow convince her. "Where'd she get cut?"

"On the arm. Averil was the one who told me about it."

He stepped back. "And how did she know?"

The door opened and his sister stepped out.

"Why didn't you tell me what happened to Talulah?" he asked her right away.

Averil stopped long enough to let her son slide down her body to reach the ground, at which point he rushed over to get back in the water. "Because I thought…" She looked to Jane for support but Jane remained silent. "We *all* thought—"

"That it was *me*?" He brought a hand to his chest. "*I* didn't do it!"

Jane was beginning to believe him. "Then who did?"

"I have no idea!" he replied.

Averil came to the pool and got in, although she stayed on the steps. "I'm so glad. I was afraid you'd get in trouble."

"I'm glad, too," Jane said. "But…who else would be mad enough to throw a rock through her window?"

"It could've been anyone," Averil said with a shrug. "We're not the only ones who hate her."

Charlie seemed genuinely bewildered. Averil did, too— or so Jane thought. But then she realized something that made her slightly uneasy. While Charlie was full of questions, it was Averil who had all the answers. That would've been fine; after all, she'd talked to Brant this morning, and he'd probably told her what had happened. That was how she knew. She'd even seen Talulah and the bandage on her arm.

The problem was…something about her manner just didn't seem right.

Paul still wouldn't answer his phone. He wouldn't even respond to Talulah's text messages.

Will you please talk to me?

I'm sorry you're upset. Can we have a conversation?

Paul? I've called the diner three times. They say you're not there.

Will you be at work tonight?

Was he going to leave the staff high and dry at the diner with no manager? Did he feel what had happened warranted that reaction? If so, why? Personal aspects aside, the diner was his business, too.

In spite of the worry and the upset—and the constant checking of her phone—Talulah had cleaned up the dishes and started on the carrot cakes she planned to serve for dessert at the funeral dinner.

She wished she didn't have to bake today, however. There was too much going on in her life. And although the weather outside had cooled slightly, having the oven on for so long heated the kitchen until it was as sweltering as it had been during the heat wave.

Fortunately, she had Brant's portable air cooler. She'd never been more grateful for it. She also had his flowers. After she'd gotten home this morning, she'd taken them from the living room and set them on the windowsill over the sink where she could see them while she worked. She'd told herself she'd done that because she needed the positivity and encouragement they offered, but she knew that wasn't all of it. She just didn't want to examine her motives any more closely.

After mopping the sweat from her face with one of her aunt's many flour sack towels, she turned her fifteenth and last cake round out of the pan and onto the counter. She could've chosen to do a simple one-layer oblong cake. That would've been easier to make, transport and serve. But she'd decided to do the food for a reason, so she was making the same tall, triple-layer round cake that was so popular at the diner. Because there was no more room in the fridge, however, she had to wait until after the sun went down to mix the cream cheese frosting. Otherwise, it might melt and the cakes wouldn't show well, even after all the extra effort.

Tired of being on her feet all day, she was sitting at the dining table eating a caprese sandwich, with olive oil and fresh herbs and spices drizzled over the buffalo mozzarella, when she finally heard her phone ping with an incoming text.

Assuming it was from Paul, she felt her stomach tense.

"Here goes," she whispered to herself. But when she picked up the phone, she saw that it wasn't her partner. It was Brant.

How's your arm?

Dared she answer him? It would be smarter to break contact completely. Today, she'd thought of him almost as many times as she'd thought of Paul, and she knew that wasn't a good sign. But a simple text exchange seemed innocuous enough.

Okay, I guess.

It doesn't hurt when you cook?

Not too badly.

How'd it go with Paul?

This was the real question. She believed Brant was concerned about her arm. He'd taken care of her last night. But they both knew chances were the wound would heal without a problem. What the past few days might mean to her future was the bigger issue.

He won't respond to me, she told him.

You haven't talked to him yet?

Nope. I've even tried to catch him at the diner. He's not there.

What does his lack of response mean?

I have no clue. Nothing like this has ever happened before.

I'm sorry.

It's not your fault. I chose to be with you.

But I don't want you to regret it. That sucks.

She only regretted the consequences. That was an important distinction. But telling him so felt as though it would put her at risk for backsliding. I'll deal with the fallout. You have your own problems. Have you heard from Charlie?

No.

Do you think you will?

Your guess is as good as mine.

I'll try to dismantle my aunt's house as soon as possible so I can get it up for sale and leave. Things should be easier for you once I'm gone.

That doesn't make me feel any better. I still want to see you.

He was direct, as usual. She felt the revelation tear out more of her resolve and struggled to galvanize herself against an entire unraveling. We always knew it was temporary, she wrote. How do you feel about Averil?

She's like a kid sister to me.

She obviously feels less...familial about you.

In case I haven't been clear, I'm not interested in her—
not in that way.

After a few moments, her phone dinged with an addition to his response. Do you wish I was?

No, but she knew he was trying to get her to admit that she still wanted to see him. And she couldn't do that. Even if she was willing to face the disapproval of everyone in Coyote Canyon while she was here, she had to protect what was left of her relationship with Paul, as well as their business. She's going to blame me, and I don't want her to hate me any more than she already does.

You dodged the question.

Because it was one thing to wonder if their relationship had crossed certain boundaries, something she definitely felt when they were making love, and quite another to drag what she was feeling out into the open. She'd never been able to fully trust her heart when it came to men. Her track record proved that. The last thing she needed was to start something serious with Brant only to realize she'd ruined her life in Seattle for nothing.

Because I don't know what to say.

I'm asking if the past week has meant anything to you—
if I mean anything to you.

Her heart started to beat harder. She should say no. "No" would put an end to whatever was going on between them. But she couldn't bring herself to lie.

Yes.

When he sent her a heart emoji, she nearly dropped her phone. He didn't mean anything by it, she told herself. She couldn't get hung up on a man who struggled with commitment himself. And she couldn't establish any more ties to this area. She'd broken away from Coyote Canyon, moved on and built a life somewhere else—and she would return to that life once she finished settling her great aunt's estate.

And yet she kept picking up her phone to stare at that heart.

"You've lost your mind," she muttered and ate her sandwich. Then she went back into the kitchen and finished the cakes. It was midnight before she drove the last one to the church so she could squeeze it into the refrigerator. She didn't have enough space to fit all five, even using the church fridge, so she was counting on the cooler night air to help keep the ones she had to leave on the counter fresh. Sarah Carrier had asked several members of Phoebe's church to come before the funeral to transfer the rest of the food. That would help.

Talulah had to be up early. She still had to prepare her remarks, which was the most daunting aspect of the funeral. She had no idea how to eulogize a woman she'd respected and admired but also feared and never truly understood or connected with. And doing this in front of her greatest critics... But she refused to think about that right now. After she cleaned the kitchen, she went out to sit on the porch because she needed a few minutes to decompress before going to bed.

As she rocked in her aunt's swing, she twisted around to frown at the broken window, which she'd covered with cardboard until the replacement she'd ordered online came in, and kept an eye on the driveway in front of her, too, just in case Charlie returned.

Fortunately, she didn't see any sign of trouble. Steering her mind away from him, she breathed in the familiar scent of the dust that covered everything in late summer and the Mimosa Tree near the porch that still had its pink blossoms. It was beautiful in Montana. She had to admit that. She'd forgotten just how bright the stars were in her hometown...

Her phone buzzed in her lap. Again, her mind jumped to Paul. He hadn't shown up at the diner tonight. Three staff members had to muddle through without him. But Selma, who was in her fifties and their most experienced employee, had assured Talulah that all had gone well.

Bracing for an argument, she picked up her phone. But once again, it wasn't Paul. This time it was her mother.

Talulah had put too much work into the funeral to tolerate any disapproval from Carolyn. And yet she knew her mother couldn't be happy with what she'd heard since Talulah had returned to town. Talulah didn't want to explain the rumors—or admit that they were true.

Listening to the creak of the wooden swing, she considered ignoring the call. It'd been a hard day. Why not let her parents think she was asleep? She could contact them after the funeral and provide the recap they'd be looking for.

But it had to be painful for her mother to miss Phoebe's funeral. Carolyn probably just wanted to feel as much a part of it as she could. So Talulah answered in spite of her reservations. "Hello?"

"You're still up? I thought with the funeral tomorrow you might've already gone to bed."

"No, I just finished up for the night."

"Finished what?"

"The carrot cakes I made for the funeral dinner."

"You made the cakes yourself?" her mother asked.

"Yeah." Talulah didn't add that she'd prepared the rest of the meal, too. She didn't want to pander for praise.

"That was nice of you, honey. I know Phoebe would've loved that."

"I hope so. How are things in Sierra Leone?"

"Hot!" she said with a laugh.

"Temps have been hot here, too."

"Montana can't even compare to the heat in Africa."

That was probably true. "How's Dad?"

"He's doing great. It's early here. He hasn't gotten up yet."

"What are you doing awake?"

"I couldn't sleep."

"Because…"

"I've been thinking about Phoebe. In some ways, she was like a mother to me. Your grandma was so often sick with lupus, so Phoebe helped out *a lot*. And then your grandma passed when I was still in college, so…"

Phoebe had been all she'd had from that point on. "Was she kinder and gentler back then?" Talulah asked.

"I don't think I'd ever call Phoebe kind or gentle," her mother said and they both chuckled. "She was gruff. But that was just her way. Deep down, she had a heart of gold and would always come through when you needed her."

"I found some old photographs in the attic of you and Grandma and Phoebe that you're going to like. Phoebe's holding you and looking as excited as I've ever seen her."

It grew quiet and a telltale sniff told Talulah her mother was weeping.

"Thanks for being there for me since I can't be there myself," her mother said once she'd regained her composure.

"Of course," Talulah said. "Are you going to be okay?"

"Oh, yeah. It's just…hard to lose someone who's been such a big part of your foundation."

"The timing hasn't made it any easier."

"You're right. I wish I could be there."

"I bet." But then Carolyn would probably feel some

guilt and question whether she was as committed to the mission as she should be.

"Have you seen Charlie?"

"As a matter of fact, I have."

"How's he treating you?"

Talulah peered under the bandage on her arm. She knew her mother would hear about what'd happened at some point. She might even tell Carolyn herself. But she wasn't going to do it now. She preferred to give Carolyn time to grieve for Phoebe without making her worry about Talulah's situation, too. "He's not friendly, of course, but it's nothing I can't handle."

"You're such a strong woman. I'm so proud of you."

Surprised that her mother hadn't brought up the gossip swirling around her, Talulah stopped rocking. "You are?"

"What mother wouldn't be?" Carolyn said, sounding equally surprised.

"Even though I walked out when I was supposed to marry the son of one of your best friends?"

"I won't lie—I wish you'd backed out a little earlier," she said, "but at least you didn't marry a man you wouldn't be happy with."

Sinking back into the swing, Talulah started to rock again. "That makes me feel a lot better. Thanks, Mom."

"I love you."

"I love you, too."

"I should let you go so you can get some sleep. Tomorrow will be a big day."

Talulah was about to say goodbye when she saw headlights on the road in front of her aunt's house. A vehicle was approaching. Normally, she wouldn't have thought anything of it. Anyone could be passing by, even teenagers out screwing around like she used to do with her friends. But it was a bit late for that. "Talulah?" her mother prompted.

"I'm here," she said into the phone, but jumped to her feet and hurried back into the house. "I'm heading off to bed," she added, trying to keep the alarm out of her voice. "I'll call you after the funeral tomorrow."

"Don't worry that it might be late in this part of the world. I'll be anxious to hear from you."

"I understand." She disconnected and pressed her back flat against the wall as she peered carefully around the edge of the small side window next to the one that'd been broken last night.

It was a car, not a truck. She could tell by the general size and shape.

Whoever it was didn't turn down her drive, like the vehicle last night. It slowed to a crawl as it passed, however, which led her to believe the driver had come by her house intentionally and wasn't just out driving around.

Who was it? And what did they want? Talulah was afraid to stick her head out too far for fear that whoever it was would see her and decide to turn in and throw something else or terrorize her in some other way. It wasn't until after the car had passed and started to speed up again that she tried to get a better look.

Then she didn't know if it was an inability to see clearly or prejudice that made her think it was the same car Averil had been driving when she showed up at Brant's this morning.

Fourteen

Brant had been having such a great time with Talulah that being cut off from her much sooner than should've been necessary—because of Charlie—made him mad. It also upset him that Charlie would try to hurt her by throwing a rock through her window and messaging Paul.

After spending several hours fixing the feed for the cattle on the ranch to minimize the bloat problem they'd been having, he quit around noon, showered up and drove over to his ex-best friend's.

Charlie lived on the opposite side of town in a double-wide mobile home on two acres. It was a nice piece of land he'd purchased himself, but he hadn't spent any time or money improving it, which was ironic, given his profession. When Brant pulled in, he saw the same things he'd seen for the past five years—a stack of old tires cast to one side of a barn that needed a fresh coat of paint, if not some structural reinforcement, a used motorcycle Charlie had bought several years ago that hadn't run from the beginning, an old El Camino he planned to restore one day and an ATV. Brant knew the ATV worked because he owned one himself and occasionally he and Charlie took them out for some fun.

He hadn't been sure he'd find Charlie at home. Most people were at work this time of day. But Charlie didn't put in a whole lot of hours, so Brant wasn't all that surprised to see his car in the drive.

He pulled in behind the Explorer and got out, and Charlie's front door opened before he could even reach the steps leading up to it.

"What are you doing here?" Charlie demanded, walking out onto the wooden landing.

Brant stopped on the grass that'd been worn down to bare dirt near the bottom step. "I certainly haven't come to apologize."

That Brant was still angry seemed to shock Charlie. "You're really going to let a bitch like Talulah come between us?"

Brant flinched at Charlie's words. He knew they probably shouldn't bother him, but they did. "Don't call her that."

Charlie's jaw sagged at the menace in his voice. "Are you kidding me? What's gotten into you? Do you *really* like her that much? More than me?"

"This isn't about who I like and who I don't like. It's about the bullshit way you're behaving. I never saw you as the type of man who'd pick on a woman."

Charlie looked confused. "Letting her boyfriend know she's been cheating on him is picking on a woman?"

"They aren't together."

"Tell *him* that."

"I don't have to," Brant bit out. "She already has."

Charlie drilled him with a penetrating look, after which he started to laugh. "Oh my God. You've fallen for her! I kept telling myself that couldn't be it. You never fall that hard for anybody, but that's what's happening here, isn't it? That's the only thing that could explain your behavior."

"You're reaching," Brant said. "She's hardly been here a week."

"Doesn't matter. You've already spent a lot of time with her."

"Not really."

Charlie's eyebrows arched at the way Brant had immediately discounted the statement. "How many nights has it been?"

"That's none of your business. I'm just here to tell you that you'd better not do anything else to her, or the little skirmishes you and I have had recently will turn into something a lot more serious."

His eyes flew wide. "You're *threatening* me?"

"I'm being straight up with you," Brant corrected.

"You think I threw that rock through her window, don't you?"

"I do," Brant stately flatly. "Because you did."

Charlie's face turned beet red. "How do you know? Were you there?"

"It's a simple process of elimination. Who else would do it?"

"How am I supposed to know? But I'm telling you it wasn't me. I admit I wrote Paul on Instagram. I already told you that. I think he should know what she's doing while she's here. I'd want to know if I were him—"

"That's an excuse," Brant interrupted with a wave of his hand. "You don't give a shit about Paul. You've never even met him. You did it to mess with Talulah."

"If she's cheating, she deserves what she gets," he said, as enragingly stubborn as ever. "And if she's not cheating, I didn't do anything wrong, because Paul won't care."

"You know he cares!"

"Then she should've considered how he'd feel. She's

leaving town after she sells her aunt's house. You realize that, don't you?"

"Of course I realize that."

"So what's your plan here? Do you think she'll fall in love with you, sell her business and move back to Coyote Canyon?"

"All I want is for you to leave her alone," Brant said. "You got that? No more stitches or other injuries. No more screwing with her relationships. Go on about your business as you should've done from the beginning and don't try to hurt her again." Message delivered, Brant turned on his heel and strode back to his truck. But just as he was getting behind the wheel, Charlie yelled.

"She's going to break your heart into a million tiny pieces, and I'm going to laugh my head off when she does!"

Ignoring him, Brant shifted into Reverse and whipped out of Charlie's rutted drive. Talulah wasn't going to break his heart. He'd have to be in love with her for that.

Talulah couldn't stop fidgeting. She'd been too anxious about the funeral to sleep, so she'd gotten up well before dawn and written her speech. Then Jane had come over to see how her arm was and to help with the food, and they'd managed to finish everything before noon.

After Jane left, Talulah had jumped into the shower and she was now ready with forty-five minutes to spare. She'd even spoken briefly to her sister—no labor pains yet, just her best wishes for a smooth funeral—and painted her fingernails, something she rarely did because she used her hands so often in her work.

It didn't matter how prepared she felt, however; nerves were still getting the best of her.

Wearing a black sleeveless dress with a strand of pearls at her neck and matching stud earrings, she pulled her hair into a low ponytail and stared at herself in the bathroom mirror, wondering if she should've worn something else for the day. She looked like she was going to a swanky cocktail party in Seattle and didn't want to be overdressed. Some of the people here might assume she'd gone "big city" or was trying to show off. And funerals did seem, generally, to have grown more casual since she was a kid. But her whole goal was to make her aunt proud, and she knew Phoebe believed strongly in convention. In her aunt's opinion, nothing short of a nice black dress would be appropriate for a funeral, so that was what Talulah was going to wear.

Fortunately, if she had her guess, many of the women from Phoebe's church would also be in dresses, so she shouldn't feel *too* out of place—or any more out of place than she would for other reasons.

As she slipped her feet into a pair of Christian Louboutin heels—shoes Paul had purchased for her when they were out celebrating the first anniversary of their business and she happened to see them in a store window—she mentally rehearsed the remarks she planned to make when it came time for her to speak. Sarah Carrier had emailed her the program. She'd be last, which came as both a relief, because she'd have a chance to get accustomed to the room and summon her nerve, and a concern, because she'd have so long to dread it.

Grabbing a small black clutch, she put her lip gloss inside, along with some tissues. Since all the food had been picked up, she didn't have to worry about that. She dabbed perfume on her neck, hurried downstairs and locked the front door behind her without having to carry anything awkward or heavy.

She was trying not to twist an ankle while crossing the uneven ground to the garage when her phone signaled an incoming text.

Preparing to let her mother know that everything was set for the funeral and all was well, she looked down. But it was Brant who'd messaged her.

You feeling okay about the funeral?

Since she was so early, she took the time to respond. As good as I can feel.

Are you sure you don't want me to be there?

It'll only make the divide between you and Charlie wider. Let's at least leave the possibility of you two becoming friends again for after I return to Seattle.

I doubt that's going to happen.

Why?

He didn't answer her question. Instead, he asked another one of his own. What about Jane? She going?

No. I told her the same thing—not to drive a bigger wedge between her and Averil.

Will you call me after it's over and let me know how it went?

She bit her lip as she tried to decide how to respond. Maintaining a friendship with him meant she'd only keep thinking about him, missing him, wanting to see him again. And she still hadn't heard from Paul. He refused to pick up when she called. He wouldn't text her back, either. She was afraid she was facing a major rift with him

and was worried that he might be hiring an attorney to try
to take control of the dessert diner.

That thought caused terror to rise inside her, but she
quickly tamped it down. She couldn't think about Paul or
her business right now. She had to get through the next
several hours first. And it wasn't as if Brant had suggested
she sleep with him again. He'd merely asked her to let him
know about the funeral. How could she say no to that?

Sure, she responded and dropped the phone into her
clutch before climbing into her SUV.

The church wasn't far, only a five-minute drive, but she
planned to arrive early. She didn't want everyone staring
at her as she walked in. But the parking lot was already
half-full when she got there.

"Shoot," she mumbled as she pulled into a stall.

Sarah Carrier was crossing the blacktop as she left her
car. When Talulah waved, she smiled. "I saw all the food
in the kitchen when we were setting up," she said. "It looks
amazing, especially those gorgeous carrot cakes."

"Thank you. I hope there'll be enough for everyone."

"I'm sure there will be. We might even have some to
spare."

Crossing her fingers, Talulah held them up in response.

Sarah assured her that the programs had been printed
and the tables, chairs, tablecloths, paper plates and plastic cutlery were in a separate room, awaiting the food,
and Talulah thanked her once again before someone else
called Sarah's name and she turned away as they entered
the building.

Here we go, Talulah thought. The afternoon would be
long and torturous, but she'd get through it somehow.

Bracing for whomever she might see, she pasted a smile
on her face as she greeted various people who were milling
around, waiting for the viewing to start. Her aunt's casket

had been placed in the foyer, along with a plethora of funeral arrangements, a large picture on an easel of Phoebe sitting at her beloved piano dressed in green and red, suggesting it'd been taken at a church Christmas program. There was also a side table that held a guestbook where people could write their sympathy to the family or share a memory of Phoebe.

Talulah understood that as Phoebe's only family present at the funeral, she was to stand next to the casket. But she wasn't ready to take her place quite yet. She ducked into the kitchen to spend a few more minutes by herself—and to avoid the cloying, overpowering scent of the carnations, plus make sure the food had been prepped according to her specifications. She'd turn on the ovens when it was time to drive behind the hearse to the cemetery so the lasagna could be heating up while they were gone.

She lingered in the kitchen, out of sight, until she heard the organ. Then she threw back her shoulders and made her way to the casket, where she stared down at her aunt's drawn face. The mortician had done a decent job with her hair and makeup. Always tall and thin, with high cheekbones, clear eyes and a direct manner, Phoebe looked almost regal against the satin interior of the casket. She'd aged well overall, but she still had the paper-thin cheeks that seemed to come with age, and her hair was ratted and styled on top of her head the way she'd worn it since Talulah could remember.

It was a strange, almost surreal moment, when she felt, for perhaps the first time—since she'd been so concerned with the funeral logistics and getting through the necessary work—the tremendous loss of a person who'd been accomplished in many ways. Times had changed, and Phoebe had refused to change with them, so she represented a bygone era, and the memories she held of almost an entire century would be lost with her.

"I'm sorry," someone said, reminding her that she had a duty to perform, and she turned to greet Phoebe's friends and fellow church members as they streamed past to offer their condolences.

Some of the people she recognized. They were not only friends of Phoebe's, they were longtime friends of her parents'. Many of them mentioned seeing her at church or school when she was a child. A few of her teachers, her volleyball coach from high school and loads and loads of Phoebe's piano students spoke to her. Talulah couldn't help but be impressed by the number of lives her aunt had touched. She hoped Phoebe was somehow aware of the size of her funeral.

Fortunately, none of Charlie's family showed up. Had she been wrong in assuming they'd attend the funeral?

As the viewing ended and everyone began to wander into the meeting hall, Talulah held back, giving herself a short break until almost everyone else was seated inside. When she couldn't stall any longer, she drew a deep breath and started for the door.

Dr. Gregor stood there, handing out the programs. He greeted her again, even though he'd spoken to her during the viewing. "Would you like a program?" he asked before she could continue past him.

She smiled as she accepted one, and a glance inside confirmed that she'd be the final speaker. Her talk was simply titled "Tribute to Phoebe Christensen by Talulah Barclay."

She'd seen nothing but friendly faces so far, but she suspected her luck wouldn't hold, and she was right. As she made her way down the aisle she could feel the steely gaze of Dinah and George Gerhart, Charlie's parents. They must've entered the church, along with several other members of their family, from the far side. Although she was careful not to look in their direction, Talulah was fairly confident Averil wasn't with them, and once she got to the raised dais, she could see that Charlie wasn't, either.

She was just breathing a sigh of relief and feeling encouraged about getting through the rest of the day when Charlie walked in wearing a beautifully tailored button-down shirt, a classy tie and stylish black slacks. Averil was with him, leading her son, Mitch, by the hand. She was also dressed in black slacks, except that hers were paired with a pretty pink blouse. They both cast her a look that told her they hadn't come to grieve the loss of her mother's aunt; they were there to make her as self-conscious and uncomfortable as possible.

Refusing to let them intimidate her, she sat taller as she searched the crowd for Jane. She was halfway hoping Jane would be there, after all, but she wasn't. So Talulah searched for other people she liked. There was Dr. Gregor, of course, but he was speaking to someone at the door, and she could see only a small slice of him, so she located Sarah Carrier, who was smiling at her from one of the middle pews.

Talulah was just finding her center again when a small stir over by the Gerharts drew her attention back to the door, since that was where they were all looking, and she was shocked to see Brant stride in.

Holding a program in his left hand, he winked at her as he made his way down the aisle.

He'd barely known her great aunt. He hadn't come for Phoebe. He'd come to support her, and she was feeling so vulnerable that his small kindness nearly brought tears to her eyes.

Both Averil and Charlie strained to get a better look at him as he took a seat by himself in the very front pew, but

Brant ignored them. Clean-shaven, he had his hair combed back with some product to hold it in place.

She found the fact that he'd put some effort into his appearance so endearing that she could feel the brittle smile she'd been wearing soften and become genuine. He was incredibly sexy in his Wranglers and work boots, even though they didn't go with his dress shirt, which had fold lines that made it obvious he'd taken it out of the package right before putting it on.

The pastor started the service with a hymn, an opening prayer and some remarks of his own. Then two of Phoebe's best piano students spoke about how Phoebe had influenced them, and three young women sang a beautiful rendition of "How Great Thou Art."

Talulah watched the clock, growing more and more anxious about getting up in front of everyone when she was persona non grata to the Gerharts and any friends who sided with them. They seemed to think they owned the town. But she felt Brant silently encouraging her, and when the time finally came, she did her best. She talked about Sunday dinners at Phoebe's when she was small, how Phoebe would accept nothing less than the maximum effort from her piano students and how particular she was about her house and person. Talulah also talked about what a wonderful pianist her great aunt was, that she could cook or can anything and how much her garden had meant to her. She finished with the important role Phoebe had played in her mother's life, and before she knew it, her speech was over.

Grateful to have it behind her, she braved a glance into the audience as she sat back down and saw several people drying their eyes. Only Charlie and his family were glaring at her. They would've preferred she embarrass herself in some way.

The music swelled as they sang "The Lord is my Shepherd," and Dr. Gregor gave the closing prayer before everyone got up to leave.

Talulah knew she couldn't show too much interest in Brant or, given the rumors, the residents of Coyote Canyon would think they were now an item. But after several people approached her to say how much they'd enjoyed her tribute, and she'd escaped to the kitchen to turn on the ovens and put in the lasagnas, she found him waiting for her at the door to the parking lot, and she was so grateful to him for coming, she couldn't stop herself from walking right up to him. "I can't believe you came," she said, her voice low. "Funerals are miserable enough when you know who's died."

He scanned the foyer. "I didn't mind it. I enjoyed hearing you talk."

"Really?"

He'd already loosened his tie. "You made your mother's aunt sound…admirable, strong. Since I know she was also difficult, you had to walk a fine line to still be honest, and you did a good job with it."

"I admit I struggled a little when I was figuring out what I wanted to say."

He was looking at her with more interest than a typical friend, and she felt her face heat as his gaze moved down over her dress. "You look good."

So did he. What he'd worn wasn't going to win any fashion awards, but he was so attractive it didn't matter. "Thanks. What made you change your mind about coming today?"

"I knew Charlie was planning to be here, and I wasn't about to let him intimidate you."

"How'd you know? Did he tell you?"

"He did a few days ago. He could've changed his mind

since then, but I had a little talk with him at his place earlier, and as I was leaving, I realized he was getting dressed up for something. I figured it was the funeral."

"You went to his house today? What'd he say?"

"That he didn't throw that rock through your window. Are you sure it was him?"

Talulah remembered the car that'd come by last night while she was sitting out on the porch swing. She thought it might've been Averil, but she wasn't going to say so. She didn't want to come between Brant and any more of his friends. "I'm not positive. Like I told you before, all I saw was a pair of headlights."

The hearse was ready to go. Talulah could see it through the glass doors of the church. The driver from the mortuary sat behind the wheel, waiting. "I've got to get going, or I'll hold up the entire procession. But I appreciate you coming. It…it made the service a lot easier for me," she admitted.

"No problem." The crooked smile he gave her made her think of him naked in bed, leaning above her, and the way her body reacted to that memory, with a flood of awareness and excitement, surprised her.

"If you'd like to hang around," she heard herself say, "I managed to finish preparing all the food for the dinner. I even have homemade carrot cake for dessert. We'll eat here as soon as the graveside part is over."

His eyes scanned the foyer, once again taking in the few people who were lingering behind. "Do you think Charlie and his family will be going to the cemetery?"

"Since coming here didn't give them the satisfaction they were looking for, I wouldn't doubt it." She knew the Gerharts were too curious and upset about Brant's showing up not to go. They'd want to see if he came to the cemetery, too, and how she and Brant acted around each other.

"Then I'll go. Do you want to ride with me?"

"I wish I could, but—" she twisted around to see behind her, and, fortunately, didn't find any of the Gerharts "—I don't dare."

He didn't press her. He knew why she was refusing. "Have you heard from Paul?"

"Not yet."

"What about the diner?" he asked with a frown. "Is he there, taking care of things?"

"No. One of our best employees has been acting as manager in his absence."

"Shit." He unbuttoned the top button of his new shirt, revealing more of his smooth tanned neck. "You gotta be worried about that."

"I am. But she seems to be getting by at the moment, and knowing she's there is helping me hold myself together."

"It'll all work out," he said. "See you at the cemetery."

She hesitated. "You don't have to go. Really."

"It's fine," he said. "I'm easily bought and you did promise to feed me after."

Laughing, she rose up to give him a hug as she would any friend. But no contact with Brant ever turned out to be as casual as it was intended. She felt his big hands slide up her back and briefly press her to him and couldn't even look at him as she pulled away, for fear he'd see the effect he had on her. Instead, she ducked her head and started to open the door.

"Talulah?"

Stopping, she forced herself to look back at him and, as his eyes locked with hers, a huge smile spread across his face. He knew she was feeling something. Maybe he felt it, too.

Fifteen

Brant stood behind everyone else as the pastor dedicated Phoebe Christensen's grave. He didn't feel he should be up in the front. He'd barely known the old lady. But he was glad he'd decided to attend this part of the funeral, too, because the way Charlie and Averil were glowering at Talulah certainly wasn't anything she should have to endure at a family member's funeral. They kept turning around to glower at him, too, and whenever they did, he'd give Charlie a look to let him know he'd better not do anything unkind.

Although there were several people between them, Brant could see part of the bandage that covered the stitches on Talulah's arm and once again wondered who'd thrown that rock through her window. Averil was the only other person, besides Charlie, who might feel strongly enough about Talulah's return to hurl something at her house. But he hated to think Charlie's sister, who'd been one of Talulah's closest friends for years, would do that.

Averil wasn't a vengeful person, was she?

He eyed her speculatively as she turned to look at him once again. He told himself to smile, to be friendly. They'd known each other most of their lives, and he adored her son. But the way she and Charlie were behaving made him mad enough that he gazed coolly back at her, challenging her hostile attitude, and when the ceremony was over and everyone started to drift off to their cars, she walked over to him.

"I didn't expect to see you at the funeral," she said. "I didn't realize you even knew Phoebe Christensen."

"I didn't realize you knew her all that well, either." They'd both had ulterior motives in coming. He wasn't about to let her pretend she'd cared about Talulah's great aunt.

"Hey!" Mitch had wriggled out of Charlie's grasp and was weaving through those who were left to get to Brant. "Can we go riding today?" he asked, reaching out to be picked up.

Brant lifted the kid into his arms. "Not today, buddy. This isn't your lesson day. But maybe on Sunday. You'll have to ask your mom about that."

Averil glanced from her son, who'd put his hands together in a prayer-like pose, begging her to agree, to Brant. "I didn't know if you'd be free on Sundays now that you're so caught up with Talulah."

Brant had avoided even acknowledging the extra attention she'd been giving him and what it meant, but he wasn't sure he could continue that way. It had to be addressed. "Averil, I'm sorry if my involvement with Talulah upsets you. I care about you, but I've never done anything to make you think—"

"It doesn't upset me," she broke in before he could finish.

He could tell she'd figured out where he was going with what he was saying and didn't want to hear it. "Good," he said. "Because I should have the right to see anyone I want. Why you or Charlie would have a problem with it, I don't know. I'm supposed to stay away from Talulah even though she broke off her relationship with Charlie fourteen years ago?"

He thought she'd argue about the circumstances, so it surprised him when her shoulders slumped. "Charlie was right, then. It's not just physical between you. You really like her."

"I don't know how I feel, exactly," he admitted. "But I'd like to continue seeing her while she's here, and I don't think that's anyone else's business."

Averil seemed even more crestfallen. "She doesn't care about her boyfriend in Seattle?"

Brant was tempted to say she didn't have a boyfriend. But he'd already told Charlie, and it hadn't made a damn bit of difference. "You'll have to ask her about that."

Her expression grew dark. "I have nothing to say to her."

"Because..."

"She's a terrible person."

"The kind of person who'd throw a rock through someone's window?" he asked.

She took a step back. "What are you saying? You think *I* threw the rock?"

"I don't know anyone, other than Charlie, who hates her more. It seems like a plausible conclusion."

"Well, it's the *wrong* conclusion," she snapped and pulled Mitch out of his arms. "Let's go," she said as she set her son on his feet. "You won't be seeing Brant ever again."

Mitch looked up at him in confusion. *"Why?"*

Averil grabbed her son's hand so he couldn't escape. "Because he... Because he..."

"Because of you, not me," Brant said softly, and she didn't stay long enough to argue. She dragged Mitch away, stuffed him in his car seat and was in such a hurry to get out of the lot she nearly collided with a Toyota sedan that was leaving at the same time.

"What was that all about?"

Brant turned to see that Talulah had walked over from where she'd been thanking the pastor. "I hope it's not true," he said, "but I think she may be the one who threw the rock through your window."

Talulah gazed after Averil's car as it turned out of the lot. "I know."

Charlie and his family didn't come to the dinner at the church, so it was the first part of the day Talulah was able to enjoy. She'd worked so hard to make the meal; her heart felt lighter just watching everyone appreciate it. The pleasure good food brought was part of the reason she liked to cook.

Maybe she'd gotten that from Phoebe, because her mother hadn't been a particularly good cook...

As soon as people began to finish their meal, Talulah moved from helping serve the lasagna to slicing the triple-layer carrot cake and was gratified by how many of her great aunt's friends exclaimed about the taste. Handling the funeral had turned out to be worth the extra effort, she decided. She'd given Phoebe a nice sendoff—one Talulah felt would meet even Phoebe's stringent standards.

"Are you really smiling?" Brant said, feigning shock as he came over to get a slice of cake.

"All of this is almost over. That makes me euphoric," she admitted. She had other problems waiting in the wings—problems seemed to be piling up there—but at least the funeral was nearly done.

"Charlie and Averil missed the best part," he said. "This dinner was better than any funeral dinner I've ever had."

He'd made the day so much easier for her—had been

willing to stand by her even if it meant risking his relationship with the Gerharts. He was intensely loyal and a person who stuck to his ideals. But his support surprised her, considering that when she first bumped into him at the café last week she would've put him firmly in the enemy camp.

During the graveside service, when she'd felt so much hostility coming from Charlie and Averil, she'd seen Brant raise his eyebrows at Charlie whenever Charlie made a move toward her and knew Brant was the reason Charlie hadn't attempted to speak to her. She was thankful for that, because anything Charlie had to say wouldn't be nice. "Thanks for coming. I can't tell you how much I appreciate it."

He raised his dessert plate with the slice of cake she'd given him. "I've been well-rewarded."

"I'll send whatever's left home with you for your brothers."

"I'm sure they'd appreciate it. Sometimes I think that, pound for pound, they eat more than the cattle on the ranch."

Her phone went off, startling her. She'd silenced the ringer except for calls coming from her sister's number, so she knew who it had to be. "It's Debbie," she told him as she put down the knife she'd been using to cut the cake and dug her phone out of the small clutch she'd left on the table beside her.

"Do you think the baby's coming today?" Brant asked.

Talulah shrugged. "Maybe she just wants to hear about the funeral," she said. But as soon as she hit the talk button, there was no more doubt. Her sister yelled, "Hurry! It's time!"

Talulah couldn't keep her eyes open. After all the late nights with Brant, the stress of the funeral and the constant worry over the diner, especially now that Paul wasn't taking care of it or responding to her, the relief of her nine-pound niece being born whole and healthy, and Debbie coming through the delivery without a problem, made it almost impossible to stay awake. Hospital personnel scurried up and down the corridor outside, talking, laughing and calling out information, and a nurse frequently came into the room to take Debbie's blood pressure or try to get the baby to nurse. But none of that disturbed Talulah. It didn't even faze her that she was in a rather uncomfortable chair.

"Hey, would you like to go to the house?" Scott asked, jiggling her shoulder to wake her.

She managed to lift her heavy eyelids. The proud father was holding his tightly bundled newborn in the crook of his arm like a football. "Um…sure. Why? Does your mom need to bring the kids home? I can watch them for you."

"We don't need you to babysit." He kept his voice down so that he wouldn't wake Debbie, who was sleeping in her hospital bed a few feet away. "They're staying with my mother for a couple of days. I just thought you'd be more comfortable."

Debbie stirred. "Is everything okay?"

"It's fine," her husband told her. "I'm just telling Talulah she can have our bed at home if she wants it."

"Yeah. Feel free to go to the house, Lu," her sister mumbled. "You'll sleep better there." After adjusting the blankets, Debbie drifted off again. She was obviously even more exhausted than Talulah was, and for good reason.

Talulah covered a yawn as she checked the time on her phone. It was nearly one in the morning. Debbie had been in the final stage of labor when she arrived, so it'd taken only another forty minutes for the baby to be born. "I'm not ready to leave yet—unless you'd like me to go so you can have some privacy with your wife and little Abby."

"No," Scott assured her. "We like having you here with us. We hardly get to see you these days."

She gave him a sleepy smile. "I'm glad I could make it. I'd never seen anyone have a baby before." She'd been so far away when Debbie had had her other children that by the time she'd arrived at the hospital, the deliveries were already over. "It was an incredible thing to witness." It'd also made her keenly aware of what she had and didn't have in her own life. Would she ever get married and have a child? Would she regret it later if she didn't?

She'd believed she was slowly moving in the direction of marriage and family with Paul. And yet now…who could say? She cared about him, but was she capable of feeling anything stronger? That had always been the problem. She liked all the men she'd had relationships with, but never seemed to fall as hard as she should. At least settling down with Paul meant the diner would remain on solid ground.

Still, that wasn't any reason to marry someone—or not the *right* reason, anyway. She remembered how appalled Brant had been when she'd said Paul was a nice guy.

She tried texting Paul one more time. Are you done giving me the silent treatment? She was beginning to lose patience with him. While she felt bad that he was upset, she'd never promised him her fidelity. They'd had many long talks about her inability to make a commitment to him. She hadn't wanted to risk ruining the friendship they already had by creating expectations—which was exactly what had happened.

She'd given up waiting for a response and dropped her phone in her lap so she could nod off again when her screen lit up. Someone had sent her a text. But it wasn't Paul. It was Brant.

Is everything okay?

He'd asked her to let him know when she'd arrived safely in Billings, but the whole baby thing had over-whelmed her and somehow the idea of sharing it with him had made her feel…strange—as though she was get-ting too close to him and needed to back away.

All is good. Little Abby weighs almost nine pounds and has a great set of lungs. Debbie is fine, too, she wrote back.

Did you arrive in time to witness the birth?

I did.

When will you be coming back?

Not sure. Depends on whether Paul shows up at the diner tomorrow. If he doesn't, I'm thinking I may have to go back to Seattle before I empty my aunt's house. We have great employees, but we've never left them alone for this long.

How's business? Have you been checking the daily re-ceipts?

I have. So far they're remaining consistent.

That's encouraging, at least.

When he didn't write anything else, she assumed that was the end of the conversation. It was late, after all; he was probably in bed and had drifted off to sleep. So she was surprised when her phone lit up again. She thought it was Brant, saying good-night, but this text wasn't from him.

She'd finally heard from Paul.

Where are you?

What do you mean? she asked. Where are YOU? You just disappeared off the planet.

I think I'm at your aunt's house. Someone at the gas station in town told me how to find it, so I'm pretty sure this is the right place. But there's no one here.

Talulah clapped a hand over her mouth. "Oh, no," she whispered into her palm. Paul had gone to Coyote Canyon.

Sixteen

The next morning, Talulah bent over Debbie's hospital bed to kiss the fuzzy head of the new baby. Scott was out hunting down something for breakfast, which had given Talulah a moment alone with her sister and niece. "I have to go. But it was great getting to spend the night with you."

"Really?" Debbie said, sounding surprised. "Because I don't think you slept very well."

"It was comforting just to be with family, especially for such a special event."

"I'm glad you could make it. That means a lot to me."

"I'm sorry Mom's not here," Talulah said, taking her hand.

"It's okay," she insisted. "She'll see Abigail when she gets home."

Talulah refrained from pointing out that Abby would be a year old by then.

"Are you heading back to Coyote Canyon?" Debbie asked.

"Not yet." After what had happened with the broken window and that car creeping by her place so late, Talulah had locked up the house as tightly as she could and removed the Hide-A-Key. She'd thought she'd be coming back alone and wanted to do what she could to avoid any nasty surprises from Charlie or Averil. But that meant Paul hadn't been able to get into the house, not without breaking out more of the window and trying to climb in over the sharp glass. When she returned his message last night, he'd told her he just rented a motel room for the night so he could get some rest. "I'm going to shower at your place, if that's okay. Then I'll meet Paul for breakfast."

"Here in Billings?"

"Yeah."

"I thought I was dreaming last night when you told me he'd driven to Montana."

"Unfortunately not."

"Why isn't he waiting for you in Coyote Canyon?"

"He wanted to keep coming so I wouldn't feel I had to rush back."

She hadn't heard from him yet this morning, but he was probably already awake and on his way.

"That's nice of him."

It *was* nice of him. Except Talulah wasn't happy that he'd left the diner in the hands of their employees and driven all the way from Seattle. Why couldn't they have talked over the phone? She'd tried to reach him so many times. And now she was in the uncomfortable situation of having Paul and Brant in the same town—once she and Paul returned from Billings, anyway. "We'll see how it goes. He also wanted to come so he could meet you. I tried telling him you probably wouldn't feel very comfortable, considering you'd just had a baby, but—"

"It's fine," her sister interrupted. "Bring him by."

"Okay."

"Good luck."

Talulah let go of her hand and blew her a kiss. "Thanks." She passed Scott on her way out. "Hey, are you leaving already?" he asked. "Because they had egg burritos at the cafeteria, and I got you one, in case you needed a little something to tide you over until Paul can get here."

Apparently, he'd absorbed more of what she'd said last night than Debbie, but then he'd been a little more coherent at the time. "That was kind of you, but I think I'll wait."

He grinned. "If Debbie doesn't want it, either, I guess I'll just have to eat two."

"Why not? This *is* a celebration, isn't it?"

"Damn right," he said and waved before disappearing into his wife's room.

Taking a deep breath, Talulah hiked her purse higher and hurried out of the hospital. She'd had such success with Phoebe's funeral. And the birth had gone perfectly, far better than she'd even dared to hope. She figured she shouldn't be too upset with Paul for not responding to her for so long and then showing up out of nowhere.

Not everything could go her way.

Talulah held her breath as she watched Paul's truck turn into the lot. They'd agreed to meet at a local pancake house that had a slew of five-star reviews. She was hungry, but she was no longer convinced that meeting him in public was the best thing to do. Maybe they needed more privacy for the type of discussion they would likely have.

Bracing for what could easily turn into a public argument, she managed a tentative smile as he got out and strode toward her.

"There you are," he said and swept her into his arms, surprising her with a big hug and a long, passionate kiss. "God, I've missed you."

She'd expected him to be angry. She knew he *had* been angry, because he hadn't responded to any of her attempts to reach him. So what was this about? Why the sudden change of heart?

"It's good to see you, too," she murmured. "But…what made you leave Seattle and the diner and come clear to Montana?"

"I decided you were worth the trip—that *we* were worth it."

Just the way he said "we" assumed too much. They hadn't made anything official. In her mind, things had barely started to heat up between them. "What about the diner?"

"The diner is fine. I put Selma Roberto in charge. You know how dependable she is."

But they'd agreed to take turns going out of town expressly because they didn't feel they should require any of their employees to take on that much responsibility. "The problem is you didn't even let me know you were coming."

"I decided to surprise you."

He'd decided to come and defend his claim, and he was doing it at the expense of the diner. But she felt bad that he always seemed to want more from her than she could give, so she didn't point that out. "You definitely surprised me."

"What happened to your arm?" he asked.

She glanced down at the bandage; she'd been so caught up in everything else she'd forgotten about her injury— and that she hadn't had a chance to tell him about it. "You saw the broken window at the house?"

"Yeah."

"Someone threw a rock through it."

"Since you've been in Montana? Who would do that?"

"I thought it might be Charlie, but…I don't know for sure."

"What an asshole! I can't believe *anyone* would do that!"

She didn't really want to talk about it. It was old news,

something she was dealing with herself. There was nothing Paul could do about it, anyway. "I'm okay. Just needed a few stitches."

"Why didn't you tell me?"

Partly because she'd been in good hands already, she realized. Brant knew, and he'd been looking out for her. She'd felt protected enough that she'd felt no need to drag anyone else into it. But maybe she would've told Paul if he'd still been talking to her. "I couldn't," she said. "You weren't answering any of my calls or texts, remember?"

"You never sent anything about getting hurt!"

Apparently, he had been reading her messages; he just hadn't been responding to them. She'd guessed as much. "I thought you were mad at me, Paul."

He scowled. "I was," he admitted. "I was shocked and hurt and mad as hell when Charlie told me what was happening here. You'd been away from me for less than a week—and already you were messing around with another guy? I couldn't believe it. But after a couple days of going out of my mind, I realized if it happened *that* fast, it was probably nothing serious. I know how long it takes to get you into bed when you're considering a relationship," he joked. "So…what made you do it?"

Desire. She couldn't remember ever wanting a man like she'd wanted Brant. But she knew that answer would only make matters worse. Paul had been chasing her for so long. Of course he'd want her to feel that kind of desire for him. And she'd been hoping she would—with time. "I've been trying to figure that out. I'm afraid I don't have a good answer."

Another couple came out of the restaurant. As they walked past, he lowered his voice. "It was just physical, though, right? An outlet for the stress you're under being back here by yourself and facing people—Charlie and his family—who are so hostile to you?"

He was feeding her the excuse he felt he could accept. He wanted her to say that the time she'd spent with Brant hadn't meant anything to her, that it was just a mistake and nothing had changed between her and Paul. But she wasn't sure that was the case. Something *had* changed, because whenever she thought of Brant, she still felt that same desire.

"Talulah?"

After quickly considering her other options, she decided to go with what Paul had suggested, for now. She could sort out her real feelings later, once they were home. She and Paul had such a good thing going with the dessert diner. She had to be careful, thoughtful—and most of all *certain*—before she stated anything too strongly, especially right now. "Maybe. I don't know. Like I said, I can't really explain it. Nothing like that has ever happened before."

He gave her a searching look. "But...you're coming back to Seattle, aren't you?"

"Of course," she said and that seemed to help.

Taking her hand, he smiled in apparent relief. "Then let's put the past behind us. Forget it. As far as I'm concerned, what happened last week never happened, and we won't talk about it again."

"Okay," she agreed. But she knew it wouldn't be that easy.

It was only forty-five minutes later, when she was in the bathroom after breakfast and Paul was waiting for her to leave the restaurant so he could follow her back to the hospital, that she got a text from Brant.

How's it going? Any pics of the new baby you can share?

She wanted to respond, to send him one of the many photos she'd taken of her beautiful new niece, and she would've done so had Paul not shown up. She might even have asked Brant if he was going to be around when she got back. That was what felt natural to her.

But because she couldn't—because she didn't know what to say—she didn't reply at all.

Brant had texted Talulah three hours ago—and gotten no response. He told himself she was probably busy with her sister and wasn't checking her phone, but as the hours passed, he began to grow concerned. Did she have an accident or something driving home?

He couldn't bring himself to believe that Charlie or Averil would seriously harm her, so he doubted *that* could be the problem. But then, he never would've thought either of them would throw a rock through her window...

Hey, you okay?

He sent that message after he finished work. Then he showered and had dinner—and there was still no word from her. Her silence seemed odd, and he began to worry about Paul. What kind of man was he? Could it be that he was obsessed with Talulah—and angry enough to harm her?

The longer it went, the more uneasy he became. Around eight, he sent her another message: Can you just let me know if you're safe?

It took about fifteen minutes, but he finally received an answer.

Sorry. Didn't mean to make you think something terrible had happened. I'm fine. We'll have to talk later, okay? I can't use my phone at the moment.

Why not? he wanted to ask. He also wanted to see if she was at home or still in Billings. But he refrained from being the kind of pain in the ass who'd text again after she'd said she couldn't use her phone.

"What're you doing tonight?" Kurt asked, coming into the living room, where Brant was sprawled in their father's old recliner.

It was poker night, something Brant typically enjoyed, but he was so tired he'd decided not to go. He was also fairly certain Charlie would be there, and Brant preferred not to deal with him right now. "I'm probably going to turn in early."

His brother scowled. "That's bullshit, bro. You can sleep when you're dead. Why not go to Hank's with me? We could grab a drink, play some pool."

Although Brant wasn't too interested in spending another evening playing pool, he let his little brother talk him into going. He didn't have to worry about running into Charlie since he would be at poker night.

Brant usually liked pool. But once they arrived, and he'd won three games in a row, he grew bored.

"One more," his brother insisted when he said he was ready to leave.

"Why? You'll never beat me," Brant teased.

"I win sometimes. Not often," he admitted sheepishly. "But if you're not afraid of losing, why not give me another chance?"

Brant played again and didn't try as hard so his brother could win. He thought that would satisfy him, but Kurt still wanted more. "Come on," he said when Brant started to return his cue stick. "That went way too fast."

"I'm done," Brant insisted, and was relieved when some of Kurt's friends showed up so his brother could stay and he could go. "Call me if you need a ride," Brant told him, but Mason, a friend of Kurt's since grade school, spoke up to say he'd make sure Kurt got home safely.

It was still fairly early, only ten, as Brant started for home. He was at the edge of town when he decided to turn the other way and swing by Talulah's house. He told himself he was just checking to make sure there'd been no more trouble at her place. But the truth was…he wanted to see her. He hadn't been able to get her off his mind all day, and that was becoming an alarming pattern.

Once he got there, he guessed she hadn't returned from Billings, after all. Other than the porch light, the place was completely dark.

Just to double-check, he went to the door. He certainly wouldn't mind if she invited him in and wanted him to stay over. He'd been craving contact with her all day. But he would've been happy with a conversation. They hadn't had a chance to talk about the funeral, the birth of her new niece or how her arm was healing.

But no one answered his knock. And when he tried the door, hoping to stick his head in and call out her name, he found it locked.

Assuming she was staying over at her sister's again, he started to leave, but the screen door was hanging so crookedly on its hinges he decided to fix it while he was there. He'd been meaning to do it; it wouldn't take long, and he had a hammer and screw gun in his truck.

A cool breeze ruffled his hair as he returned to the drive, hauled his tools out of the back of his truck and carried them to the porch. He was enjoying the work—and thinking about her coming home to find it able to latch— when two cars turned into the drive.

* * *

Talulah stomped on the brake the second she saw Brant, but then had to ease up and keep going so Paul wouldn't rear-end her. He was right behind her in the Lexus sedan his mother had left him when she passed away two years ago. There was no chance he'd miss seeing Brant, which meant she couldn't avoid a meeting between the two of them. And it would happen on her great aunt's front porch, not even on neutral ground somewhere in town.

"Shit." She didn't bother to pull into the detached garage. She was afraid Paul would get out and confront Brant before she had a chance to reach them and do whatever she could to mitigate any problems.

Still, she had to park farther away from the house than Paul did so Brant would be able to leave without any need to move their cars, so she was a few steps behind Paul when he charged toward the porch.

"Who the hell are you?" he demanded. "And what are you doing here?"

"Paul!" Talulah cried, trying to warn him with her voice to go easy, but he wasn't paying any attention.

Brant took his time setting the screen door he'd taken off the hinges against the house. She could tell by the tightening of his jaw and the narrowing of his eyes that he wasn't any happier to meet Paul than Paul was to meet him.

"Just doing a friend a favor," he said simply.

His words were carefully calibrated—pleasant, but barely so—and the way his gaze raked over Paul suggested he was sizing him up. Talulah could easily guess why. He was wondering what would happen if he had to fight, what his chances were of winning, and that made Talulah even more anxious. She *definitely* didn't want this to go in that direction. There'd already been more than enough trouble with Charlie.

"Paul, this is Brant. Brant, this is Paul." An introduction was unavoidable, so Talulah got on with it, hoping they'd both be civil, and they could all get through this without any serious drama.

"I know who he is," Paul grumbled. "I knew it the second I saw him."

Attempting to ignore Paul's response, which was less polite than she'd wished, Talulah forced a smile for Brant's sake and held it in place only with enormous effort. "Thanks for fixing the door. That screen was driving me crazy."

Brant didn't take his eyes off Paul, but Paul cast her an exasperated, even irritated look, letting her know he wasn't happy she was being so friendly to the man she'd slept with. "It's almost ten thirty," Paul said, turning his attention back to Brant. "Do you help out all your friends when it's this late or just the female ones you're hoping to crawl back into bed with?"

A muscle moved in Brant's cheek. "Out of respect for Talulah, I'm not going to answer that question."

"You don't think I should be upset?"

Talulah put a hand on Paul's arm. "Please, stop. Really. This isn't necessary, especially when Brant's just being nice."

"He's *not* 'just' being nice," Paul snapped. "That's the problem."

Brant raised his eyebrows. "I don't blame you for not liking me. But you only get to act like an asshole if I've done something wrong."

Paul jerked his arm away from Talulah as he stepped forward. "You know exactly what you've done. I've been with Talulah for four years!"

"We've been *business partners* for four years," she tried to clarify, but Paul talked right over her.

"And I've known her even longer than that, since culinary school."

"You haven't known her longer than I have," Brant pointed out.

"What does that matter?"

Talulah knew what Paul had been getting at. He meant they'd been growing closer and closer for years and Brant should respect that. But it was a flimsy argument, and Brant had immediately called him on it.

"It *doesn't* matter," he said with a shrug. "That's my point. But you're the one who brought it up." He bent to pick up his tools, but when Paul came toward him, he left them on the porch and straightened. "Are we going to have a problem here?"

"That depends," Paul replied. "Are you going to stay away from Talulah?"

Talulah grabbed Paul's arm again. "Stop it! I'll decide who I associate with. You don't have the right to decide for me."

"I just want to know!" he said to her. "Is that asking too much? Am I going to have to worry about this douchebag coming over here, trying to get in your pants again, as soon as I'm gone?"

The hair stood up on the back of Talulah's neck. She'd never seen Paul act so territorial, but she'd never really seen him when he felt threatened, either. She'd been too caught up in their business to date other men. He'd probably assumed they were exclusive—even though she'd always said otherwise—because he'd never encountered any competition, especially in the last couple of years when she'd devoted herself so completely to launching the dessert diner. "We're *not* together, Paul."

He rounded on her. "You think this guy cares about you the way I do? He just wants a good fuck! You told me yourself he goes from woman to woman without ever feeling much. We, on the other hand, have a successful business. I'm willing to offer you marriage, babies, anything you want and everything I have."

Talulah had the vague feeling that her inability to commit was once again going to come between her and the people she cared about, but she couldn't seem to help it. She couldn't pretend to feel something she didn't. She could only try to be careful and not say or do anything rash until she was certain of her own mind and heart. And who knew when that would be? "I asked you earlier to give me more time, Paul. I'm not ready for this. It's been one hell of a week coming back here, facing my past. Please... don't treat my friends badly."

The way Brant's eyes cut to her made her realize how he might interpret what she'd just said. *One hell of a week*, as if it'd *all* been insufferable. But it hadn't, and *he* was the reason. He'd shielded her from the worst of it, even at the cost of his best friend.

She wanted to clarify her statement. But Paul didn't give her the chance, which was just as well, since it probably would only have made matters worse. "Even if you've slept with them?" he demanded.

Whatever Brant was thinking, his attention snapped back to Paul. "Watch how you talk to her," he warned.

Paul threw back his shoulders, and his hands curled into fists. "Oh, yeah? What're you going to do about it?"

Talulah's pulse was racing as she squeezed between them. "What's happening here? Quit it! Please. Both of you. This is childish."

Paul's eyes glittered with anger. "This dude thinks he can come out here, on *your* property, and tell *me* what to do."

"Paul, you know that—" Talulah started, planning to

remind him, once again, that he had no real claim on her, but Brant broke in before she could finish.

"You should be careful," he said to Paul.

Hearing the steel in Brant's voice, Talulah hoped Paul would back down. But he didn't. *"Why?"* he said with even more challenge.

"Because you're really beginning to piss me off."

They might've come to blows right then. Paul shoved her to get her out from between them, but in the same second, she heard a female voice say, "Hey, you're back?"

They all turned to see Ellen crossing the grass toward them, the end of the cigarette she held in one hand glowing in the darkness.

"I am back," Talulah said, breathing a sigh of relief. "Looks like you are, too."

"Finally." Ellen squinted at the two men as she stopped and took a long drag. "I came by earlier but couldn't get anyone."

"I was in Billings. My sister just had a baby."

"Everything go okay?"

"It did—thank goodness."

As Ellen drew closer, the light from the porch illuminated her pixie-like face, and Talulah could see that she'd changed the color of her hair to a whitish blond. "What's going on here?" she asked, gesturing at the men with her cigarette. "Are you having some sort of disagreement?"

"Who are you?" Paul asked.

Talulah frowned at him for not being more courteous. From his perspective it had to be a bit odd that this person would seemingly materialize out of nowhere. He didn't know she and Ellen were neighbors. But still… "Ellen, this is my business partner—Paul Pacheco. He drove here from Seattle. Paul, Ellen lives next door."

Paul glanced around as though he was surprised there

was another house in the immediate vicinity. It was hard enough to see the structures on the adjacent property during the day, since so many trees and the garage obstructed the view. He probably hadn't noticed it earlier. And at night, it was virtually impossible.

"Why are you trying to fight Brant?" Ellen asked him calmly.

Paul stiffened. "That's none of your business."

"Well, maybe it isn't," she said, exhaling on a long stream of smoke. "But it's lucky I came by. I might've just saved your ass."

"He's lucky indeed," Brant said and picked up his toolbox. "I'm out of here. Good to see you, Ellen."

"You wouldn't have to fight anyone if you want to come to *my* house," she joked, but there was too much tension for any of them to laugh. They all watched Brant stalk away, climb into his truck and drive off.

"Looks like you're busy," Ellen said. "I'll come over sometime when this guy is a little more open to company." She indicated Paul with her cigarette before dropping it, stamping it out and picking up the butt. "'Night."

Talulah sagged, completely exhausted, as she studied the screen door Brant had left leaning up against the house. "You *had* to almost cause a fight?" she asked, finally turning her attention to Paul.

He looked somewhat abashed. "Maybe I went too far."

Talulah didn't say anything. She just walked past him, pulled the key out of her purse and opened the door. "There are two bedrooms besides the master upstairs. You're welcome to get your bag and take one of them. I need some time to myself," she said and wearily climbed the stairs to her room.

Seventeen

Brant couldn't believe it. He wasn't even sure how he'd gotten himself into such a mess. That night at Talulah's, when he'd had the concussion, was supposed to be a one-time thing. Easy. Fun. No repercussions. It might've ended that way. But one night had turned into two, and two had turned into three, and they'd been some of the best nights he'd ever had.

Added to that, Charlie or Averil had thrown that rock through her window, cutting her and making him mad, and he'd had to take a stand against that sort of behavior, which pulled him further into Talulah's life. That was the reason he'd had to go to the funeral, to keep an eye on them. He knew no one else would make sure she got through it. And he'd decided to fix her door because…

He couldn't say why he'd decided to fix her door.

Anyway, here he was, lying in bed, feeling like a fool—as if Paul had hit him in the stomach even though the confrontation hadn't come to blows. And the crazy thing was…it bothered him much more than it should to think that Paul was the one who was with Talulah right now, sleeping…where?

"I'm turning into Charlie," he muttered, punching his pillow.

With a sigh, Brant rolled over to check the time on his phone. Nearly three. On weekdays, he got up in two hours, but tomorrow was Saturday. He could sleep in if he needed to. At least he had that going for him. He had to do a few things around the ranch—move the cattle to another paddock for Kurt, since Kurt had taken his last turn—but he'd have most of the day off. He could finally change the oil in his truck. And after lunch, he and his brothers could take the boat to the lake and enjoy one of the last days of summer.

That should've sounded like fun. Boating and water-skiing were some of his favorite activities. But knowing Paul was in town, and that he couldn't see Talulah again, had changed him in some way. Nothing seemed to have the same appeal it did before, even going to the lake.

This had to be what a crush felt like, he decided. He was miserable. Everything that'd once been important to him—everything he used to love doing—no longer seemed to matter. He'd give up the lake in a heartbeat if it meant he could go over and hang out with Talulah.

Emotions aren't that simple, Brant. She's a man-eater. And if you're not careful, you might find that out the hard way.

Averil had told him that. He didn't believe Talulah was a man-eater. She just happened to have more than her fair share of sex appeal. Thanks to that, and her beauty, and her sweetness, and the fact that she wasn't remotely clingy or grasping, she attracted more than her fair share of men. And because he'd never run into anyone else who'd captured his attention quite like she had, he'd fallen right into the trap Averil had been warning him about. That was all. He didn't find what Averil had said there to be too significant. But his response that day was: *Trust me, I can take care of myself.*

He'd been too cocky for his own good.

You've never had your heart broken, have you?

Not really. I guess I've been lucky.

Yeah, well, let's hope your luck isn't about to run out.

This part of the conversation weighed more heavily.

But his luck *wasn't* about to run out. He'd caught himself in time, hadn't he? All he had to do was keep his distance and let the effect she had on him slowly wear off. Eventually, it would have to. And with Paul in town, staying away from her would be easy since he couldn't see her even if he wanted to.

You think this guy cares about you the way I do? He just wants a good fuck! You told me yourself he goes from woman to woman without ever feeling much.

Paul had said that, and Talulah hadn't corrected him. Apparently, even she would be surprised by how he felt.

But he refused to be like Charlie. He'd take firm control of himself, yank his attention back to his regular life, where it should've been all along, and let her go on her way.

When Talulah woke up, the first thing that popped into her mind was the memory of arriving home last night to find Brant fixing her screen door. He'd been good to her since she'd come back—in so many ways. It made her cringe to remember Paul jumping out of the car to accost him.

Paul's behavior had embarrassed her. And yet she could hardly blame him. She understood what he was going through—and that she was the reason. Having him in her life for such a long time, with daily contact since they'd opened the diner together, had undermined all her good intentions to avoid getting into another situation like those in the past. Somewhere along the line, he'd stopped believing what she said and started to assume she felt more than she did, simply because he wanted her to.

Fortunately, she didn't have to worry about hurting Brant. He was probably relieved to have such an easy exit. They were having a good time, enjoying each other, but she imagined him shrugging her off the moment he got into his truck and was willing to bet he wouldn't think of her again.

I've never left anyone standing at the altar, he'd said that day in the town diner.

Because you bail out before it even gets that far, she'd told him.

That's what you're supposed to do. I can teach you how, if you want me to.

He didn't need to teach her; he was going to show her. But knowing that the brief interlude they'd enjoyed had already come to an end created such a strange sense of loss—like a breakup, really, even though they'd never been together in the first place. Whatever they'd had, it was too bad it had to end so soon. They'd been having a wonderful time, one that felt natural and spontaneous and next-level when it came to sex. Everything with him, including his touch, was more exciting.

Movement from down the hall made her tense. Paul was awake. She figured she should get up and say hello, but she wasn't looking forward to another day spent reassuring him that nothing had really changed while fending off every attempt he made to get her to agree she'd never look at another man again.

She kicked off the covers and was just going into the bathroom when she heard a creak behind her. Paul had come out of his room and was standing in the hall, barefoot and shirtless, in a pair of basketball shorts.

Talulah had slept with him once, only a week before she came to Coyote Canyon, but she was wearing nothing except a pair of panties and a spaghetti-strap top and instinctively wanted to shield her body from his view.

"Morning," he said, raking his hands through his thick dark hair as it fell around his shoulders.

"Morning." She continued into the bathroom, so she could stand behind the door and peer out at him. "Are you hungry?" she asked.

A frown indicated he'd noticed her reaction and that made her feel as bad as everything else. He had to be wondering why they couldn't simply pick up where they'd left off. After all, it'd been easy enough for her to go to bed with Brant—someone she'd known in high school and hadn't seen since—proving it wasn't a long process for some guys.

But coming to Coyote Canyon and getting involved with him had removed the possibility of sleeping with Paul again, at least for the time being, and she couldn't even explain why.

Fortunately, Paul didn't remark on it. He seemed to be trying, once again, not to pressure her too much. "I am hungry. What about you?"

"I'm starving. Why don't I make some buttermilk pancakes? You like my mother's recipe, don't you?"

"Do you have buttermilk?"

"No, but we could buy some easily enough."

He waved that option away. "I'd rather just go out."

Talulah wasn't too keen on that idea. She didn't want to be seen in town with Paul after all the rumors that'd been circulating about her and Brant. She knew that being seen with Paul would only supercharge the gossip and make it more difficult for her to stay here after he left. "It won't take long to go to the store."

"But I'd like to see your hometown while I'm here. Don't you want to show me around?"

What could she say that wouldn't make him accuse her of doing exactly what she *was* doing—trying to keep him out of sight as much as possible?

She cleared her throat. "Okay. Let me get cleaned up," she said and shut the door.

Unless they went to a restaurant in a neighboring town, odds were good they'd run into *someone* she knew. It was a weekend, after all, and a lot of people would be eating out, picking up groceries or running errands.

Chances were much lower that they'd run into Brant. She had to acknowledge that. But even a small chance made her uneasy, because he was the one she wanted to avoid most of all.

Talulah took her time getting ready. Depending on who was out and about, she'd probably draw attention and wanted to look her best. But when they got to Urban Remedy, a farm-to-fork restaurant that was new and trendy and something she thought Paul would be more likely to appreciate than the traditional greasy spoon where she'd run into Brant shortly after she'd arrived, there was no one she recognized.

Feeling the tension coiled tightly inside her slowly begin to unravel, she ordered the mushroom toast with fresh leeks, shiitake mushrooms and lemon aioli, and Paul chose the eggs benedict with local farm-fresh eggs and hollandaise sauce. And of course they both ordered coffee.

"It was hard not to get the chorizo scramble, but I can't pass up eggs benedict," Paul commented as a tall young man with dreadlocks entered their order into an iPad.

Talulah glanced at the menu painted on a wooden sign behind the counter as she stuck her credit card in the reader. Paul had offered to pay, but she'd insisted it was her turn. She didn't want him to be able to accuse her of taking advantage of him if their relationship didn't develop as he hoped. She was now especially glad she'd always been careful about that. "I was tempted by the biscuits and gravy and fried sage," she said as she reclaimed her card.

"You love biscuits and gravy."

"I do, but I went with the mushroom toast because I've never had anything like it before."

Food was one area where they were a natural fit. They loved trying new things—whether it was someone else's cooking or their own. Overall, they did well as business partners, too. And Talulah liked hiking and hanging out with him. She'd even enjoyed it when they'd had sex—well enough, anyway. She'd thought that maybe she'd broken through a barrier, and that she'd be interested in getting more serious when she returned.

But then she'd slept with Brant and that had somehow demolished the small amount of desire she'd begun to feel for Paul.

She hoped she could get back to where she'd been before. If not…

She didn't want to think about the ramifications. She'd worked so hard to establish herself in the restaurant business. And she was fairly certain she wanted a family. If she married Paul, it would be easy to maintain what they already had. They could even trade off working at the diner and taking care of the kids.

If only she could get her stubborn heart to cooperate.

They each poured some water from a carafe set out for people to help themselves and chose a two-seater table in the outdoor section near the garden.

"I'm surprised to find a cool place like this in such a small town," Paul said.

Talulah put her water on the table. "It's definitely more Bozeman than Coyote Canyon, but it just opened last year, so maybe Coyote Canyon will become more hip over time."

"There're enough people around to support it?"

"I think it pulls customers from the surrounding area, too. I saw several people on Yelp say they drove over from various places an hour or two from here."

"Opening this kind of restaurant in such a backward town is ballsy."

"Are you trying to be insulting?" she asked.

He looked surprised. "No. You've called it backward yourself, on numerous occasions."

She supposed she had. Coyote Canyon wasn't anything like Seattle. She'd often joked about coming from "nowhere." But it irritated her when *he* belittled her hometown. "Well, from what I read online, the owners already had the farm," she said, veering away from an argument. "The restaurant's just an extension of that."

"I hope they can make it work."

At the moment, Talulah was more worried about their own restaurant. "How many days have you been away from the diner? Four? Five? Isn't that kind of long?"

"I was there Tuesday and Wednesday," he told her. "I didn't leave until early Thursday morning, after I finished the baking."

She felt her eyebrows pull together. "But I called…"

He looked away. "I told everyone that if you called to say they hadn't seen me."

He had? And what reason had he given them? Had he also told everyone at the diner that she'd slept with someone else? At the very least, Selma, Beth and the others had to be aware that there was now a problem between them, something she'd purposely avoided making apparent herself. Not only was it unprofessional to drag them into the middle of an argument, she hated to think of the people they'd hired speculating on her personal life, or choosing sides.

What Paul had done bothered her for another reason, too. "You wanted me to worry about the diner when you knew there was nothing I could do, other than head home, if our employees had a problem?"

He toyed with the condensation on his glass. "Not really. I just wasn't ready to talk to you."

No, he'd tried to make her worry; she could tell. He knew how much she cared about the diner. It wasn't the worst revenge anyone could devise, but turning their employees against her, having them lie for him and making her fear for the diner was revenge all the same. "You could've told me you needed time. I would've respected a request like that. Then we wouldn't have had to involve our employees."

"They actually helped talk me through it," he said as if that made it okay.

"You told them about Brant?"

"Was I supposed to keep it a secret? I was shocked and hurt, Lu. I thought it was over between us."

But did their employees also know that she didn't owe him her fidelity? That he was expecting more than she'd ever promised? Talulah doubted he'd shared that part, because it would make him so much less sympathetic.

She could've called him out, but it was possible he'd taken the night they'd been together to mean more than it did—although she remembered at least two conversations afterward in which she'd said she still wasn't sure and wanted to take things slow before making any sort of commitment.

She couldn't help being annoyed, even angry, but she

decided to let it go. "How long do you plan on staying here in Coyote Canyon?"

He stiffened. She hadn't chosen the best time to ask that question, but she'd been wondering since he arrived. "Why? Are you in a hurry to get rid of me?" he asked.

"Not at all," she replied, trying to sound as convincing as possible. "It's just…someone should be at the diner. Weekends are our busiest days."

"You're underestimating our employees."

She'd picked up her water glass, but at this, she put it back down. "I am? Because I thought you agreed with me. When I said I had to come to Coyote Canyon to take care of my great aunt's funeral and belongings, I suggested you join me for a few days—at least for the funeral so I wouldn't have to face everyone from my past alone—and you said the funeral would only last a couple of hours and it wouldn't be worth having you come out for that. We agreed it would be smarter for you to be there while I'm gone, and I'd be there while you're gone."

"The diner's *fine*, Talulah."

He sounded exasperated that she kept pushing the issue, but he hadn't addressed her argument. What she was trying to make him see was that he hadn't been willing to come to Coyote Canyon because of what *she'd* been worried about, but he'd certainly been willing to come for something *he* was worried about.

Once again, Talulah told herself it wasn't a huge deal, she was being sensitive, but it bugged her, especially when she thought of Brant showing up at Phoebe's funeral and sitting right in the front row, just to give her some support—all the while knowing it would risk several of his relationships here in town.

"Can I ask you a question?" Paul said.

She knew by his tone of voice that it would require patience, but she made the attempt to be courteous. "Sure."

"What attracted you to that hayseed in the first place?"

Talulah felt her nails curve into her palms. Everything Paul did and said seemed to get on her nerves today. Was it him? Or was it her? "I thought you said we wouldn't talk about Brant again."

"That was before I found him on your porch last night, and then you acted so weird after."

"I didn't act weird," she said. "I was tired and went to bed."

"I'm just curious. He has a powerful build. I'll give him that. But I'd never expect you to be attracted to someone like him."

"Someone like him?" she echoed. "He might live a different lifestyle than we do, but he's quite successful at what he does."

Paul didn't seem impressed. "Maybe he is. But admit it—you'd be bored living out here. You two have nothing in common. What would you even talk about?"

So far, the conversation between her and Brant had been easy, natural and as enjoyable as everything else they'd shared. She wanted to tell Paul that, but she knew it wouldn't help. "Let's drop it, okay? But I *will* tell you this. If we happen to run into him again, I wouldn't try to start another fight."

Talulah heard her name and stood up to get their food, but Paul caught her by the wrist. "Why? You don't think I can take him?"

"Ranching is hard work—much more physical than anything we do. And he's been competing with his three equally rugged brothers for most of his life."

"Which means…"

"He's used to wrestling and pitting his strength against other men."

"I'm not scared of him," Paul scoffed.

But Talulah knew he'd be a fool to start trouble with Brant. Hopefully, he'd listen to her.

Eighteen

There was still part of one carrot cake in Brant's refrigerator. His brothers had devoured everything else he'd brought home from the funeral, and they'd eat this, too, if he didn't get to it first. But allowing himself to enjoy it somehow made him feel as though he'd be capitulating—accepting that he was beginning to care way too much for Talulah.

"What're you doing?" Ranson had just entered the kitchen to find Brant staring into the fridge. "The TV's out there, bro."

Brant grabbed a beer instead. But when his brother opened the fridge the second he closed it and reached for the cake, Brant stopped him. "That's mine."

A scowl darkened Ranson's face. "*All* of it?"

Brant considered the sizable chunk that remained. He *could* share, but he wasn't amenable to that or much of anything else at the moment. "I'll let you know if there's any left when I'm done."

"What are the chances of that?" Ranson asked. "Tell you what. I'll arm wrestle you for it."

"You wouldn't want to take me on tonight," Brant told him.

"Why not?"

Brant cracked open his beer. "Because if I arm wrestle you, I'm going to make you put a hundred bucks on it. Then you stand to lose something, too."

Ranson took one look at him, and Brant saw his confidence fade. "Yeah, that's a bet I won't bother with." He shut the fridge. "So...do you think you can get Talulah to bake us another one?"

"No, he can't," Kurt said, joining them from the living room. "Her boyfriend's in town, so Brant's lost his privileges. Ain't that right, Brant?"

"I'm already in a bad mood," Brant warned. "It might be smart to watch your mouth."

"Oh, I get it," Ranson said as he nudged Kurt in the ribs. "He's jealous."

"I'm not jealous," Brant said. "This thing between Talulah and me was never meant to be anything serious. I knew that going in."

"So why are you acting like you're ready to tear someone's head off?" Kurt asked as he opened the fridge.

When he tried to reach for the cake, Brant knocked his hand away, too. "Don't touch that. Like I told Ran, it's mine."

"All of it?"

"All of it. For now, anyway."

"Well, if you're going to be stingy like that, I won't tell you what Kate just told me on the phone," Kurt said.

"Jane's sister? Who's close friends with *Talulah*?" Ranson clarified.

Brant already knew which Kate Kurt had been referring to. Kate and Kurt had been friends for years, and recently their relationship seemed to be turning into more than that. Ran was just trying to be funny. "Why would I care?" Brant asked, feigning indifference. But he did care, and the fact that his brother was dangling this particular carrot in front of him proved Kurt knew it.

"Because, in case you haven't guessed, it's about Talulah."

Brant told himself not to fall for this, but there really wasn't anything to be gained by continuing the "it makes no difference to me" charade. "What'd she say?"

"It'll cost you the rest of the cake..." Kurt reminded him.

Brant arched his eyebrows. "I'll give you *half*."

Ranson nudged Kurt. "The way he's feeling about her? I think you can get it all—and then give *me* half."

Brant ignored that. "What did Kate say?" he asked Kurt. "If half the cake isn't good enough, I could always beat it out of you. That'd be your other option."

Pretending to be shocked, Kurt gaped at Ranson. "Have you ever seen him like this? Damn! I think he really likes her."

"He *definitely* likes her," Ranson concurred.

"That's it. I'm out of here." Brant had taken enough of their razzing. He turned to leave, but before he could reach the door to the living room, Kurt spoke up.

"Fine, I'll tell you. Kate saw Talulah in town earlier while we were at the lake."

Brant swung around. "And?"

"She was with her boyfriend from Seattle."

"He's *not* her boyfriend," Brant bit out.

"Okay, she was with some dude who had a man bun."

"That's better. What were they doing?"

"Just walking down the street, window shopping and stopping at various places. Kate said the dude kept trying to touch her, but she'd move away, as if she wasn't into him."

"That could be Kate's interpretation," he pointed out.

"Except that Kate followed them into the ice cream parlor and heard them get into an argument. He said she was acting different toward him, that she wouldn't even let him hold her hand."

Brant's mood was miraculously improving. "And how did Talulah respond to that?"

"Unfortunately, she spoke too softly for Kate to hear without being obvious about it. But he didn't like her response. That was clear, which tells you something."

"Is that it?"

"That's it."

"And you think that tiny bit of gossip is worth the last piece of cake?" he asked.

"Don't give me that crap," Kurt said, calling him on his shit. "I know you're happy to hear it."

"Fine. You two can share the cake," he said and flashed them a grin, because he *was* happy to hear it, before taking his beer and walking out.

When he got to his room, he closed the door, set his beer on the dresser and pulled his phone from his pocket. Would it make any difference if he told Talulah how he felt?

Is there any chance you're missing me as much as I'm missing you?

As soon as he typed that, he realized he'd be a fool to send it and erased it instead. She was going back to Seattle after she took care of Phoebe's house. It wasn't as if he had a real chance with her, as if *they* had a real chance, even if she didn't get back with Paul.

"Shit," he muttered and tossed his phone on the bed, only to hear it ding with an incoming message.

He grabbed it right away, hoping it was Talulah. But it was Charlie, who must've heard Paul was in town: I told you so.

Talulah spent a restless night tossing and turning and beating herself up for the way things had gone with Paul since he arrived. It seemed as though they'd argued over everything. As soon as they'd agree to let one thing go, something else would crop up. If it wasn't Brant, it was how long she had to stay to take care of the house. And if it wasn't about the house, it was that she'd never made much of an effort to introduce him to her family. No matter what they were talking about, Paul's underlying resentment found some fissure through which to erupt. They couldn't even agree on whether to eat in or go out for dinner. Although Talulah had allowed him his choice on almost everything since he'd arrived, by the time evening came around, she'd preferred to retreat from town, was tired of being on display.

The argument that ensued because of it had been pretty bad, but it wasn't anything like the one they'd had after they ate out and got home, and he tried to put on the screen door. It'd looked like an easy enough job, even to her, but when he couldn't get it to hang right or swing level, he'd started saying Brant shouldn't have removed it in the first place, that he'd had no business touching anything that belonged to her.

Unable to abide his tirade for long, she'd stood up for Brant by saying he'd only been trying to help, at which point Paul had made his attacks more personal. He'd accused her of using him to fulfill her dream of owning a restaurant, using him to take care of the diner while she was out messing around with other guys and blaming her for leading him on.

That was when Talulah had really lost her temper. How was she using him? They were splitting all the profits on the diner, taking turns looking after the place, and she'd always been careful to pay her own way when any costs were involved. She'd done nothing wrong. But pointing that out only made him angrier. He even got mad that she wasn't as upset as he felt she should be that *he* was upset.

In the end, Talulah had asked him to go back to Seattle. She'd told him she was too worried about the diner to focus on their relationship, and she had too much work to do on Phoebe's house to take any more time away from getting it done. In her opinion, they were doing more harm than good to keep going the way they were. She was becoming more and more convinced that the best chance they had of salvaging their friendship, and possibly their partnership, was to separate, for now, and give each other some space.

Considering how the night had gone, Talulah had no idea how Paul would behave when he got up this morning. Maybe he'd leave without even speaking to her.

In an attempt to part on friendly terms, she dragged herself out of bed at dawn to shower and dress and make him some breakfast. But it was after nine when she finally heard movement overhead, so he didn't seem to be in any hurry to get on the road. It'd been so long since she made breakfast she'd had to cover his food and put it in the fridge—and she was beginning to worry that he'd decided not to go home today, after all.

She couldn't take another twenty-four hours of their bickering…

When he came downstairs, she took his plate out of the fridge and put it in the microwave.

He poked his head in the tiny kitchen. "You made breakfast?"

"I did—the orange marmalade French toast you liked when I tried the recipe a couple of months ago," she said while they waited for his food to heat. "I don't want to fight with you anymore. I hope you know that I honestly *want* to get along and…and make you happy."

He leaned against the doorway. "That would be easy

enough to do. You know what I want, Lu. But for some reason you can't give it to me."

Even the sulkiness of his voice bothered her. She couldn't figure out what was going on. "Not right now," she admitted as the microwave dinged. She took out his plate and slipped past him to reach the dining table, and he pulled out a chair and slouched into it.

"I thought you'd eventually realize that we're perfect for each other. I mean…what do you plan to do with your life if you don't marry me? Do you want to remain single indefinitely? Give yourself only to your work?"

She went back into the kitchen to pour him a cup of coffee. "That isn't the future I'm hoping for, no."

"Then what? You're fighting your own happiness. You know that, don't you? Brant isn't looking for anything more than a good time. That makes him seem safe. That's what made it possible for you to sleep with him so easily. And here I am, willing to offer you what most girls want, and you're not interested. It's too ironic."

"Talulah?" someone called from the front door, surprising them both. "Anyone home?"

Talulah leaned around Paul to peer through the living room. "Ellen?"

"What the hell's wrong with your screen door?" she asked, having to wrest it open to get in.

"It's not fixable," Paul said before Talulah could respond. "It needs to be replaced."

Ellen glanced over at him. "I thought that was your car in the drive."

"Is it a problem that I'm still here?"

She shrugged. "Not for me. But some people are making a big deal out of it."

"Would 'some people' be Brant the rancher?" he asked drily.

"Actually, I was referring to Charlie and his family."

Paul took a drink of his coffee. "Why would they care?"

"They make everything that has to do with Talulah their business."

"Well, you can tell them I'm leaving."

"Damn. Now who'll keep the gossip mill running?" Ellen joked, and Talulah breathed a little easier, secretly glad that he hadn't changed his mind.

"In a town this size, I'm sure there'll be someone," he said.

Ellen held up the measuring cup she'd brought over. "Can I borrow a cup of sugar?" she asked Talulah.

"Of course." Talulah went to the pantry and grabbed what was left of the bag she'd purchased for the carrot cakes. "Just bring back what you don't use. No worries."

"Okay," she said, but she was standing behind Paul when she gave a slight gesture with her head that let Talulah know she wanted to be walked out.

"Do you need anything else?" Talulah asked, following her through the living room.

"I don't think so," she said as Talulah forced open the recalcitrant screen door.

When Ellen hesitated, Talulah waited until they were both out on the porch before whispering, "Is something wrong?"

Ellen leaned to the right to glance past her. Paul had his back to them as he ate, but she seemed to realize they didn't have enough privacy for whatever she wanted to say. "Call me later," she said, and Talulah knew she meant *after he goes*.

Nineteen

As soon as Paul finished eating, he went upstairs to get his bag while Talulah waited nervously in the living room. She had the feeling he was hoping she'd ask him to stay and didn't want to have that conversation. At this point, she was so glad he was leaving she dreaded going back to Seattle.

As hard as it had been for her to face coming home to Coyote Canyon, she'd never dreamed she'd begin to feel the same about Seattle.

Telling herself they'd just gotten on each other's nerves, that once her stint in her hometown was behind her all would go back to normal, she packed up some of her mother's aunt's strawberry preserves as she heard him coming down the stairs.

"You're going to love this jam my great aunt put up. I'm sending a few jars home with you."

"Thanks." He peered into the bag she handed him before meeting her gaze. "I'm sorry I couldn't put what happened with Brant behind me. I tried, but…maybe with more time."

"Don't worry about it." She managed a smile. "Every relationship has its rough patches. We'll get through this."

He seemed relieved. "Yeah, I guess they do. See you when you get home."

She walked him out to his car, gave him a stilted hug and waved goodbye as he backed down the drive.

After he was gone, she waited for the remorse to hit her, a desire to chase him down and bring him back, but she felt only relief—the same kind of relief she'd felt when she'd escaped her three engagements, as if all she wanted to do was run and run and never look back.

Except this time she *had* to go back. They had a business together.

It wasn't until she stepped onto the porch and once again encountered Paul's botched fix on the screen door that she remembered Ellen wanted to hear from her.

Paul's gone, Talulah texted her neighbor. What's going on? Do you want to come back over?

Can't. Just got an out of water call.

What's that?

The pump's broke on a well I drilled. I need to get over there and fix it. I just wanted to show you a conversation I had with Brant this morning.

About?

You.

She sent a few screenshots of a text exchange she'd had with Brant and Talulah sank into the closest chair before making it larger so it'd be easier to read.

Brant: Any chance you can see if Paul's car is still at Ta-lulah's?

Ellen: What for?

Brant: I just want to know.

Ellen: Because you're jealous?

No answer.
A few minutes later, Ellen texted him again: Why don't you drive by like Charlie always does? [laughing emoji]

Brant: I'd rather not give in to that impulse.

Ellen: Asking me to check for you is the same thing. You realize that.

Brant: Never mind.

Ellen: OMG! Is this for real? You want to be with her?

No answer.

Ellen: The fact that you're skipping all the hard questions tells me something.

Brant: I don't want to talk about it.

Ellen: Because you don't like the answers?

Brant: Because I don't know the answers.

Ellen: You're acting strange. How can you not know what's causing your obsession?

Brant: The only thing I know for sure is that I wasn't ready for what we had to be over—and I want more carrot cake. Lol

Every beat of Talulah's heart seemed to reverberate through her body as she reread Brant's last text. She hadn't been ready for what they'd had, however brief it was, to end, either. But what'd happened so far had all but destroyed her relationship with Paul.

No way could she see Brant again.

"Paul's gone," Kurt said. "You know that, right?"

Brant was in the barn, oiling a new saddle, and refused to look over at his brother, who'd just finished brushing down the horses and mucking out the stalls. "So?" he said. It'd been four days since Paul went back to Seattle. Brant knew because Ellen had sent him a message when Paul left last Sunday, and Brant had spent every day since then watching his phone, hoping to hear from Talulah.

But she hadn't been in touch. That right there told him she wasn't feeling the same thing he was. And if she wasn't feeling the same thing, he had to let her go. Otherwise, he'd only get himself in deeper. Then when she went back to Seattle he'd feel even worse than he did now.

"I just thought you'd want to know." Kurt tossed the brush he'd been using onto a shelf. "You haven't been yourself since he came into town. I thought if you knew he was gone, maybe it'd help."

"I'm fine," Brant insisted.

His brother responded with a skeptical snort. "If that's

the case, why are you acting like a bear with a thorn in its paw?"

Brant straightened. "I'll get over it, okay?" He was trying to make that happen sooner rather than later, but it wasn't easy with Talulah still in town. Knowing she was *that* close kept him hanging on to the possibility that he'd see her again, even if he only bumped into her somewhere.

"Turns out I have just the thing to help," Kurt said.

Brant could hardly imagine what his brother was about to suggest. "I'm not interested."

"You'd rather keep sulking?"

Was that how he was coming across? Brant didn't want to be as annoying as Charlie. "What do you want me to do?" he asked grudgingly.

"I told Kate I'd take her and some of her friends to the lake on Saturday. I was hoping you'd come along."

"You need a wingman?"

"Sort of. Ranson's going to that bachelor party, but Miles will be joining us."

"Then why do you want me to go?"

Kurt grinned. "There'll be more girls than even I can handle, bro."

Brant couldn't help laughing. He considered Kate and her friends too young for him. But he figured waterskiing would be better than moping around the ranch, continuing to hope he'd hear from Talulah. "Okay, I'll go."

It was Friday afternoon when Jane came over to help Talulah pack up Phoebe's house, but they'd stopped working over an hour ago, prepared a big salad for dinner and were now sitting on the porch swing, enjoying the sunset with a glass of wine.

"You're really not going to call him?" Jane asked.

Talulah puffed out her cheeks before letting her breath

go. Jane had been trying to get her to open up about Brant for hours. Although Talulah had been able to dodge those questions so far, they weren't busy anymore, which meant she couldn't act too preoccupied to answer. "No."

"Why not? Kurt told Kate he'd never seen his brother quite so down. Brant cares about you, Lu. You're breaking his heart."

Talulah rolled her eyes. "That's a little dramatic. Are you forgetting that this is a man who's never had a steady girlfriend?"

"You're saying he doesn't have a heart?"

"I'm saying he guards it far too well to give me even a small piece of it. He'd *never* allow himself to fall for the woman he calls the runaway bride, because then the joke would be on him."

"I get the impression he's as surprised as we are—and that he knows the joke is on him."

Talulah gazed at the incredible array of lavender, orange and red on the horizon. She had to admit that, just like the stars, the sunsets here were some of the most beautiful she'd ever seen. "I doubt that. But even if it's true, it's better if he forgets me sooner rather than later."

Jane took a sip of her wine. "Why do you say that? You don't care about him?"

"Of course I do. That's why I'm staying away. I don't want to hurt him, too. I seem to hurt every man I get involved with. Paul and I can hardly say a civil word to each other these days."

"I heard you on the phone earlier," she said with a grimace. "I'm sorry."

"It's sad." Talulah drained her glass. "We got along so well before. And I have no idea how to patch things up. He still calls me every day, but we can barely get through a conversation without an argument." She stopped the swing long enough to put her glass down where she wouldn't knock it over. "Now we're even arguing about what's best for the diner. I swear…when I see his name pop up on my phone, I feel sick inside."

"But if you can't continue as you were with Paul, why not let yourself see Brant while you're here?"

Because there was something wrong with her. Because they wouldn't really have a chance. And because he'd be stupid to open his heart to someone like her. She didn't even want him to take the chance. "There are too many reasons to list," she said with a sigh. "You don't hop onto a train that's speeding toward a brick wall."

"How do you know this time won't be different?"

"Because now you have *two* people who aren't any good at commitment. Besides that complication, we live in different states. And…"

When she let her words dwindle away, Jane twisted around to face her. "And?"

"I've decided to try, once again, to make up with Averil, and I know I'll never be able to do that if I'm still seeing Brant."

Jane's eyes went wide. "Are you kidding me? After how she's treated you?"

"I think she might've been willing to let the past go. It was my involvement with Brant that made her hate me all over again. She wants him herself."

"You're assuming if you back off, she can have him? What was stopping them from getting together before you got here?"

"Even if they don't get together, at least she can't blame me for taking him from her. I wouldn't be happy if the woman who stood up my brother at the altar returned to town and started sleeping with the guy I've wanted since forever. Who would?"

"I get that. And you know I care about Averil, too. But…giving up Brant for her might be a bit much to ask."

"Not if it could never work out anyway."

"What did he say when you took the carrot cake over to him on Tuesday?" she asked, stopping the swing to put down her glass as Talulah had done.

She'd been talking to Jane on the phone while she was baking or Jane wouldn't have known about the cake. Talulah sort of regretted telling her. She wasn't sure why she'd been baking for him in the first place, except that she was dying to see him again. He was on her mind constantly. "I didn't take it to him."

"Why not?" she asked in surprise.

"Ellen had some friends over. When I drove past her place and saw all the cars, I decided it'd be better to give it to her for her company."

"But you made it for him!" Jane protested.

Talulah had actually baked another cake for Brant last night, and she hadn't delivered that one, either. Knowing it would be a mistake starting things up again, she'd bailed out and left it on Averil's doorstep instead. "I know, but… like I said, if I could make up with Averil while I'm here, I'd have a better chance of keeping that kind of a relationship than a romantic one." She frowned. "Averil's the only friend who's ever become an enemy. I can't say that about the men I've dated."

Jane scowled. "I hope she appreciates what you're doing."

"It's possible she won't. But even if she doesn't, I couldn't take a cake to Brant."

"Because…" Jane prodded.

"I was afraid it would start something again." Deep down she'd been dying for it to start something again. "And I don't want to disrupt his life. He was happy before I got here. I prefer to leave him that way." It was difficult enough to cope with the guilt she felt for crushing the three men she'd almost married. Now Paul, like them, was claiming he'd never forgive her. She didn't want Brant to end up hating her, too.

"I think you're making a mistake, Lu," Jane said. "I've never heard of Brant acting like this over a woman."

"If I back off now, he'll get over it in, like…a week." She snapped her fingers for emphasis. "And it's for the best. I'm not to be trusted. He'd be the first to tell you that."

"You could be selling yourself short."

"In what way?"

"Maybe it's just that you haven't met the right guy. For all you know, Brant could be the one. And, selfishly, I'd like to see you two get together, because then you'd move back to Coyote Canyon."

"And leave my business?" Talulah said with a laugh.

"You never know." She nudged Talulah's leg with hers. "How're your stitches healing?"

"They're starting to itch."

"That's a good sign. Can you get them wet?"

"I do it every day in the shower."

"I mean, like…in a lake?"

"I think so. Why?"

"Kate has a friend with a boat. She's invited us to go waterskiing with her tomorrow. Any interest?"

Talulah was feeling so much pressure to finish her great aunt's house in time, she didn't dare. "I'm behind. I should stay here and keep working. The attic was so full of junk it took me all week to sort through it."

"The rest should go quicker," Jane argued. "Come with me. Who knows when you'll be back in Coyote Canyon. We might as well have some fun while you're here. Besides, we won't be going until four."

Maybe she was taking life too seriously—always pushing, always worried. Telling herself to relax and live a little, Talulah smiled as she looped her arm through Jane's. "Okay."

Averil closed her eyes as she savored the buttery rich taste of the big slice of carrot cake in front of her. Her parents had taken Mitch to the grocery store with them, so she had a moment to enjoy it uninterrupted—until the front door banged opened and Charlie called out a hello.

Sheltering her plate with her arm, she stuffed a huge bite into her mouth, trying to finish before he could discover what she was eating. But, of course, he sniffed it out like a bloodhound and came directly into the kitchen. "Where'd you get that?" he asked.

She couldn't talk because of the food in her mouth, so she gestured at the fridge.

He pulled out the rest of the cake. "This looks delicious," he exclaimed as he cut himself a big piece. "Did you or Mom make it?"

She was tempted to say *she'd* made it. That would stop all the questions and let her go back to eating in peace. But she was afraid he'd mention the cake in front of their parents, who would know better. It was her mother who'd answered the doorbell last night to find no one there and the cake on the mat. "No."

"You bought it? Where?"

She swallowed the rest of what was in her mouth. "Someone left it on the doorstep last night."

"Who?"

She shrugged. "Someone from the church, I guess."

"What for?"

"I don't know."

He seemed mildly surprised, but willing to accept what

she'd said, at first. Then he looked back at the cake and a puzzled expression came over his face. "Wait a minute… It couldn't be someone from church. No one we know makes cakes this fancy, except…*Talulah*."

Averil had come to the same conclusion the moment her mother had carried it in last night. It was just easier to let herself enjoy it if she pretended there was still some question. "I don't think it was her," she said, adding a dose of skepticism she didn't really feel. "Why would Talulah bake for *us*?"

"I couldn't tell you, especially since she believes one of us threw a rock through her window and cut her arm."

Averil shot him a glance. "You're saying you didn't?"

He looked affronted. "Of course not. Did *you*?"

"No!" she said. "Why would I do something like that?"

"We both know why. You've always had a thing for Brant. When we were younger, anytime he came over, I couldn't get rid of you."

"I thought you wanted to see us together, too. You've told me a million times that he'd make a great father for Mitch."

Charlie seemed tempted to argue, but Averil knew he couldn't. He'd said that on numerous occasions. He just wasn't eager to pay Brant such a high compliment now that they weren't getting along. "This is definitely a Talulah cake," he said, changing the subject. "I've seen it on her website. And I've heard several people talk about the dinner she made for the funeral. They always mention the carrot cake as if it was something special."

And they were right. Averil had never tasted anything better. "So…if it *was* Talulah who gave it to us, does that mean you won't eat it?" she asked.

"After what she's done to me, I shouldn't," he said sulkily. "Was there a note?"

"No."

"Are you sure? It could've blown away. Because it's strange she wouldn't want credit for this."

"The cake itself tells us who it's from, right? But for all Talulah knows, we dumped it in the trash."

"That's how you justify eating it? Where are your ideals?" he asked, but grinned as he carried his plate over to the table.

She raised her eyebrows as he sat across from her and took his first bite. "Apparently in the same place as yours."

"Like you said, she'll never know."

Averil felt a slight twinge of discomfort for rolling over so easily. She'd been furious with Talulah since forever. But she wasn't nearly as upset as she'd been before. Word was going around town that Talulah had dumped Brant, and that brought so much relief she no longer cared about the ruined wedding fourteen years ago. *Current* disaster had been averted, and once Talulah left town and everything returned to normal, maybe Brant would realize he'd overlooked the one woman who'd loved him the longest and would make him the happiest. "We should let the past go," she said.

Charlie gaped at her. "You don't care about what she did to me anymore?"

Averil finished the last of her cake, even scraped the crumbs off her plate. What she'd never voiced to her brother was how much she'd missed Talulah. She just hadn't allowed herself to admit it over the years for fear she'd break down and call her. "I gave up one of my best friends because of what she did to you," she said softly. "But she's never done anything to me. And it's been fourteen years. Isn't that long enough to show my loyalty, Charlie?"

He didn't answer right away. "It doesn't make things any easier on me that everyone else likes her so much," he finally said, using his fork to move the frosting around on his cake.

"I know. And I'm sorry. But I've been feeling left out myself. Jane keeps going over to Phoebe's, where Talulah's staying, and the honest truth is I'd like to go with her."

He frowned, but eventually, regretfully, shrugged. "If you want to be friends with her again, I'll understand."

"I think it would be nice to at least explore the possibility." She imagined hanging out at Phoebe's—imagined it once again being the three of them, laughing and enjoying each other like old times—and felt a flicker of hope. With a little forgiveness and a lot of effort, they might be able to salvage what they'd once had.

As long as Talulah stayed away from Brant.

Once Talulah had agreed to go to the lake, she started getting excited about it. But she hadn't brought a swimsuit to Coyote Canyon. She had to wake up early and run over to Bozeman to find one.

She ended up buying a bikini with a top that laced up in back, and she chose white because it made the most of the slight suntan she'd been able to get this summer hiking with Paul. She also picked up some white-framed sunglasses, a pair of red flip-flops and a red-and-white tote bag she could use to carry her sunblock, a T-shirt and a pair of shorts.

It was noon by the time she finished shopping, but she hadn't heard from Paul all morning. He was probably extra-busy at the diner, trying to get ready for the busiest night of the week—he'd had a lot of catching up to do after being away—but the relief she felt was weird. She was glad she didn't have to talk to him...

She hated that something so important to her future had changed, but Jane kept sending her funny memes in anticipation of their getaway, and Talulah was somehow happier than she'd been in a long time. She'd thought she was perfectly satisfied in Seattle. But she was realizing just how out of balance her life had become. She'd allowed it to narrow down to her work and the hikes she went on with Paul. Being away from it all—not even hearing from him—left her feeling as though she'd broken free from something oppressive.

She called Debbie on the drive back to see how things were going. She'd been checking on her sister every day, so she knew both mother and baby were home, trying to adjust to their new schedules, and felt guilty that she hadn't been back to see them. "You get any sleep last night?" she asked.

"It wasn't too bad," Debbie told her. "Abby got up twice to nurse, but went right back down each time."

"That's lucky. Does Scott ever get up with her?"

"No. Since he can't nurse her, anyway, he says one of us might as well get some sleep."

"He could bring the baby to you and take her back to bed," Talulah pointed out. "Some dads do that."

"He never did anything like that with our other kids, and he's not going to change now. At least he kicks in later, when they get a little older."

"Women have to do *all* the hard stuff," Talulah joked. "It's so unfair."

"It really is," her sister said, laughing with her. "Any word from Mom?"

"Not since I gave her a recap of the funeral. I'll check in with her again tomorrow. Sunday's our day to catch up. Have you heard from her?"

"She's called a few times to ask about Abby. And I've sent pics. How's everything going with the house?"

"It's getting there, but slowly."

"Once I'm back on my feet, I'll bring the kids and come help."

Talulah couldn't imagine they'd get anything done with three kids to care for and a newborn, as well, but she was eager to see them. "You don't need to help. I'd love to see you all. Let me know when you can make it, and I'll prepare dinner for everyone."

"That sounds good. No one can cook like you do. Have you heard from Brant?"

Her question dimmed the bright glow of Talulah's happiness. "No. I'm trying to stay away from him, remember?"

"I remember. But part of me is like…when will you ever get this opportunity again?"

"What?" Talulah said, cracking up. *"This* is coming from my straitlaced sister?"

"Well, we are talking about *Brant*, and you only live once," she joked.

"I've been tempted to look at it that way," Talulah admitted. "But what about Averil?"

"What about her? The fact that she could hold a grudge for so long doesn't speak highly of her."

"I hurt her brother, Deb."

"From what you've told me, the way she's behaved lately has more to do with Brant."

"That's partly why I've decided to back away from him."

"Even though it's an unnecessary sacrifice? Let's face it. If he wanted her, he's had plenty of opportunity."

"That's not the point. The point is that even if she doesn't get him, she wouldn't want him to be with *me*."

"Then what kind of friend could she be?"

Talulah slid her new sunglasses higher on her nose. "I don't know. All I can say is that I miss having her in my life." She missed Brant, too. Every night she had to overcome the urge to call him. But she didn't add that. "Anyway, I'm only here for another week or two, so it's very likely neither one of them will end up being part of my life."

"Well, if you have to pick one or the other, I vote for Brant."

Talulah pulled into the parking lot at the lake, where she was supposed to meet Jane, Kate and whoever else Kate had invited. "Duly noted." She turned off the car and grabbed the tote where she'd stuffed a towel and all the things she wanted to bring with her. "I have to hang up. Jane's invited me to go boating."

"That sounds like fun. Have a great time."

She said goodbye to Debbie, climbed out and headed down to the water, where she immediately spotted Jane and Kate on shore. Jane was wearing a black one-piece cut high on the leg and Kate looked great in the skimpiest string bikini Talulah had ever seen. Both of them wore sunglasses and held big striped towels.

"You look incredible," Jane said as Talulah approached.

"Thanks. So do both of you. Where're your other friends?" Talulah asked Kate.

"At the boat launch." She gestured to a ski boat two men were taking off a trailer not far away.

"Wait! That's Brant's brother," Talulah said as soon as they got close enough for her to see Kurt clearly.

"Yeah, of course," Kate said as if she was surprised Talulah wouldn't be expecting him. "It's the Elways' boat. Miles is Brant's brother, too."

She would've turned to Jane to see what was going on. But it'd dawned on her that the truck attached to the trailer belonged to Brant. He was sitting in the driver's seat, looking at her through the open window he'd been using to help back the boat down the launch. His gaze connected with hers. Then his jaw hardened and he looked away.

Twenty

"I can't believe you did this," Brant muttered, keeping his voice low so no one else could hear.

Kurt had walked back to the truck to get the cooler. "Did what?" he said, but the grin stretching across his face made it obvious he was playing games.

"You *know* what, damn it."

"Whoa! What's wrong with you?" Kurt said, sobering. "I did you a favor, bro. You've been moping around for a week, and now she's right here. You can thank me later."

Thank him? You didn't get over a woman by staring at her in a bikini. But Kurt had already hefted the cooler out of the back and was carrying it to the boat, so Brant didn't have the opportunity to voice any more of his displeasure.

"All clear," Miles called out a moment later, letting Brant know he could go park.

Briefly, Brant considered driving off and leaving them all at the lake. He hadn't signed on for an entire evening with Talulah, especially because she'd looked just as shocked to see him as he was her.

Cursing the entire time he circled the lot, he finally found a spot big enough for both the truck and the trailer and sat there for a few minutes, trying to regain his equilibrium. He couldn't leave. Someone who didn't care whether Talulah was around or not would never react in such a volatile way, which meant he could only slap a smile on his face and act as though she was no different to him than any other woman.

He could manage that for four to five hours, couldn't he?

Since the answer had to be yes, he got out and strode down to the boat, where everyone was waiting for him. He could feel Talulah's gaze as he approached, but he refused to glance her way. He'd just ignore her, he told himself, and try to enjoy the sun, the water and the skiing.

Then, when it was all behind him and he got back home, he'd let his brother know he didn't appreciate being tricked.

Talulah felt unwanted and out of place. Brant wouldn't even look at her. He took the driver's seat, which put his back to her most of the time, and found a section of calm water so everyone could ski.

Kurt and Miles skied like pros, and Jane and Kate weren't bad, considering they'd had far less experience. Jane tried to talk Talulah into going when they were done, but she insisted she preferred to ride in the boat and watch others. She'd only been skiing one other time in her life, many years ago, and it hadn't been a success.

Miles took over at the wheel so Brant could ski, and like his brothers, he did so flawlessly.

"Are you mad at me?" Jane whispered while he was out of the boat and couldn't hear her. After getting out of the water, she'd wrapped herself in a towel.

Talulah frowned. She didn't want to say anything in front of the Elway brothers, who kept glancing over. "We'll talk about it later."

"I'm sorry," she murmured. "I thought it would be a fun surprise."

It wasn't that Talulah didn't want to see Brant. She did. She was just so conflicted about how her actions would affect the people around her, including him. "It was definitely a surprise," she said.

When Brant signaled that he was done, Kurt made his way over to her. "Aren't you at least going to *try* to ski?"

She could tell he was frustrated by her refusal. "I'm not good at it. I tried once before."

"It'd be worth trying again," he said, and after Brant got back in the boat, even Kate and Jane insisted she make the effort. Jane said that all she had to do was grip the rope handles and push the ski against the pressure of the water once the boat started to accelerate, and she'd "pop up."

They made it sound easy. They made it look easy, too. But once she got out in the cold water and was hanging on to the rope, she found she'd been right all along: it wasn't easy. Brant had taken over driving again—she had the impression he was their main driver—but as soon as he gave the boat some gas, the ski wobbled beneath her, then cut out to the side, where it was ripped off by the rushing water, and she was dragged behind the boat until she remembered to let go of the rope.

She'd tried four times and drank far more lake water than she deemed healthy by the time she decided to give up. When Brant circled around, and Kurt lifted the rope to throw it out to her again, she yelled, "I can't do it. I feel like an idiot, making you go in circles. It's okay. Someone else can take a turn."

The ski had come off again during her last spill, but she'd managed to grab it. She was trying to hand it up to Miles when Brant said something to Kurt that must've been, "Here, you drive," or something like that, because he suddenly dived off the side and swam over to her.

"What are you doing?" she asked. "You don't have to help me. I can tell you don't even want me to be here."

"You have no idea what I want," he said with a scowl. "But back to skiing. You're trying too hard. Relax and lean back. Let the boat do the rest."

"I hate that you're mad at me," she said.

"I'm not mad at you. I—" He seemed to think better of making that statement. "Never mind. Come here."

She shivered as he adjusted the shoes on the ski, making them fit more snugly. "Remember, let the boat do the work," he said as he helped her put the ski back on. "Just sit in the water, draw your knees into your chest and let the tension slowly pull you up. I wish I had two skis, so I could start you out that way. It'd be easier for you. But it's been a long time since we brought a beginner. I don't even know where those old skis went."

He motioned for Kurt to throw him the rope and held on to it for her as the boat taxied slowly away from them, far enough to straighten the line. "You've been crashing right before you succeed. If you could keep the ski under you for another second or two, you'd have it."

Getting behind her, he pulled her into the chair he formed with his body so she could get in the proper position. "See? Like this," he said. "Now relax. Are you relaxed?"

"I'm kind of scared, to be honest," she said, her teeth chattering.

"There's nothing to be scared of. If you get in trouble, all you have to do is remember to let go of the rope. But that won't be necessary this time because you're going to get up."

"What about you?" she asked. "Why aren't you swimming back to the boat?"

"Because you're shaking too badly. I'm going to hold you steady, so you'll have a better chance."

"Is that safe? What if another boat comes along and doesn't see you?"

"My brother won't strand me out here. If you get up, he'll just pull you in a circle around me until you're tired."

"Are you *sure* that's okay?"

He didn't answer. He seemed to know she wasn't only worried for his well-being, she was throwing up another excuse to procrastinate her next attempt. Holding her against the firm framework of his body, he signaled for Kurt to hit the gas and let go.

The engine roared, the rope yanked her arms and the pressure of the water hit her ski at all once, causing her to wobble like she had before. She thought she was going down again, but remembering what Brant had said, she fought to straighten her ski and keep it underneath her for a little longer—and it worked. The next thing she knew, she was flying across the water like those who'd skied before her.

She wanted to look at Brant in triumph, but she knew she'd fall if she did. She hung on for dear life as Kurt made a wide circle, exactly as Brant had predicted he would. They went around twice. Then, once she got close to Brant again, she let go.

"I did it!" she said as she sank into the water, this time with her ski intact. "Did you see me?"

He swam the short distance between them since she couldn't maneuver very well. "I did."

"You're smiling," she pointed out in surprise.

"I'm proud of you. And I figure you have enough people mad at you," he added with a shrug.

"I do. Thanks for not piling on."

He sobered as he studied her. "Did you give Paul the commitment he's been after? Is that why you haven't called me?"

She wiped the water from her face. "No. I haven't called because I suck at romantic relationships, and you know it. You're better off without me."

He lowered his voice. "What if I don't want to be without you? You have a phobia about getting stuck with the wrong person, but I don't care. I want you. What do you say to that? Do you ever think of me?"

"Only every second," she told him glumly.

His smile reappeared, this one much broader. "That's my girl."

His girl. When Paul said things like that, it bothered her. But when Brant did it, she went positively gooey inside. "The odds are stacked against us, and I don't want it to end badly."

He met her gaze. "I wish I could promise you it wouldn't. Maybe I'll get my heart broken for the first time. Maybe you will. But we'll have one hell of a good time before the big crash."

"Do you have to use the word *crash*?" she asked.

"We're brave enough," he insisted. "Don't you think? We'll risk it together."

She was in an impossible situation. And yet her hand found his hand, and a sense of contentment filled her as they laced their fingers together. "What about Charlie and Averil and Paul?" she asked. "There will definitely be repercussions."

"If it'll make you feel safe enough to give our relationship a chance, we'll be more careful this time. No one else will have to know we're seeing each other."

"Okay."

"Hey! What're you guys doing out there?" Miles yelled. "Are either of you ever going to ski?"

"Do you want to ski again?" he asked her.

Talulah didn't bother to answer. Her mind was on something else entirely—all the times in the past few days she'd talked herself out of calling Brant, and yet here she was with him anyway. That effort had turned out to be a waste. It hadn't changed anything. She still wanted him as badly as she ever had.

Almost before she knew what she was going to do, she leaned over and brushed her lips against his.

He looked shocked when their eyes met afterward, and everyone on the boat started cheering. "What happened to keeping it a secret?" he asked as he started to laugh.

She didn't have a good answer. "I don't know. I've wanted to do that since I first saw you glowering at me from inside your truck. I guess I acted impulsively."

"That's fine with me. I actually prefer full transparency. If anyone has a problem with us being together, they'll just have to get over it," he said and, ignoring the fact that they had an audience, he grabbed her by the life vest with both hands, hauled her up against him and kissed her soundly.

Brant had never had so much fun. After they quit skiing, they docked the boat and had a barbecue on shore, where he grilled hot dogs and burgers and Kurt pulled a potato salad and a fruit salad he'd purchased at the local grocery store out of the cooler.

"We should all have brought something," Talulah said as she sat next to Brant on a tree trunk, her plate in hand.

"We have everything we need," Brant said and leaned over to whisper something else. "Kurt took care of it all. In case you couldn't tell, he's trying to impress Kate."

She gave him a sly smile. "After watching them together today, I think it's working, don't you?"

"I don't know. It can be hard to tell with a woman."

When she elbowed him in the ribs, he laughed and said, "Ouch! Here I am, nice enough to take you back, and you do *that*?"

"You're lucky to have me back," she said, shooting him a sulky look.

She was obviously teasing, too, but Brant *did* feel lucky. He was also grateful that they had this time away from town, that they were with people who had their best interests at heart and that they didn't have to worry about all the drama that'd caused Talulah to shut him out.

After they finished eating, Talulah got up and went to the edge of the water to wash her hands, since Kurt had forgotten to bring napkins, while Brant remained on the tree trunk, unable to take his eyes off her.

"If that isn't a dreamy expression I don't know what is," Jane said, sitting down beside him.

He slid over to give her more room. "I can't believe you and Kurt planned this out in advance. What a dirty trick."

"We had to do something! You were both being so damn stubborn."

"I'm glad it worked out."

"So am I."

She picked up a stick and began to draw in the dirt. "So...you have two weeks before she has to go. Will that be enough?"

"I don't know," he said. "I'll think about what comes next later. At least I have two weeks. That's more than I had this morning."

"I've never seen you like this," she said, looking mildly bemused.

He didn't like other people getting involved in his business, so he usually held his cards much closer to his chest. It wasn't entirely clear to him why he hadn't done a better job of that when it came to Talulah. She'd taken him by surprise somehow—in every way. "Yeah, well, let's hope I don't end up like Charlie."

"Mad at her, you mean?"

Seeing Talulah shake the water off her hands and start back toward them, he lowered his voice. "Mooning after her for the rest of my life."

Jane chuckled. "If anybody can convince her to stay, it'd be you."

"You might have too much confidence in me."

Jane looked from Talulah to him and back again. "I don't think so."

"What are you two talking about?" Talulah asked, grabbing her beach towel so she could finish drying her hands.

"I was saying that the world is full of possibilities," Jane said with a wink and went to get more food.

Twenty-One

Talulah was so caught up in the afterglow of a wonderful evening spent sitting on the shore of the lake, watching the sun go down with Brant, that it took her a moment to snap out of that heady, euphoric zone when she returned home at seven thirty and found a beige Altima in her drive. At first, she thought the car was sitting empty. But as she pulled past it to reach the garage, the driver lifted her head, and by the time she'd parked, Averil had gotten out and taken her little boy from his booster seat in back.

Talulah felt the smile she'd been wearing for the past several hours slip from her face, and a lump grew in the pit of her stomach. "Averil."

"Surprise!" Averil said with an uncomfortable chuckle. "Sorry to just…show up. It probably would've been less awkward to call, but I felt it was only right to pay you a visit."

Talulah could still taste the kiss Brant had given her when he'd walked her to her car. Because she knew how Averil would feel about their being together, guilt washed over her as she knelt to speak to Averil's child. "This is your little boy? I mean, I know it is. I saw him at the funeral. What a cutie!"

Averil ruffled his hair. "Yeah, this is Mitch. Can you say hi, buddy?"

"Hi," he mumbled shyly, staring at his feet.

Talulah tilted up his chin. "I can see so much of you in him," she told Averil.

Averil continued to smooth his hair. "He looks a lot more like his daddy than he does me."

"Where does his daddy live?"

"Cash is in California, doing his own thing." She sighed. "We don't hear from him very often."

It'd been so long since Talulah had looked Averil square in the face that she couldn't help noticing the slight changes a decade and a half had wrought in her former friend—the crow's-feet starting to form at her eyes, the faint smile lines around her mouth, the few silver strands of hair mixed in with the brown. "I'm sorry things didn't work out for the two of you. Divorce is never easy. Where'd you meet him?"

Averil didn't seem comfortable holding Talulah's gaze and watched her own fingers move through her son's hair as she responded. "At Montana State. He was on the baseball team. I thought he was such a good catch—pun intended," she said with the quirky expression Talulah remembered so well. "But he was a player all the way around."

Despite their differences since the botched wedding, Talulah hated the thought of Averil being hurt. "He liked the ladies?"

She nodded. "And they liked him."

"I'm so sorry."

"I'm mostly over it," she said with a shrug and glanced at the house. "Do you mind if we come in for a few minutes? I think it's time you and I had a talk."

Talulah's mouth went so dry she could hardly speak. She was expecting Brant in an hour, as soon as he'd helped take care of the boat and grabbed a shower. She'd been planning to shower herself and then bake a carrot cake, since he hadn't gotten either of the two she'd made for him this week. But how could she deny Averil a few minutes, when this was the first friendly overture she'd made in fourteen years? "Um… Sure. Of course. The house is a bit of a mess… I've been…packing."

Averil made a face. "I don't care about that."

"Okay." Talulah withdrew her house key, and as they started up the walk, Averil gestured at the cardboard-covered window.

"I'm sorry about what happened, by the way. And I'm aware of the rumors that've been going around. But I want you to know it wasn't me who threw that rock."

"I'm glad to hear it." She knew Averil had been unhappy with her, but unhappy enough to do something like that? This was the friend who, besides Jane, had been closest to her. The three of them had spent almost every Friday night together. Talulah had even received her first kiss at Averil's house—and not from Charlie. Allen Bond, a boy in their Spanish class, had snuck over to play spin the bottle when they were only thirteen. Talulah had her first period that same week, and it was Averil who'd shielded her all the way to the girls' bathroom and then gone to the principal's office to call Talulah's mom.

Talulah had so many fond memories of Averil, including the planning and shopping they'd done together for the wedding. They'd been excited to become sisters as well as best friends—until Talulah had ruined it, of course. But Averil was part of the reason Talulah hadn't been able to back out sooner. Their friendship had held her fast. And once she *did* break the engagement, she'd felt so adrift she'd grabbed on to two different men, one after the other, searching for an anchor—her place in the world—and wound up realizing they weren't right for her, either.

She'd had to learn how to make it on her own, separate from her family and her hometown and her longtime friends, and without the security of being with a man who was in love with her. Now she'd accomplished that, but she was still so traumatized by her early foray into adulthood that she wasn't convinced she could promise *anyone* forever. She already knew she'd never felt anything like what she felt for Brant—that level of excitement, the deep satisfaction that came from just looking at him. But she had no idea whether it would or could last. She'd have to give up so much to be with him, only to find herself right back in the same town she'd left. And he could easily "bail out," as he put it, before things got *too* serious, all of which meant the decisions she was making were more difficult than they should've been.

Would it be a mistake to risk losing Averil again for two weeks with Brant? Or did what she felt for Brant deserve a chance, no matter what it did to her odds of reconciling with Averil?

"Would you like something to drink? A glass of wine?" Talulah asked, unlocking the door and flipping on the light. "I have some orange juice for Mitch."

"That'd be great. Thanks."

Averil gestured at the settee in the living room. "Have a seat. I'm going to run up and change, but I'll make it quick."

"You've been swimming?" Averil seemed to notice her bikini for the first time. It'd been dark outside, and her mind was probably on other things. After all, showing up here meant she was breaking ranks with Charlie and the rest of the family—which wouldn't be easy to do.

"Jane and I went to the lake." Talulah held her breath, hoping Averil would let it go at that. A lot of people went up to the lake to hang out, swim and barbecue. But if Averil knew that Jane's sister and Kurt were starting to see each other, she might've made the connection to the Elways' boat, and Brant, which was why Talulah hadn't mentioned Kate's name.

Fortunately, Mitch reached for a porcelain rose Phoebe had displayed on a side table, distracting Averil. "No, buddy. Don't touch. That could break," Talulah heard her say as she hurried up the stairs.

Talulah *was* eager to get out of her suit, which was damp and uncomfortable, especially given the cooler temperatures at night, but she also craved a moment of privacy she could use to text Brant.

Hey, you're never going to believe it, but Averil was sitting in my drive when I got home. She wanted to come in and talk. Do you mind holding off for a while?

Hoping for a quick response, Talulah tossed her phone on the bed while she changed.

Fortunately, he'd answered by the time she'd yanked on a pair of yoga pants and a Pike Place Market sweatshirt.

I can wait. No worries. Hope it goes well. Are you going to tell her about me? [grimace emoji]

If I tell her about you, it won't go well. I think I'll just see what she has to say, at least for tonight.

Okay.

Talulah pulled her hair into a quick ponytail before leaving her phone in her room—on purpose—and hurrying back down to the living room.

Averil was looking at the photographs of old relatives that lined the walls, including one of Talulah's grandma and grandpa. "What are you going to do with the house once you get everything packed?" she asked.

"Put it up for sale."

"That's kind of a shame, isn't it? This is such a cool place."

Talulah had been so focused on burrowing through what she had to get done that she'd taken little time to consider the house itself, only the clutter inside it. She had to admit, however, that refurbished and updated, it could be as nice as some of the farmhouses depicted in decorating magazines. "It doesn't have a master bedroom, but that could be fixed."

"I wish *I* had the money to buy it."

Talulah went into the kitchen to get Mitch's juice and pour them each a glass of wine. "How's it going living with your folks again?" she called out.

"It's not easy. I mean…it's great that I have people around who can help with Mitch. My parents watch him while I'm working at the bank. But being home has its downside, too."

"It *would* be difficult to go back once you've been out on your own." Talulah knew she wouldn't like it, either.

"Exactly. If I give Mitch a treat, I feel like they're thinking he shouldn't have it. If I let him stay up past his bedtime, I can feel their disapproval. If I don't wake up to feed him breakfast right away, they jump up to do it, then get mad at me, when he would've been fine for thirty minutes without their intervention, you know? I hate not having my own place."

"You'll get out on your own again soon."

"I hope so. For now, staying with them is helping me a lot—especially with babysitting and my finances—so I feel bad even complaining." She threw up her hands. "There's no winning."

"Here you go, honey," Talulah said to Mitch as she gave him a small plastic cup partially filled with orange juice.

Averil tapped his shoulder. "What do you say?"

"Thank you," he murmured, mostly into the cup.

Talulah handed Averil her wine in a tumbler. "These aren't wineglasses, but they'll have to do."

"No problem." She took a sip. "This is good. So was that carrot cake you made, by the way."

Talulah sat on a side chair and tucked her legs underneath her. "I'm glad you enjoyed it."

"Charlie came by. He had some, too."

"He did?" Talulah said in surprise. "Did he know *I* made it?"

Averil sank onto the settee across from her, and Mitch demanded to be pulled into his mother's lap. "He did."

"I'm sorry about the wedding, Av," Talulah said. "I hurt Charlie, and I hurt you, too, and I feel terrible about it."

"You know... I was up most of last night thinking about the wedding and everything that led up to it."

Talulah caught her breath. "And?"

Averil stared at the carpet for a moment before responding. "We were so young—just kids, really. It's hard to get anything right at that age. Heck, getting things right can be hard as an adult. Take my marriage, for example." She lifted her gaze. "I owe you an apology, too—for holding you so accountable for your mistakes. Lord knows I've made a few of my own."

Talulah smiled, but she wasn't sure how or what to feel. She was so torn. She was grateful for the forgiveness Averil was offering her and eager to welcome someone she'd loved so much back into her life. And yet...what did making up with Averil mean for her and Brant?

* * *

Despite having her five-year-old with her, it was almost eleven by the time Averil woke Mitch, who'd fallen asleep while they talked, and left. Talulah thought it was probably too late to see Brant. She was disappointed, and yet it had been cathartic catching up with her old friend, hearing about Averil's marriage and motherhood and sympathizing with the part of Averil's story about returning to Coyote Canyon with a broken heart. Talulah had dreamed about a conversation just like the one they'd had, sharing their joy and pain as if they'd never lost their friendship.

She loved Averil *and* Brant, she realized—loved Brant in a way she'd never loved Paul. But after finding it hard to fall in love, she was skeptical that what she was feeling could be real. Could it happen that fast and that easily? Or was this another false reading, the excitement of a new relationship snatching her out of the doldrums? Something she'd regret later?

She sighed as she watched Averil's taillights disappear down the road. Then she climbed the stairs to check her phone. It'd been four hours since she'd messaged Brant, and yet he'd texted her only once in all that time.

I hope everything's going okay with Averil. Heading to bed. Left a key under the mat for you, if you're interested. [heart emoji]

Instead of being mad at her for not getting back to him sooner, he'd been kind and understanding and supportive. She was trying to find the place where she truly belonged—if it wasn't with Paul in Seattle—but she didn't want to hurt anyone. Brant seemed to take her good intentions for granted, to assume the best, and didn't feel the need to rail at her because of his own disappointment or the inconvenience she'd caused him. Maybe that wouldn't have been a big deal to anyone else, but Talulah knew Paul would've complained that she hadn't told Averil she had previous plans, and was grateful for Brant's generosity. It made her love him all the more.

"What am I going to do?" she said with a groan. She had no answer to that question. But she knew that for now, she was going to risk a visit to the ranch, even though someone could see her and tell Averil. She craved Brant's warm body pressed reassuringly against hers.

His text had come in at ten. He was most likely asleep by now. But she wrote him back, anyway: I'm coming.

The moment Talulah climbed into bed with him, Brant reached for her. He hadn't planned on waking up, not fully. He was just going to pull her into his arms. But she was completely naked. That was the first thing he noticed. And the way she kissed his neck and face let him know she was interested in more than sleeping.

"Everything go okay with Averil?" he mumbled.

"Yeah." She nuzzled his neck. "It lasted longer than I expected, though. I'm sorry."

"It's okay. What happened?"

"It was actually good. She seems willing to move on and forgive me."

But they both knew if they kept seeing each other, that probably wouldn't last. Which reminded him… "Where'd you park?"

She pressed her lips to his temple, his forehead, his jaw. "I pulled around behind the barn. I hope that's okay."

"It's fine. I'd be willing to camouflage your car with tree branches, if I had to," he said.

"You think Charlie might be watching us that closely?"

"I wouldn't put it past him. But let's not talk about Charlie." He kissed her arm where she had her stitches, still angry that Charlie or Averil had thrown that rock.

"I'm sorry for waking you up. I should've waited until tomorrow to see you, but I couldn't," she admitted.

He let his hands slide up over her soft curves before rolling her beneath him. "Believe me, I'm glad you're here."

"Do you think we're out of our minds to trust each other?" she asked, catching his face so he had to look at her.

It was dark, but moonlight cast everything in a silvery glow, providing just enough light that he could see she was worried. He couldn't blame her. When it came to love, she didn't have the best reputation and neither did he. "Who said I trust you?" he teased.

"You don't?"

"Hopefully trust will come for both of us. I *am* crazy about you, though, so there's that." Pinning her hands above her head, he pressed inside her and was shocked, as her body accepted his, by the strength of his own emotions. He'd been joking around, but there was something very serious going on between them. How could she have come to mean so much to him—and in such a short time? Charlie's runaway bride?

"Yes, this is what I need." She drew his face down to hers. "I need *you*," she said, and kissed him.

Twenty-Two

Talulah's phone went off, waking her early Sunday morning. She yawned and stretched, and Brant began to stir, too, but she could tell he wasn't eager to wake up when he covered his head with a pillow.

She wished she could do the same, wished she could fall back into the comfortable, warm, dreamless sleep she'd experienced since they'd made love. But the person blowing up her phone wouldn't stop. As soon as her voice mail picked up, whoever it was would hang up and call again.

"Sounds like someone's anxious to reach you," Brant said with a yawn, shoving aside the pillow.

"Might be my mother. The time difference between here and Sierra Leone is so big she tends to call at odd hours. And Sunday is our day to catch up." The last thing she wanted was to speak to her mother while she was naked in bed with Brant, though. "I'll call her back."

Rolling over, she got her phone from her purse on the nightstand to turn off the ringer, at least—but hesitated when she saw who'd been so determined to reach her. It was Paul.

He hadn't called all day yesterday. What could he want

this early in the morning? It was even an hour earlier in Seattle.

"Don't tell me it's Averil," Brant said.

"No, but it's not my mother."

"Let me guess. Paul?"

"Yeah."

"You going to answer it?"

She didn't want to. She'd enjoyed the break. But… "It could be about the diner."

"Wouldn't he text you if it was an emergency?"

The way he'd behaved the last time he was upset with her, leading her to believe their business had no managerial support, didn't give her a great deal of confidence that he'd go to the extra effort. She could already hear him justifying himself for not texting. *"I tried to reach you. You wouldn't pick up."*

"To be honest, I don't know," she told Brant.

He got out of bed. "I don't mind if you feel you should take the call. I have to go to the bathroom, anyway."

Just in case Paul needed to talk to her about an employee emergency, or a myriad of other potential problems, she hit the talk button. "Hello?"

"You couldn't call *me* for once?" he demanded without preamble. "Not even to check on the diner?"

Damn it. This was more personal bullshit. "Paul, I'm half-asleep. Are you really going to start an argument at… what?" She checked the time on her phone. "Six in the morning? *Five* your time?"

"I'm up doing all the baking for *our* diner. Why shouldn't you be up, too?"

He did have quite a bit of work to accomplish each morning, work they typically did together. But she was going to return the favor, and he knew it. "I'll be handling all the baking on my own next month, won't I?"

"Yeah, but I'll be hiking with friends, not banging other women."

Talulah squeezed her eyes closed. "I'm going to ignore that." She cleared her throat as Brant came back to bed. "I've been preoccupied, I admit. There's a lot going on here."

"A lot going on? You call packing up your aunt's junk on a Saturday a lot going on?"

"I didn't pack yesterday. I spent the majority of my time with Jane. I don't get to see her very often when I'm in Seattle. And then Averil showed up at my place last night. We talked until late."

"Are you saying you're no longer seeing Brant? That he isn't part of what's keeping you so busy?"

Paul knew she hadn't talked to Averil, her former best friend, for fourteen years. It'd been a source of pain and loss all that time, since before he met her. And yet he didn't care enough about that to let what she'd said even register. "Paul…"

"Are you still seeing him?" Paul said, raising his voice.

Talulah could tell Brant had heard, because he lifted his head from the pillow in sudden interest. "Paul, please," she said.

"Answer the question," Paul insisted.

She considered the implications of her response, how an admission could potentially impact the diner—*their* diner. But doing the right thing was more important than any business. She wanted to be fair and honest with Paul. "Yes."

Brant was watching her closely as he slid up against the headboard.

"You're sleeping with him," Paul said as if he'd known it all along and yet couldn't believe it.

Talulah gripped her phone tighter. "Paul, I never expected this to happen. I—"

"You know what? That's it. As far as I'm concerned, you can go to hell," he said and hung up.

Dropping her phone in her lap, she leaned her head back and closed her eyes.

Brant took her hand and kissed her fingers. "Are you okay?"

She didn't open her eyes, but she nodded.

"I can't believe you told him about us."

"Should I have lied?" she asked miserably, finally looking over at him.

"I'm glad you didn't."

"Because…"

"It proves that you're taking what's happening between us seriously."

But…should she? That was the question.

A knock sounded on Brant's door. "Hey, Talulah!"

Shocked that anyone else knew she was in the room, Talulah turned to Brant for an explanation.

"It's Miles," he said, seemingly unconcerned.

"I know who it is. But how does he know I'm here?"

"Maybe he heard us talking. Or he went out to check on the cattle and saw your car behind the barn."

In case Miles opened the door, she pulled the bedding higher before answering him. "Yes?"

"So many people have told me you can cook."

"Um… I have a culinary degree," she said. "I'd like to think I can cook."

"Great. Any chance you'd consider making breakfast?"

"Whoa, Miles," Brant said, but Talulah waved him off. The prospect of getting to know Brant's brothers, of cooking them a meal, appealed to her, enough that she decided to put her most recent spat with Paul out of her mind. Whenever she was with Brant, she had a wonderful time.

And they had only fourteen days left. Why let anything ruin it?

She'd just have to pick up the pieces of her life after that. "Sure," she called back. "When do you want to eat?"

"Any time you'd be willing to leave Brant's bed," he said.

"It might be a while," Brant called out, jumping into the conversation.

"*If* I can force myself," Talulah said, joining in on the joke, "what do you want me to make?"

"We'll eat anything," Miles told her. "You choose."

"If all you have in the fridge is a jug of milk, there might not be much I can do."

"We're pretty well-stocked," Brant volunteered.

"So you're supportive of this plan?" she said to him.

A boyish grin crept onto his face. "I'm starving."

"Then I'll see what I can do." She got up and pulled on her panties along with one of Brant's T-shirts, which came halfway to her knees, and opened the door.

"You're going to do it?" Miles said when he saw her.

"I'm going to do it," she confirmed and went down the hall to see what they had in the kitchen.

She found a package of English muffins on the counter, something she hadn't expected them to have, which gave her an idea—as long as she could find the rest of the necessary ingredients.

Brant came into the kitchen a few minutes later, wearing only a pair of faded jeans and looking as sexy as she'd ever seen a man look. "Do we have everything you need?" he asked. "If not, I could run over to the Quick Mart at the gas station."

The gas station would just have the basics, but the brothers had eggs, butter, Dijon mustard, lemon juice and cayenne pepper—everything she needed to make a good hollandaise sauce. "I've got it," she said.

Brant scratched his chest. "What can I do to help?"

"Nothing, really," she said as she measured various ingredients into a saucepan.

He came up behind her while she was using a fork in lieu of a wire whisk to mix the sauce, slid his arms around her waist and nuzzled her neck. "You look so damn good in my shirt. I can't believe I didn't try to keep you in bed a little longer."

She leaned back into him. "You must like food as much as sex."

"No way."

"Well, you haven't tasted my eggs benedict," she said.

"I've tasted *you*. And nothing could be sweeter." She got goose bumps as he pulled her earlobe into his mouth. But then he stepped away; they heard someone coming.

"Smells great in here." Ranson stopped dead in his tracks when he saw her at the stove. "Well, damn. I didn't realize we had so much company. Apparently, everyone who went to the lake yesterday got lucky. I can't believe I missed out."

Talulah could tell he was kidding, and she knew the joke involved her staying over, but she didn't fully understand his meaning until Kurt walked in half a second later with a sleep-tousled Kate. Obviously, she'd spent the night, too.

"Oh, now I get it," Talulah said. "We're just missing Jane."

Miles, who joined them a second later, had obviously heard them talking because he scowled when he said, "Jane thinks she's too old for me."

Brant mussed his brother's hair. "Poor Miles, trying to overreach," he said, and they all laughed.

* * *

To Brant, it felt perfectly natural to have Talulah at the house. She fit in well with his brothers and seemed to enjoy their jokes. They showed her no mercy, but she teased them right back, and there was plenty of laughter. It was definitely a plus that she loved to cook, because it created a direct path to their hearts. By the end of breakfast, when they were thanking her and telling her how delicious the meal had been, Brant could tell they really liked her in spite of being conditioned to think the worst because of Charlie.

He made his brothers clean up the kitchen, since he and Talulah had done the cooking. Claiming he *and* Talulah had prepared the meal was a bit of an overstatement, and they were quick to point that out. But he'd told them he'd ask her to bake another carrot cake if they let him off the hook, and that silenced all complaints.

"I actually made you two carrot cakes last week," Talulah informed him as they walked back to his room.

"You did?" he said. "Are they at your place? If so, let's go get 'em."

"Sorry. I gave one to Ellen and the other to Averil."

"You gave them both away?" he complained. "Why didn't you give one to me? I was miserable without you."

"I was trying to avoid starting something."

Their situation was a problem. And he didn't know what they were going to do about it. But not being with her while she was in town wasn't an option, not if she was willing to be with him. "Then I was even luckier than I realized that Jane got you to the lake yesterday," he said as he went into the bathroom and turned on the shower. "Who knows how many other cakes I might've missed?"

She grinned at him when he came back into the room. "So you want me for my cooking?"

He tugged off the T-shirt she was wearing and drew her bare chest up against his. "Among other things."

She rose up on tiptoe to kiss him. "I'll never forget the mean look on your face when you were in the truck yesterday. You were *so* mad I was there."

He gave her a mock scowl. "I wasn't mad, exactly. I was…feeling sorry for myself."

"Because you're used to getting what you want and didn't think it was going to happen this time?"

He rested his forehead against hers. "Because I'm falling in love with you." Those words slipped out so quickly, so easily and so unexpectedly that he caught his breath after he said them.

Her eyes widened. "You can't mean that…"

He'd never made that declaration before, and yet he'd just done it with a woman who had such a strong fear of commitment he'd call it a phobia. What was wrong with him?

He considered taking the words back while he could, turning them into a joke or qualifying them in some way. But he felt how he felt. He'd dated enough women to know the difference. "I do," he said. "I know you're worried about what's happened in the past and that it'll happen again. But you've done all you can, Lu. You've warned me and warned me. I'll take responsibility for myself from here on out."

She shook her head. "You say that now…"

He gripped her shoulders. "I mean it. I want you badly enough to accept the risk. And that's on me. So just…feel what you feel without holding back, at least for *that* reason, and maybe one day you'll be able to say those words to *me*. If not, it's okay. I only want to hear them if you truly mean it."

"It's too soon. I—"

"I know. You're in a difficult situation, and I'm sorry." He tucked her head under his chin as he embraced her. "So don't even think about it. Not today. Let's just have fun while we're together."

He felt her chest rise as she drew a deep breath. "Okay…"

"What do you want to do?" he asked.

"I'm not sure. If we go out, Averil will see us—or someone who knows her will see us and then tell her. I'm not ready for that, either."

"That's only if we stay in Coyote Canyon."

When the tension left her body, he knew she felt some relief. Out of town she wouldn't have to worry about Averil or Charlie or anyone else. They could have the day together without any of those concerns, and Brant thought that was important. "Where should we go?" she asked.

"Why don't we go to your sister's? I haven't seen a newborn in ages."

"Debbie would love that," she said. "And I've been meaning to get back over there."

"Today's the day, then." He let go of her and jerked his head toward the bathroom, which was steaming up because he'd left the water running for so long. "Would you like to use the shower first, or do you want me to?"

He knew giving her the choice to shower on her own would probably surprise her. But he didn't want to take anything for granted, didn't want to make her feel smothered or cornered. If he'd learned anything in all his years of ranching, it was that any kind of creature reacted best to a kind, patient, slow hand. Now that Talulah knew how he felt, it was even more important he give her the opportunity to come to him on her own, or not at all, and trust that he'd accept her choice without blaming or mistreating her.

What she did next proved to be a good sign. Maybe it was a small one, but it was the kind of thing he hoped to see more of. She took his hand, kissed his palm in the very center and drew him into the bathroom with her. "Why do we have to take turns?"

The level of emotion Talulah felt whenever she made love with Brant was greater than she'd ever experienced before. And yet she was afraid to put a label on it. An "I love you" would be a big deal, especially now that Brant had declared himself. It would make everything mutual, which would naturally constitute a commitment and maybe even lead to a future together—or at least an attempt to achieve that.

She had to be careful. What they had was too new to rely on it, for one thing. And there was still so much standing between them.

Besides, what she'd felt for other men had worn off over time—as soon as they began to get serious. That always marked the beginning of the end, an end that probably should've come more quickly than it did. Instead of breaking up, however, she'd talk herself into trying to make it work so she wouldn't disappoint anyone, which meant that by the time she bolted, she created even more damage.

Would her relationship with Brant go down a similar path?

The water pounded down in the shower, and the muscles in Brant's shoulders stood out like thick ropes beneath her fingers as he lifted her in his arms. When he drove inside her, she was surprised that their connection felt so unique on an emotional level.

Except this was a terrible time and place to fall in love, so she'd be stupid to allow it. Brant was also a very inconvenient choice. Averil would hate her. Paul would hate her. The future of the diner would be uncertain.

Why couldn't she make things easy and feel more for Paul?

After Brant reached climax, he dropped his head on her shoulder, trying to catch his breath, but he didn't put her down. Reluctant to separate, they stayed wrapped up in each other's arms for several minutes, with her back to the slick tile and her legs around his narrow hips. "Please know that I will always let you leave me, without any blame or anger," he said. "I just hope it doesn't go that way."

She kissed his temple. But she didn't dare say anything. Words created expectations; she'd learned that the hard way. She'd never meant to hurt anybody, but she especially didn't want to hurt him.

Twenty-Three

"He's even better-looking than he was in high school," Debbie whispered to Talulah as soon as they were in the kitchen and away from Brant and Scott, who were chatting in the living room while watching the kids.

"He's definitely put on more muscle," Talulah said.

Debbie took out a large tray as well as all the ingredients for the charcuterie board they planned to prepare. "He looks strong enough to lift a house. And he seems so into you."

Talulah started arranging rows of Gouda cheese on one corner of the tray, saving the gorgonzola for a spot closer to the center. "What makes you say that?"

After washing some red and green grapes, Debbie placed the red ones next to the Gouda and the green ones on the other side of the board. "The fact that he was willing to come here, for one thing. No man offers to visit someone's sister, not unless he's serious about the woman he's with."

"He knew you in high school, Deb. He probably wanted to see how you're doing."

"I'm sure that never crossed his mind," she said with a laugh. "He ignored me in high school, didn't even realize I was there. But the way he looks at *you*…"

"Oh, stop." Talulah washed her hands before spreading out thin slices of salami and arranging them between the two cheeses. "You just want me to move back to Montana."

"I'm not going to lie—I would love that." She opened a jar of green olives and filled one of the ramekins. "But I'm being honest about Brant."

"Falling for him would really screw up my life," Talulah said.

"Still, you are falling for him, right?"

"I don't know. How can I be certain?" She added some pine nuts and almonds while her sister filled another ramekin with raspberry jelly and spread water crackers near a block of brie. "I can't make another mistake."

"You won't."

"How do you know?"

"Because you're being extra-cautious—probably overly so."

"A woman with my reputation can never be *too* cautious." She washed a handful of strawberries and placed them strategically on the board. "How'd you know you wanted to marry Scott?"

"That's tough to say. I just...did."

Talulah tucked raw spinach leaves around some of the ramekins and the brie to add a little green. "I wish I could be as decisive as you."

"If you choose Brant over Averil and Paul and even the diner, you must want him pretty bad. I'd say then you'll have your answer." She winked as she picked up the large charcuterie board. "Are we done? What do you think?"

"It looks great. I'll bring in another bottle of wine—and some juice for you and the kids."

"The sacrifices I make for breastfeeding," she grumbled and left the room.

Talulah stayed in the kitchen a few minutes longer, listening to her sister, brother-in-law and Brant talk in the other room. Brant was playing with the kids at the same time, so there were snatches of conversation she couldn't hear above the screaming of whichever child he was tossing around or tickling. But she had to smile at how casual and comfortable he seemed—and how good he was with her nieces and nephew.

"Hey, Lu! You bringing more wine or what?" Scott called out, and she pulled herself from the well of her thoughts long enough to uncork a new bottle.

"Coming," she told him, but her phone buzzed with a text before she could pour.

Setting the wine down, she pulled her phone from her pocket, whispering, "Please don't let it be Paul." If it was, she wasn't going to answer. He had as much invested in the diner as she did. She could only hope he'd safeguard their business until she could get back. While he was in Europe, she'd have a whole month to decide what to do about their deteriorating relationship—whether or not he'd be able to settle for friendship so they could continue to make their partnership work.

Fortunately, the text wasn't from Paul. It was from Averil.

What are you doing today?

Talulah stifled a groan. Every decision she made seemed harder than the one before. But, fortunately, she could answer Averil's question honestly.

I'm in Billings, visiting my sister and her new baby.

Fun! You should've invited me to go with you. I'd love to see Debbie again. She has some kids close to Mitch's age, right?

She does, Talulah wrote. Next time.

Okay. Send me a pic of the new baby.

Talulah had one on her phone from the day Abby was born, but she wanted to get a recent one. Newborns changed so quickly.

When she brought Scott and Brant their wine, she expected to see Debbie or Scott holding the new addition to their family. But Abby was cradled in Brant's arms.

"Looks like she's sound asleep," Talulah said as he accepted his glass.

He smiled as he set it on the table beside him. "I want to see what she's like when she's awake, so I keep jiggling her, hoping she'll open her eyes, but she won't."

Debbie laughed. "She's too warm and comfortable."

"Do you mind if I take a picture?" Talulah asked, and he smiled as she snapped one on her phone. This wasn't a photograph she'd ever send to Averil, of course. But it was definitely one she wanted to keep for herself.

"You're quiet," Talulah said. "Are you tired? Want me to take over?"

She was sitting next to Brant in the middle of the bench seat, her hand on his thigh as he drove them home. He liked having her there, so close. It felt like she was his in a way no other woman had been. But he couldn't get his mind off what might or might not happen in the future. He'd told her she could leave him at any time without blame or anger, but he had to admit that every minute he spent with her made the prospect of losing her harder. "I'm fine," he said. "Just thinking."

"About…"

Should he tell her? He'd promised himself he wouldn't

pressure her. But they were running out of time. He could easily imagine her getting swept up in her old life and forgetting about him after she went back to Seattle, so coming up with a plan seemed important. "Today, I guess."

"What about it?"

"It was nice."

"I enjoyed it, too," she said. "But I'm surprised you did. The kids wouldn't leave you alone."

"That was my fault. I kept riling them up. I love kids. I'd like to have a couple of my own." He glanced over at her. "What about you?"

"I'd like to have kids, too—someday."

"We're in our thirties," he pointed out.

"Meaning what? We're getting old, and it'll soon be too late?"

He could tell she was joking—sort of. She seemed reluctant to have too serious a conversation, and he could understand why. He was the one who'd said they'd just have fun today. But after holding Abby and feeling the peach fuzz on her head and smelling that sweet, baby-powdery smell on her skin and clothes, he realized just how ready he was for something beyond work, hanging out with his brothers and drinking with his friends. It felt like he'd been stuck in one place for the past few years, waiting for something he needed before he could move on, and now he'd found it.

"I've been giving the prospect of a family some thought, too," she told him.

He passed a slow-moving semi. "And?"

"I get where you're coming from. If I'm going to do it, it should probably happen in the next five or six years."

"Is that why you were thinking of settling down with Paul?"

"I guess. Partly. Then I wouldn't have to try to meet someone else. I could give him what he wanted. And it would be easy, or at least comfortable, to share our responsibilities—taking care of both the diner and the children."

"Paul would be the most convenient choice." Brant couldn't argue with that.

"So it's a good thing I came home," she said. "Or I might've gone through with it. I wouldn't have let myself back out *again*. And now I know for sure that I don't want to marry him or have his baby."

Brant turned down the radio. "What about mine?"

She looked shocked. He was kind of shocked himself. He was saying things to her he'd never said to any other woman. "We don't even know how our lives would fit together, Brant. I mean… I don't see you moving to Seattle…"

"No," he admitted. "What would I do there? My brothers and I own the ranch. It's not just my livelihood, it's the only thing I'm good at, the only thing I've been trained to do."

She loosened her seat belt so she could turn slightly toward him. "Exactly."

"I'd hate to ask you to give up the diner. But if it came down to that, I'd be able to take care of you." He knew how much she loved her business, but he had to at least try to convince her to fight for what they could have together.

"As kind as it is that you'd be willing to do that, I doubt I'd be satisfied letting *anyone* take care of me," she said.

"What if I helped you open another diner—in Coyote Canyon? Or I guess I could sell my part of the ranch to my brothers, and we could go somewhere else, like Billings or Bozeman, where we could buy more land. The only problem with that is success in ranching is a matter of scale. We'd have to work extra-hard just to get to where I'm at now. It would be much more of a struggle if we went out on our own."

"If we moved to Bozeman or Billings, I'd still have to leave the diner," she said.

"True, but you wouldn't have to be around Charlie or Averil."

"They don't seem like a good enough reason to make you sell your interest in the ranch."

He was impressed with how reasonable she was being. But he almost wished she'd said, "Okay, let's go to Bozeman." At least then they'd be making plans to stay together. As it was, he felt as though she was standing on one side of a wide canyon, and he was standing on the other. "So... would you ever consider coming back to Coyote Canyon?"

"I don't know," she replied. "If I could open a dessert diner in Coyote Canyon, I might. But it doesn't have nearly the population of Seattle. Who knows if it'd take off the way the first one did? Or if I'd have the money to get it going to begin with?"

"Wouldn't Paul have to buy you out?"

"He doesn't have the cash to pay me what it's worth."

"I have some money saved. I could help with the start-up costs and he could pay you monthly."

She slipped a hand around the arm he had slung over the steering wheel and kissed his biceps. "That's very generous of you, but I couldn't let you take that risk. And Paul could just as easily get spiteful and make it so difficult to separate our interests that we'd end up destroying what we've created. Then he and I would both have nothing."

Brant frowned as he watched the dashes in the middle of the road rush toward them. "You really think he'd do that? Even though it's not in his best interest, either?"

"I couldn't tell you. You never truly know people unti

you try to break up with them—even if it's only a business partnership."

Brant pictured the man who'd come storming toward him when he'd been trying to fix the screen door. Talulah could be right. Sometimes jealousy caused people to do terrible things, and there was no question that Paul was jealous. The way he'd acted this morning when he called Talulah served as further proof. "That doesn't give me a lot to offer you," he said and knew in that moment he needed to prepare himself for goodbye.

"Oh boy."

Talulah had fallen asleep before they could get back to Coyote Canyon, but hearing Brant say that woke her up. "What is it?"

His eyes flicked to the rearview mirror. "I'm pretty sure Charlie's behind us."

A shot of adrenaline chased her grogginess away, and she ducked down in her seat. "We're back in Coyote Canyon?"

"Just rolled in."

"And he's following us?"

"He was stopped at the light on Main when I came through. I think he saw my truck and turned to come after me."

"You're kidding…"

"No. Hard to tell from headlights alone, but…that's got to be him. I know he saw me. And he'll see you if you don't stay down."

Being careful not to let her head pop up above the seat, she unsnapped her seat belt and slid into the passenger-side foot well of Brant's truck. "What's he doing now?"

"Coming up alongside," he said as they stopped at the

only other light in town. "Be quiet. He's motioning for me to roll down my window."

She burrowed even lower. Brant's truck was higher than Charlie's SUV, and it was dark out, but she had no idea if Charlie had already caught a glimpse of another person inside the truck.

"Hey," Charlie said.

Talulah couldn't see him, just as he couldn't see her, but she recognized his voice.

"What's up?" Brant asked.

"Been looking all over for you."

"What for?"

"I feel bad about how I've acted lately. I'm sorry. I guess I let Talulah get the best of me again. But it's stupid to allow any woman come between us, especially one who doesn't even live here."

"It's fine," Brant said. "Everything's fine."

"You're still pissed. I can tell."

Brant gestured at the light. "There're people behind us. We gotta go."

"Want to head over to Hank's?" Charlie called as Brant gave the truck some gas.

"Not tonight," Brant called back and rolled up his window.

"Is he still following you?" Talulah whispered a few seconds later.

"For now." Brant kept watching his mirrors, but as they left town, and the businesses and buildings gave way to rolling countryside, he relaxed. "He's turning back."

"You know, if you and I get together, you'll lose Charlie for good," she pointed out as she climbed back into the seat—this time on the passenger side so anyone coming up from behind wouldn't wonder who was sitting so close to Brant.

"I know," he said.

She fastened her seat belt. "Won't that be hard?"

He slowed, driving under the arch in front of his home and around the barn to her car. "Of course it will be."

"But…"

He shut off the engine. "I'd choose you over anyone else, Lu."

She was so stunned she almost couldn't find the words to respond. "How can you sound so sure? I've only been in town a couple of weeks."

"I've dated a lot of women through the years. I feel like I've done enough market research to know when I've found what I've been looking for," he quipped.

"It doesn't frighten you that you could be making a mistake? You've never even been in a committed relationship."

"Not because I *can't* commit. Because I hadn't found the one person I want to spend the rest of my life with."

She pointed to herself. "You're saying that's me?"

"You know it is. I may be oversimplifying, but if you want someone badly enough, you put that person first, make whatever sacrifices are necessary."

She gaped at him. "Are you asking me to give up the diner and my life in Seattle?"

He looked troubled as he considered his answer. "I hate that being with me would cost you so much," he replied. "So I'd never ask that of you. It would have to be your decision and yours alone. Otherwise, you'd resent me for it later." He lowered his voice. "But if you made that choice, I'd do whatever I could do to make you happy."

She started to point out all the things he had to worry about. That she hadn't proven to be the most reliable love interest. That with more time, he might change his mind. That he might be blowing up his relationships with Averil and Charlie for nothing. But he waved her words away.

"You seem to think I'm not truly capable of love," he said. "That you can't rely on me or what I feel because I don't have a history of long relationships. But if being with you means I need to sell my interest in the ranch, I'll do it. If it means I lose my relationship with Charlie, I'll make that sacrifice, too. Aside from my brothers, those are the things I loved most before you got here. If that's not commitment, I don't know what is."

He climbed out and came around the truck to open her door, but she didn't move. She felt frozen to the seat.

Had Brant Elway—hard-to-get Brant Elway—just offered her forever?

Twenty-Four

It was the timing. That was Talulah's biggest stumbling block. She was as caught up with Brant as he was with her, and she knew it. But their relationship seemed to be moving at the speed of light. Could they rely on their feelings? Or in three months, six months, a year, would the intensity of what they felt for each other fade or suddenly deflate like a punctured balloon?

Because *she* was willing to make sacrifices for him, too; she just didn't want to sacrifice her business and everything she'd established in life for nothing.

She forced herself to imagine what it would be like to live in Coyote Canyon *after* being dumped by Brant. What would she do then? How would she face the heartbreak, the disappointment, the humiliation and the prospect of having to start all over again—either here or somewhere else?

There was so much hanging in the balance; she was taking a wait-and-see approach. But they spent as much of the next week together as they could, dodging Averil and Charlie and being careful not to let anyone else in town see them, either. She cooked for Brant and, sometimes, his brothers. He took her to the lake for an evening alone, and they enjoyed a long boat ride before making love in a secluded cove. Another night they camped out on the ranch, under the stars. When they weren't together, they texted each other constantly. She even started bringing him lunch because she couldn't wait until the end of the day to see him.

Paul wouldn't accept her calls, even when she tried to reach him at the restaurant, which seemed rather immature, considering they owned a business together. Fortunately, her employees assured her that all was well at the diner. She got the impression they'd heard an earful about her, but she tried not to react to that. She preferred to behave as professionally as possible, even if Paul was stretching the truth and telling everyone she'd cheated on him.

At least Debbie and the baby were thriving. And Talulah was getting along well with Jane and Ellen, both of whom came over to help pack whenever they could. Averil was so involved in fighting with her ex over unpaid child support and dealing with extended family visiting from out of town that, other than an occasional text, she was too busy to contact Talulah. Which was lucky for Talulah, given the amount of time she was spending with Brant. Averil did call on Thursday to invite her over for dinner on Sunday, however. She said their company would be gone by then. She also said she'd had a talk with her parents, who felt it was time to sit down and speak with Talulah themselves.

"You're not really going to have dinner with the Gerharts, are you?" Brant asked when she told him about the call. It was late Friday afternoon, and he was guiding Sadie, the reins held loosely in one hand, while she rode on the saddle behind him, both arms around his waist. Brant had received a call from their neighbor, saying an Elway steer had gotten out, so Brant had to check the fencing in the south forty to see how that had happened before quitting work. Since Talulah was mostly prepared for the estate sale she planned to hold tomorrow, she'd snuck over so she could go on this errand with him.

"I said I would," she told him.

"You might want to rethink that one, Lu."

He was more protective of her than any guy she'd ever been with. But he was protective of everyone he loved—without being possessive or overbearing. He gave her the feeling he'd stand by her no matter what she decided, which engendered so much trust. That was one of the things she loved most about him. "I can understand why you'd be worried about the Gerharts." Sunday dinner at their place *did* sound daunting. And yet… Talulah had shared many, many meals with Charlie's family in the past. They'd been a big part of her childhood. She'd even gone on several camping trips with Averil—could still remember seeing Yellowstone for the first time when she was with them. "But…how could I say no? Besides, Dinah sets the tone for the whole family, and I doubt she'll treat me *too* badly, not now that Averil and I are speaking again. She's also a good friend of my mother's."

"But what do you hope to achieve by going?" he asked. "You don't think they'll be happy when they find out we're together, do you?"

Brant had made his feelings about her clear the night they'd returned from Billings, and to her surprise he hadn't wavered since. There'd been no second thoughts, no back-tracking. She got the impression he'd decided on her and that was that.

Even to Talulah it felt as though they were meant to be together. She had zero desire to see any other man. But they both knew she had to go back to Seattle and take care of the diner while Paul was gone. She was waiting to see how she felt while she was away from Brant and back in the place she'd thought she was happy before. "If they can get past what I did to Charlie, I don't see why they'd care who I'm with."

"That might be true for anyone else you might be with, but it won't be true for me."

He was right. But what if she didn't end up with Brant? Then she'd regret not taking advantage of the chance to *finally* have her apology accepted. She'd felt bad about Charlie and Averil for so long… "I can see that, but…the invitation caught me off guard. I didn't know how to respond, except to agree and act excited to see everyone."

"Did she say if Charlie will be there?" he asked.

"She didn't."

"I bet he comes. This will be like the funeral. He seems to think that, at some point, you're going to regret your decision to cut him loose."

Talulah wouldn't put it past Charlie to show up. But she cared enough about Averil and the other Gerharts to risk it. "That'll never happen."

"I bet he's still driving past your place every chance he gets."

"Maybe," she said. "Since I've been sneaking out to meet you every night, I wouldn't know. I haven't been there to notice any headlights." She and Brant felt safer seeing each other at the ranch, where they were less exposed. She usually hurried across the field behind her house to Ellen's barn, where he picked her up. She always left a few lights on at Phoebe's to make it appear that she was home. But if Charlie had been checking consistently, he might be wondering why she never passed in front of the windows anymore. "If he's at dinner, I'll simply be polite and hope he'll do the same," she said.

Sadie tried to turn back to the barn. She obviously knew it was the end of the workday and wanted to be home. But

Brant redirected her. "What will you say if they ask you about me?"

"I'll tell them you're so good in bed you're irresistible," she teased, slipping her arms tighter around his waist.

"I'm serious," he said.

She was surprised by *how* serious. "What do you want me to say?"

It took him a moment to respond. "I don't know. Sometimes it feels like you love me so much you'll never leave me. The way you act when we're together—it's like you're already part of me. And other times…"

"I'm just trying to be careful, take it slow," she said.

They continued in silence for several minutes. Then he said, "If you *do* come back to me after Seattle, where would you like to live?"

"Here in Coyote Canyon, I guess."

"Where in Coyote Canyon?"

"That's hard to say. I haven't really thought about it." She'd been trying to avoid that kind of daydreaming. Creating an idyllic picture of life with Brant could tempt her into making the wrong decision.

"You've been talking about your aunt's house as though you really like it," he said. "And she's got a few acres, which I like."

"Are you suggesting we buy her property?"

"I'd be open to it—if it would make you happy. It's far enough away from the ranch that we could have our own lives separate from my brothers and parents. And yet it's not too far of a drive each day to get to work."

They reached the fence and started ambling along it, looking for the break. It didn't take more than a few minutes to find it. As soon as he saw the problem, Brant hopped down and helped her off the horse, and she held Sadie's reins while he examined the damage.

After pulling a hammer from his saddlebag, he reattached the boards that'd fallen off. But one board was broken in half. He used duct tape to hold it together before hammering it back in place, too.

"That won't hold for long, will it?" she asked.

"Not if it rains. But it should hold until Monday, when I can haul a new board out here," he said as he strode toward her.

He was about to climb onto the horse when she stopped him and kissed him.

"What's that for?" he asked.

She admired the vivid blue of his eyes and the smile lines that creased his tanned face. "Just to let you know that—" She hesitated. She wasn't used to taking the emotional risk inherent in saying what she was about to say.

"That…" he prodded.

"There are times when it feels as though I could never live without you."

It'd been a big admission for her, and yet he started to laugh. "Was that really so hard?"

"No," she said grudgingly. "But that doesn't mean it won't come back to haunt me."

"You're going to be just fine." Smiling, he got on the horse and pulled her up behind him.

Averil checked her phone again. There'd been no response to her last text to Talulah, asking if she wanted to hang out tonight. Aunt Kathy and Uncle Chester were in town until Sunday morning, but Averil's parents had taken them to Bozeman for a couple days, and they'd left early this morning while Averil was heading to the bank.

Averil didn't mind missing the trip. Now that the workweek had ended, she was eager to cut loose with friends, which was why she'd hoped Talulah would be able to join her and Jane at Hank's tonight. The three of them hadn't been together since before the wedding. But there'd been no word, even when Jane had tried to reach her, so Averil and Jane had gone on their own like they'd been doing for the last fourteen years.

Now it was almost midnight. Averil had picked up Mitch from her oldest brother's house, where he'd been playing with his cousins, and still there was no response from Talulah.

Where was she? Was she out of town?

She had to be. Since they'd made up, and Talulah had responded about dinner on Sunday, Averil couldn't think of any other reason she wouldn't be checking her phone.

Unless...

"Mommy, where are we?" Mitch asked, waking up as she brought the car to a stop in Talulah's drive.

After going to Hank's and having a couple of beers—with some chili cheese fries and hot wings—and watching a baseball game with Jane, she'd grabbed Mitch and gone home, only to back out of the drive as soon as she pulled into it. She kept picturing Talulah with Brant, even though she knew Talulah had broken it off. Talulah wasn't the only one who was mysteriously missing tonight. Averil had seen Miles at Hank's, and when she'd asked what Brant was doing, he'd mumbled something vague and turned away, as though he didn't really want to address the question.

"I'm just checking on a friend, okay?" she said as she cut the engine. "Stay here. I'll be right back."

"I don't want to stay!" he protested. "Why can't I go with you?"

Averil supposed it would be better to have him with her, in case Talulah invited her in. She didn't want to leave him crying for her.

"Fine. You can come, too," she said and got him out of his booster seat before leading him to the front door.

The porch light was on. So were several other lights in the house, but everything seemed still and quiet. Averil would've worried about ringing the doorbell so late, but Talulah would've turned off at least some of the inside lights if she was going to bed, wouldn't she?

When no one answered to the bell, Averil knocked loudly, and Mitch copied her by shoving the teddy bear he'd taken from the car into his left arm so he could knock with his right hand.

No response. "Talulah?" Averil yelled, knocking again.

Still nothing. Pulling Mitch along behind her, she went to the garage and used the flashlight on her phone to peer through the window on one side.

Talulah's car was parked there.

She had to be asleep, Averil told herself, but when she went around to the back door, in case Talulah was in the kitchen where she could be seen through the windows, there was no sign of her.

"I'm tired," Mitch said, starting to cry. "Can we go home?"

"Yes. We're going now," she said, but when she stooped to pick up her son, she saw a dirt path leading from Talulah's house toward Ellen's house next door. And the weird thing was that there were footprints in it, and one set was far too big to belong to Ellen or Talulah.

Could she see herself living in Aunt Phoebe's house?

As Talulah got ready for the estate sale the following morning, she studied the old Victorian with a more discerning eye. It had diamond-pane windows, tall ceilings, wainscoting and plenty of built-in cabinetry. It would look great, renovated in the modern farmhouse style, which would be the direction she'd take it if she and Brant were to move here. But she certainly hadn't expected to be in the market for a home in Coyote Canyon, least of all *this* home. What would Debbie and the rest of her family think of her buying Phoebe's house and moving back?

She wasn't about to ask them. Not until she'd been in Seattle for a few weeks and had the chance to determine if she was out of her mind for even considering such a big change. Brant hadn't mentioned marriage—other than joking that he knew better than to propose—so she still wasn't sure what their relationship would look like. Would they simply live together? If so, for how long? He'd mentioned that he wanted kids. So did she. What would happen when babies came along?

She couldn't imagine they wouldn't marry then. Brant was far too traditional for anything other than the standard nuclear family. She wasn't stuck on keeping her own name. But the prospect of facing another wedding scared her. From the way he joked, it scared him, too.

With a quick glance at the clock on her phone—it was just after six—she finished arranging all the things she was putting up for sale. She was exhausted and running out of energy, but she was almost ready. Some of the more sentimental stuff she'd stored in the attic to keep it safe from would-be shoppers. She'd take those boxes to Billings and store them at Debbie's for when her mother returned. Carolyn could go through it all then and dispose of whatever she didn't want to keep. What didn't sell and didn't go in that special pile, Talulah would donate.

Brant had offered to help her today, but she couldn't even consider that. She'd heard from both Averil and Jane last night and sent them a reply this morning, saying she'd been caught up in getting ready for the estate sale and gone to bed early. She felt that was a fairly safe cover, but if they came to see how the sale was going, and Brant was around, Talulah had little doubt they'd put two and two together.

She navigated to the text she'd sent them a few minutes earlier to see if they'd responded. Neither of them had. But it was very early yet…

Slipping her phone into the pocket on her yoga pants, she did a final walkthrough to make sure everything was tagged with a price. She should get a good turnout. She'd put up a sign advertising the sale on the community bulletin board near police headquarters, and she'd added the information to the town website, which had a calendar feature. Thanks to Mrs. Carrier, news of the sale had also been sent in a churchwide email. Knowing some folks might come early, eager to get first pick of whatever was available, she hadn't even dared let Brant stay for more than a few minutes when he dropped her off this morning. There was no point in getting careless now, the day before she was to have dinner with the Gerharts.

He'd taken the time to fix the screen door before he left, however. And he hadn't said anything about the botched job Paul had done. She was glad he didn't mention Paul very often—other than when he was referring to their business.

Her phone dinged with a message. Brant was home. Knowing that they'd gotten away with one more night together helped her to relax. But she was glad he'd left when he did, because early birds began showing up less than an hour later, even though the sale didn't officially start until eight.

She'd sold quite a bit of her aunt's furniture and various small household items before Ellen pulled up, carrying to-go cups from the tiny but popular drive-through coffee shop that'd opened on Grove Street sometime after Talulah had moved away.

"How's it going?" she asked as she sauntered up the walk wearing cutoff sweats, Birkenstocks and an Ahimsa T-shirt she'd turned into a midriff.

Talulah had already had coffee. But she'd only gotten a few hours of sleep, so she welcomed another cup. "Thank you," she said as Ellen handed one to her and gestured toward the cars lining the drive. "It's been steady."

"You making money?"

"I'm doing okay. I priced everything on the low side so it would sell." Talulah slid over and patted the extra space on the swing beside her. "Want to sit down?"

Ellen glanced toward the house. "You don't need to watch what's going on inside?"

There were several small groups milling through the various rooms on the main floor, spare bedrooms and basement, but the door stood open, and Talulah wasn't going to follow people around, regardless. "No. Everything's tagged. Anyone who wants to buy something knows where to find me."

Ellen lowered her voice as she sat down. "What's Brant up to today?"

"Washing his truck, doing laundry, that sort of thing."

"Did you guys spend the night here?"

"No. We came back early this morning, though."

A puzzled look appeared on Ellen's face. "How early?"

"Five thirty or so," Talulah replied. "Why?"

"I could've sworn it was close to midnight when I saw a car turn down your drive. That wasn't you?"

"No. I was at the ranch. Did you happen to catch the make or model?"

A woman walked out of the house holding a pair of antique mantel luster lamps. "Will you take ten dollars for these?" she asked.

While Talulah was eager to get rid of almost everything,

she shook her head. This person wasn't just asking for a bargain; she wanted a steal. "No, I'm sorry."

"Why not?" the woman pressed. "I don't think they're worth a hundred dollars."

"Then put them back," Ellen said with a shrug.

The woman lowered the lamps. "Well, you don't have to be rude about it!"

Ellen scowled at Talulah. "Was *I* the one being rude?"

Eager to return to the conversation they'd been having a moment earlier, Talulah didn't want to get too distracted. "I'm charging much less than they're worth," she told the woman. "Feel free to do the research yourself if it makes you more comfortable."

The shopper thrust a hundred-dollar bill at Talulah. *"Here,"* she said and marched down the walkway to her car.

"Ten dollars? Seriously?" Ellen said, shaking her head.

Talulah watched the woman edge past another vehicle as she maneuvered down the long, crowded drive. "It's how the game's played at an estate sale, I guess."

"If you want to be an asshole," Ellen muttered and Talulah laughed. Her neighbor was quickly becoming one of her favorite people. Even the way Ellen had acted when it came to Brant impressed Talulah. She could've been as jealous and possessive as Averil. Instead, she'd told Talulah that she wouldn't want him if he wasn't all that into her, anyway.

Talulah took a sip of her coffee. "Back to what you were saying before. Did you happen to notice the make and model of the car that was here last night?"

"No."

"But it was a sedan?"

"I'm pretty sure it was. The headlights weren't high enough for it to have been a truck."

"How long did whoever it was stay?"

"I watched for about five minutes while I had a smoke outside. But when nothing happened, I figured it was you and Brant, after all. It wasn't until this morning that I found something odd behind my barn."

"What was it?"

"A teddy bear."

"A teddy bear?" Talulah had been around that barn herself quite a bit lately, and she'd never noticed a teddy bear. "Did it look as though it'd been on the ground for very long?"

"No, that's the thing," Ellen said. "It's obviously brand-new, not weathered at all. And when you press its paw, a recording comes on."

"What does it say?" Talulah asked.

"'Grandma loves you, Mitch.' You don't happen to know anyone named Mitch, do you?"

Talulah stopped the swing. "Yes, I do."

"How'd it go?" Brant asked.

Talulah switched the phone to her other ear as she ambled around the house, taking stock of the items that were left over from the estate sale. "It went well. Most of the things I wanted to sell are gone. The rest won't be hard to get rid of. The only thing that has me stumped is my aunt's piano."

"I'm surprised that didn't sell," he said. "Pianos, especially baby grands, are worth some money."

"I marked it as not for sale," she admitted.

"Why?" he asked. "Are you planning to take it to Seattle with you?"

"No. It would never fit in my apartment, even if I could get it to the tenth floor. It's just…sentimental—what I associate with her the most. I couldn't bear to let it go."

"That's a big keep for someone you said you weren't very close to."

"It's strange, but…the more I live in her house, the stronger the kinship I feel. I found a bunch of journals under the bed and started reading the earliest one. It's interesting and is helping me get to know who she really was—not just the stern face she turned to the world."

"Debbie might like to read them, too. She might also want the piano?"

"She already has a piano. She plays and plans to give her children lessons."

"If you need to store it someplace, I can bring it over here, cover it so it doesn't get damaged and stick it in one of the barns."

She leaned against the wall in the music room. She'd sold the two chairs and side table that'd been next to the piano, where Phoebe's students had waited for the previous appointment to end, so it looked oddly bare. "Thanks, but I'm considering offering it to whoever buys the house. I can't see it going anywhere—it belongs here."

"The next owner might not agree," he pointed out. "It's possible they'd want to do something else with that room— maybe knock out a wall or two and open the place up."

"That's what I'd do if I bought it, but I'll be sad if I have to get rid of the piano."

"There's no rush, I guess. You can make arrangements to sell it or store it if and when it comes to that. At least everything else will be handled."

She shoved off the wall and headed through the living room and dining room to the kitchen. "It looks weird having so much of her stuff gone. But at least you can move around easier in this place now." She started to make herself a sandwich. She'd been so busy and had had so many people come through the house she hadn't taken the time to eat. "Ellen stopped by earlier," she told him, changing the subject.

"To check out the sale?"

"To tell me something."

"What was it?" he asked curiously.

Talulah cut up an onion for her chicken salad sandwich. "She found a teddy bear behind the barn this morning."

"A what?"

"You heard that right," she said and explained what Ellen had told her and how she'd determined it had to belong to Averil's son.

"But even if Averil *was* attempting to spy on you, why would she bring Mitch?"

"Who knows? Maybe she was picking him up from whoever was babysitting while she was out last night."

"That could explain the car Ellen saw in your drive. But why would Averil take Mitch to the barn?"

"I'm guessing she came by to make sure I was home, and when I didn't answer the door, she started to get suspicious and snoop around."

"Bottom line—you think she knows about us."

"She has to at least suspect, doesn't she?"

"It's possible. But what led her to the barn?"

"I don't know. Something did."

"Have you heard from her today?" he asked.

"No."

"Are you still going to dinner at the Gerharts' tomorrow?"

She carried her sandwich into the dining room. "I guess so. We have to address the fact that I'm still seeing you at some point."

"You're going to tell her?"

Talulah drew a deep breath as she sat down. She'd been trying to preserve her relationship with Averil. Something as special as what they'd once had seemed like it *should* be saved. But at what cost? She'd told Paul about Brant. Now, regardless of the consequences, she needed to tell everyone else. "I think I will."

Twenty-Five

Charlie *was* there. Talulah saw his car as she pulled in and wished it wasn't too late to cancel. What had she been thinking, accepting this invitation? She should've had Averil over to her place so they could talk alone. But the opportunity to finally offer an apology to the people who'd hated her for so long, people who'd been such a big part of her life as a child, had been too enticing.

Besides, she still didn't know for sure that she'd end up with Brant. It'd be a shame if she told everyone she was in a relationship with him, then went back to Seattle and decided not to give up her life there. If that happened, she'd blow her chance at reconciliation for nothing, and she wanted to put her past behind her at last. She'd come to realize just how much she'd missed her hometown and no longer wanted to feel like an outcast.

It was unfortunate that she couldn't put Averil on hold for a few months until she figured out what she was going to do with her life. She'd never expected to fall in love with Brant, never expected to be facing the decision before her. But—just like with her prior fiancés—she couldn't control how she felt. She couldn't make herself love them, and she couldn't make herself stop loving Brant.

Gathering her courage, she stepped out of the car, retrieved the chocolate molten lava cake she'd baked early this morning and approached the Gerhart house.

Apparently, Charlie had been watching for her, because he opened the door before she could balance the cake well enough to knock.

Ultra-self-conscious, being under direct scrutiny from only a couple of feet away, she drew a deep breath. "Hello."

His eyes swept over her with a tinge of contempt, as though he was eager to find any small flaws in her appearance—a wrinkle, a wart, a slight bulge here or there. She wasn't sure if he found the blemish he seemed to be looking for, but he didn't return her intrepid smile. He did, however, step back as Averil appeared beside him and exclaimed over the cake. "Oh, my gosh! That looks delicious!"

Talulah let her take it. She was nervous enough that she was afraid she'd drop it otherwise. "Thanks." Chocolate had been Charlie's favorite back when they were together. She'd made the cake as a peace offering of sorts, since the carrot cake seemed to have gone over so well.

"Do you serve this one at your diner?" Averil asked.

"I do. It's one of the most popular items on the menu."

"Yum! I can't wait to try it." She turned to Charlie. "Excuse me. Can you please get out of the way so Talulah can come in?"

Averil sounded slightly irritated with him for standing so close, but he didn't react to the edge in her tone. He shifted a few feet to the left, and Talulah moved past him into the house, which didn't appear to have changed much in the past fourteen years. A brick rambler with light blue carpet and drapes, it'd been built in the seventies. Although it was rather dated, Dinah kept everything neat and in good repair, so the house felt lived-in and comfortable rather than shabby.

The scent of rosemary and garlic permeated the air. "Smells good in here," Talulah remarked, painfully aware that Charlie was still watching her closely.

"It's my mom's famous rosemary chicken," Averil informed her.

Eager to put some more space between her and Charlie, Talulah followed Averil toward the kitchen. "I think I might've tried it once or twice in high school."

"Probably. She's been making it for years."

The familiarity of the home and everything in it, including the people, made Talulah nostalgic enough that she was glad she'd come—and once again uncertain whether she should mention Brant. Would Averil bring him up? She wasn't acting upset that she hadn't found Talulah at home last night, hadn't launched any accusations. Maybe she'd only been checking up on things and hadn't found anything amiss and was, therefore, not suspicious.

Talulah got the feeling that was how it had gone. But she had Mitch's teddy bear in her car so she could give it back when it was time to leave. She planned to wait until later, though, after they'd had dinner and a chance to talk.

Dinah turned when they entered the kitchen. "Hello, Talulah."

Although the warmth of her greeting wasn't what it had once been, she sounded polite.

George, Averil's father, sat at the table, shucking corn. He looked up and seemed more genuinely happy to see her. "It's been a while, kiddo," he said. "How're you doing?"

Talulah offered him a grateful smile, thankful for his kindness and happy that Charlie hadn't followed them into the kitchen. "I'm managing, thanks."

Dinah took a pan of rolls from the oven. "Averil tells us you own a dessert diner in Seattle these days."

"I do. I wanted to open my own place after I graduated from culinary school, but it took me a few years to make that happen."

"You did it with a partner, right?"

Considering what Dinah had most likely heard about her, Talulah suspected there could be some subtext in that question, but she decided to take it at face value. "A friend, yes."

"And he's there taking care of the place now?"

"He is. I'll do the same for him next month when he attends a family reunion in Iowa before going on to Europe to hike with some buddies."

"Sounds like a lot more fun than planning a funeral," George commented.

"I admit I wasn't too excited about getting that assignment, but now I'm glad I had the opportunity," she told him. "Going through Phoebe's stuff—all the cans of fruit and preserves and other food she put up, the sheet music she collected, the keepsakes and the scrapbooks she made of her childhood—taught me quite a bit about her."

"Did she keep a journal?" Dinah asked.

"She kept a lot of them. I found a whole trove under the bed when I started on her bedroom three days ago. Whenever I take a break from packing, I read a little more about what it was like for her growing up in Coyote Canyon before her parents had running water and electricity."

"What happened to your arm?" George asked, catching sight of her stitches. The cut was healing so well, she no longer used a bandage to cover it, but she would've done so to come here tonight had she thought of it.

Talulah looked down as though it was the first ti

she'd seen the stitches, too, as she struggled to formulate a reply. "Um… Someone threw a rock."

"And it hit you?" Dinah said.

"It shattered the window at Phoebe's, and a piece of glass landed in my arm."

"No kidding!" George said. "When was that?"

"A few days after I returned to town," she mumbled.

"That's terrible!" Dinah exclaimed, taking her wrist to get a better look. "Does your mother know?"

Talulah shook her head. "I haven't told her. With Phoebe passing away, and Debbie having the new baby, I didn't want to worry her."

"Who would do something like that?" George asked, obviously appalled.

Talulah tried not to look at Averil, who was putting ice in two glasses and acting as though she wasn't paying attention. "I don't know. It's okay, though, really. It's healing."

George's eyebrows shot up high on his bald head. "That's not okay at all! I hope you called the cops."

"No."

"Why not?" he demanded.

Talulah cleared her throat. "Whoever did it probably didn't realize how badly it could hurt me. They just… picked up a rock and threw it out of…you know…rage and frustration."

"*Rage?* Who would be that angry with you?" Dinah asked and seemed to realize the answer to her own question the second it was out of her mouth. "Charlie?" she yelled, calling her son into the kitchen.

He poked his head into the room. "What?"

Dinah gestured at Talulah's arm. "Please tell me you didn't throw the rock that hurt her."

"No," he said with a scowl. "Of course I didn't."

"I sincerely hope not," Dinah said, visibly relieved.

Charlie shot Averil a look that suggested his mother had asked the wrong child, but Dinah didn't pick up on it and was instantly distracted when Mitch came running into the kitchen. "Grandma! Grandma! I found a pincher bug!"

Dinah's expression warmed the instant she saw her grandson. "Did you catch it?"

"I tried." He wrinkled his nose. "It got away."

"Well, I promise you there are plenty more where that one came from." With a chuckle, she ruffled his hair. "This kid loves bugs," she told Talulah.

"Hi, Mitch," Talulah said, and he gave her a quick, distracted wave before running off—presumably to find another pincher bug.

Voices in the entry indicated that other people had arrived. From what she could hear, Talulah guessed it was more family. No one had bothered to ring the bell. Charlie had two older brothers and two older sisters who'd been married and starting families when she and Averil graduated from high school. Back then, some of the Gerhart siblings still lived in Coyote Canyon, but others had moved to various parts of Montana. If she remembered correctly, one had moved to California.

As the newcomers filtered into the kitchen to say hello to Dinah and George, Talulah slipped to the outer edge of the party and stood against the wall, grateful that she was no longer the center of attention. But she had only a short reprieve before Bob, Averil's oldest brother, noticed her. "Wow. What are *you* doing here?" he asked.

Before Talulah could come up with an appropriate answer, Averil slugged him playfully on the arm. "Oh, stop," she said. "*I* invited her."

Bob didn't seem mollified. The family had probably been talking viciously about the woman who'd stood up their brother at the altar—and doing it for so long and as recently as the funeral—that he wasn't willing to welcome the runaway bride back into their circle. "Oh, yeah? What'd Charlie have to say about that?"

"It was his choice to come today," Averil replied. "I told him she'd be here."

"You expected him to miss a family meal for *her* sake?"

"Bob, that's enough," Dinah said.

"Charlie comes over all the time," Averil said in her own defense. "He's a big boy. Missing one meal wouldn't kill him. And Talulah was one of my best friends growing up. I haven't associated with her since we graduated, because of Charlie. I deserve some consideration in this, too, don't you think?"

Wishing she could simply disappear, Talulah shifted from one foot to the other. "I'm sorry," she started to say, but Bob spoke over her.

"She didn't have to wait until the wedding to break up with him," he said. "There's no excuse for that."

Talulah was certain they'd been saying that to each other for fourteen years. And they were right. She didn't know how to make them understand what went on in her head and heart back then, but she wasn't willing to let Averil continue to stand up for her, especially against family members. "I owe you all an apology," she said, loudly enough that even Bob's wife and two kids, both preteens, suddenly stopped talking and began to pay attention. "I was barely eighteen when I almost married Charlie. It might be easy to say I should've handled it differently. And I sincerely wish I had. But… I couldn't. I didn't want to disappoint him."

Charlie had come all the way into the kitchen, too, behind his big brother. When he heard what she said, he made a sound that indicated he was incredulous, but she'd come this far—she could only persevere with her speech. "I didn't want to disappoint Averil, either," she continued. "After all, it's not every day you have the chance to become a sister to one of your best friends." She looked around at the rest of the family, all of whom were staring at her. "To be honest, I didn't want to disappoint *anyone*. I did express some reservations privately to Charlie and suggested we hold off on getting married. But he said we just needed to start our lives together and everything would be okay."

"I don't remember saying that," Charlie grumbled.

"We had that discussion," Talulah insisted. "What I did—it doesn't happen out of nowhere. There were signs. You just didn't want to see them, and I kept trying to forge ahead—for your sake and Averil's and my family's."

"Because marrying me would be so terrible?" Charlie said.

"No. I knew it wouldn't be," Talulah replied. "Or I would've backed out sooner. What I'm saying is that you deserved more than I could've given you. You deserved someone who was madly in love with you and devoted to you and would stick with you through thick and thin—not a woman who had to talk herself into staying in the relationship. I loved you," she said, and his gaze dropped to the floor. "Part of me *still* loves the boy you used to be, even after all the years you've hated me. But I've never been *in* love with you, Charlie. Not the way I'm in love with Brant."

His family, most of whom had been unable to meet her eyes as she spoke, suddenly looked up. "Did you say *Brant*?" Bob asked and focused on Averil for confirmation. "Did you hear that?"

Talulah felt sick inside. Instead of waiting for the right time and place, she'd just blurted out her true feelings before they could even eat dinner.

"That can't be true…" Averil said, her voice barely above a whisper. "You only want him because I do."

Closing her eyes, Talulah kneaded her forehead. "That isn't why, Averil. That's the reason I've been trying to talk myself *out* of loving him. Do you think I want to disappoint you again?"

Tears instantly filled her friend's eyes, and she pushed her way through the people crowded around them as she left the kitchen.

"You can't be serious!" Charlie exclaimed. "What does he have that I don't?"

She shook her head. "I can't explain it, Charlie."

"But…you're not going to stay here and marry him, are you? I bet you'll back out at the last minute, like you did to me. You can't handle commitment. That's what it is. But I don't care. He deserves to know what it feels like."

"We haven't even talked about marriage."

"You'd have to give up your dessert diner to move back here."

"I realize that."

"And what about Paul? He thinks you're coming back to him."

She ignored the "to him" part, even though she knew Charlie had phrased the statement to make her look and feel as bad as possible. "I don't know what I'm going to do," she admitted, and after mumbling yet another apology to the others—who were all gaping at her—she hurried through the kitchen so she could let herself out of the house.

Before she drove away, however, she retrieved Mitch's teddy bear from her back seat and left it on the doorstep.

It was the first time they'd been together in public as a couple. Brant was relieved that all the sneaking around was over, that he and Talulah could go wherever they wanted, whenever they wanted. It would now be much more obvious—to everyone—that Talulah had dropped him just like she'd dropped Charlie if she never returned from Seattle after she went home. But he wasn't one to worry too much about what other people thought. If she didn't come back to him, embarrassment would be the least of what he'd suffer.

"You haven't heard from Averil since you walked out last night?" he asked as he put down the menu. It was a Monday. She'd spent the night with him, but he'd gotten up early and gone to work, and this was the first time he'd seen her today. She'd messaged to see if he had time for breakfast, and he'd taken an hour off. This was her last week in town; he was going to see her whenever he could. He also knew she felt bad about how things had gone at the Gerharts' and was hoping to cheer her up.

"No," she said. "Nothing."

"Do you think they've found Mitch's teddy bear by now?"

"Bob and his family would've seen it when they left."

He leaned back as the waitress brought them coffee. "I wonder what she's thinking."

She added a dash of cream to her cup. "She probably hates me more than ever."

"I feel bad she's so upset. But neither one of us meant to hurt her. There were times when I sort of wondered if Averil was feeling something I wasn't, but I never knew it would play out like this."

"Would you feel differently about her if I hadn't come back?" she asked earnestly.

"Would you feel differently about Charlie if you and I hadn't hooked up?" he asked instead of answering.

She grimaced. "Of course not."

"There you go," he said. "Stop looking for things to feel guilty about." He got up and swung around the booth to sit on her side.

"Be careful," she joked when the waitress looked over as he dragged his place mat, water glass and coffee across the table. "Everyone will know you're in a relationship with the runaway bride."

"The cat's already out of the bag. Besides, I've made up my mind, and I've been clear and up-front about it. You're the one who's undecided."

"I'd have to give up a lot more than you would," she muttered.

Taking her hand, he kissed her fingers, and the many nights they'd spent together, the feel of her beneath him, the way her smile made his heart melt, how much he looked forward to being with her again whenever they were apart—it all went through his mind at once. "I can only hope I'm worth it," he said jokingly.

She took a sip of her coffee. "If I do come back, how do you see things going, Brant?"

He was afraid to mention marriage. He purposely left that out of any discussion about their future. But that was exactly what he wanted. Maybe he was old-fashioned, but he dreamed of building a life with her the way his parents had built a life together. He wanted her to take his name, bear his children and know that he'd always be true to her and protect her no matter what. "How do you want it to go?" he asked, turning the question back on her.

When she bit her lip instead of responding, he said, "We could buy a house together."

"And not get married?"

"Not if you don't want to. But if you begged me to marry you, I might consider it," he teased. "As long as we eloped. No way would I want to be standing at an altar with everyone we know looking on, wondering if I'll be the one exception to the rule."

When he started laughing, she almost shoved him out of the booth. "You know I wasn't in love with those men!"

He righted himself and sobered as he looked into her pretty but troubled eyes. "Do you love *me*?" He'd promised himself he wouldn't ask. He wanted her to tell him on her own. But he was terrified of losing her and found himself trying to grab hold of something solid in the middle of all the uncertainty.

"You know I do," she said. "It's just…"

"A question of how much," he filled in.

Her eyebrows furrowed. "No! If not for the diner, it wouldn't be nearly as difficult a choice."

He couldn't fault her for not wanting to sacrifice her business. He picked up his water glass. "Are you excited about going back to Seattle?"

She shook her head. "I don't want to leave you."

Would her feelings change once she got back into her normal surroundings? "The fact that Averil and Charlie live in Coyote Canyon has to make you less likely to come back," he said.

"I admit it won't be *pleasant* to run into them…"

He frowned as the waitress started toward them with their food. "I have a lot working against me."

She slid her arm through his and pecked his shoulder. "You have a lot working for you, too."

He smiled. But he couldn't help fearing it wouldn't be enough.

Twenty-Six

One week later

I never planned on living my life alone. Does anyone ever really plan on that? I don't think human beings are meant to be single. If not for certain choices, maybe I would've had a husband and children like most other women. But I can't complain. I've had a good life overall, with supportive parents, a roof over my head, plenty to eat. That's more than a lot of people have.

"What are you doing?" Brant asked, poking his head into the bedroom.

Talulah closed the book as she glanced up. She'd dropped one of Phoebe's journals while trying to slip them into a box she was going to put in her SUV. It'd fallen open to a page halfway through, which she'd started reading. "I'm packing up Phoebe's journals. I haven't read this one yet, but I was curious to see if I should put it in the box for later or keep it closer at hand."

"And? What's the verdict?"

"The box. She's much older in this one. It'll take me a while to get to it."

"Did she keep a journal of her whole life?"

"Not day by day. Not even year by year. But there are probably ten volumes."

He leaned against the doorjamb. "Where are you at in her story?"

"Volume two. I'm right where she joins the military as a nurse to help in the war effort in 1941."

"She was a nurse in World War II?" he asked in surprise.

"She didn't have any training. But back then, training wasn't required."

"Did she see combat?"

"She did. According to what I'm currently reading, she's working in a makeshift hospital in Bataan, which is in the Philippines somewhere, shortly after the bombing of Pearl Harbor."

"Did she ever talk about being stationed in the Philippines?"

"No. Never mentioned the war, either. Her early life is all new to me. Maybe that's why I find it so interesting. She was my great aunt, and yet she was almost a stranger to me."

"So many people saw things they'd rather forget," he said.

"When I mentioned her stint in the military to my mother yesterday, she said she was too little to remember much about it, but that Phoebe had once told her a large number of the nurses she'd worked with were captured by the Japanese after she came back to the States."

"They became POWs?" he said. "For how long?"

"Something like three years."

"Did any of them survive?"

"According to my mother, they all did."

"Sounds like you've got some interesting reading ahead."

Talulah leafed through some pages of the journal, examining her aunt's spidery script, before putting it in the box. "Growing up, I saw Phoebe as a crotchety old lady—someone who was demanding and unyielding and not that relevant to my own life. But…"

"You're starting to like her?" he said.

"I am. She was an incredible woman."

"So are you." Coming up behind her, he slipped his arms around her midsection. "It's so hard to let you leave me."

"I'd like to say it won't be for long, but…"

"I know. I won't push you. If you come back to me, I want it to be because you love me, not because you don't want to disappoint me."

"Thank you for that," she murmured. Brant was the first man she'd been with who seemed to care whether her feelings were as strong as they should be. And the fact that he was willing to give her the space and time she needed made her love him all the more.

"I've got the portable AC unit in my truck."

Talulah sighed heavily as she glanced around the bedroom. It was bare, but not nearly as empty as the other rooms in the house. She purposely hadn't sold the bed, in case she needed to use it in the future. She hadn't sold the dressers, either, since they matched the bed.

"I can move this stuff out of here and store it for you, or sell it once you list the house," he said, gesturing at the furniture that remained. The window he'd ordered for her had come in, and he was going to install that, too.

She turned to face him. "Thank you, Brant. I can't tell you how grateful I am to you—for everything."

He rested his forehead against hers. "I wish you weren't leaving."

"So do I. I don't know what's waiting for me in Seattle, or how I'll deal with it."

"You'll call me, though, when you get in, to tell me you're safe?"

He'd offered to drive her to Seattle and fly back, but if he did that, one of his brothers would have to go to Bozeman to pick him up at the airport. And if he took her home, that would only cause more problems with Paul, who wouldn't be leaving for his family reunion until Friday. He'd messaged her to ask if she was still returning on time, so they could talk and she could get back in the groove of taking care of the diner; she'd agreed, hoping that accommodating him might mitigate some of his anger. "I will," she promised.

"Paul had better treat you right," Brant muttered.

She closed her eyes as she held him close. "Whether I come back or not, I want you to know this." She looked up into his face. "I love you."

The drive through Missoula and across Idaho was some of the prettiest country Talula had ever seen. She'd admired it the entire time she was coming to Coyote Canyon. But she paid little attention to it on her way back. She didn't seem to be the same person who'd made this trek a month ago, before the funeral, before getting closer to her family, before confronting her past—*before Brant*. But she had so much unfinished business in Seattle. She had to go back, regardless of how it all played out.

As she was passing through Coeur d'Alene, a message came in from Paul, which the computer in her car read to her. Are you coming today?

She used Siri to reply. On my way.

When will you get in?

Late. I didn't leave Coyote Canyon until after noon.

Just had to fuck Brant one more time, huh?

He had no idea how much work she'd had to do while she was in town. But he didn't care about that.

Really? Do you have to be so crude?

Call me when you get here. I'll be up.

Talulah wasn't convinced she'd have the reserves to deal with Paul tonight. It wasn't until midnight that the lights of the city appeared in the distance ahead of her. But she decided she might as well see him right away— get it over with.

I'll be at my place in thirty.

See you there.

He had a key to her apartment. He'd agreed to bring in the mail and water the plants. Since he'd become so hostile to her, having him inside her house felt like an intrusion, but when she'd made the arrangements, she'd never anticipated that their relationship would go in this direction. Now he seemed like too big a part of her life in every aspect.

Once she parked in the underground lot and grabbed what she could of her bags, she dragged them to the elevator and pushed the button for the tenth floor.

Sure enough, when she let herself into her apartment, she found the lights and TV on—and Paul sitting on her leather couch with a beer.

"Welcome home," he said sarcastically.

"Are you going to make this terrible?" she asked, leaving her bags in the entryway and proceeding to the kitchen to get a glass of water.

"Do you think the last few weeks have been fun for me?"

"No, and I'm sorry for that. But I couldn't have changed anything."

"You could've refrained from cheating on me."

"I didn't cheat on you. I made it clear that we weren't together."

"You slept with me right before you left!"

Because she'd felt so much pressure to finally advance the relationship, and she'd hoped it would bring her some clarity as to whether she wanted to be with him for the rest of her life. "One time! And when we talked about it afterward, I told you I wasn't sure about us, that I needed to take it slow."

"You were worried about how it would impact the diner."

"Not only the diner, Paul. I didn't know my own heart. I made no secret of that. You said, 'Take as long as you like.'"

"Which was nice of me. I've been patient all these years, but that was obviously a mistake. I had no idea you'd—"

"Stop." She lifted her hand. "Just…stop. Let's not do this. What happened in Coyote Canyon happened. I can't change it now. So where does that leave us?"

He turned the beer can in his hand. "You tell me," he said, coming to his feet. "Are you finished having your fun? Are you home for good?"

"What do you mean by *home for good*?"

"Is everything going to go back to the way it was before?"

She walked over to the window and stared out at the city lights. She loved Seattle, enjoyed her life here and had never dreamed she'd consider leaving. She also loved the dessert diner. But she'd left her heart with a cowboy in Coyote Canyon. "I'm hoping to have the answers we both need by the time you get back from Europe."

He set his beer can aside and walked over to her. "I'm sorry for how I've behaved," he said as he came up behind her. "If…if we could just forgive each other and start over, maybe we'd be able to save everything."

"I'm sorry. That's not possible," she said. Because now that she knew what love really felt like, she could easily say her feelings for Paul had never progressed beyond friendship.

When Brant saw Charlie come into Hank's with some of the guys they played poker with, he turned away. It'd been three weeks since Talulah left. She'd stayed in close touch, but he knew Charlie didn't believe she was coming back. Charlie was probably *hoping* she wouldn't. He wanted Brant to feel the heartache and rejection he'd felt, and the longer her absence went on, the more confident he became that Brant would be the next guy to get burned.

"Nice shot," Kurt said as Brant banked the four ball into the side pocket. Brant had needed that shot and could stand to make a few others like it. Kurt was winning for a change. But Brant could tell his brother was equally distracted by Charlie, who was making a big deal about buying drinks for everyone in his party. "Look who's here," Kurt muttered after he missed what should've been an easy shot.

"I saw him," Brant said.

Doug Stringham, who'd gone to high school at the same time they did, had come in with Charlie, but the moment he saw Brant, he walked over to say hello.

"Hey, man," he said as Brant sent the cue ball into the three ball with a solid crack that sank it into the side pocket. "Where've you been lately? I haven't seen you at poker in ages."

Brant hadn't felt like being around Charlie. He'd been busy at the ranch, too, getting ready for fall. It wouldn't be long before they were once again facing the cold winter months. And there was the window to repair and some dry rot he'd been taking care of for Talulah at Phoebe's place. "I've decided to let you keep a little more of your money for the time being," he told Doug, who was married and had three kids.

"But now there's no challenge," Doug joked. "Tell me you're coming back. It's not the same without you."

"I'll be there eventually," Brant told him. "I've just been busy."

Doug lowered his voice. "Charlie says it's because of him. That the two of you aren't speaking."

Brant shrugged. "I don't have anything to say to him."

"He can be a dick sometimes," Doug said, but he was grinning, making the statement more playful than derogatory.

"Maybe I'm the dick," Brant said. "I fell in love with the wrong woman, but I didn't do it on purpose."

Doug watched Kurt set up a tricky shot. "You and Talulah are for real, then?" he said. "She always was gorgeous. But she has one hell of a reputation. I hope you won't get hurt."

Brant didn't say anything. It was his turn at pool. He sank one ball, but missed the second, and by the time he looked up again, everyone Doug had been with had joined them, including Charlie.

"Hey, are you two ever going to let this Talulah thing go?" Leo Spagnoli said, gesturing between the two of them. "Because it's really starting to get in the way."

Leo had moved to Coyote Canyon after Talulah left, so he'd never even met her.

"I'm happy to let it go," Brant said. "But we might have another problem when she comes back."

"Poor deluded bastard," Charlie joked. "He doesn't know she's not coming back. Why the hell would she move all the way out here when she has a thriving business in Seattle?"

He'd kept his voice down, as if he was talking to the guys standing next to him, but Brant would easily hear. "You don't know what the hell you're talking about," he told him, instantly angry.

But deep down, after Talulah's conversations about the diner and all the daily details of running it, he was beginning to believe Charlie might be right.

Talulah sat in the diner long after the employees had left. It was late on a Saturday night. She'd turned the open sign facing the busy street to Closed over an hour ago. But she hadn't been able to make herself leave. She'd wanted to stay in this place she'd created—amid the many tables and chairs she'd chosen, glass cases she'd helped to purchase and confections she'd baked herself. She'd selected the name, the location, the logo and the look she'd wanted for the diner, as well as putting together the menu. Paul had come in to share the risk, join his credit to hers and split the rent. He also helped with the baking each day. But the idea, the entire concept, was hers.

As she sat behind the counter, she navigated to Yelp, where she read the many wonderful reviews posted by customers who'd tried her cakes, pies and ice cream creations. She'd worked so hard. With Paul's help, she'd made the diner into what she'd hoped it would be. A dream like that rarely became a reality, not for someone as young as she'd been—someone who'd started with nothing.

The business was finally bringing in some good cash, too. If they were careful and managed their money wisely, she and Paul probably *could* open a second location, as he'd been nagging her to do.

They could serve twice as many people and make twice as much money. Maybe they could even become a chain one day.

But opening a second store would only create another bond to the Seattle area—and to Paul.

What was she going to do?

Her phone buzzed with a text. She glanced down to see that Brant had sent her a message. Miss you.

She missed him, too, but she didn't know when she'd be able to go back. She'd spoken to Paul several times to assure him that all was well at the diner, but he refused to talk about the future. He said he had the right to take a month off and enjoy himself, just as she'd done, and they'd go over anything business-related once he got home. But she already knew he'd make it as difficult as possible if she wanted out of the partnership.

"It's so ironic," she mumbled. She'd *finally* fallen in love—and it had to be with one of the boys from her hometown.

She wished she could call her sister. She knew that both Debbie and Abby were doing great. She checked in often. But if it wasn't so late she would've called again. She needed to talk to someone besides Brant. She didn't want him to know how much. She didn't want him to know how much she was struggling with the decisions she had to make.

She glanced at the giant clock on the wall. Although it was nearly midnight on the west coast, it was morning in most of Africa. She hadn't turned to her mother for advice in years, especially when it came to men, but she found herself eager to hear Carolyn's voice.

"Hey," she said when her mother answered.

"Hi, honey. How are you?"

"Good."

"Everything's okay at the dessert diner?"

"Yep. Things are going well."

"Even without Paul?"

Despite all the extra work, which now fell on her, she'd been enjoying the peace and calm—the absence of any animosity or pressure. "Even without Paul."

"There's something wrong," her mother replied. "I can hear it in your voice."

Talulah slumped over. She was sitting on a stool while leaning her elbows on the counter. "I don't know what to do," she admitted.

"About what?"

"About Brant."

"Do you love him?"

"Absolutely. For once, I'm sure about that."

"Okay, then. Where would you be the happiest?"

"If I knew that, I'd have my answer." She sat taller and busied herself straightening the items around the register. "Do you ever regret making the sacrifices you've made for Dad over the years?" she asked.

She'd expected her mother to immediately say she didn't regret a thing, so she was surprised when her mother didn't answer right away.

"Mom?" Talulah said, confused.

"It was different back when I married," Carolyn hedged.

"What does that mean?"

"It means I probably *did* make more sacrifices than I

should have. But I believed it was the woman's place to put her husband first, and I took that to heart."

Was she still doing that? Talulah had wondered if the mission—at least such a long one—had been her father's idea. "You're saying you *do* have regrets."

"If I'm being honest, I have a few."

"What am I supposed to make of that?"

"Don't give up the diner too soon," her mother said, and then her father must've come into the room because she immediately changed the subject.

"Dinah called me recently and told me that while you were in Coyote Canyon, someone threw a rock that shattered the window and you were cut."

"Yeah. I bet you can guess who did that."

"Charlie?"

"Or Averil."

"You think *Averil* would do something like that?"

Talulah remembered finding Mitch's teddy bear behind the barn, so she knew Charlie wasn't the only one coming by late at night. "I don't want to believe it. But it would have to be her or Charlie. There's no one else it could be."

"Dinah says Averil insists it's Charlie. But she doesn't believe it. She says it has to be someone else."

"Of course she'd say that. She's his mother. But no one else was mad at me. Not enough to—" Talulah let her words drift off as she remembered that there *was* one other person who was mad at her. Paul had been mad at her, and he hadn't been picking up his phone for several days right about the time it happened.

He was in Seattle at the time, though, wasn't he?

A strange feeling came over her as she jumped to her feet. "I'd better go, Mom. It's getting late, and I'm still at the diner."

"Okay, honey. I'll talk to you again on Sunday," Carolyn

said, but after she disconnected, Talulah didn't pack up her tote. Her heart was pounding as she considered possibilities that'd never occurred to her before. Could Paul have come to Coyote Canyon earlier than he'd said? "This is a long shot," she muttered, and yet the hair on her neck was standing on end. Since someone wouldn't be likely to drive that far twice in such a short time, she grabbed her laptop from under the register and logged into his Southwest account. It was only an hour-and-forty-minute flight. Because they had a Rapid Rewards credit card they used for the business, which earned travel miles, and those miles belonged equally to both of them, Talulah had the username and password.

She kept telling herself that she was being ridiculous, that this was the most unlikely of scenarios. Paul had acted so surprised when he saw her arm. He'd asked about the stitches. It couldn't be him.

And yet…

She sank onto the stool, scarcely able to believe what she saw. He'd booked a ticket to Bozeman, where he must've rented a car, the day she'd been cut.

Brant hadn't heard from Talulah today. She hadn't even responded to his text. He could feel her slipping away from him and didn't know what to do next.

"What's wrong with you?" A gust of wind slammed the door as Ranson came into the living room from outside, followed by Miles. They'd just returned from a friend's house. They'd invited Brant to go with them to play beer pong, but he'd said he had stuff to get done.

"Nothing," Brant replied. "Just tired. I'm about to go to bed."

"Whatever show you were watching is over, dude."

Miles gestured at the TV. "In case you haven't noticed, the screen's frozen."

"I told you, I'm about to go to bed," Brant responded, but he couldn't have said how long it'd been since the show ended. He couldn't even have explained what the show had been about. He'd been lost in his own thoughts for so long, trying to figure out what he was going to do if he had to go on without Talulah.

"You've been moping around all week," Ranson said, grabbing the remote and diving onto the couch.

"I haven't been moping," Brant said, but he was feeling so terrible he couldn't mount much of a defense.

Miles seemed to understand, because he gave Brant's shoulder a squeeze. "Don't worry, bro. She's coming back."

"Yeah, I know that," Brant said, but once he got to his bedroom, he pulled out his phone and texted Charlie.

Go ahead and laugh, dude. I think you were right.

Twenty-Seven

A week later, Brant still hadn't heard from Talulah. She'd simply gone silent. He knew Paul was scheduled to be back this past Thursday, but he couldn't even get her to confirm that he'd returned. Brant could only assume she felt too bad to tell him the truth—that she'd decided to stay in Seattle for the sake of the diner, and she must not want to be with him, or he would've heard from her.

He deserved all the misery. He'd known from the beginning that Talulah wasn't likely to stick around Coyote Canyon. Why he'd let himself fall for "the runaway bride" in spite of all the warning he'd had, and then hope against hope he'd be different from Charlie, he couldn't say. Arrogance had gotten the best of him, he supposed.

"I'm a fool," he told Kurt as they ate dinner together on Saturday night. Ranson and Miles had already left to go somewhere else for the evening—Brant had no idea where—leaving them alone with the meat loaf and mashed potatoes and gravy his mother had dropped off. "I can't believe I did this to myself."

"You're giving up too soon," Kurt told him.

"She's not responding to me. I haven't heard from her

for a week. It doesn't take a rocket scientist to figure out that's a hard no."

Kurt shoveled another bite into his mouth. "If she's saying no, she should tell you that."

"Maybe it's too hard for her. Maybe moving on without bothering to say goodbye is the easiest way to go."

His brother took a big drink of milk. "Or she got back with Paul…"

"She was never *with* Paul!" Brant said, nearly yelling. But that didn't mean Paul hadn't finally prevailed. Had she decided to get into a relationship with him at last? Brant had admitted all along that Paul would be the easiest and most convenient choice.

"Forget about her," Kurt said. "She's not worth what you're going through."

"Don't say anything negative about her," Brant warned, but that only made his brother laugh.

"Come on, bro. Let's get showered and go out. We'll have some fun. And if you're *not* having fun, we'll drink until you won't have to think about her anymore, at least for tonight."

"I don't feel like going out," he grumbled.

"Don't let Charlie gloat. Show your face around town and act like what's happened doesn't bother you."

Brant swallowed the potatoes in his mouth, even though he didn't feel much like eating these days. "I don't care enough about what Charlie thinks to put on a show."

"Then I don't know what else to say. Maybe we should get you laid."

"No, thanks," he said. "I'm not interested in that, either."

Kurt gaped at him. "Holy shit. She's really done a number on you."

Brant shot him a dirty look. "I'd love nothing better than to find a deserving target. You should keep that in mind."

Kurt scraped his plate clean. "Don't get mad at me. You'll move on and find someone you love as much as Talulah eventually. There are plenty of other fish in the sea."

"Is that how you feel about Kate?" Brant asked.

His little brother lost some of his cockiness. "No, but…"

"Just don't offer me any advice," Brant told him. "You're not helping."

"Fine," Kurt snapped. "Stay here and feel sorry for yourself if that's what you want to do."

The doorbell rang.

"Aren't you going to answer that?" Brant asked.

Kurt didn't even look up. "Nope. I'm gonna rinse off my plate and get ready. You're not doing anything tonight. Why don't you grab it?"

Cursing under his breath, Brant went into the living room. He wasn't in the mood to be social, and Kurt could've saved him this encounter—if he wasn't being such an ass. Even as Brant reached for the door handle, he had half a mind to go back and haul his little brother out of the kitchen to *make* him handle it. But Kurt would be gone in a few minutes. Then, as soon as he could get rid of whoever was at the door, Brant would have the house to himself.

No one was standing outside when he opened the door. "Hello?" he called.

No response.

He was about to step out so he could see the driveway but caught himself before he nearly crushed a large bakery box on the doormat. It looked like someone had delivered some sort of food.

He hoped to hell it wasn't Averil. After he'd given Charlie the satisfaction of knowing he'd been right, Averil had texted to say she was sorry about what Talulah had done. Brant hadn't responded to her. But then, he hadn't responded to Charlie, either, who'd also sent him a surpris-

ingly conciliatory message: I'm sorry. I know what it feels
like. Call me if you want to talk.

It'd be a cold day in hell when he called Charlie to discuss Talulah, Brant thought as he picked up the box and
carried it inside.

Kurt twisted around from where he was rinsing his plate
at the sink as Brant came back into the kitchen. "What's
that?"

Brant set it on the table. "I'm about to find out," he said
and grabbed a knife to slit the tape holding the top shut.

Once he lifted the lid, he put the knife down and stepped
back.

"What is it?" Kurt, hands dripping water, came over to
see what was inside the box, too.

"It's a carrot cake," Brant replied. One of Talulah's carrot cakes. Brant had eaten enough of them to know. But
the most shocking thing wasn't that she'd baked him his
favorite cake, or that she was probably in town to deliver it.

It was what she'd written across the top.

Will you marry me?

Talulah waited in the driveway, nervously pacing next
to her SUV. Paul hadn't been happy when she'd confronted
him about what she'd learned. At first, he'd tried to deny
it—had been adamant that there was no way he'd thrown
that rock. But he had no answer for the flight he'd taken
and, in the end, had finally sagged against the counter and
stared glumly at his feet, only finding his voice again several minutes later to say, softly, that he'd meant to come
and win her back, but the idea of her being with someone
else had upset him so badly he'd reacted impulsively when
he saw her—had never meant to hurt her.

He'd begged her to forgive him and to stay, but she'd
packed up all the belongings she could fit in her vehicle

and left for Coyote Canyon. She'd *had* to do it. She felt like she couldn't breathe in Seattle anymore—that was how desperate she'd become to get home to Brant. Still, even after ten hours of driving, there were moments when she couldn't believe she was doing what she was doing. The risk of it, the daring, made her queasy. At least the uncertainty she'd always felt when it came to whatever man she was seeing was gone. She'd made her choice—and it gave her peace of mind because it felt right.

When Brant came out of the house again and walked in her direction, she wiped her damp palms on her jeans.

"*You're* proposing to *me*?" he said, obviously stunned.

She felt a sheepish smile tug at her lips. "Well, I knew better than to expect *you* to propose to *me*."

He laughed as he reached her, pulled her into his arms and buried his face in her neck. "God, you scared me," he said as he twirled her around. "I thought I'd lost you."

"I'm sorry." She placed her hands on his cheeks as he set her down. "I had to shut out the noise. Close down all communication with you and Paul and just…search my heart."

"And this is what you want?" he asked beseechingly. "You've decided for sure? I can count on it?"

The words were surprisingly easy to say, considering the angst she'd gone through to get here. "*You* are what I want. No matter what happens, I'm there. You can count on it."

She admired the beautiful blue of his eyes as he squinted against the sun sinking behind her. "How did you finally decide?"

Part of it was finding out that it was Paul who'd thrown that rock. But she knew if she said that it would only tempt Brant to knock some sense into him, so she decided not to tell him about that today. Instead, she was going to focus on the more positive catalyst. "I guess, in a way, Phoebe told me what to do."

"Since Phoebe's dead, I think I could use an explanation," he said with a laugh.

"You know I was reading her journals, right? Well, I came to a part where she met this amazing man while she was serving in the military—a doctor."

"They fell in love?"

"They did but never married. After the war, he went back to Georgia, and because my grandmother was getting old and sick, and my mother was still only a young teen and didn't really have anyone to look after her, Phoebe decided her place was here in Coyote Canyon with her family."

"And that was it? They were doomed, she and the doctor?" Brant said. "Why couldn't *he* have come here?"

"He was divorced and had an ex-wife and two children in Georgia. Phoebe hoped to join him eventually, once my mother got a little older. But Phoebe couldn't quite pull loose from what she felt was her responsibility as a sister and an aunt, and he eventually met someone else. Phoebe wrote in her journal that choosing Coyote Canyon over going to be with him was one of the hardest decisions she ever made. She couldn't regret it because she truly felt my mother needed her. But I read the rest of her journals this past month, and she mourned that doctor—Jim Fritz—for the rest of her life and never met anyone else she loved nearly as much."

"Wow," he said. "That's a sad story."

"It is. And I didn't want that to be *our* story. I figured I could try to build another business, but there's only one of you. We might be looking at the chance of a lifetime."

"You're everything I've ever wanted," he told her frankly. "But what about Paul and the diner? Did he agree to buy you out?"

"No. He won't even make me an offer. He's too pissed off that I'm leaving the area and that we won't be opening another location together. But over the past month, I trained our best employee to help him with the baking, so he'll be able to get by without me. And I'll take him to court, if necessary, if he won't pay me a fair price for everything I've contributed to the business in terms of money, ideas, time—even my recipes. I won't let him or anything else stop me from being with you."

"I can't tell you how happy I am to hear it," Brant said. "No matter what happens, whether he buys you out or not, I'll help you start another diner right here in Coyote Canyon. I promise. And we'll do all we can to make it a success."

"You already work hard enough. I'll do it on my own. And even if it doesn't succeed, at least I'll have you."

He touched the compass tattoo on her forearm—as if he was remembering what she'd told him about how it represented her internal compass that had led her away from Coyote Canyon—and she felt compelled to explain. "I followed my heart when I left this place," she said. "And now I've followed it back home."

Kurt startled Talulah by interrupting them when they were kissing. "Damn, that's a good cake!" he said.

Brant whipped around to confront him. "You're *eating* my proposal cake?"

"Didn't think you'd mind." He gestured at Talulah. "You've got what you want."

"That's true," Brant said, immediately backing off. "I guess nothing could really make me mad right now."

Talulah drew a deep breath. "So…what do you say?" she asked Brant, drawing his attention back to her. "I'm offering you everything I've got. *Will* you marry me?"

A wry grin twisted his lips. "Will you show up for the wedding?"

"I will if you will," she said, and they all started to laugh.

It was only the third time in Brant's life that he'd worn a tuxedo. He'd rented one for junior prom, and he'd gone to the same dance as a senior. Now he was in a simple black tux without tails for his own wedding.

"Don't be nervous," Charlie muttered. "She's coming."

Brant couldn't help being nervous. They were standing in Talulah's parents' church—Charlie's family's church, too—and Talulah was ten minutes late for the ceremony. Normally, ten minutes wouldn't be a big deal, not at a wedding. There were always last-minute details that slowed things down. Ten minutes was merely a hiccup, a heartbeat. He'd been to one ceremony that'd started thirty minutes late. But the memory of being in the same place fourteen years ago, while they waited just like this and Talulah didn't show up, loomed large in Brant's mind.

Like they had before, her mother and brother-in-law sat in the front pew, only this time Debbie's children were with them. According to Talulah, her mom had absolutely refused to miss the wedding, so her dad had agreed to return from Africa. They were staying in town for Christmas, which was only a week away, before going back to finish their mission in Sierra Leone. Carolyn had been more assertive than usual, which had surprised Talulah, so Brant didn't want Carolyn to be disappointed—or embarrassed again.

Brant's parents sat on the other side of the aisle. A professional photographer snapped pictures as Brant struggled with the temptation to loosen his bow tie. A videographer smiled encouragingly, trying to get *him* to smile every time

Brant's anxious glance sought the doors at the back where Talulah was supposed to enter, and flowers adorned the aisle at every pew.

Brant told himself it was the overpowering scent of so many white roses and not the fear that he and Talulah had stupidly set themselves up for an epic failure that was making his stomach roil.

"Yeah. She'll be here," he confirmed to Charlie. He'd responded belatedly, but he had to say *something*. Why he'd asked Charlie to be his best man, he had no idea. Any one of his brothers would've happily taken that role. But how would he have chosen between them? And it'd seemed petty not to let bygones be bygones with Charlie, who'd paid him a visit more than two months ago to apologize and ask if they could reclaim their friendship.

Brant had apologized, too, for falling in love with the woman Charlie had always wanted, and healing the rift had somehow entailed asking Charlie to be his best man, since Brant had once been Charlie's. That it was the same bride was…weird—ironic even—so having Charlie next to him in this moment only made Brant more uncomfortable. Their friendship wasn't quite the same as before, and realistically, Brant knew it probably never would be—although, once Charlie fell in love with someone else and got married, maybe any underlying jealousy and resentment would disappear. Brant supposed that was the hope that'd led him to include Charlie in the wedding. He'd done it for the sake of the past and the future.

Talulah *would* show up, he told himself. He was just experiencing déjà vu, standing at the same altar with mostly the same people in the same church waiting for the same bride. He and Talulah should've eloped. He'd suggested it. But Talulah had said she was only going to say "I do" once,

and she wanted to do it right. For Phoebe. For her parents.
For everyone in Coyote Canyon who'd ever doubted her.

Brant knew he'd forgive her even if she stood him up.
They'd been happy together, living in Phoebe's house,
which they planned to buy, for almost three months. During that time, Talulah had proved how much she loved him.
But he sincerely regretted letting her talk him into a big
wedding. There'd been no need for it…

From the corner of his eye, he saw Debbie's smile grow
strained. As Talulah's maid of honor, she was searching
for any sign of her sister and father starting down the aisle.
She kept turning to murmur to Jane, Ellen and Averil, Talulah's bridesmaids, all of whom were beginning to look
as concerned as she did—except Averil. Even though it
was Paul who'd thrown the rock, Brant couldn't quite trust
that she sincerely had Talulah's best interests at heart. He
could tell by the way she looked at him that she was hoping he'd change his mind. Still, he hadn't argued with
Talulah when she'd said she wanted to include Averil as
one of her bridesmaids. She felt the same as he did with
Charlie—was simply hoping this might lead them back to
real friendship at some point.

At last, Talulah's father appeared. After a moment of relief, however, Brant's heart sank. Talulah wasn't with him.

What was going on? Brant knew from the rehearsal that
this wasn't how the wedding was supposed to go.

He watched as Talulah's dad came down the aisle and
leaned over to whisper to Carolyn, who quickly handed
off little Abby and followed him back out of the chapel.

The level of ambient noise rose as the congregation
whispered among themselves. Everyone was obviously
wondering about the holdup. Brant could almost hear them
asking each other: *Has the runaway bride taken off again?*

He wanted to know what was wrong himself. Was Talulah okay? Having second thoughts?

She didn't have to go through with this if she didn't want to. He'd just marry her in Vegas one day. He loved her enough to wait, if that was what he had to do.

He was about to follow her parents to make sure she understood that when Talulah and her father appeared at the entrance, and "Here Comes the Bride" swelled so loudly he could hardly hear himself think. The organist was playing such an enthusiastic rendition that Brant got the impression she was afraid Talulah would bolt if she didn't get down the aisle fast enough.

Talulah looked stunning—gorgeous enough to take Brant's breath away. She'd shown up, after all. For him.

But he could tell that something was still off when people in the audience started to laugh as she passed by. The chuckling grew so loud it could almost compete with the music.

It wasn't until Talulah's father grinned as he put her hand in Brant's and said, *"Finally,"* that Brant started laughing, too.

"What's going on?" he whispered to Talulah.

"I had a little wardrobe malfunction," she explained and turned to show him what their guests had already seen. The zipper on the back of her dress had broken, and her mother had used pins and even some duct tape—to make sure everyone knew what had been going on—and to hold it closed long enough for her to get married.

"Would you rather go back and fix it?" he asked with a halt gesture to the pastor to give her time to make the decision. "You've put so much work into this wedding. I want it to be exactly as you envisioned it."

"Seeing you in that tux is exactly how I envisioned it," she said. "I'm not walking out of here until I'm your wife."

Impulsively, he kissed her, even though it wasn't time for that, and everyone started to clap.

Epilogue

"Come on out and take a look at this," Brant said.

Talulah had been so busy cleaning the kitchen of her new dessert diner, so she could be at the register once she opened the doors for the first time, that she hadn't been in front for thirty minutes or more.

"What's going on?" she called back, too determined to finish the dishes to allow herself to be interrupted. They were due to open in just a few minutes.

"I think this is something you need to see for yourself."

The tone of his voice made her wonder if she'd missed some small detail she'd need to remedy before they could welcome any customers. Leaving what remained of the dishes, she wiped her hands and hurried into the front of the restaurant. "What's wrong?"

Brant grinned as he gestured outside.

A line was forming, and Ellen, Jane and Averil were at the front. Brant's brothers were right behind them. "Aw, look at my friends and your brothers," she said, waving as they made funny faces at her through the glass. "They're so good to us."

In the six months she and Brant had been married, she'd grown closest to Ellen. Since Ellen lived next door, she came over often, and she had a knack for decorating unlike anyone Talulah had ever met. She could make something look fantastic for pennies. Together, they'd fixed up Phoebe's house on a tight budget, since she and Brant had decided to put off any major remodeling—other than the few improvements he could manage in his spare time—to save money for the next iteration of Talulah's Dessert Diner.

She gazed at the logo they'd had painted on the window. She and Brant had brainstormed changing the name and/or the logo, since Paul wouldn't relinquish either. But in the end, Talulah had decided to keep everything the same. She didn't care if there was another Talulah's Dessert Diner in the world. Paul's location was far enough away that it wouldn't impact her. At least they'd come to an agreement on the financial end of things. She'd forced him to negotiate with her by threatening to call the police on him for throwing the rock that'd cut her arm.

He'd been difficult to deal with even though they had the evidence to prove it was him. Talulah had given him almost everything he'd demanded in the dissolution of their partnership just to get out of it as quickly and cleanly as possible. She'd get only forty percent of net profits for the next three years. But she had Brant. And he meant more to her than anything or anyone else. She'd made the right decision when she left Seattle, even though it'd meant walking away from her first restaurant. Now, other than receiving a monthly check from Paul, she was free of him.

"It's not just friends and family coming to support you, Lu." Brant took her by the elbow and tugged her closer to the window. "Look at that line! It goes three blocks down Center Street."

Talulah felt her jaw drop. Half the town had to be waiting on the sidewalk. She and Brant had done a lot of work to advertise the grand opening. They'd stressed the success and rave reviews of the Seattle location as though Coyote Canyon was getting its own version of the diner everyone loved in the big city, and the citizens of her hometown were responding as if they were excited about it. "This is unbelievable," she mumbled, overwhelmed.

"I'm sure you'll have every bit as much business here as you did in Seattle," he said. "There's a lot less competition, and no one bakes as well as you."

She didn't dare comment. The dream of having another successful restaurant was important enough to her that she was growing emotional. Slipping her arms around his lean waist, she rested her head against his chest.

"You okay?" he said, smoothing her hair.

"I'm just happy," she said when she was able to speak around the lump in her throat.

"I'm glad." He leaned back so he could look into her face. "I've been afraid that if this flops you'll regret your decision to marry me."

"Never," she said. "Even if these people weren't here, or they don't come back after today, I would still be happy. Marrying you was the best thing I've ever done."

Pulling her even closer, he pecked her lips. "I'm glad. Because I feel exactly the same way."

A surge of excitement went through Talulah. "Let's open the doors!" she said, and with a final glance at the many cakes and pies she'd baked this morning and displayed in their new glass case, she grabbed the keys.

* * * * *

Get 3 FREE REWARDS!

We'll send you 2 FREE Books plus a FREE Mystery Gift.

Both the **Romance** and **Suspense** collections feature compelling novels written by many of today's bestselling authors.

HARLEQUIN
PLUS

Try the best multimedia
subscription service for romance
readers like you!

Read, Watch and Play.

Experience the easiest way to get
the romance content you crave.

Start your **FREE TRIAL** at
<u>www.harlequinplus.com/freetrial</u>.